THE COMPANY OF STRANGERS

THE COMPANY OF STRANGERS

Robert Wilson

HARCOURT, INC.

New York   San Diego   London

www.harcourt.com

*This novel is entirely a work of fiction. The names, characters, and incidents
portrayed in it are the work of the author's imagination. Any resemblance to actual
persons, living or dead; events; or localities is entirely coincidental.*

Library of Congress Cataloging-in-Publication Data
Wilson, Robert, 1957–
The company of strangers/Robert Wilson—1st ed.
p.   cm.
ISBN 0-15-100846-9
1. World War, 1939–1945—Portugal—Lisbon—Fiction.
2. Women mathematicians—Fiction. 3. Germans—Portugal—Fiction.
4. British—Portugal—Fiction. 5. Lisbon (Portugal)—Fiction. 6. Berlin
(Germany)—Fiction. 7. Women spies—Fiction.   I. Title
PR6073.I474 C6 2001
823'.914—dc21   2001024186

First U.S. edition
A C E G I K J H F D B

Printed in the United States of America

For Jane
and
in memory of my father
1922–1980

ACKNOWLEDGEMENTS

I would like to thank Col. Peter Taylor (retd), Mrs Pam Taylor and Elwin Taylor for helping me with books, maps and information on Berlin in the 1960s and 1970s.

Ah, love, let us be true
To one another! For the world, which seems
To lie before us like a land of dreams,
So various, so beautiful, so new,
Hath really neither joy, nor love, nor light,
Nor certitude, nor peace, nor help for pain;
And we are here as on a darkling plain
Swept with confused alarms of struggle and flight,
Where ignorant armies clash by night.

Dover Beach by Matthew Arnold

THE COMPANY OF
STRANGERS

Book One

Outlaws of the Mind

Chapter 1

30th October 1940, London. Night 54 of the Blitz.

She was running, running as she had done before in her dreams, except this wasn't a dream, even though with the flares dropping, as slowly as petals, and the yellow light, and the dark streets with the orange glow on the skyline it could easily be a dream, a horror dream.

She flinched at a tremendous explosion in a nearby street, staggered at the shudder in the ground, nearly ploughed into the paving stones face-first, legs kicking back wildly. She pushed up off a low wall at the front of a house and her feet were slapping against the pavement again. She ran faster as she saw the Auxiliary Fire Service outside the house. New hoses uncoiled from the engines and joined the spaghetti in the black glass street as they trained more water on the back of the house, which was no longer a house but half a house. The whole of one side blown away and the grand piano with two legs over the startling new precipice, its lid hanging open like a tongue lapping up the flames, which set off a terrible twanging as the fire plucked at the piano strings and snapped them, peeled them back.

She stood there with her hands over her ears to the unbearable sound of destruction. Her eyes and mouth were wide open as the back of the house collapsed into the neighbour's garden, leaving the kitchen in full view and oddly intact. A hissing noise of escaping gas from the ruptured mains suddenly thumped into flame and burst across the street, pushing the firemen back. There was a figure lying in the kitchen, not moving and with clothes alight.

She jumped up on to the low wall at the side of the house and screamed into the blistering heat of the burning house.

'Daddy! Daddy!'

A fireman grabbed her and hauled her roughly back, almost

3

threw her at a warden, who tried to hold her but she wrenched herself free just as the piano, the piano that she'd been playing to him only two hours before, fell from its precipice with a loud crack and a discord that reached into her chest and squeezed her lungs. Now she saw all the sheet music going up in flames and he was lying on the floor at the foot of the wall of fire, which the AFS where hosing down so that it hissed and sputtered, but didn't go out.

Another crack and this time the roof dropped, spitting whole window frames into the street like broken teeth, and crashed down on to the floor below, shedding great sledges of tiles which shattered on the pavement. There was a momentary pause, then the roof smashed through to the next floor and, like a giant candle snuff, suffocated the flaming music, crushed his supine body and dropped him amongst shafts of flaming timber into the bay window of the ground floor.

The warden lunged at her again, got a hold of her collar, and she wheeled round and bit his wrist so that he flinched back his hand. She's a wild one, this black-haired, gypsy-looking girl, thought the warden, but he had to get her away, poor thing, get her away from her daddy burning in the bay window in front of her. He went for her again, got her in a bear hug, her legs flailing, lashing out and then she went limp as a rag doll, bent in the middle over his arms.

A woman, white-faced, ran up to the warden and said that the girl was her daughter, which confused him because he'd seen the man who she'd been calling Daddy and the warden knew that the man's wife was dead in the kitchen.

'She's been calling for her daddy in the house there.'

'That's not her daddy,' said the woman. 'Her father's dead. That's her piano teacher.'

'What's she doing out here, anyway?' he asked, getting official. 'The All Clear hasn't sounded . . .'

The girl wrestled away from her mother and ran down the side of another house and into the garden, lit by the still falling flares. She ran across the yellow lawn and threw herself into the bushes growing against the back wall. Her mother followed. Bombs were still falling, the ack-ack was still pumping away on the Common, the searchlights swarming over the black velvet sky. Her mother was screaming at her, roaring over the noise, screeching with fright, savagely begging her to come out.

The girl sat with her hands over her ears, eyes closed. Only two hours before he'd held her hands, told her she was as nervous as a cat, stroked each of her fingers, squared her shoulders to that same piano and she'd played for him, played like a dream for him, so that he'd told her afterwards he'd closed his eyes and left London and the war and found a green meadow in the sunshine, somewhere where the trees were flashing with red and gold in the autumn wind.

The first wave of bombers moved off. The ack-ack fell silent. All that was left in the cold autumn air was the roar of the conflagration and the hiss of water on burning wood. She crawled out of the bushes. Her mother grabbed her by the shoulders, shook her backwards and forwards. The girl was calm, but her face was set, her teeth gritted and her eyes black and unseeing.

'You're a stupid girl, Andrea. A stupid, stupid girl,' said her mother.

The girl took in her mother's white raving face in the dark and yellow garden, her face hard and determined.

'I hate Germans,' she said. 'And I hate you.'

Her mother slapped her hard across the face.

Chapter 2

7th February 1942, Wolfsschanze, Hitler's East Front HQ, Rastenburg, East Prussia.

The aircraft, a Heinkel III bomber refitted for passenger use, began its descent over the vast blackness of the pine forests of East Prussia. The low moan of its two engines brought with it the bleakness of the vast, snow-covered Russian steppes, the emptiness of the gutted, burnt-out railway station at Dnepropetrovsk and the endlessness of the frozen Pripet marshes between Kiev and the start of Polish pine.

The plane landed and taxied in a miasma of snow thrashed up into the darkness by its propellers. A coated figure, huddled against the icy blast, slipped into this chill world from a neat hole which had opened up in the belly of the aircraft. A car from the Führer's personal pool waited just off the wing tip and the chauffeur, collar up to his hat, held the door open. Fifteen minutes later the guard at the gate of Restricted Area I admitted Albert Speer, architect, into the military compound of Hitler's Rastenburg headquarters for the first time. Speer went straight to the officers' canteen and ate a large meal with appropriate wolfishness, which would have reminded his fellow diners, if they'd had room for empathy, just how difficult it was to keep the latest far-flung corner of the Third Reich supplied.

Two captains, Karl Voss and Hans Weber, intelligence officers in their mid twenties attached to the Army Chief of Staff, General Zeitzler, had been standing outside stamping their feet and smoking cigarettes when Speer arrived.

'Who's that?' asked Voss.

'I knew you'd ask that.'

'You don't think that's a normal question when somebody you don't know walks past?'

'You forgot the word "important". When somebody important walks past.'

'Piss off, Weber.'

'I've seen you.'

'What?'

'Let's get back,' said Weber, chucking his cigarette.

'No, tell me.'

'Your problem, Voss . . . is that you're too intelligent. Heidelberg University and your fucking physics degree, you're . . .'

'Too intelligent to be an intelligence officer?'

'You're new, you don't understand yet – the thing about intelligence is that it doesn't do to be too inquisitive.'

'Where *does* this rubbish come from, Weber?' asked Voss, incredulous.

'I tell you one thing,' he said, 'I know what powerful people see when they look at you and me . . . and it's not two individuals with lives and families and all the rest.'

'What then?'

'They see opportunities,' he said, and barged Voss through the door.

They went back to work in the situation room, up the silent corridor towards Hitler's apartment where the Führer was still entertaining the Armaments Minister, Fritz Todt, whose arrival had terminated the situation meeting of that afternoon. As the young captains resumed their seats the two older men were still just about talking. Food had been served to them earlier by an orderly grown accustomed to glacial silences, split only by the odd cracking of a wooden chair.

Voss and Weber worked, or rather Voss did. Weber's head started toppling again almost as soon as they sat down in the airless room. Only the snap of his neck muscles jerked him awake and prevented him from flattening his face on the desk. Voss told him to go to bed. Weber's eyes ground in their sockets.

'Go on,' said Voss. 'This is nearly finished anyway.'

'Those,' said Weber, standing and pointing at four boxes of files, 'have to go out on the first flight in the morning . . . to Berlin.'

'You mean unless the Moscow flight is open by then.'

Weber grunted. 'You'll learn,' he said. 'Back to the monk's cell for me. It's going to be hard tomorrow. He's always bad after Todt's given his report.'

'Why's that?' asked Voss, still keen, still capable of doing an all-nighter for the East Front.

'The first place you lose a battle is up here,' said Weber, leaning over Voss and tapping his head, 'and Todt lost that one last June. He's a good man and he's a genius and that's a bad combination for this war. Good night.'

Voss knew Fritz Todt, as everyone knew him, as the inventor of the *autobahnen*, but he was much more than that now. Not only was he running all arms and munitions production for the Third Reich, but he and his Organization Todt were the builders of the West Wall and the U-boat pens that would protect Europe from invasion. He was also in charge of building and repairing all roads and railways in the Occupied Territories. Todt was the greatest construction engineer in German history and this was the greatest programme of all time.

Voss surveyed the situation map. The front line stretched from Lake Onega, 500 kilometres south-west of Archangel on the White Sea, through Leningrad, the Moscow suburbs and down to Tagan-rog on the Sea of Azov, off the Black Sea. From Arctic to Caucasus was under German control.

'And he thinks we're *losing* this war?' asked Voss out loud, shaking his head.

He worked for another hour or more and then went out for another cigarette and to wake himself up in the freezing air. On his way back he saw the good-looking man who'd arrived earlier, sitting on his own in the dining room and then, coming towards him outside the situation room, another figure, shuffling along with sagging shoulders as if they were under some penitential weight. The face was grey, soft and slack, falling away from its substructure. The eyes saw nothing beyond the immense calculation in his mind. Voss moved to avoid the man but at the last moment they seemed to veer into each other and their shoulders clashed. The man's face was reanimated in shock and Voss recognized him now.

'Forgive me, Herr Reichsminister.'

'No, no, my fault,' said Todt. 'I wasn't looking.'

'Thinking too hard, sir,' said Voss, dog-like.

Todt studied the slim, blond young man more carefully now.

'Working late, Captain?'

'Just finishing the orders, sir,' said Voss, nodding at the open door of the situation room.

Todt lingered on the threshold of the room, his eyes roved the map and the flags of the armies and their divisions.

'Nearly there, sir,' said Voss.

'Russia,' said Todt, his eye swivelling on to Voss, 'is a very large place.'

'Yes, sir,' said Voss, after a long pause in which nothing more was forthcoming.

'Maps of Russia should be room-sized,' said Todt. 'So that army generals have to *walk* to move their divisions, with the knowledge that each step they take is 500 kilometres of snow and ice, or rain and mud, and in the few months of the year when it's neither of those things they should know that the steppe is shimmering in silent, brutal, dust-choked heat.'

Voss shut up, mesmerized by the thunderous roll of the older man's voice. Todt backed out of the room. Voss wanted him to stay, to continue, but no questions came to mind other than the banal.

'Are you on the first flight out tomorrow, sir?'

'Yes, why?'

'To Berlin?'

'We'll stop in Berlin on the way to Munich.'

'These files need to go to Berlin.'

'In that case they'd better be on my plane before seven thirty. Talk to the flight captain. Good night, er . . . Captain . . .'

'Captain Voss, sir.'

'Have you seen Speer, Captain Voss? I was told he'd arrived.'

'There's someone in the dining room. He arrived earlier.'

Todt moved away, shuffling again down the corridor. Before he turned left to the dining room he turned on Voss.

'Don't imagine for one second, Captain, that the Russians are doing nothing about . . . about *your* situation in there,' he said, and disappeared.

No wonder the Führer was bad after Todt's visits.

Another half-hour passed and Voss went to fetch coffee from the dining room. Speer and Todt sat on either side of a single glass of wine, which the older man sipped. The structural differences between the two men were marked. The one slumped with definite subsidence under the right foundation, the nineteenth century, Wilhelmine façade lined and cracked, the paint and masonry crumbling to scurf. The other cantilevered over at an impossible angle, his lines clean and defined, the modern Bauhaus front, dark, handsome, uncluttered and bright.

'Captain Voss,' said Todt, turning to him, 'did you speak to the flight captain yet?'

'No, sir.'

'When you do, tell him that Herr Speer will be joining me. He came in from Dnepropetrovsk tonight.'

Voss drank his coffee and on the way back to his work he had the strange and uncomfortable sense of silent machinery at work, out of his sight and beyond his knowledge. He turned into the situation room, just as SS Colonel Bruno Weiss came out of Hitler's apartment. Weiss was head of the SS company at Rastenburg in charge of Hitler's security and the only thing Voss knew about him was that he didn't like anybody except Hitler, and he had a particular dislike of intelligence officers.

'What are you doing, Captain?' he shouted down the corridor.

'Just finishing these orders, sir.'

Weiss bore down on him and inspected the situation room, the scar running from his left eye to below his cheekbone livid against his pale skin.

'What are these?'

'Army Chief of Staff files, sir, to go back to Berlin on the Reichsminister Todt's flight this morning. I'm about to inform the flight captain.'

Weiss nodded at the phone. Voss called the flight captain and booked Speer on to the plane as well. Weiss wrote things down in his notebook and went back to Hitler's apartment. Minutes later he was back.

'These files . . . when are they going?' he asked.

'They have to be at the airstrip by 07.30 hours this morning, sir.'

'Answer the question fully, Captain.'

'I will be taking them personally, leaving here at 07.15 hours, sir.'

'Good,' said Weiss. 'I have some security files to go back to the Reichsführer's office. They will be delivered here. I will inform the flight captain.'

Weiss left. An adjutant strode past. Minutes later he came back followed by Speer.

Voss, like Hitler (not an unconscious imitation), enjoyed working at night. He worked with the door open to hear the voices, see the men, to gain a sense of the magnetic flow – those drawn to and favoured by the Führer and those he rejected and disgraced. In the short time he'd been in Rastenburg, Voss had seen men striding down the centre of that corridor, medals, pips and epaulets flashing, to return fifteen minutes later hugging the wall, shunned even by the carpet strip in the middle. There were others, of course, who came back evangelized, something in their eyes higher than the stars, greater than love. These were the men who had 'gone', left the decrepit shell of their own bodies to walk an Elysium with other demigods, their ambitions fulfilled, their greatness confirmed.

Weber saw it differently, and said it with a cruder voice: 'These guys, they're all married with wives and families of lovely children and yet they go up there and take it up the arse every night. It's a disgrace.' Weber had accused Voss of it, too. Of sitting with his tongue out in the corridor, waiting for a tummy rub. It needled Voss only because it was true. In his first week, as Voss had laid maps down in a situation meeting while Zeitzler said his piece, the Führer had suddenly gripped Voss by the bicep and the touch had shot something fast and pure into his veins like morphine, strong, addictive but weakening, too.

The *Wolfsschanze* stilled into the early hours. Corridor traffic halted. Voss filed the orders and prepared the maps and positions for the morning conference, taking his time because he liked the feeling of working while the world was asleep. At 3.00 a.m. there was a flurry of activity from Hitler's apartment and moments later Speer appeared at the door looking like a matinée idol. He asked Voss if he wouldn't mind cancelling him from the Reichsminister's flight in the morning, he was too tired after his earlier flight and his meeting with the Führer. Voss assured him of his efficiency in the matter and Speer stepped into the room. He stood over the map and brushed a hand in a great swathe over Russia, Poland, Germany, the Netherlands and France. He became conscious of Voss studying him and put his hand in his pocket. He nodded, said good night and reminded him to tell the flight captain. He didn't want to be disturbed in the morning.

Voss made the call and went to bed for three hours. He got up just before 7.00 a.m., called a car and he and the chauffeur loaded the box files, along with a black metal trunk which had appeared in the situation room addressed in white paint through a stencil to the SS Personalhauptamt, 98–9 Wilmersdorferstrasse, Berlin-Charlottenburg. They drove to the airstrip where, to their surprise, they found Todt's Heinkel charging down the runway. Voss could already feel the lash of Weiss's fury. He went to the flight captain who told him they were just testing the plane under orders from Hitler's adjutant. The plane circled twice and relanded. A sergeant with a manifest cleared the files on to the aircraft and they loaded them. Voss and the chauffeur drank a coffee in the canteen and ate bread and eggs. At 7.50 a.m. the Reichsminister's car pulled alongside and Fritz Todt boarded the Heinkel alone.

The plane immediately taxied to the end of the runway, paused, throttled up and set off down the snow-scabbed airstrip towards the black trees and low grey cloud of another grainy military morning. It should still have been dark at this hour but the Führer insisted on keeping Berlin time at his Rastenburg headquarters.

As he left the canteen Voss was arrested by the rare sight of SS Colonel Weiss outside the Restricted Area I compound. He was in the control tower, looking green through the glass, his thick arms folded across his chest, his pale face lit by some unseen light below him.

The continuous roar of the plane's engines changed tone and the wings tipped as it banked over the pine forest. This was unusual, too. The plane should have continued west, piercing the soft gut of the grey cloud to break through into the brilliant, uncomplicated sunshine above, instead of which it had rolled north and appeared to be coming back in to re-land.

The pilot straightened the wings of the plane and settled the aircraft into its descent. It was just reaching the beginning of the runway, no more than a hundred feet off the ground, when a spear of flame shot up from the fuselage behind the cockpit. Voss, already gaping, flinched as the roar of the explosion reached him. His driver ducked as the plane tilted and a wing clipped the ground, shearing away from the body of the plane, which thundered into the snow-covered ground and exploded with hideous violence, twice, a fraction of a second between each full fuel tank igniting.

Black smoke belched, funnelling out into the grey sky. Only the tailplane had survived the impact. Two fire engines stormed pointlessly out of their hangar, slewing on the icy ground. SS Colonel Weiss dropped his arms, jutted his chest, stretched his shoulders back and left the observation platform.

Voss grew into the iron-hard ground, his feet drawing up the numbing cold, transporting it through to the bones and organs of his body.

Chapter 3

8th February 1942, Wolfsschanze HQ, Rastenburg, East Prussia.

Voss was driven back to Restricted Area I in silence, the dead hand
of a full inquiry already on his shoulder. He pieced together the
ugly fragments of information in his brain and felt his mind recoil
in disgust. He began to see, for the first time, how a man could
shoot himself. Until then it had been a mystery to him, on hearing
of someone's suicide, how a man could bring himself to such a
disastrous conclusion. He smoked hard until he was quite faint and
prickling. He staggered up the path to the main building and realized on entering that the horrific news had preceded him by some
minutes.

The dining room was full, but rather than being morbid with
the news of the death of the most important and capable engineer
in the German Reich, it was rife with the rumour of a successor.
The monochrome mass of braid and band, oak leaf cluster and iron
cross seethed like the bullring of the Bourse. Only one man was
silent, head up, hair swept back, dark eyes shining under the thick
straight eyebrows – Albert Speer. Voss blinked, sure as a camera
shutter, and captured the image – a man on the brink of his destiny.

Voss took a coffee, fed himself into the knots of conversation
and soon realized that anybody with anything to do with construction and transportation was in the room.

'Speer will take the Atlantic Wall, the U-boat pens and the
Occupied West. It's already been talked about.'

'What about the Ukraine? The Ukraine is more important now.'

'You didn't forget that we declared war on the United States
before Christmas.'

'No, I didn't, and nor did Todt.'

Silence. Heads swung to Speer's table. People were putting
things to him and he was managing vague replies to their questions,

14

but he wasn't listening. He was coming to terms with a price. Appalled at the animal troughing around him, unwilling to accept anything that they attempted to confer on him, he was trying to justify to himself not only his presence there (for the first time and on such a tragic occasion), but something else whose nature he couldn't quite grasp. He seemed to be coping with a strong, unpleasant smell which had reached his nostrils only.

'He won't give it all to him . . . the Führer wouldn't do that. No experience.'

'He'll split Armaments and Munitions away from Construction.'

'You wait . . . the Reichsmarschall will be here any moment. Then we'll see . . .'

'Where is Goering?'

'At Romiten. Hunting.'

'That's only a hundred kilometres away . . . has anybody called him?'

'Goering will take Armaments and Munitions into his Commission for the Four Year Plan. He's in charge of the war economy. It fits.'

'The only thing that fits, if you ask me, is that one's face over there.'

'What's Speer *doing* here, anyway?'

'He was stuck in Dnepropetrovsk. He flew in with Captain Nein last night.'

'He *fetched* him?' asked a voice, aghast.

'No, no Captain Nein flew in there with SS General Sepp Dietrich and offered Speer a lift.'

'Did Speer and the general . . . talk?'

There was silence at that probability and Voss moved across to some air force officers who were picking over the details of the crash.

'He must have pulled the self-destruct handle.'

'Who? The pilot?'

'No, Todt . . . by accident.'

'Did it have a self-destruct mechanism on board?'

'No, it was a new plane. It hadn't been fitted.'

'What was he doing in a two-engined plane in the first place? The Führer has expressly forbidden . . .'

15

'That's what Todt was told yesterday. He was furious. The Führer waived it.'

'That's why they took the plane up for a practice spin.'

'And you're sure there was no self-destruct mechanism?'

'Positive.'

'There were three explosions . . . that's what the flight sergeant said.'

'Three?'

'There must have been a self-destruct . . .'

'There was none!'

Voss went to the decoding room to pick up any positional changes in the field. He took the decodes to the situation room. The corridor was silent. Hitler rarely moved before eleven o'clock, but on a day such as this? Surely. The apartment door stayed closed, the SS guards silent.

Weber was already working on supply positions in the Ukraine. He didn't look up. Voss leafed the decodes.

'SS Colonel Weiss was looking for you,' said Weber.

'Did he say what he wanted?' asked Voss, bowels loosening.

'Something about those boxes of files . . .'

'Have you heard, Weber?'

'About the plane crash, you mean?'

'The Reichsminister Todt is dead.'

'Were those files on board?'

'Yes,' said Voss, stunned by Weber's insouciance.

'Shit. Zeitzler's going to be mad.'

'Weber,' said Voss, amazed, 'Todt is dead.'

'*Todt ist tot. Todt ist tot.* What can I say, other than it will brighten the Führer's day not to have that doom merchant on his shoulder.'

'For God's sake, Weber.'

'Look, Voss, Todt never agreed with the Russian campaign and when the Führer declared war on America, well . . . poof!'

'Poof!?'

'Todt was a very cautious man, unlike our Führer who is . . . what shall we say . . . ?'

'Bold.'

'Yes, bold. That's a good, strong adjective. Let's leave it at that.'

'What are you saying, Weber?'

'Keep your head down and your ears out of that corridor. Do

16

your job, don't blabber, this is all that matters,' he said, and drew a circle around himself. 'You haven't been here long enough to know what these people are capable of.'

'They're already talking about Speer. Goering taking over . . .'

'I don't want to know, Voss,' said Weber, closing his hands over his ears. 'And nor do you. You've got to start thinking about those files, how they got on that plane and why SS Colonel Weiss wants to talk to you, because if he wanted to talk to me after such a morning I'd have been in the toilet an hour ago. Start thinking about yourself, Voss, because here in Rastenburg you're the only one who will.'

The mention of the toilet sent Voss out of the room at a brisk pace. He sat in one of the stalls, face in hands, and passed a loose, hot motion which, rather than emptying him, left his guts writhing.

Colonel Weiss caught up with him while he washed his hands. They talked to each other via the mirror, Weiss's face disturbingly wrong in reflection.

'Those files . . .' started Weiss.

'General Zeitzler's files, you mean?'

'Did you check them, Captain Voss . . . before you took them into your care?'

'Took them into my care?' Voss asked himself, chest wall shuddering at the impact of this implication.

'Did you, Captain? Did you?' persisted Weiss.

'They weren't mine to check, and even if they were I wouldn't know why I would have to check a large amount of documentation irrelevant to me.'

'So who filled those boxes?'

'I didn't see them filled.'

'You *didn't*?' roared Weiss, throwing Voss into free-fall fear. 'You put boxes on to a Reichsminister's plane without . . .'

'Maybe you should ask Captain Weber,' said Voss, desperate, lashing out at anything to save himself.

'Captain Weber,' said Weiss, writing him down in his book of the damned.

'I was doing him a favour putting the files on the plane in the first place, as I was for . . .' He coughed at a garrotting look from Weiss and changed tack. 'Is this part of the official inquiry, sir?'

'This is the preliminary investigation prior to the official inquiry which will be conducted by the air force, as it is technically an air force matter,' said Weiss, and then more threatening, 'but as you know, I'm in charge of all security matters in and around this compound . . . and I notice things, Captain Voss.'

Weiss had turned away from the mirror to look at him for real. Voss stepped back and his boot heel hit the wall but he managed to look Weiss straight in his terrible eye, hoping that his own stress, from the G-force steepness of the learning curve, was not distorting his face.

'I have a copy of the manifest,' said Weiss. 'Perhaps you should read it through now.'

Weiss handed him the paper. It started with a list of personnel on the flight. Speer's name had been added and then crossed out. Underneath was the cargo. Voss ran his eyes down the list, which was short and consisted of four boxes of files for the Army Chief of Staff, delivery Berlin, and several pieces of luggage going with Todt to Munich. There was no mention of a metal trunk for delivery to the SS Personalhauptamt in Berlin-Charlottenburg.

Voss had control of his panic now, the horizon firm in his head as he came up to the moment, or was it the line? Yes, it was something to be crossed, a line with no grey area, without no man's land, the moral line, which once stepped over joined him to Weiss's morality. He also knew that to mention the nonexistent trunk would be a life-changing decision, one that could change his life into death. It nearly amused him, that and the strange clarity of those turbulent thoughts.

'Now you understand,' said Weiss, 'why it's necessary for me to do a little probing on the question of these files.'

'Yes, sir,' said Voss. 'You're absolutely right, sir.'

'Good, we have an understanding then?'

'Yes, sir,' said Voss. 'One thing . . . wasn't there . . . ?'

Weiss stiffened in his boots, the scar dragging down his eye seemed to pulsate.

'. . . wasn't there a self-destruct mechanism on the plane?' finished Voss.

Weiss's good eye widened and he nodded, confirming that and their new understanding into him. He left the toilets. Voss reverted to the sink and splashed his hot face over and over with cold water, not able to clean exactly, but able to revise and rework, justify and accommodate the necessity for the snap decision he'd been forced to make. He dried his face and looked at himself in the mirror and had one of his odd perceptions, that we never know what we look like to others, we only know our reflection and that now he knew he would be different and it might be all right because perhaps he would just look like one of them.

He went outside for a smoke and to pace out his new understanding, as if he was wearing different boots. Senior officers came and went with only one topic of conversation on their hungry lips and two names, Speer and Todt. But by the end of that cigarette Voss had made his first intelligence discovery in the field, because the officers still came and went and they still had those two names on their lips but this time they were shaking their heads and the words 'self-destruct mechanism' and the 'incidence of failure' had threaded their way amongst the names.

It comes out of here and goes in there, thought Voss. The inestimable power of the spoken word. The power of misinformation in a thunderstruck community.

Voss went back to work. No Weber. He replotted the latest movements from the decodes. Weber returned, took a seat, braced himself against the desk. Voss kept his head down, looked at Weber through the bone of his cranium.

'At least I know you can listen now,' said Weber. 'You've passed the first Rastenburg test with an A and you don't have to worry about me and those files. I didn't fill them. I didn't seal them. I didn't even sign for them. Learn something from that, Voss. They're saying now that somebody must have accidentally pulled the self-destruct handle in the plane. We're all in the clear. Are you hearing me, Voss?'

'I'm hearing you.'

Voss did hear him, but only through the reel of film in his head which was full of the black metal trunk with its white stencilled address. His hands lifting the trunk and taking it into the plane where he jams it between the seats so it won't slide about – two of Zeitzler's boxes of files on top and two on the seats by the trunk. Todt comes on to the plane, preceded by his luggage, impatient to be away from the scene of his disastrous politicking and up into the light of the sunshine and the clear air where everything is comprehensible. He straps himself into his seat, not next to the pilot but in the fuselage where he might be able to do some work. The hold darkens as the door closes. The pilot taxis to the end of the runway. The plane steadies itself, the wings rock and stabilize. The propellers thrash the icy air. The pressure kicks in behind the old man's back and they surge down the runway flashing white, grey and black at the snow and ice patches on the strip. Then Todt sees the black trunk and some low animal instinct kicks in the paranoia and a terrible realization. He roars at the pilot to stop the plane but the pilot cannot stop. The velocity is already too great. He has to take off. The wheels defy gravity and Todt has a moment of weightlessness, a premonition of the lightness of being to follow. They bank in the steep curve, the trunk tight against the wall of the fuselage. Todt staring into the black Polish pine trees, or are they East Prussian pine trees now, Germanic Empire pine trees? Todt's weight has come back to him and he's in a panic now. He's seen the trunk before. He's seen it in his head and he knows what's in it. He knew what would be in it the night before and he woke up with the knowledge this morning and it was further confirmed by the flight captain who told him that Speer would not be on the plane. What was Speer *doing* here anyway? Todt and Speer. Two men who knew their destiny and had no hesitation in obeying. The plane's wings are still perpendicular to the ground. The black forest is still flashing past Todt's care-worn eyes. The wings flatten. They're going to make it after all. The pilot is hunched and roaring at the control tower. The altimeter winds its way down through three hundred to two hundred to one hundred and fifty and Todt is praying and the pilot is praying too, although he doesn't know why and that is how they enter the biggest noise, the whitest light. Two men praying. One who didn't like war enough and the other unlucky to be flying him.

And then silence. Not even the wind whistling through the shattered fuselage. Pure peace for the man who didn't like war enough.

'Everything all right in there, Voss?'

Voss looked up, dazed, Weber a blur in his eye.

'There was something else . . .'

'There was *nothing* else, Voss. Nothing that anybody wants to know. Nothing that I want to know. Those words stay in your head. In here we talk about military positions. All right?'

Voss went through the decodes. The black metal trunk slid into a dark recess, the murky horror corner of his mind, and soon the white stencilled address was barely readable.

At 1.00 p.m. Hitler sent an adjutant to bring in his first caller of the day. The adjutant returned with Speer in his wake. Fifteen minutes later the Reichsmarschall Goering appeared in the corridor smiling and resplendent in light blue, his smooth jowls, shiny perhaps from the patina of last night's morphine sweat, juddered with each step. Half an hour later it was out. Speer had been appointed Todt's successor in *all* his capacities and the Reichsmarschall Goering's humour was reclassified as unstable.

Men from the Air Ministry sifted the wreckage for days and found nothing but seared metal and black dust. The black metal trunk with its white stencilling had ceased to exist. SS Colonel Weiss, under Hitler's instructions, conducted an internal investigation into the airport personnel and ground crew. Voss was required to supply his initials to the manifest alongside the four box files – posterity for his perjury.

The ice began to thaw, tanks whose tracks had been welded to the steppes broke free and the war rolled on, even without the greatest construction engineer in German history.

Chapter 4

18th November 1942, Wolfsschanze HQ, Rastenburg, East Prussia.

Voss wanted to remove his eyeballs and swill them in saline, see the grit sink to the bottom. The bunker was silent with the Führer away at the Berghof in Obersalzberg. Voss's work had been finished hours ago but he remained at the situation table, chin resting on his white, piled fists, staring into the map where a rough cratering existed at a point on the Volga river. Stalingrad had been poked and prodded, jabbed and reamed until it was a dirty, paper-flaked hole. As Voss looked deeper into it he began to see the blackened, snow-covered city, the cadaverous apartment buildings, the gnarled and twisted beams of shelled factories, the poxed façades, the scree-filled streets littered with stiffened, deep-frozen bodies and, alongside it, growing to midnight black in the white landscape and becoming viscous with the cold, the Volga – the line of communication from the south to the north of Russia.

He was sitting in this position long after he could have gone to bed, contemplating the grey front line that was now stretched to the thinness of piano wire since the German Sixth Army had ballooned it over to Stalingrad, because of his brother. Julius Voss was a major in the 113th Infantry Division of the Sixth Army. This division was not one of those fighting like a pack of street dogs in the ruins of Stalingrad but was dug into the snow somewhere on the treeless steppe east of the point where the river Don had decided to turn south to the Sea of Azov.

Julius Voss was his father's son. A brilliant sportsman, he'd collected a silver in the *epée* at the 1936 Berlin Olympics. He rode a horse as if it was a part of him. On his first day's hunting at the age of sixteen he'd tracked a deer for a whole day and shot it in the eye from 300 metres. He was a perfect and outstanding army officer, loved by his men and admired by his superiors. He was intelligent and, despite his life of brilliance, there wasn't a shred of arrogance in the man. Karl thought about him a lot. He loved him. Julius had been his protector at school, sport not being one of Karl's strengths and, having too many brains for everybody's comfort, life could have been hell without a brother three years older and a golden boy, too. So Karl was taking his turn to watch over his brother.

The German position was not as strong as it might first appear. The Russians had trussed up ten divisions in and around the city in bloody and brutal street-to-street fighting since September and now, unless they could hammer home the death blow in the next month, it looked as if the rest of the German army would be condemned to spend another winter out in the open. More men would die and there would be little chance of the Sixth Army being reinforced until the spring. The situation was doomed to a four-month deep-frozen stalemate.

The door to the situation room crashed open, cannoned off the wall and slammed shut. It opened more slowly to reveal Weber standing in the frame.

'That's better,' he said, trying to put some lick on to his lips, clearly drunk, steaming drunk, his forehead shining, his eyes bright, his skin blubber. 'I knew I'd find you in here, boring the maps again.'

Weber swaggered into the room.

'You can't bore maps, Weber.'

'*You* can. Look at them, poor bastards. Insensate with tedium. You don't talk to them, Voss, that's your problem.'

'Piss off, Weber. You're ten schnapps down the hole and not fit to talk to.'

'And you? What are you doing? Is the brilliant, creative military mind of Captain Karl Voss going to solve the Stalingrad problem ... tonight, or do we have to wait *another* twenty-four hours?'

'I was just thinking ...'

'Don't tell me. Let me guess. You were just thinking about what the Reichsminister Fritz Todt said to you before his plane crash ...'

'And why shouldn't I?'

'Because it's morbid in a man of your age. You should be thinking about ... about women ...' said Weber and, placing both hands

23

on the table, he began some vigorous, graphic and improbable thrusting.

Voss looked away. Weber collapsed across the table. When Voss looked back, Weber's face was right there, giving him the wife's-eye view, head on the pillow, husband sweaty, lurid, tight, pink skin and wet-eyed.

'You shouldn't feel guilty just because Todt spoke to you,' said Weber, licking his lips again, eyes closed now as if imagining a kiss coming to him.

'That's not why I feel guilty. I feel . . .'

'Don't tell me, I don't want to know,' said Weber, sitting up and shunning him with a hand. 'Bore your maps, Voss. Go on. But I'll tell you this,' he came in close again, devil breath, 'Paulus will take Stalingrad before Christmas and we'll be in Persia by next spring, rolling in sherbet. The oil will be ours, *and* the grain. How long will Moscow last?'

'The Romanians on the River Don front have reported huge troop concentrations in their north-west sector,' said Voss, flat and heavy.

Weber sat up, dangled his legs and gave Voss the gab, gab, gab with his hand.

'The fucking Romanians,' he said. 'Goulash for brains.'

'That's the Hungarians.'

'What?'

'Who eat goulash.'

'What do Romanians eat?'

Voss shrugged.

'Problem,' said Weber. 'We don't know what the Romanian brain consists of, but if you ask me it's yoghurt . . . no . . . it's the whey from the top of the yoghurt.'

'You're boring me, Weber.'

'Let's have a drink.'

'You're stinking already.'

'Come on,' he said, grabbing Voss around the shoulders and barging him out of the door, their cheeks touching as they went through, horrid lovers.

Weber slashed the lights out. They put on their coats and went back to their quarters. Weber crashed about in his own room while Voss moved the chess game, which he was playing against his father

24

by post, away from the bed. Weber appeared, triumphant, with schnapps. He crashed down on to the bed, hoicked a magazine out from under his buttocks.

'What's this?'

'*Die Naturwissenschafen.*'

'Fucking physics,' said Weber, hurling the magazine. 'You want to get into something ...'

'... physical, yes, I know, Weber. Give me the schnapps, I need to be braindead to continue.'

Weber handed over the bottle, bolstered his wet head with Voss's pillow, whacking it into position with his stone cranium. Voss sipped the clear liquid which lit a trail down to his colon.

'What's physics going to do for me?' burped Weber.

'Win the war.'

'Go on.'

'Give us endless reusable energy.'

'And?'

'Explain life.'

'I don't want life explained, I just want to live it on my own terms.'

'Nobody gets to do that, Weber ... not even the Führer.'

'Tell me how it's going to win us the war.'

'Perhaps you haven't heard talk of the atom bomb.'

'I heard Heisenberg nearly blew himself up with one in June.'

'So you've heard of Heisenberg.'

'Naturally,' said Weber, brushing imaginary lint from his fly. '*And* the chemist Otto Hahn. You think I don't stick my ear out in that corridor every now and again.'

'I won't bore you then.'

'So what's it all about? Atom bombs.'

'Forget it, Weber.'

'It goes in easier when I'm drunk.'

'All right. You take some fissionable material ...'

'I'm lost.'

'Remember Goethe.'

'Goethe! Fuck. What did *he* say about "fissionable material"?'

'He said: "What is the path? There is no path. On into the unknown."'

'Gloomy bastard,' said Weber, snatching back the bottle. 'Start again.'

'There's a certain type of material, a very rare material, which when brought together in a critical mass – shut up and listen – could create as many as eighty generations of fission – shut up, Weber, just let me get it out – before the phenomenal heat would blow the mass apart. That means . . .'

'I'm glad you said that.'

'. . . that, if you can imagine this, one fission releases two hundred million electron bolts of energy and that would double eighty times before the chain reaction would stop. What do you think that would produce, Weber?'

'The biggest blast known to mankind. Is that what you're saying?'

'A whole city wiped out with one bomb.'

'You said this fissionable material's pretty rare.'

'It comes from uranium.'

'Aha!' said Weber, sitting up. 'Joachimstahl.'

'What about it?'

'Biggest uranium mine in Europe. And it's in Czechoslovakia . . . which is *ours*,' said Weber, cuddling the schnapps bottle.

'There's an even bigger one in the Belgian Congo.'

'Aha! Which is ours, too, because . . .'

'Yes, Weber, we know, but it's still a very complicated chemical process to get the fissionable material out of the uranium. The stuff they'd found was called U 235 but they could only get traces and it decayed almost instantly. Then somebody called Weizsäcker began to think about what happened to all the excess neutrons released by the fission of U 235, some would be captured by U 238, which would then become U 239, which would then decay into a new element which he called Ekarhenium.'

'Voss.'

'Yes?'

'You're boring the shit out of me. Drink some more of this and try saying it all backwards. It might, you know, make more sense.'

'I told you it was complicated,' said Voss. 'Anyway, they've found a way to make the "fissionable material" comparatively easily in an atomic pile, which uses graphite and some stuff called heavy water, which we used to be able to get from the Norsk Hydro plant in Norway – until the British sabotaged it.'

'I remember something about that,' said Weber. 'So the British know we're building this bomb.'

26

'They know we have the science – it's in all these magazines you're throwing around my room – but do we have the capability? It's a huge industrial undertaking, building an atomic pile is just the first step.'

'How much of this Ekarhe— shit do you need to make a bomb?'

'A kilo, maybe two.'

'That's not very much . . . to blow up an entire city.'

'Blow up isn't really the word, Weber,' said Voss. 'Vaporize is more like it.'

'Give me that schnapps.'

'It's going to take years to build this thing.'

'We'll be rolling in sherbet by then.'

Weber finished the bottle and went to bed. Voss stayed up and read his mother's part of the letter, which contained detailed descriptions of social occasions and was strangely comforting. His father, General Heinrich Voss, sitting out the war in enforced retirement, having made the mistake of voicing his opinions about the Commissar Order – where any Jews or partisans encountered in the Russian campaign were to be handed over to the SS for 'treatment' – would add an irascible note at the bottom and a chess move. This time his move was followed by the word 'check' and the line: 'You don't know it yet but I've got you on the run.' Voss shook his head. He didn't even have to think. He dragged the chair with the chessboard to him, made his father's move and then his own, which he scribbled on to a note and put in an envelope to post in the morning.

At 10.00 a.m. 19th November the first conference of the day got underway with a discussion over an enlarged map of Stalingrad and its immediate vicinity. No attempt had been made to alter the map to show the true state of the city. All it indicated was neatly packaged sectors, red for Russian, grey for German, like peacetime postal districts.

At 10.30 a.m. the teleprinters shunted into life and the phones started ringing. General Zeitzler was called from the room, to return minutes later with the announcement that a Russian offensive had started at 05.20 a.m. He showed how a Russian tank force had broken through the Romanian sectors and was now heading south-east towards the river Don, and that activity had broken out along the whole front to hold German forces in their positions. A panzer corps had been sent to engage the advancing Russians. Everything was in hand. Voss made the necessary alterations to the map. They went back to the Stalingrad situation leaving Zeitzler fingering the small flag of the panzer corps and rasping a hand over his sandpaper chin.

By lunchtime the next day news reached Rastenburg of a second large Russian offensive starting south of Stalingrad, with such huge numbers of tanks and infantry it was inconceivable that they'd had no intelligence.

The Stalingrad map was rolled and stacked.

It was clear that full encirclement of the Sixth Army was the Russian intention. Voss felt sick and empty as Zeitzler dragged him and his inexhaustible memory around wherever he went. Voss stood over Zeitzler's telephone conversations to the Führer, vomiting information which the Army Chief of Staff would use in a desperate bid to impress on Hitler the dire circumstances and the need to allow the Sixth Army to retreat. The Führer paced the great hall of the Berghof swearing at Slavs and hammering tables into submission.

Sunday, 22nd November was *Totensonntag*, the day of remembrance for the dead, and after a subdued service they heard that the two Russian forces were about to meet and that encirclement was a foregone conclusion. The Führer left the Berghof for Leipzig to fly on to Rastenburg.

As Voss began the monumental task of drafting orders for the phased withdrawal of the Sixth Army the Führer stopped his train en route to Leipzig and called Zeitzler expressly to forbid any retreat.

Zeitzler sent Voss back to his room and, to take his mind off the disaster, Voss pored over the chess game. In doing so he suddenly saw his error, or rather, he perceived his father's strength of position. He searched for the letter he'd scribbled days ago and found that one of the orderlies had posted it for him. He took out another sheet of paper and wrote one word on it. Resigned.

The Führer arrived in Rastenburg on 23rd November and after the initial shock of the Russian success nerves steadied. In the days and weeks that followed the disaster, Voss witnessed the transformation of the Rastenburg HQ. It ceased to be a military installation and became instead the stuff of legend. Men would arrive, tear off their cloaks and capes and perform miracles in front of their glassy-eyed leader. Vast and powerfully armoured divisions, miraculously supplied, would appear and drive up from the south to relieve the stricken army. When, as in some bizarre game of three-card monte, this force failed to materialize, another maestro would whisk away a silken sheet and show fleets of aircraft supplying and resupplying until, brought back up to full strength, the Sixth Army would take Stalingrad, break the Russian encirclement and assume their position in Germanic legend. Everything became possible. Rastenburg became a circus where the greatest illusionists of the time came to perform.

At this stage, in the weeks leading up to Christmas, a sickness settled itself in Voss's gut. The news of men dying of starvation and cold, and the back to back shows from prestidigitators from all the forces, sealed off his stomach. His blue eyes sunk back into his head, his uniform hung off his ribs. He sipped water or schnapps and smoked upwards of fifty cigarettes a day.

In mid December an attempt was made to relieve the army from the south. The Russians stalled the attack and proceeded to smash the Italian army and decimate the air transport fleet. Still the Führer refused permission for the Sixth Army to retreat; his eyes seared the situation maps demanding deliverance.

Voss listened, first to the quality of the silence in the situation conferences, which were black, crushing and hideous, and then to the boot-licking apostles of the High Command who would pledge the impossible for one look of love from the Führer. He asked for a transfer to the front. Zeitzler refused him and, perhaps after seeing the bones appearing through the skin of Voss's face, went on Stalingrad rations himself. They became known as 'the cadavers'.

There had been no improvement in the German Sixth Army's position by the beginning of January 1943 and Voss, pale with his facial skin drawn tightly over his skull, found himself on his bed in his room smoking and sipping some of Weber's violent schnapps. He had two letters in front of him on the seat of a chair where he used to keep the chess games he played with his father. There'd been no chess since his resignation back in November. The two letters, both short, one from his father and the other from his brother, had presented him with a problem whose only solution involved calling on SS Colonel Bruno Weiss.

The *Kessel*, Stalingrad

1st January 1943

Dear Karl,

You know better than anyone our situation out here. I can only thank you for trying to send us the sausages and ham for Christmas but it was a lost cause. They probably never got off the airstrip. Real meat has not been seen for weeks. Krebs and Stahlschuss came up with some shreds of dried mule so that we managed to have some kind of celebration for the New Year. It wasn't as good as Christmas which, whatever happens to me now, will have been one of the greatest military experiences of my short career. It's difficult to believe in this unbearable environment that men can find (I've thought about this a long time to try to find the right word) such sweetness in themselves. They gave each other things which were their last and most important possessions and if they had nothing they made something from bits of metal or carved bone retrieved from the steppe. It was remarkable to find the human spirit so undaunted. Glaser has tried to have me taken to the hospital again (I'm yellow, and the legs are still badly swollen so that I can't move about) but I've refused. I never want to see that vision of hell again. I won't tell you. You must have heard by now.

I listen to the men and there's been a change in their mood now. Before the New Year they would say that the Führer will rescue them. Now, if they still think that, they don't say it. We are resigned to our fate and you might be surprised to hear that we are cheerful because, and I know this will sound absurd in the circumstances, we are free.

I think of you and am always your brother,

Julius

Karl read this letter over and over. His brother had never been one for the examination of the soul and his discovery of the nobility of man in these desperate circumstances was a revelation. Karl was sickened by the thought of playing on Weiss's side of the fence to get what he wanted.

Berlin

2nd January 1943

Dear Karl,

We have had another letter from Julius. His are not censored like some of the junior officers'. Your mother cannot read them even though he makes light of the terrible things around him. He seems so inured to the desperate circumstances that he doesn't see that what he considers normal is, to people in Berlin, unimaginable horror. I do not ask this of you lightly. I only ask this of you because I saw some of this pointlessness in the Great War. It goes against every military instinct I have but I would like you to do everything you can to get your brother out of that place. I know it is forbidden. I know it is impossible but I must ask this of you on behalf of your mother and for myself.

Your father

Voss lay back on the bed, his boots up on the metal bar at his feet, the two letters on his chest resting against his protruding ribs. He lit another cigarette from the one he'd been smoking. He knew that if anything happened to Julius it could potentially destroy his family. Since his father had been 'retired', he'd invested all his hopes and aspirations in his first-born son. He thought it possible that his father might be able to bear Julius's death in glorious victory but not, definitely not, in miserable defeat.

Voss swung his feet off the bed and slapped a sheet of paper on to the chair. He would have preferred to ask this favour of General Zeitzler but knew that he could not possibly grant him the request. SS Colonel Weiss was the only man with whom he had any leverage, if that was a word he could use when it came to the SS.

He began writing in his horrible, cramped scrawl, handwriting

31

that had developed because his brain always worked faster than his fingers. He balled his first attempt and tried again. He screwed that one up, too. He didn't know what he wanted for his brother. He wanted to save him, of course, but on what terms? Julius, his state of mind heightened to rare acuity, would not be easily duped.

Rastenburg

5th January 1943

Dear Julius,
The officer who will give you this letter will be able to get you out of your predicament, fly you out of the *Kessel* and eventually into hospital back in Berlin. You have a stark and terrible decision to make. If you stay, our mother and, you know this to be true, more especially our father will be heartbroken. You, his eldest son, have always been his lodestone, the one to whom he is naturally drawn, from whom he derives his energy and now, since his retirement, in who he has invested all his hope. He would be a broken man without you in his life.

If you leave, your men will not despise you but you will despise yourself. You will bear the guilt of the survivor, the guilt of the chosen one. This is possibly, and only you can answer this question, reparable damage. Whatever happens in our father's mind will not be.

I cannot believe I am having to deliver the burden of this choice to you in your desperate circumstances. In earlier attempts I tried to dress it up nicely, a temptation for Julius, but it refused to be pretty. It is an ugly choice. For my part, all I can say is that, whatever you decide, you are always my brother and I have never felt that there's any better man living.

Karl

Voss buttoned his tunic, put on his coat and went out under the icicle fringes of his hut into the frozen air. His boots rang on the hard, snow-packed ground. He entered Restricted Area I and went

straight to the Security Command post from where he knew SS
Colonel Weiss would be running his brutal régime. The other
soldiers looked at him as he entered. Nobody came willingly into
the Security Command post. Nobody ever wanted to talk to SS
Colonel Weiss. He was shown straight in. Weiss sat behind his
desk in a state of livid surprise, his white skin even whiter against
the deep black of his uniform, his crimson stepped scar from his
eye to cheek redder. Voss's nerve ricocheted around his stomach
looking for a way out.

'What can I do for you, Captain Voss?'

'A personal matter, sir.'

'Personal?' Weiss asked himself; he didn't normally deal with
the personal.

'I believe we reached a very special understanding between each
other last February and that is why I have come to you with this
personal matter.'

'Sit,' said Weiss, as if he was a dog. 'You look ill, Captain.'

'Lost my appetite, sir,' said Voss, lowering himself into a chair
on shaky thighs. 'You know . . . the situation with the Sixth Army
. . . is traumatic for everybody.'

'The Führer will resolve the problem. We will win the day,
Captain. You will see,' said Weiss, giving him a wary look, already
at work on the subtext of the words.

'My brother is in the *Kessel*, sir. He is extremely sick.'

'Haven't his men taken him to the hospital for treatment?'

'They have, but his condition did not respond to the treatment
they have available in the field hospital there. He asked to be taken
back to his division. I believe his condition is only treatable *outside*
the *Kessel*.'

Weiss said nothing. The fingers he ran over his scarred cheek
had well-cared for nails, glossy, packed with protein but tinged blue
from underneath.

'Where are you quartered, Captain?' asked Weiss after a long
pause.

It caught him off guard. He wasn't sure where he was quartered
any more. Numbers tinkered in his brain.

'Area III, C4,' he said.

'Ah yes, you're next to Captain Weber,' said Weiss, so quickly
that it was clear that his question hadn't been necessary.

33

The chair back cut into Voss's newly exposed ribs. You didn't build up any credit in Weiss's world, you always had to pay.

'Captain Weber is not a careful individual, is he, Captain Voss?'

'In what respect, sir?'

'Drunken, loose-tongued, curious.'

'Curious?'

'Inquisitive,' said Weiss. 'And I notice you don't disagree with my first two observations.'

'Forgive me for saying so, sir, but in my opinion Weber is the least inquisitive man I know, very concentrated on his task,' said Voss. 'And as for drinking ... who doesn't?'

'Loose-tongued?' asked Weiss.

'Who's there to be loose-tongued with?'

'Have you been with Captain Weber on any of his trips to town?'

Voss blinked. He didn't know anything about Weber's trips to town.

Weiss played the edge of his desk one-handed, a tremolo finished with a rapped flourish.

'He has a very sensitive position right in the heart of the matter,' said Weiss. 'What do you two talk about when you're drinking together?'

Voss shouldn't have been shocked, but he was, at Weiss's apparent omniscience. A squirt of adrenalin slithered through his veins, panic tightened his neck glands.

'Nothing of importance.'

'Tell me.'

'He's asked me to explain things to him.'

'Like what? Chess?'

'He hates chess.'

'Then what?'

'Physics. He knew I went to Heidelberg before I was called up.'

'Physics?' repeated Weiss, eyes glazing.

Voss thought he sensed a nonchalance that made him think that this was perhaps dangerous ground, mine-sown.

'The evenings are long here in Rastenburg,' said Voss to cover himself. 'He teases me. He says I should be thinking of things more *physical*. You know, women.'

'Women,' said Weiss, laughing with so little mirth it became something else.

'He's more frustrated than he is inquisitive,' said Voss, aware that Weiss wasn't listening any more.

'So you would like to get your brother out of the *Kessel*,' said Weiss, opting for an alarming change of direction which left Voss thinking he'd said things he hadn't. 'Yes, in view of our earlier understanding I think that could be arranged. Do you have his details?'

Voss handed over his letter, wondering if the tiny morsel about Weber he'd offered was as good as a whole carcass to Weiss's paranoia.

'Rest assured,' said Weiss, 'we will get him out. I look forward to continuing our special understanding, Captain Voss.'

Voss heard nothing more from Weiss and he didn't put himself in the man's way. He wrote a note to his father saying that he'd put the process of getting Julius away from Stalingrad in motion, he was waiting for news and it might take a little time because of the shambolic state inside the *Kessel*. He avoided Weber and began to play against himself at chess without, curiously, ever being able to win.

A week later there was a conference in the situation room with all the senior officers in the *Wolfsschanze* present. It was a meeting that would change Karl Voss. A captain had flown in from the front and Voss had heard that he had been primed to deliver a speech on the real situation on the ground. Voss slipped into the meeting in time to hear the captain deliver his vision of horror. Lice-ridden men living off water and shreds of horse meat, others jaundiced with their limbs swollen to twice the size, hundreds of men a day dying of starvation in the brutal cold, the wounded at the airstrip left out in the open, their blood congealed to ice, the dead stacked on the impenetrable ground. The Führer took it, shoulders rounded, lids weighed down.

And then the moment.

The captain moved on to a complete rundown of the decimated fighting strength of every unit within the *Kessel* and without. Hitler nodded. Slowly he turned to the map and squeezed his chin. As the Führer's slightly shaking hand moved out from his side the captain faltered. Hitler stood a flag up which had fallen over and began to talk about an SS panzer division, which was three weeks from the action. The captain's words still came out as he'd no doubt rehearsed again and again, but they had no meaning. It was as if all the conjunctions and prepositions had been stripped out, all the verbs had become their opposites, all nouns incomprehensible.

Silence, as the captain's boot squeak retreated. Hitler surveyed all his officers, his eyes beseeching, the terrible violence of red on the map below him flooding his face. Field Marshal Keitel, face trembling with emotion, stepped forward with a thunderous crack from his boot heel and roared over the deadly silence:

'*Mein Führer*, we will hold Stalingrad.'

At breakfast the next day Voss ate properly for the first time in weeks. Afterwards, as he headed to the situation room, he was called to the Security Command post. He sat down in Weiss's hard chair. Weiss leaned over and gave him an envelope. It contained his own letter to Julius unopened and with it a note.

The Kessel

12th January 1943

Dear Captain Voss,
An officer arrived today saying that he had come to pick up
your brother. It is my sad duty to inform you that Major
Julius Voss died on 10th January. We are his men and we
would like you to know that he left this life with the same
courage with which he endured it. His thoughts were never
for himself but only ever for the men under his command . . .

Voss couldn't read on. He put the note and letter back in their envelope, saluted SS Colonel Weiss and went back to the main building where he found the toilets and emptied his first solid breakfast in weeks into the bowl.

The news that afternoon, of the final assault on the abandoned Sixth Army, reached Voss from a strange distance, like words penetrating a sick child's mind. Did it happen or not?

There was nothing to be done and he finished work early. The sense of doom in the situation room was unbearable. The generals crowded the maps as if coffin-side at a vigil. He went back to his quarters and knocked on Weber's door. A strange person answered it. Voss asked after Weber. The man didn't know him. He went to the next door, found another captain sitting on his bed smoking.

'Where's Weber?' he asked.

The captain turned his mouth down, shook his head.

'Security breach or something. He was taken away yesterday. I don't know, don't ask. Not in this . . . climate, anyway. If you know what I mean,' said the captain, and Voss didn't move, stared at him so that the man felt the need to say more. 'Something about . . . well, it's only rumour . . . don't hold with it myself. You wouldn't if you knew Weber.'

Voss still said nothing and the captain was sufficiently uncomfortable to get off his chair and come to the door.

'I know Weber,' said Voss, with the certainty of someone who was about to be proven wrong.

'They found him in bed with a butcher's delivery boy in town.'

Voss went to his room and wrote to his mother and father. It was a letter which left him exhausted, drained of everything so that his arms hung hopeless and unliftable at his sides. He went to bed early and slept, waking twice in the night to find tears on his face. In the morning he was woken up by an orderly and told to report to General Zeitzler's office.

Zeitzler sat him down and didn't stand behind his desk but leaned against the front of it. He looked avuncular, not his usual military self. He gave Voss permission to smoke.

'I have some bad news,' he said, his fingers pattering his thigh. 'Your father died last night . . .'

Voss fixed his eyes on Zeitzler's left epaulette. The only words to reach him were 'compassionate leave'. By lunchtime he found himself in the half-dead light, standing away from the edge of the dark pine trees alongside the railway track, a grey sack of clothes on one side and a small brown suitcase on the other. The Berlin train left at 1.00 p.m. and although he was heading into his mother's grief he could only feel that this was a new beginning and that greater possibilities existed away from this place, this hidden kingdom – the *Wolfsschanze*.

Chapter 5

'No, no, they sent somebody to see us,' said Frau Voss. 'They sent Colonel Linge, you remember him, an old friend of your father's, retired, a good man, not too stiff like the rest of them, he has something, a sensitivity, he's not a man that assumes everybody's the same as himself, he can differentiate, a rare trait in military circles. Of course, as soon as your father saw him he knew what it was about. But you see . . .' She blinked but the tears fattened too quickly and rolled down her cheeks before she could get the clutched, lace-edged handkerchief to her face.

Karl Voss leaned over and took his mother's free hand, a hand that he remembered differently, not so bony, frail and blue-veined. How fast grief sucks out the marrow – some days off food, three nights without sleep, the mind spiralling its dark gyre, in and out, but always around and around the same terrible, hard point. It was a force more destructive than a ravaging illness where the body's instinct is to fight. Grief provides all the symptoms but no fight. There's nothing to fight for. It's already gone. Stripped of purpose the mind turns on the body and reduces it. He squeezed her hand, trying to inject some of his youth into her, his sense of a future.

'It was wrong,' she said, careful not to say 'he'. 'He shouldn't have placed so much hope in your letter. I didn't to start with, but he infected me with his . . . Having him around the house all the time, he worked on me until we became these two candles in the window, waiting.'

She blew her nose, took a deep, trembling breath.

'Still, Colonel Linge came. They went into his study. They talked for quite some time and then your father showed the colonel to the door. He came in here to see me and he was calm. He told me that Julius had died and all the wonderful things that Colonel

38

Linge had said about him. And then he went back to his study and locked himself in. I was worried but not so worried, although now I see what his calmness was. His mind was made up. After some hours sitting alone here I went to bed, knocking on his door on the way. He told me to go up, he'd join me, which he did, hours later, maybe two or three o'clock in the morning. He slept, or maybe he didn't, at least he lay on his side and didn't move. He was up before I was awake. In the kitchen he said he was going to see Dr Schulz. I spoke to Dr Schulz afterwards and he did go to see him. He asked him for something to keep him calm and Dr Schulz, he's very good, he gave him some herbal teas, took his blood pressure, which was high but to be expected. Dr Schulz even asked him, "You're not thinking of doing anything stupid, are you, General?" and your father replied "What? Me? No, no, why do you think I'm here?" and he left. He drove to the Havel, into Wannsee and out again, parked the car, walked along the waterfront and shot himself.'

No tears this time. She just sat back and breathed evenly, looking at nothing beyond the short horizon of her own thoughts which were: he didn't do it in his study, nor in the car, always a considerate man. He went out on the cold, hard ground and pointed the gun at the offending organ, his heart, not his head, and fired off two bullets into it. He froze out there. He was set solid by the time he was found, no walkers at this time of year, and short, bitter after-noons. She'd gone a little crazy that night he didn't come home. She woke up in the morning to find all the gardening tools laid out in the kitchen. What had she been thinking? She came to, her son's pulse thudding into her.

'On his desk are the letters he wrote,' she said. 'There's one there for you. Read it and we'll talk again. And put some coal on the fire. I know it's valuable but I'm just too cold today ... you know how it gets into the marrow some days.'

Karl threw some pieces on the fire, put his hands in there for a second until the heat nipped them. He went to his father's study, his boots loud on the wooden floor of the corridor the way his father's were, so that Julius and he could hear them from the top of the house. Louder as he got heavier with the years.

He found the letter and sat in a leather armchair by the window, which still offered dim, late afternoon light.

Berlin-Schlachtensee

14th January 1943

Dear Karl,

This action I have taken is as a result of my unique perception of a series of events in my life. It has nothing to do with you. I know you did everything possible to get Julius out and it was typical of him to make light of the seriousness of his physical condition so that none of us could have known how close to death he was. Your mother, too, is blameless in this. She has given of her strength constantly and in the last two years I have been an even more difficult man to live with than I was before.

I have been overwhelmed by despair, not just because of the sudden termination of my career, but also because of my helplessness in the face of what I fear will be the direst consequences for Germany as a result of our aggression and the extent of our aggression over the past three years.

Don't misunderstand me. I, as you know, approved of Hitler in those early years. He returned to the nation the belief in ourselves which we had lost in that first terrible war. I encouraged Julius into the Party as well as the army. I, like everybody else, was inspired. But the Commissar Order, which I vehemently opposed, was for a very important reason. Certain things have happened and will continue to happen in Germany and the rest of Europe while the National Socialists are in power. You have heard of these things. They are truly terrible. Too terrible, in so many ways, to believe. My stand against the Commissar Order was an attempt to prevent the army from acquiescing to these other, darker, politically motivated and utterly dishonourable actions. I failed and paid the penalty, a small one compared to the eternal damnation of the German Army for conspiring in these appalling deeds. If we lose this war, and it is possible, given the extent to which we have stretched ourselves over so many fronts, that the defeat of the Sixth Army at Stalingrad is the beginning, then our army officers will face the same retribution as the brutes and thugs in the SS. We have all been tarred by obeying the Commissar Order.

This was the beginning of my despair and my removal from the battlefield compounded it in helplessness. When this abandonment of principle was combined with the leadership's utter failure to respond to the predicament of a far-flung army I realized that we were lost, that fundamental military logic no longer applied, that more than honour had been handed over with the acquiescence to the Commissar Order. Our generals have been emasculated, we will be run by the Corporal from now on. That this abysmal state of affairs should have resulted in the death of my first-born son was more than I could bear. I am no longer young. The future looks bleak amidst the wasteland of my shattered beliefs. Everything I stood for, believed in and cherished has fallen.

Two more things. At my funeral there will be a man called Major Manfred Giesler. He is an officer with the Abwehr. You will either talk to him if you believe in what I have said in the early part of this letter or you will not. That is your decision.

My body will be cremated and I would like you to scatter my ashes on a grave in the Wannsee church cemetery belonging to Rosemarie Hausser 1888–1905.

I wish you a happy and successful life and hope that you will once again be able to pursue your aptitude in physics in more peaceful times.

Your ever loving father

PS It is absolutely imperative that this letter be destroyed after you have read it. Failure to do so could result in danger for yourself, your mother and Major Giesler. If my predictions as to the course of this war prove to be correct you will see that letters containing such sentiments will carry heavy consequences.

Voss reread the letter and burnt it in the grate, watching the slow, greenish flames consume and blacken the paper. He sat by the window again in a state of shock at this, his first intimate sight of the workings of his father's mind. He gathered himself for a few moments; the conflicting emotions needed to be reined in before he went to speak to his mother. Anger and grief didn't seem to be able to sit in the same room for very long.

He went back to his mother who still sat in the same position, the light poorer but her scalp visible under her grey hair, which he'd never seen before.

'So,' she said before he had sat down, 'he told you about the girl.'

'He told me he wants his ashes cast on her grave.'

His mother nodded, and looked over her shoulder as if she'd heard something outside. The light caught her face, no sadness, only acceptance.

'She was somebody he knew, an army officer's daughter. He fell in love with her and she died. I think he knew her for all of one week.'

'One week?' said Voss. 'He told you this?'

'He told me about the girl, he was a totally honourable man, your father, incapable even of omission. His sister filled in the details.'

'But you're his wife and . . . I can't do this.'

'You can, Karl. You will. If it's his wish, it's mine too. Just think of it as your father being in love with the idea, or rather an ideal, that was not complicated or tarnished by the grind of everyday life. That is the purest form of love you can find. Perfection,' she said, shrugging. 'I can think of no better thing after what your father went through, than for him to rest with his ideal. To him it was a vision of peace that he failed to attain in life.'

The funeral took place three days later. There were few people, most of his father's friends were at one front or another. Frau Voss invited the few back to her house for some tea. Major Giesler was one who accepted. At the house Karl asked for a private word with him and they went into his father's study.

Voss began to tell him the contents of his father's letter. Giesler stopped him, went to the phone, followed the line to the wall and removed the pin from the socket. He sat back down in the leather chair by the window. Voss told him of his willingness to talk. Giesler said nothing. He had his hands clasped and was chewing on a knuckle, one of the few hairless regions of his body. He was very dark and his thick black eyebrows joined over his nose. He had a large, full-lipped, sensual mouth and his cheeks, razored that morning, already needed to be reshaved.

'I would understand,' said Voss, 'if you needed to make some inquiries about me before we talk.'

'We've already made our inquiries,' said Giesler.

Voss thought for a moment.

'In Rastenburg?'

'We know, for instance, how you felt about the . . . the death of the Reichsminister Todt,' said Giesler, 'and your . . . disappointment with the way in which good soldiers died needlessly at Stalingrad and, of course, you have an impeccable pedigree.'

Voss frowned, replayed some reels in his mind.

'Weber?'

Giesler opened his hands, reclasped them.

'Weber disappeared,' said Voss. 'What happened to him?'

'We didn't know he was a homosexual. There are some things that even the deepest of inquiries will not unearth.'

'But where is he?'

'He is in very serious trouble, which he brought on himself,' said Giesler. 'He behaved recklessly in a climate where scapegoats were eagerly sought.'

'He must have been under pressure . . .'

'Drinking is one thing.'

'How do you know I'm not homosexual?'

Giesler looked at him long and hard, that sensual mouth becoming unnerving.

'Weber,' he said after some time, as if perhaps that source hadn't been as reliable as he'd have liked.

'Well, he should know, although I'm not sure how. Women were not abundant in Rastenburg and those that were available . . .' he drifted off, disheartened by the turn the conversation had taken; this dip into the ignoble was not what he'd had in mind. This was supposed to be a courageous act and here they were parting the dirt.

Giesler had his answer. He didn't need to pursue this discussion further. He gave Voss an address of a villa in Gatow with a meeting time for the next day and stood. They shook hands and Giesler hung on, which at first Voss thought was another sexuality test but, no, it was a sincerity hold, a brotherhood clasp.

'Weber won't talk,' he said. 'It's possible he will survive, although he will never get back into Rastenburg. But it is something for you to think about before you come to Gatow tomorrow. It's not easy to be an enemy of the State – not, I hasten to add, an enemy of the nation, but *this* State. It is dangerous and lonely work. You will be lying to your colleagues every day for perhaps years. You will have no friends because friends are dangerous. Your work will require a mental fortitude, not intelligence necessarily, but strength and it is something you may feel you do not have. If you do not come to Gatow tomorrow nobody will think any the less of you. We will go our separate ways, praying for Germany.'

Voss slept badly that night in a torment over his part in Weber's arrest. At four in the morning, the death and debt hour, he found his mind crowded with thoughts of his father and mother, Julius and Weber, and it was then that he had a sudden perception of the power of words, of the business of communication. Once words are said nothing is the same. His father didn't have to tell his mother about Rosemarie Hausser, but he did. It must have established an unrecoverable distance, instilled a lifelong sense of disappointment in his mother with a short line, some words and a name. In his own crucial conversation with Weiss, which he had not been prepared for, he realized that it was not physics that had alerted him but the words 'physical' and 'women'. It had been a confirmation. It made him think that in talking to people you never know what they know, you never know what they think, and innocuous words can take on huge importance. He stopped writhing in his bed – he hadn't served up Weber, he'd just handed Weiss the spoons.

He went to Gatow the following afternoon, nervous as if it was a visit to the doctor, who might find a mild symptom the precursor of something deadly. He was met by a housekeeper who took him to a book-lined room at the back of the house. She gave him real coffee and a homemade biscuit. Giesler came in with a large man of military rectitude but who was dressed in a blue double-breasted suit. He was bald with a brown, clipped fringe of hair at the back and sides. He wore gold-rimmed spectacles. Voss was introduced but the man's name was never given.

They talked about his work at Heidelberg University and recent developments in physics. The man was knowledgeable, not expert, but he understood. The words 'fissionable material', 'critical mass', 'chain reaction' and 'atomic pile' were not mysterious concepts.

The conversation switched from physics to the Russians. Voss expressed his fear of them:

'They have no reason to be forgiving after what we have done to them. We have broken a pact, invaded their country, and brutalized the population. After the defeat we have suffered at Stalingrad it is possible that they will have the confidence to drive us back. If they succeed I believe they will not stop until they reach Berlin. They will punish us.'

'So you would see it as advantageous that we negotiate a separate peace with the Allies?'

'Imperative, unless we want to see Germany or a part of Germany in the Soviet Union. Perhaps we can even persuade the Allies that we are not the real enemy in this war and that . . .'

The man held up his hand.

'One step at a time,' said the man firmly. 'First we will work on your transfer away from Rastenburg. You will need some training, too. The Abwehr headquarters along with the Army High Command has moved south to Zossen and we now live for our sins in a concrete citadel out there called Maibach II. You will spend some months with us. The work you will be doing is very different – gathering information, running agents in the field – it's not the military intelligence that you know. After that we will send you to Paris and from there we will try to position you in Lisbon.'

'Lisbon?'

'It's the only place in Europe now where we can talk easily with the Allies.'

Voss lived with his mother while he completed his training in Zossen. She looked after him as if he was at school again and it was a comfort for both of them. It was a wrench when he was transferred to France in June.

He spent eight months in the Abwehr's French headquarters at 82 Avenue Foch in Paris and, furnished with his new perception of the power of words, saw the horrific consequences for others who hadn't yet come to the same understanding.

French and British men and women were arrested, sent to concentration camps, tortured and executed for what was, more than half the time, a totally imaginary situation. Both the Abwehr and the SD/Gestapo, who operated from next door, were playing what became known as radio games. Voss never worked out whether it was merely Allied stupidity or German infiltration into their intelligence operations at a very high level which enabled these deadly games to be played. Once an Allied radio operator was captured and his codename and signal extracted an Abwehr operator would continue broadcasting to London. Later when there were two security signals required, the Allies would reply simply reminding the operator that he'd forgotten his second signal but to continue. The baffled and angry radio operators soon supplied the second security signal to the Germans. Following these fictitious Abwehr broadcasts more agents and supplies would be flown into some misty French field and a reception from the Occupying force. These new agents' codenames were then used to build fictitious networks operated by the Abwehr and Gestapo, dispersing vast quantities of misinformation to the Allies. Meetings convened by operational Allied agents were frequently attended by Abwehr men using captured agents' codenames.

Occasionally Voss would stage arrests in the street to maintain verisimilitude.

Most intelligence activity was mirage and artifice. Very little was real. Intelligence, he discovered, was built on the foundations of the imagination and, in the case of the radio games, a blind belief in the veracity of technology. It was a terrifying concept, as terrifying as if the basic principles of physics or maths were completely wrong and whole academic disciplines had been built on falsehood and thus all discoveries were intrinsically wrong, all achievements bogus.

Voss also learned never to fall in love in this world. Lovers betrayed each other easily. Torture, the Gestapo's preferred method, was unnecessary. Just the insinuation of a lover's infidelity to a prisoner was as powerful as any of their appalling applications. The emotional betrayal played such devious and teasing tricks on the mind. Jealousy was inevitable in the loneliness of a cell. The darkness, with only the infected mind for company, created powerful images that at first disheartened and later so enraged and ravaged the prisoners that they would grasp at a new strength and in their vindictiveness bring down not just the lover, but all the connections as well.

This did not mean that Voss was celibate in his time in Paris – that was impossible and there was something to prove to Giesler too – but he kept his distance. A Frenchwoman called Françoise Larache taught him a different and darker lesson about love in the intelligence game.

They met when using the same bar. He would take a coffee in the mornings and find her watching him. He would stop off in the evening for a glass of something and she was often there at a table, smoking her strong cigarettes. They exchanged words and began to share a table, where he would watch her red lips connect with the thick tip of her cigarette, and her fingers pick off the flakes of tobacco from her pointed tongue. One night they went for a meal and back to his apartment where they made love. She was energetic and inventive, doing things on their first night which surprised him.

They became regulars of each other's company in bed, and as Françoise was quick to demand, out of bed as well. She pushed him to do things which were at first exciting and then became increasingly more reckless. She liked to make love on the balcony with people passing in the street below. She would lean back over the rail, her arms around his neck, and then suddenly let go so that he nearly lost her over the edge. They would have sex in doorways and on landings while people ate their dinner and table-talked. She would even cry out and the talk would stop inside. Voss would have to close his hand over her mouth. The greater the chance of being discovered, the more excited Françoise became.

Then one day in the autumn with the dried leaves rustling over the balcony, her mischievous eye, the one that glinted when she looked up at him from under her eyebrow, became darker, as if he was seeing deeper in and what was there was more sinister, taboo.

It started with a request that he spank her for being a naughty girl. Voss felt stupid with a grown woman over his knees and she had to encourage him to be serious and to be more severe. It didn't seem to be fun any more. He still lusted after her, but for Françoise the sex was being driven by something else. He became reluctant to play her games, she angry. They had furious arguments, monumental rows with flying objects, which would end in brutal love-making where each thrust into her seemed to be a payment back. He found himself reeling out of his apartment into the docility of occupied Paris, unable to believe what he'd participated in the night before, only knowing that it was powerful, intense and degrading.

Françoise's goading became worse. There was no fun now. She said terrible, unforgivable things and, although he could see what she was doing, he was a part of it too. There was no stepping back. She was forcing him to slap her, and not just a hysteria-breaking slap, a punishing slap. She wanted to be hit hard. She drove her face at him. The words came out slicing the air, lacerating, stabbing, each one honed to cut deep to the bone. They grappled and wrestled each other to the floor. She sunk her nails into his neck. He wrenched himself free and found his fist cocked back to his shoulder. He swayed, dizzy at what this had come to. Her face was suddenly soft, her eyes dreamy. This was what she wanted. He stood up, straightened his clothes. All lust gone. Her face hardened. He gave her his hand, she took it and he pulled her to her feet. She spat in his face. He pulled her to the door, grabbing her coat and handbag on the way, and threw her out of the apartment.

He made discreet inquiries. She was an informer, a collaborator. She delivered her countrymen, neatly trussed, to the Gestapo. The SD man Voss spoke to tapped the side of his head, shook it.

He saw her once more before he left Paris, walking in a snow-covered street on the arm of a huge, black-coated SS sergeant. Voss hid in a doorway as they went past. She was holding snow to the side of her face.

In mid January 1944 Voss was called to a meeting at the Hotel Lutecia. It was at night and the room in which the meeting was being held was dark. Only a small lamp lit one corner. The man he was meeting sat in front of the light, he had no face, only the silhouette of hair combed back, maybe grey or white. His voice was old. A voice that spoke as if under pressure, as if the chest was tight with phlegm.

'There are going to be some changes,' he said. 'It seems our friend Kaltenbrunner at the Reich's Main Security Office is going to get his way and bring the Abwehr under the direct control of the SD. God knows, they've been trying long enough. It is something we are going to have to live with. We want to be sure that you are in position with the right information for negotiation with the Allies before it happens. I understand you have been following the activities of a French communist intellectual, Olivier Mesnel, here in Paris.'

'We are in the process of disentangling his network. We haven't found out yet how his information is reaching Moscow or how his orders come in.'

'He has now applied for a visa to go to Spain.'

'He is ultimately heading for Lisbon,' said Voss. 'We were lucky enough to intercept the courier sent by the Portuguese communists asking him to go there.'

'Do you have any idea why he is required in Lisbon?'

'No, and I don't think Mesnel does either.'

'You will take this opportunity to follow him to Lisbon and to install yourself as the military attaché and security officer in the German Legation. When these changes come through, which could be next month, you will find yourself directly answerable to SS Colonel Reinhardt Wolters. He is not one of us, needless to say, but you must make him your friend. Sutherland and Rose are running the Lisbon station of the British Secret Intelligence Service, you will be talking to them directly, procedure is in the brief. There are some documents here which you should look at and memorize before you go and a letter which contains important information on microdot. You will use this information to open negotiations with the British. You must show them that we can be trusted, that our intentions are honourable and that the reverse is true of the Russians.'

'I'm not sure how the latter will be possible. I understand there is no Soviet legation in Lisbon.'

'That's true. Salazar won't allow them in. No atheists on Catholic Portuguese soil – which reminds me, we must make sure the Portuguese don't deny him a visa.'

The man seemed to laugh for no particular reason, or perhaps it was a wheeze that became a cough. He lit a cigarette.

'It is possible that Olivier Mesnel will lead you somewhere. He must be going to Lisbon for a purpose which I don't think, given his political beliefs, will be to take a ship to the United States.'

'At the Casablanca Conference it was decided that our surrender would have to be unconditional. We will have to offer something extraordinary for the British and the Americans to even consider breaking with the Russians.'

A long silence. Smoke rising from the chair drifted towards the lamp behind.

'Believe me, the Americans will be looking for any reason they can to cut themselves away from Stalin at the first opportunity, especially after the Russians have invaded Europe. At the Teheran Conference Stalin said that up to a hundred thousand German officers would have to be executed and he would need four million German *slaves* – that was his word – to rebuild Russia. This kind of talk is unacceptable to men of humanity such as Churchill and Roosevelt. If we can provide a catalyst . . .' he paused, struggled in his chair as if suddenly cramped, '. . . the Führer's death, I think, would be sufficient.'

Voss shivered even though it was warm in the room. The water he was easing himself into now felt deep and cold.

'Is that a planned action?'

'One of many,' said the man, as tired as if he'd planned them all.

Voss wanted to get away from contemplating the enormity of the statement.

'I've lost track of the development of our atomic programme. That could be important to the Allies. They've seen that we have the potential . . . can we put their minds at rest?'

'It's all in the documents.'

'How much time have we got?'

'We hope to make progress . . . like all things, in the spring, but by the end of the summer at the latest we must have results. The Russians have retaken Zhitomir and have crossed the Polish border – they're no more than a thousand kilometres from Berlin. We are being bombed to rubble by the Allies. The city is a ruin, the arms and munitions factories working at barely fifty per cent. The air force can't reach the new Russian arms factories on the other side of the Urals. The bear gets stronger and the eagle weaker and more short-sighted.'

There didn't seem to be any need of more questions after that and Voss was gestured towards the table where three fat files awaited him. He sat down and reached for the lamp. A hand landed on his shoulder and squeezed it in the same way that his father's used to – reassuring, giving strength.

'You are very important to us,' said the voice. 'You understand what is written in these files better than anybody, but we have chosen you for other reasons too. I can only ask you, please, when you are in Lisbon, do not make the same mistake you made with Mademoiselle Larache. This is too important. This is about the survival of a nation.'

The hand released him. The man and his pressurized voice left the room. Voss worked until 6.00 a.m. going through the files on the atomic programme and the V1 and V2 rocket programmes.

On 20th January 1944 Olivier Mesnel was issued with an exit visa to travel to Spain. On the 22nd January Voss boarded the same night train as Mesnel, which left the Gare de Lyon heading south to Lyon and Perpignan, crossing the border at Port Bou and then on to Barcelona and Madrid. Mesnel rarely left his compartment. In Madrid the Frenchman stayed in a cheap pension for two nights and then took another train to Lisbon on the night of 25th January.

They arrived in Santa Apolónia station in Lisbon late the following afternoon. It was raining and Mesnel in his oversized coat and hat walked at funereal pace from the station to the massive square of the Terreiro do Paço, which Voss was surprised to see sandbagged and guarded in a neutral country. He followed the Frenchman through the Baixa and up the Avenida da Liberdade to the Praça Marquês de Pombal where Mesnel, dragging his feet, seemingly weak with hunger, entered a small *pensão* on the Rua Braancamp. Voss was relieved to take a taxi to the German Legation on the Rua do Pau de Bandeira in Lapa, a smart quarter on the outskirts of the city. SS Colonel Reinhardt Wolters had been expecting him two days earlier but welcomed him all the same.

On 13th February the Chief of the Abwehr, Admiral Canaris, was escorted out of the Maibach II complex by officers sent from the Reich's Main Security Office by Kaltenbrunner. He was taken to the house within the grounds where he packed and was then driven to his own home in Schlachtensee. On 18th February the Abwehr was dissolved and brought under Kaltenbrunner's direct control. The rain was clattering against the windows of the German Legation in Lapa when Wolters came into Voss's office to deliver the good news. As the SS man left the room, Voss was overwhelmed by a sense of loneliness, a man out on a limb at the westernmost tip of Europe with only the enemy to talk to.

Chapter 6

10th July 1944, Orlando Road, Clapham, London.

Andrea Aspinall collapsed on her bed in her room with the windows open, just back from another trip to the air-raid shelter – the doodlebugs a menace, flying over at all times of day, not like the good old predictable nights of endless bombing raids in the Blitz. Sometimes she toyed with the idea of not going to the shelter – listen for the low drone of the diesel-powered rocket, wait for its engine to cut out, take pot luck under its silent falling, test her boredom threshold.

She went to sit on the window ledge, her room at the top, old servants' quarters. She looked over the back garden through the lime trees to Macauley Road, four houses along, direct hit from a doodlebug, not much left, blackened beams, piled rubble but nobody home at the time. She caught sight of herself, only her head in the bottom corner of the mirror on the dressing table across the room. Long black hair, dark, nearly olive skin, twenty-year-old brown eyes wanting to be older.

She opened a packet of Woodbines, rested the filterless cigarette on her lower lip, let it stick. She struck a match on the outside wall, warm brick. Her hand came into the frame, she turned her face and accepted the light. She flicked her head back, unstuck the cigarette, let out a long stream of smoke and came back to herself in the mirror with her tongue on her top lip – being sophisticated. She shook her head at herself, looked out of the window – still a silly girl playing romantic games in the mirror. Not a spy.

She'd spent most of her life at the Sacred Heart Convent in Devizes where she'd been sent at seven years old when her great aunt had died and there'd been no one to look after her while her mother worked. That was why the piano teacher and his wife, who'd been bombed in their home during the Blitz, had been so important to her, they'd become family, looking after her through school holidays. The piano teacher was her father. She'd never known her own, the one who'd died of cholera before she was born.

They knew about discipline and religion at the Sacred Heart and not much else, but it hadn't prevented her from getting a place at St Anne's, Oxford to read maths. She'd done nearly two years of her degree when her tutor invited her to a party at St John's. At the party a large quantity of drink was served and consumed by dons, undergraduates and other people not directly associated with the university. These people floated around the room and occasionally moored themselves to some young person or other and engaged them in short intense conversations about politics and history. She went to more parties like this and met a man who took a particular interest in her, who was called simply – Rawlinson.

Rawlinson was very tall. He wore a three-piece suit, charcoal grey, a starched collar attached with studs to his shirt and a school tie which, if she'd known more, would have said Wellington and the military. He was in his fifties with all his hair, which was black on top, grey at the sides and combed through with tonic. He had only one leg and his prosthesis was stiff so that when he walked that leg swung in a semi-circle and he had to support himself with a duckhead-topped cane. She felt lucky because, while his conversation was the usual penetrative stuff, he participated with the charm of an uncle who shouldn't really take a fancy to his niece but couldn't help it.

'Tell me something,' he said. 'Mathematics. Has anybody ever asked you why mathematics? Interesting.'

Andrea, a little drunk, shrugged. Unprepared for the question, her brain ticked. She spoke with her mind elsewhere.

'You can get things to work out, I suppose,' she said, feeling instantly stupid, embarrassed.

'Not always, I shouldn't think,' said Rawlinson, surprising her, taking it seriously, taking her seriously even.

'No, not always, but when you do it's . . . well . . . there's a beauty to it, an inconceivable simplicity. As Godfrey Hardy said, "Beauty is the test. There's no place in this world for ugly mathematics."'

'Beauty?' said Rawlinson, baffled. 'Not something I remember from maths class. Fiendish is more the word. Show me beauty . . . beauty that I can understand.'

'The number six,' she said, 'has three divisors – one, two and three – which if added together come to . . . six. Isn't that perfect? And, seen in that same light, isn't Pythagoras's theorem beautiful too? So simple. The square of the hypotenuse is equal to the sum of the other two sides squared. True for all right-angled triangles ever created. What seems terribly complicated can be resolved into equations . . . formulae which go towards completing the . . . well, at least part of the puzzle.'

He tapped his cheek with a long finger.

'The puzzle?'

'How things work,' she said, hysteria mounting as the banality took root.

'And people,' he said; question or agreement, she wasn't sure.

'People?'

'How do *people* fit into the equation?'

'There are infinite possibilities in maths. Every number is a complex number. It can be real or imaginary, and real numbers can be rational or irrational. Rational like integers or fractions, irrational like algebra or transcendental numbers.'

'Transcendental?'

'Real, but non-algebraic.'

'I see.'

'Like π.'

'What are you saying, Miss Aspinall?'

'I'm talking to you in the simplest way possible, at the most basic end of mathematics, and already there are things you don't fully understand. It's a secret language. Only very few people know it and can speak it.'

'That still doesn't explain how people fit into your world.'

'I was just showing you that numbers can be complicated in the same way that people can be. And something else . . . I'm a person, too, with all the normal human needs. I don't always speak in algorithms.'

'Numbers are more stable than people, I'd have thought. More predictable.'

'I haven't come across an emotional number . . . yet,' she said, her hands feeling huge at her sides, flapping like albatross's wings, 'which is why, I suppose, it's possible to get things to work out . . . every so often.'

54

'Are solutions important to you?'

Andrea studied him for a moment, the question carrying interview weight. His eyes didn't flinch from hers. She lost the match.

'I do like to solve problems. That's the reward. But it's not always possible and working towards something can be just as satisfying,' she said, not believing it, but thinking it might please him.

After this string of parties her tutor sent her over to Oriel to talk to someone about 'matters pertaining to the war effort'. He sent her to a doctor who gave her a half-hour medical examination. She didn't hear anything for a week until she was called back to Oriel and found herself signing the Official Secrets Act, so, it seemed, that they could give her a course in typing and shorthand. She thought she was headed for a code-cracking centre, where she'd heard lots of other maths graduates had been sent, but they gave her some additional training instead. Dead-letter drops, invisible ink, using miniature cameras, following people, talking to people while pretending to be someone else to find out what they knew – role-playing, they called it. The minuscule arts of deception. They also taught her how to fire a gun, ride a motorbike and drive a car.

They sent her home at the beginning of July to wait for an assignment. A week later she was contacted by Rawlinson, who told her he was going to come to tea to meet her mother. It was important to establish normality at home, her mother had to be given something official about what her daughter would be doing but not, of course, the reality.

'Andrea!'

Her mother shouted up the stairs from the hall. She dabbed the coal of the cigarette out on the wall, put the butt back in the packet.

'Andrea!'

'Coming, Mother,' she said, ripping open the door.

She looked down the stairs to her mother's moon-white, but not so luminous, face at the curve of the bannisters.

'Mr Rawlinson's here,' she said in a stage whisper.

'I didn't hear him arrive.'

'Well, he's here,' she said. 'Shoes.'

She went barefoot back to the bedroom, put on her mother's

horrible shoes, laced them up. She sniffed the air, still smoky, still behaving like Mother's little girl. Definitely not a spy.

'She's very young, you know . . .' She overheard her mother in the drawing room. 'I mean, she's nineteen, no twenty, but she doesn't act it. She went to a convent . . .'

'The Sacred Heart in Devizes,' said Rawlinson. 'Good school.'

'And out of London.'

'Away from the bombing.'

'It wasn't the bombing, Mr Rawlinson,' her mother said, without saying what it had been.

Andrea braced herself for the tedium of her mother behaving properly in front of strangers.

'Not the bombing . . . ?' said Rawlinson, feigning mild surprise.

'The influences,' said Mrs Aspinall.

Andrea rattled her heels on the tiles to announce herself, to stop her mother talking about 'goings on' in the air-raid shelters. She shook hands with Rawlinson.

Her mother's bra creaked as she poured the tea. What rigging for such a tight little ship, thought Andrea, feeling Rawlinson's bright, nearly saucy eyes on her neck, which heated up. Teacups rattled, raised and refitted on to saucers.

'You speak German,' he said to Andrea.

'*Frisch weht der Wind / Der heimat zu, / Mein Irisch kind / Wo weilest du?*' said Andrea.

'Don't show off, dear,' said her mother.

'And Portuguese,' said Andrea.

'She taught herself, you know,' said Audrey Aspinall, interrupting. 'Pass Mr Rawlinson some cake, dear.'

Andrea had been sitting on her hands and now found that the ribbing of her dress was printed on the back of them as she passed the cake. Why did her mother always do this to her?

'You have secretarial skills,' said Rawlinson, lifting the cake.

'She just did a course, didn't you, dear?'

Andrea didn't contribute. Her mother's porcelain face, still beautiful at thirty-eight years old but unyielding, turned hard on her. Andrea hadn't told her mother anything about what had gone on at Oxford other than what they'd told her to say.

'It's my job to find suitable staff for our embassies and high commissions. My department is very small and when we find someone with a foreign language we tend to snap them up. I have a position for your daughter, Mrs Aspinall . . . abroad.'

'I'd like to go abroad,' said Andrea.

'How would you know?' said her mother. 'That's the thing about young people today, Mr Rawlinson, they think they know everything without having done anything but, of course, they don't think. They don't think and they don't listen.'

'We're *relying* on youth in this war, Mrs Aspinall,' said Rawlinson, 'because they don't know fear. Eighteen-year-olds can do a hundred bombing missions, get shot down, make their way through enemy territory and be up in the air again within a week. The reason they can do that is precisely that they don't think, you see. The *danger's* in the thinking.'

'I'm not sure about abroad . . .' said Mrs Aspinall.

'Why don't you come to my office tomorrow,' said Rawlinson to Andrea. 'We'll test your skills. Eleven o'clock suit you?'

'I don't know where you'd send her. Not south. She can't stand the heat.'

This was a lie, worse than a lie because the opposite was the case. Andrea, inside her dark skin, under her starling glossy hair, glared at her mother's translucency, at the blue blood inching its way under the alabaster skin. Mrs Aspinall had a Victorian's attitude to sun. It never touched her skin. In summer she wore marble, in winter the snow would pile on her head as on a statue's in the square.

'Lisbon, Mrs Aspinall, we have an opening in Lisbon which would suit your daughter's skills and intelligence.'

'Lisbon? But there must be something she can do in London.'

Rawlinson got to his feet, hauling his stiff leg up after him, shooting Andrea a conspiratorial look.

They followed him into the hall. Mrs Aspinall fitted him into his light coat, gave him his hat, smoothed the shoulders of his coat. Andrea blinked at that small, intimate action. It shocked her, confused her.

'You're going to be hot out there, Mr Rawlinson.'

'Thank you so much for tea, Mrs Aspinall,' he said, and tipped his hat before going down to the gate and out into the sun-baked street.

'Well, you won't want to go to Lisbon, will you?' said Mrs Aspinall, closing the door.

'Why not?'

'It's as good as Africa down there ... Arabs,' she added as an afterthought, making it exotic.

'I suppose it's because I speak Portuguese,' said Andrea. 'Why do you never let me say ...'

'Don't start on that. I'm not doing battle with you on that score,' she said, heading back into the living room.

'Why shouldn't I talk about my father?'

'He's dead, you never knew him,' she said, throwing her tea dregs into the pot plant, pouring herself another cup. 'I hardly did, either.'

'That's no reason.'

'It's just not done, Andrea. That's all.'

Something wriggled in Andrea's mind, something irrational like the first half of an equation, some algebra with too many unknowns. She was thinking about her mother smoothing Rawlinson's shoulders. Intimacy and what brought that intimacy. Rawlinson's leg. And why dead Portuguese fathers can't be mentioned.

Talking to her mother was just like algebra. Maths without the numbers. Words which meant something else. A question arrived in Andrea's head. One prompted by an image. It was a question which couldn't be asked. She could think it and if she looked at her mother and thought it, she'd shudder, which she did.

'I don't know how you can be cold in this heat.'

'Not cold, Mother. Just a thought.'

In the morning her mother produced one of her suits for Andrea to wear. A dark blue pencil skirt, short jacket, cream blouse, and a hat that perched rather than sat. Her nails were inspected and passed. After breakfast her mother told her to clean her teeth and left for work firing a volley of instructions up the stairs about what to do and, more important, what not to do.

Andrea took a bus to St James's Park and spent a few minutes on a bench before walking down Queen Anne's Gate to number 54 Broadway. She went to the second floor, her feet already hurting in the borrowed shoes, and the suit, built for her mother's slightly smaller frame, was pinching her under the armpits, which were damp in the heat. A woman told her to wait on a hard, leather-seated wooden chair. Sun streamed through the lazy dust motes.

She was shown into Rawlinson's office. He sat with his leg coming through the footwell to her side of his desk. Tea appeared and two biscuits. The secretary retired.

'Biscuit?' he asked.

She took the offered biscuit. The dry half detached itself from the sodden half.

'So,' said Rawlinson, pulling himself up straight in his chair, the air clear as after a storm. 'Nice to have you on board. There's just one question I have outstanding here. Your father.'

'My father?'

'You never include your father's details on any of your forms.'

'My mother says it's not relevant. He died before I was born. He had no influence and nor did his family. I . . .'

'How did he die?'

'They were in India. There was a cholera outbreak. He died, as did my mother's parents. She came back to England and lived with her aunt. I was born here at St George's.'

'In 1924,' he said. 'You see, I was interested in the Portuguese business. Why does Miss Aspinall speak Portuguese? And I found out that your father was Portuguese.'

'My grandparents were missionaries in the south of India. There were a lot of Portuguese down there from their colony, Goa. She met . . .'

'Your mother never took his name . . .' said Rawlinson, and steadied himself to pronounce Joaquim Reis Leitão.

'*Leitão* means "suckling pig",' she explained.

'Does it?' he said. 'I see why she never took his name. Not something you'd want to have to explain every day of the week . . . suckling pig.'

He sipped his tea. Andrea chased a piece of dry biscuit around her mouth.

'You've led a cloistered life,' said Rawlinson.

'That's what my mother says.'

'The Sacred Heart. Then Oxford. Very sheltered.'

'I spent time here during the Blitz as well,' said Andrea. 'That was a sheltered life, too.'

Rawlinson took some moments to find the joke and grunted, reluctant to be amused.

'So you'll be all right in Lisbon,' said Rawlinson, launching

59

himself out of the chair, cracking his leg a stunning blow on the desk.

'You'll be working as a secretary for a Shell Oil executive called Meredith Cardew,' said Rawlinson, speaking to the sky. 'Rather a fortuitous vacancy. Last girl married a local. The husband doesn't like her working. She's pregnant. There's been some accommodation arranged for you, which I will not attempt to explain but it is the crucial element of your assignment. How's your physics?'

'School Certificate standard.'

'That'll have to do. You'll be doing some translating work. German scientific journals into English for the Americans, so you'll have your work cut out, what with being Cardew's secretary and all. Sutherland and Rose are running the Lisbon station. They'll make contact with you via Cardew. A car will pick you up on Saturday morning and take you to RAF Northolt where you'll be given your documents for travelling to Lisbon. You'll be met at the airport by an agent called James – Jim – Wallis who works for an import/export company down at the docks. He will take you to Cardew's house in Carcavelos, just outside Lisbon. Everything you need to know at this stage is in a file which Miss Bridges will give you and which you will read here and remember.'

He turned his back to the sun. His face, backlit by the window, blackened. He held out his hand.

'Welcome to the Company,' he said.

'The Company?'

'What we call ourselves to each other.'

'Thank you, sir.'

'You'll do very well,' he said.

Miss Bridges sat her in a small room off her office with the file. It wasn't a long file. The changes that had been wrought in her life were small but significant. She would now be known as Anne Ashworth. Her parents lived on Clapham Northside. Her father, Graham Ashworth, was an accountant, and her mother, Margaret Ashworth, was a housewife. Their lives to date had nearly been too boring to read. She digested the material, closed the file and left.

She crossed St James's Park and The Mall and walked up St James's Street to Ryder Street where she knew her mother worked in a government office. She stood on the other side of

St James's to the entrance to Ryder Street and waited. At lunchtime the streets began to fill with people looking for something to eat. Men dived into pubs, women into teahouses. Her mother's white face appeared in the entrance to 7 Ryder Street and walked down to St James's. Andrea tracked her from across the street, into the park. Before the lake she took a right and chose a bench with a view of Duck Island and Horse Guards Road.

Rawlinson's distinctive gait was impossible to miss. He came from the other end of the park and joined her mother on the bench. They sat and looked at the ducks. Rawlinson's hand rested on the duckhead-topped cane. After some minutes he held her hand; Andrea saw the join just below the two slats of wood at the back of the bench. A roaming dog paused to sniff at their feet and moved on. Her mother turned to look at the side of Rawlinson's face and spoke something into his ear, only inches away. They stayed there for half an hour and then walked together, but unconnected, towards the bridge across the middle of the lake where they parted.

Andrea killed time in a reference library just off Leicester Square until the late afternoon. Rawlinson was punctual about leaving work. Andrea watched him swing his boom down towards Petty France and into St James's Park tube station. She followed him to a terraced house in Flood Street in Chelsea. A woman met him at the door, kissed him and took his hat. The door closed and through the lead-glass panes Andrea saw the coat coming off his back. The same coat that her mother had smoothed on to his shoulders the previous afternoon. Rawlinson's blurred outline appeared in the frame of the sitting-room window and collapsed out of sight into a chair. The woman arrived in the window, looked out through the net curtains directly into Andrea's stunned face and then up and down the street as if she was expecting someone.

Andrea walked back down to Sloane Square and caught a bus to Clapham Common, her feet in an uproar from the hard leather of her mother's shoes. She was furious at the years spent watching her mother laying the bricks to the austere edifice of her own hypocrisy. She limped home, dragged her tortured feet up the wooden stairs and collapsed face-down on the bed.

The next morning at breakfast her mother appeared in the doorway tightly bound in a burgundy silk dressing gown. Andrea felt her contemplating six or seven lines of attack before putting the kettle on – the English solution to personal confrontation.

'I got the job,' said Andrea.

'I know.'

'How?'

'Mr Rawlinson's secretary called me at the office,' she said, 'which was very considerate, I thought.'

Andrea searched her mother's back for clues. The scapulae shifted under the silk.

'Do you like Mr Rawlinson?' asked Andrea.

'He seems very pleasant.'

'Do you think you could like him . . . more?'

'*More?*' she said, rounding on her daughter. 'What do you mean by "more"?'

'You know,' she said, shrugging.

'Goodness me, I've only met him once. He's probably married.'

'That would be a shame, wouldn't it?' said Andrea. 'Anyway, I'll be out of here by the weekend.'

'What's that supposed to mean?'

'I'll clear my room out. You could take a lodger.'

'A *lodger*,' said Mrs Aspinall, aghast.

'Why not? They pay money. You could use a few pounds extra, couldn't you?'

Mrs Aspinall sat down opposite her daughter, who had a forearm either side of her plate, hands poised on the table top like spiders.

'What happened to you yesterday afternoon?'

'Nothing. After Rawlinson, I went to the library.'

'You're going away. You've got your whole life ahead of you. I'm staying here. I'll be on my own. Don't you think I'll be lonely? Have you thought about that?'

'That depends if you're alone.'

Her mother blinked. Andrea decided that the line was her parting shot. She looked back from the bottom of the stairs, her mother was still in the same position, the kettle whistling madly in her ear.

Andrea got straight down to packing her few clothes and books. Her mother thundered up the stairs. Half a minute of antagonistic silence opened up as she hovered outside the bedroom door. She moved off. Water ran in the bathroom.

Fifteen minutes later Mrs Aspinall came into Andrea's empty

room with only the case in the middle of the floor. All vestiges of her daughter already gone.

'You've packed,' she said. 'I thought you weren't leaving until Saturday.'

'I wanted to be organized.'

Her mother's face was indecipherable, too much going on at once for any emotion to make itself plain.

The complicated world of adults.

Chapter 7

Andrea landed in Lisbon at three in the afternoon, the adrenalin from her first flight still live in her veins. The heat slammed into her at the door of the aircraft along with the smell of hot metal, tar and vaporized aviation fuel. She took out the white-rimmed sunglasses her mother had given her to protect her eyes and took her first steps on foreign soil as Anne Ashworth.

The sun slapped down on the wide-open spaces of the airfield. The landscape beyond wavered in the rising heat. The trunks of palm trees snaked up to their frayed heads. The flat ground at their feet shone mirror bright. Nobody was moving out there, not even a bird, in the torrid afternoon.

The new airport, barely eighteen months old, had straight, hard, fascistic lines, its main building dominated by the control tower affright with antennae. Armed police moved around the halls inside looking at everyone, who in turn looked at no one, sank into themselves, tried to disappear. Andrea's dark face in the white sunglasses stood out and the customs officer selected her with two beckoning fingers and a cigarette trailing smoke.

He watched her with dark, long-lashed eyes as she opened her case, his lips invisible under a heavy moustache. Other passengers passed through with cursory glances over their luggage. The customs officer dismantled her packing, shook out her underwear, leafed through her books. He lit another cigarette, felt around the lining of the case, glancing up at her so that she stared off around the empty hall, bored. His eyes were rarely on the job but more frequently on her hips, or drilling into her bust. She twitched a nervous smile at him. His smile back showed black and brown rotten teeth, lichen-fringed. She flinched. His sad eyes hardened and he left the counter. She repacked the case.

The one man in the arrivals hall left no doubt as to his nationality. Blond hair combed back in straight rails, faint pencil moustache crayoned in, tweed jacket even in this heat, school tie. All that was missing was a lanyard with a pea whistle attached for bringing boys up short of the line.

'Wallis,' he said. 'Jim.'

'Ashworth,' she replied. 'Anne.'

'Good show,' he said, taking her case. 'You were a long time in there.'

'I was being shown some local colour.'

'I see,' he said, not sure what she meant, but still keen whatever. 'I'm running you out to Cardew's house in Carcavelos. They did tell you, didn't they?'

'You sound as if they might not have done.'

'Communication's abysmal in this outfit,' he said.

He threw her case into the boot of a black Citroën and got in behind the wheel. He offered her a cigarette.

'Três Vintes, they're called. Not bad. Not a patch on Woodies though.'

They lit up and Wallis drove at high speed straight into the heart of Lisbon, which at this hour and in the heat was silent. He hung an elbow out of the window, sneaked a look at her legs.

'First time abroad?' he asked.

She nodded.

'What do you think?'

'I thought it would be ... older.'

'This is all the new building here. Salazar, he's the chap in charge, he made so much money out of us ... and Jerry – you know, what with the wolfram, sardines and the like – he's building a new city, new motorways, a stadium, all this residential stuff – *bairros*, they call them here – all brand new. There's even talk of stringing a bridge across the Tagus. You'll see, though ... when we get into the centre. You'll see.'

The Citroën's tyres squealed around a mule-drawn cart with eight people in it. The wooden wheels rattled over the cobbles. Dogs attached to the axle with string trotted in the shade, tongues lolling in the heat. The broad, dark faces of the women stared down without seeing.

'We'll take the scenic route,' said Wallis. 'The hills of Lisbon.'

Anne, as she now thought of herself permanently, leaned into him as they rounded the Praça de Saldanha, their faces suddenly close together, his with more than professional interest in them, giving her some girlish satisfaction. They shot down the hill into Estefânia, rounded the fountain and crossed high above another street on to Avenida Almirante Reis. Wallis built up speed down the long straight avenue. Overhead cables appeared, the tyres stuttered over the tramlines embedded in the cobbles. The ramparts of the Castelo São Jorge high above them were vague in the heat haze, the dark stone pines crowding a shoulder. They came into an area which looked as if it had suffered recent bomb damage and even the buildings still standing looked decrepit and crumbling, with grasses growing out of the walls and roofs, and the plaster façades scabbed and blistered.

'This is the Mouraria, which they're demolishing, cleaning the area up a bit. On the other side of the hill is the Alfama, best place to live in Lisbon when the Moors were here but they moved out in the Middle Ages. Scared of earthquakes. And, you know, that quarter was one of the few places that survived the big one in 1755. I tell you, it's like a *medina* in there, not too sanitary – and I should know, I was in Casablanca until last year.'

'What were you doing there?'

'Cooking things up in the kasbah.'

They came into a square whose centre was dominated by a massive wrought-iron covered market. Police, mounted and on foot, patrolled the area. The road was scattered with cobblestones torn up and thrown from the now pockmarked pavements. A *Manteigaria* on the corner had been half destroyed, no glass left in any of the doors and windows, and two women inside, sweeping up debris. The shop's awning was ripped but still showed the words *carnes fumadas*.

'Praça da Figueira. There was a riot here this morning. The *Manteigaria* was selling *chouriços* filled with sawdust. The rationing's bad enough without that, what with Salazar selling everything to Jerry. The locals got angry. The communists sent in a few *provocateurs*, the *Guarda* showed up on horseback. Heads got broken. There's two wars going on here in Lisbon. Us versus Jerry and the *Estado Novo* versus the Communists.'

'*Estado Novo?*'

66

'Salazar's New State. The régime. Not much different to the bastards *we're* fighting. Secret police – Gestapo trained – called the PVDE. The city's infested with *bufos* – informers. The prisons . . . well, you don't want to go to a Portuguese prison. They even used to have a concentration camp out on the Cape Verde Islands. Tarrefal. The *frigideira*, they called it . . . the frying pan. This is the Baixa, the business end of town. Completely rebuilt by the Marquês de Pombal after the earthquake. He was another hard man. The Portuguese seem to need them every few hundred years.'

'Need what?'

'Bastards.'

They rounded a square with a high column in the centre and went up a slip road off the corner. Wallis accelerated up the steep hill. A metal walkway crossed the street high above the buildings, connected to a lift.

'Elevador do Carmo, built by Raoul Mesnier. Gets you from the Baixa to the Chiado without breaking a sweat.'

They turned right, first gear up the hill. The difference of it all pouring into Anne. More policemen in khaki, guns in leather holsters. Peaked box caps. Shops with black glass and gold lettering. Jerónimo Martins' *Chá e café. Chocolates.* Broad pavements with black and white geometric patterns. Another turn. Another steep hill. Past a tram, groaning and screeching downhill. Dark impassive faces at the windows. Wallis pointed across her. The Baixa opened out below in squares of red-tiled roof. The castle still hazy, but now at the same level as them across the valley.

'Best view in Lisbon,' said Wallis. 'I'll show you the embassy then I'll take you out to the seaside.'

They drove around Largo do Rato and the Jardim da Estrela and turned left in front of a massive twin-towered, domed cathedral.

'Basílica da Estrela,' said Wallis. 'Built by Maria I at the end of the eighteenth century. She said she'd build a cathedral if she gave birth to a son, which she did. They started building it and the boy died two years before it was completed. Smallpox. Poor lad. But that's Lisbon for you.'

'That's Lisbon?'

'A sad place . . . suits those of melancholic disposition. Are you?'

'Melancholic? No. And you . . . Mr Wallis?'

'Jim. Call me Jim.'

'You don't seem to be that way inclined, Jim.'

'Me? No. No time for it. What's there to be sad about? It's only war. Let's go and see the enemy.'

He cut round the back of the basilica, up a short incline and then down into Lapa. They rolled quietly into a small square where a large mansion stood behind wrought-iron gates and high railings. A swastika flag hung from a flagpole above the door. Two limp phoenix palms stood in the garden. A flame of purple bougainvillea climbed above a window. The blue of the Tagus was visible over the rooftops. For once Wallis didn't say a word. The car dropped down a short hill, turned left and after a hundred yards Wallis nodded up the hill to where the Union Jack hung from a long pink building halfway up.

'We're practically neighbours,' he said. 'I won't drive you up there. There're always *bufos* hanging around outside looking for new faces, ready to report anything to the Germans.'

They went down the hill and came out at the Santos docks. Wallis turned right, heading west along the banks of the Tagus and out beyond the mouth of the estuary. The road hugged the coastline, the railway tracks alongside.

At Carcavelos, just by a large, brown, ancient fort they turned away from the sea and went through the centre of town and out the other side where they pulled up in front of a large, sombre house standing on its own behind a high wall. Two mature stone pines in the garden cast dark shadows over the windows. Wallis honked the horn and a gardener appeared from the shrubbery to open the gate.

'This is Cardew's house,' said Wallis, 'your boss at Shell, but your other bosses will see you first – Sutherland and Rose.'

Wallis lifted out her luggage, rang the door bell, got back in the car and reversed out. A maid came to the door, took her case inside and led her down the hall to a shuttered room where two men sat, one smoking a pipe, the other a cigarette. The maid closed the door. The two men stood. One tall and slim with brown hair swept back, introduced himself as Richard Rose. The other, shorter, with thick, black, undulating hair just said: 'Sutherland'. Both were in shirtsleeves, the room stuffy even with the french windows half-open on to the lawn.

Sutherland stared at Anne from under dark eyebrows. He had

blackberry smudges at the corners of his blue eyes. His skin was white and pasty. He pointed to a chair with the stem of his pipe.

'Wallis took his time,' he said.

'I think he gave me the introductory tour, sir.'

He worked on his pipe for a moment. His lips were oddly bluish, kissing off the pipe stem. He was a still man, no expression around his eyes or mouth and little movement in his body. A lizard, thought Anne.

'You're what they call *morena*,' said Rose. 'Dark. Dusky.'

'As opposed to *loira*,' she said. 'Blonde. Dizzy.'

Rose didn't like it, too cheeky on her first day perhaps. Sutherland smiled so fast and with such little breadth that all she saw was a brown column on the left side of his front teeth – discoloured from smoking.

'I didn't think your ability to speak Portuguese was part of your cover,' said Sutherland, his voice coming from somewhere down his throat, his lips parting to say the words but not moving.

'Sorry, sir.'

'This place ... Lisbon,' he clarified, 'is ... perhaps Wallis told you, a very dangerous city for the careless. You might think that the worst is over, now that we've landed in Normandy, but there are still some very critical situations, life and death situations, for men at sea and in the air. The idea of our intelligence operation here is to make those situations safer, not to exacerbate them with thoughtlessness.'

'Of course, sir,' said Anne, thinking – pompous.

'Information is at a premium. There's an active market on all sides. Nobody is innocent. Everyone is either buying or selling. From maids and waiters to ministers and businessmen. The overall climate is quieter. A lot of the refugees have been shipped out now, so the rumour circuit is tighter and there's less misinformation. We have won the economic war. Salazar no longer fears a Nazi invasion and he's closed the wolfram mines. We're doing our best to make sure that they don't get their hands on any other useful products. As a result we see things more clearly but, although there are fewer players on the pitch, and less complications, it has become a much more subtle affair because now, Miss Ashworth, we are in the endgame. Do you play chess?'

She nodded, mesmerized by the intensity of his passionless face,

69

her own blood zipping around her body faster now that she was close to the current, the live wire. All her training seemed like so much theory. In less than an hour a new world had been peeled open – not just the place, Lisbon, but also an immediate sense of the power of the clandestine. The privilege of knowing things that nobody else knew. Smoke trailed from the pipe held just off Sutherland's face, curled through the sparse sunlight coming through the cracks of the shutters and disappeared up to the high ceiling.

'Part of your mission is a social one. There are no lines drawn here. Who is who? Who plays for whom? There are powerful people, rich people, people who've made a great deal of money out of this war, out of us and the Germans. We know who some of them are, but we want to know all of them. Your ability to speak Portuguese, or rather understand it, is important in this respect and, equally, that nobody should know of this facility. The same applies to your German. You will only use that in the office for translating these journals.'

'What specifically is it from these journals that the Americans are interested in?'

Sutherland beckoned Rose into the conversation, who gave a historical rundown of German nuclear capability from their first successful fission experiments back in 1938 through to Weizsäcker's discovery of Ekarhenium, the vital new element that could make the bomb. As Rose spoke, Sutherland watched the young woman. He didn't listen because he didn't understand any of it and he could see that she was struggling too.

'On 19th September 1939 Hitler made a speech in Danzig in which he threatened to employ a weapon against which there would be no defence,' said Rose. 'The Americans are convinced that he meant an atomic bomb.'

'You shouldn't worry about understanding any of this perfectly. There are probably only a handful of scientists in the world who do,' said Sutherland. 'The important thing is for you to understand the significance of this endgame that we're all involved in.'

'Why would the Germans tell you all this in a physics journal and published papers? Shouldn't this be top secret?'

Sutherland ignored the question.

'The fact is that the Allies have their own bomb programme. We have our own Ekarhenium, the 94th element, which for reasons of secrecy we refer to as "49".'

Brilliant, thought Anne, to switch the numbers round like that.

'In March 1941 Fritz Reiche, a German physicist on the run from the Nazis, passed through Lisbon on the way to the United States,' Rose continued. 'He was met by the Jewish Refugee Organization here and before they put him on a ship to New York we had a meeting in which he warned us that a bomb programme did exist in Germany. We now know that they're building an atomic pile for the creation of Ekarhenium somewhere in Berlin. We also know that Heisenberg went to see Niels Bohr, the Danish physicist, and that they had an argument about whether atomic warfare was the right way for physics to be going. A rift developed between the two men over the Germans' active bomb programme. Heisenberg also sketched out, in rough, the makings of an atomic pile. Since then Bohr has left Denmark and gone over to the Americans. You've been in London since June?'

'Yes, sir.'

'So you know about the doodlebugs . . . the V1 rocket bombs?'

'Yes, sir.'

'We believe that these are the prototype rockets for launching an atomic bomb on London.'

It felt suddenly cold in the room despite the grinding heat outside. Anne rubbed her arms. Sutherland sucked on his pipe, which bubbled like a tubercular lung in the stem.

'Your day job in Cardew's office will be to microfilm the two German physics journals *Zeitschrift für Physik* and *Die Naturwissenschafen* and provide Sutherland and me with typed translations of any articles which pertain to atomic physics,' said Rose. 'More important than that is the accommodation we've managed to arrange for you in Estoril. Cardew has been working up a good social relationship with a fellow called Patrick Wilshere. He's a wealthy businessman in his mid fifties, with contacts and companies in the Portuguese colonies, mainly Angola. He is also Irish, a Catholic and not a lover of Great Britain. We have intelligence that he was selling wolfram, from his Portuguese wife's family's mining concessions in the north, exclusively to the Germans, as well as cork and olive oil from family estates in the Alentejo. He has offered Cardew a room in his considerable house for a lodger. He specified a female lodger.'

71

Sutherland looked to see the effect of this on his new agent. Her blood now felt as thin and cold as ether.

'What is expected of me?' she asked, clipping each word off.

'To listen.'

'You just said that he specified a female lodger.'

'He prefers female company,' said Rose, as if it was something he himself couldn't understand.

'What about his wife? Doesn't his wife live in the same house?'

'I understand that the relationship with his wife has . . . broken down somewhat.'

Anne began to breathe deep, slow breaths. Her thighs were sticking together under the cotton of her dress. Sweat seemed to be pricking out all over. Sutherland shifted in his chair. His first bodily movement.

'Cardew thinks she's suffered some kind of breakdown,' he said.

'You mean she's mad, too?' asked Anne, the scenario burgeoning in her mind.

'Not howling at the moon, exactly,' said Rose. 'More nerves, we think.'

'What's her name?' she asked.

'Mafalda. She's very well connected. Excellent family. Hugely wealthy. The spread they've got in Estoril . . . magnificent. Small palace. Own grounds. Marvellous,' said Sutherland, selling it hard.

'Do you mind if I smoke, sir?' she asked.

Sutherland broke out of his chair and offered her a cigarette from a silver box on the table. He lit it with a weighty Georgian silver lighter with a green baize bottom. Anne drew in heavily, saw Sutherland brightening in her vision.

'Tell me more about Wilshere,' she said, and as an afterthought, 'please, sir.'

'He's a drinking man. Likes to . . .'

'Does that mean he's a drunk?'

'He likes a drink,' said Rose. 'You do too, from the accounts of the Oxford do's. Quite a strong head on you, they said.'

'That's different from being a drunk.'

'Well, while we're about it, he's a gambler as well,' said Sutherland. 'The casino's practically at the bottom of their garden. Do you . . . ?'

'I've never had that sort of liquidity.'

'But you probably know something about probability, what with your maths . . .'

'It's not a particular interest of mine.'

'What is?' asked Rose.

'Numbers.'

'Ah, pure maths,' he said, as if he might know something. 'What drew you to that?'

'A sense of completeness,' she said, hoping that would do the trick.

'A sense or the illusion?' asked Rose.

'We might be talking about a lot of abstractions but what links them, the logic, is very real, very strict and irrefutable.'

'I'm a crossword man myself,' said Rose. 'I like to see into people's minds. How they work.'

Anne smoked some more.

'Crosswords have their own kind of completeness, too,' she said, 'if you're any good at them.'

Things were digging into her. Her bra felt tight. Her waistband knotty. She wasn't getting on with these two men and she didn't know how it had happened. Maybe that first exchange and the last one really had been too cheeky. Perhaps they'd seen one thing, imagined and extended their idea of her and she'd revealed something completely different. Was she this difficult?

'The thing about intelligence is that the picture is *always* incomplete. We deal in fragments. You, in the field, even more so. You might not always know what you're doing, you might not always appreciate the importance of what you hear. There are no solutions and, even if there were, you wouldn't have known the question in the first place. You listen and report,' said Sutherland.

'Something else for you to listen for in the Wilshere household, apart from people's names, has some relevance to the endgame we were talking about earlier,' said Rose. 'To make the doodlebugs, or any rocket for that matter, the Germans need precision tools. To make those tools requires precision cutting instruments. They need diamonds. Industrial diamonds. Those diamonds are finding their way in here on ships from Central Africa. We have tried searching those ships when they put in at our ports, like Freetown in Sierra Leone, but a handful of diamonds is not so easy to find on a 7,000-ton ship. We think, but we have no proof, that Wilshere

73

is bringing in diamonds from Angola and getting them into the German Legation, where they are sent by diplomatic bag to Berlin. We don't know how he does it or how he gets paid for doing it. So anything you hear about diamonds and payment for them in the Wilshere household must be communicated, via Cardew, to us at once.'

'How do you want me to do that?'

'Wallis will look after that. You'll see him and arrange things with him.'

He glanced at his watch.

'Cardew had better take you up to the house now. It's getting late. I've told him to brief you on Wilshere and his wife, but I've also instructed him to exclude certain details which, for the safety of your cover, it would be better for you to find out yourself. I don't want you going in there knowing too much about the situation and not reacting correctly to . . . developments. You're supposed to be a secretary. First time abroad and all that. I want you to be curious about everything and everybody.'

'That doesn't sound as if it's going to be too difficult, sir.'

Sutherland grimaced. The brown column of teeth appeared again and shut down just as fast. He went to the door and called for Cardew.

Chapter 8

Saturday, 15th July 1944, Estoril, near Lisbon.

Meredith Cardew drove Anne west past empty beaches. The sun was still high and the air crammed with heat, the sea in a flat calm, the Atlantic Ocean just licking at the sand. She didn't speak, still overwhelmed by that first meeting with Rose and Sutherland. Across the estuary Cardew pointed out the beaches of Caparica and further into the haze, discernible only as a smudge, the headland of Cabo Espichel. He was trying to loosen her up.

The saltine air that came through the windows brought back weekends by the sea before the war with her mother fully clothed and scarfed against the sun and wind, while her own young body went hazelnut brown in a day. It was easy to love this place, she thought, after London with its bombed-out, blackened houses, the drab grey streets piled with rubble. Here, by the sea, under the big sky, the palms and the bougainvillea flashing past, it should be easy to forget five years of destruction.

Cardew drove one-handed, clawing tobacco into his pipe with the other. He even managed to get the pipe going without sending them off down the rocks and into the sea. He was mid thirties, with thinning, reddish blond hair which had been razor cut up the back. He was tall, very long legs, and slim with a long nose and a facile smile working on the corners of his mouth. His baggy trousers flapped as his knees seemed to be conducting an unseen orchestra; the turn-ups were halfway up his shins, which were covered by thick beige socks. He wore heavy brogues on his feet.

What were the winter clothes like?

He smoked the pipe blowing stage kisses. His right arm had suffered a severe burn up to the elbow. The skin was shiny and patterned like sea fossils in rock.

'Boiling water,' he said, catching her looking, 'when I was a child.'

'Sorry,' she said, flustered at being caught out.

'Did Sutherland and Rose fill you in?'

'As much as they were prepared to. They said they'd purposely left some gaps.'

'Ye-e-e-s,' said Cardew, a frown of uncertainty rippling down his forehead. 'Did Rose say anything about Mafalda?'

'He said she was having a breakdown of some sort, not "howling at the moon", as he put it, just nerves.'

'I don't know what it is. Something to do with her husband perhaps, but it might just be a genetic thing. A bit of inbreeding back down the line. These big Portuguese families are known for it. Marrying each other's first cousins and the like and before you know it . . . I mean, look at the Portuguese royal family. A set of March hares if ever I saw one.'

'Isn't that all over now? The royal family?'

'Thirty-six years ago. Terrible business. The king and his son came up to Lisbon from the country, from Vila Viçosa in fact, not far from where Mafalda's family comes from, near the border. They arrived in Lisbon, trundling through the streets, both assassinated in their carriage. End of the monarchy. Well, it took a couple more years to fizzle out, but that was the effective end: 1908. Still, she might just be depressed or something. Whatever, she's not right, which is probably why Wilshere's looking for some company.'

'Female company, so I understand.'

Cardew shifted in his seat and looked as wary as a grouse on the Glorious Twelfth.

'Bit of a rum one, old Wilshere. He's broken the mould. Not your average chap.'

'Does he have children?'

'Only sons, who are away. No daughters. Probably why he wants female company. And here I am with four, for God's sake,' he said, a little gloomy. 'Sporting legacy gone . . . although the eldest one's school long-jump champion.'

'All is not lost, Mr Cardew.'

He brightened, bounced the end of his pipe by clenching his jaw.

'I think you'll like Wilshere,' said Cardew. 'And I know he'll like you. You've got that determined look about you. He likes girls with a bit of spunk. He didn't like Marjorie.'

'Marjorie?'

'My former secretary. The one who married a Portuguese and is now pregnant. The husband won't let her work, says she's got to lie down. Poor girl's got six months to go. Still, that's why you're here. Wilshere didn't take to her, anyway. She was a bit too English for his taste and he upset her. Yes, he can be a bit like that. If he takes to you, you're all right. If not he's . . . he's a difficult bugger.'

'He likes you.'

'Yes . . . in his way.'

'Aren't you a bit too English as well?'

'Sorry, old girl. I'm a Scot, both sides. Talk like a Sassenach but I'm a Scot through and through. Like Wilshere, in fact, he's Irish down to his heels but talks with a silver spoon in his mouth.'

'Or a hot potato . . . if he's Irish,' said Anne.

Cardew roared, not that he found it so funny. He was just the type who liked to laugh.

'What else is there to know about Patrick Wilshere?' she asked.

'He can be a charmer . . .'

'As well as a drinker and a gambler.'

'He rides, too. Do you ride?'

'No.'

'It's nice up there on the Serra de Sintra on horseback,' said Cardew. 'Sutherland told me you had a top-class brain. Maths. Languages. That sort of thing.'

'It didn't leave much time for anything else. I'm just not sporty, Mr Cardew. Sorry. I'm not much of a team person, I suppose. It's probably something to do with being an only child and . . .'

She pulled up short of saying 'and not having a father'. She had a father now, of course. Graham Ashworth. Accountant. She looked out of the window and ordered her mind. They passed large villas set in their own, almost tropical gardens.

'There're crowned heads of Europe sitting out the war in Estoril,' said Cardew. 'That's the kind of place it is.'

He turned off the main road at the Estoril railway station and drove into a square lined with hotels and cafés surrounding some gardens with palm trees and beds of roses, which gradually sloped up to a modern building at the top.

They passed the Hotel Palácio which Cardew told her was 'ours' and next door the Hotel Parque which was 'theirs'. They went round the back of the modern building at the top which proved to be the casino, and Cardew pointed out a narrow, overgrown passage and a gate in the hedgerow further up, which was the back way into the Wilsheres' garden. They climbed higher, right to the top of the hill, past gardens enclosed by privilege, hugging the towering phoenix palms and spiked fans of the Washingtonians, while the brash purple lights of bougainvillea tried to escape over the wall. Anne straightened her sunglasses on her nose, rested an elbow on the car window ledge, wished she had a cigarette going, which she thought would be the final detail of a leading actress's style, coming into her Riviera home.

'You didn't say whether you liked Wilshere,' said Anne, catching sight of herself in the wing mirror.

Cardew stared intently at the windscreen as if the entrails of squashed insects might lead him somewhere. They pulled up at an ornate gateway, walls curving up and scrolling against solid stone posts, each of which sported a giant carved pineapple on top. A tiled panel bore the words *Quinta da Águia* and the wrought-iron gates an elaborate *QA* design.

'Here's an insight into the man,' said Cardew. 'This place used to be called *Quinta do Cisne*, Swan House, if you like. He's renamed it Eagle House. His little joke, I think.'

'I don't get it.'

'He does business with the Americans *and* the Germans. Both countries use the eagle as their national symbol.'

'Maybe he's just being a gentleman.'

'How's that?'

'Making everybody feel comfortable . . . unless they're Marjorie,' she said.

The driveway was cobbled all the way up to the house, white with black geometric patterns, just as she'd seen on the Lisbon pavements. It was lined with pink oleanders, very mature, almost trees. They came out of the oleanders into a square in front of the house which had a fountain in the middle, water spouting from a dolphin's mouth. Lawn sloped away to distant hedges, a stepped, cobbled path ran down one side towards the bottom of the garden and the back gateway to possible financial ruin. The view reached to the hotels and palms of Estoril's main square, the railway station and the ocean beyond.

The house itself was vast and box-like, not an accumulation of extensions, not something organic that had grown with the owner's mind or fortune, but a house that had been planned, finished and never again added to. Its ugliness was disguised by the leafy frills of an ancient wisteria whose tributaries reached the eaves of the terracotta tiled roof. They walked to the pillared porch, Anne fretting about her case left in the car.

The door was opened by a grotesquely bent old man, his head at right angles to his body and turned sideways so that he could look Cardew in the eye. He wore a black tailed jacket and striped trousers. He was backed up by a small, wide woman also dressed in black with a white apron and cap. Cardew's Portuguese came out like an order for buttered scones but it was intelligible enough for the old man, who produced a length of cane from the back of his jacket and set off towards the car with the woman in tow. Another maid appeared, doing up her apron. She was even smaller than the first, with a face that had been pinched and drawn out to the length of a fox's. Tiny eyes, closed up by malnourishment in pregnancy, flickered in her head. There was an exchange and the maid set off across the black and white chequered floor of the dark hall which was surrounded by oak panelling, and stairs that joined a gallery above. A huge, tiered iron chandelier hung from the wooden roof.

On either side of the door through which the maid had disappeared were two glass cases full of brightly coloured, naïve clay figurines. Dark, uncleaned oil paintings in heavy gilt frames hung above them. In one, the stern face of a bearded ancestor appeared as if through battle smoke, the woman standing behind his chair was pale with dark rings around her eyes as if illness had been a way of life.

'Mafalda's parents,' said Cardew. 'The Conde and Condessa. Dead now. She inherited the lot.'

Behind them the old man and the maid staggered in with Anne's case suspended between them on the piece of cane. They started up the staircase and paused on the first landing. The old man held on to the shiny ball at the corner of the bannisters, panting. Anne felt the urge to get up there to help him and, sensing it, Cardew gripped her elbow. The other maid returned, taking tile-sized steps towards them, her foxy face nudging the air, suspicious, checking them for smells. Cardew steered Anne down the length of a wooden-floored corridor with a strip of carpet up the middle, tall mirrors on either side of mixed quality so that Anne appeared thin, chubby, wavy. A chandeliered dining room flashed past on the left. At the end of the corridor, just before the french windows out on to the back terrace, they turned right into a long, high room with six tall windows giving out on to the lawn. The shutters were open, the blue and gold designs on them faded from the fierce summer sun.

The quantity of furniture in the room gave the impression that there was a lot going on, that maps and compasses might have been helpful. This furniture was not in any way co-ordinated, colours clashed, brocade and velvet sat uncomfortably together, the muted carpets seemed embarrassed by the brashness and weight of it all. At the far end of the room was a carved marble fireplace which contained a frieze in bas-relief of an ancient people, Corinthians or Phoenicians, engaged in endless tussle with wild animals. Above the fireplace hung a painting, a hunting scene of wild and bloody savagery, with wild boar stuck and squealing and wounded dogs tossed in the air while mounted men with lances stared on.

Patrick Wilshere stood below this scene dressed in riding britches, boots and a loose, collarless white shirt undone at the neck. Cardew's description of him as 'rum' and 'not average' was typical understatement. Wilshere had stepped out of a novel from a different, more romantic age. His grey hair, swept back behind his ears, was long, long enough so that it rested on the first vertebrae of his back. He had a moustache whose waxed tips pointed upwards and his eyes were creased at the corners as if on permanent look-out for the source of all amusement. His hands had long elegant fingers and they cradled a cut-glass tumbler half-full of amber liquid. He nudged himself away from the fireplace where he'd been leaning.

'Meredith!' he called down the room, pleased to see him, hearty.

The maid stepped back and Anne followed Cardew through the watercourse between the furniture to the small backwater where Wilshere stood, still with the faint reek of horse about him.

'Sorry, haven't had time to change,' said Wilshere. 'Been out on the hills all day, just got back and needed a blast to put the wind back in my sails. You must be Anne. Pleased to meet you. Been travelling all day, I expect. Could do with freshening up. Get yourself out of that suit and into something more comfortable. Yes. MARIA! If you can't remember the maids' names just shout Maria and you'll get two or three.'

The maid came back and stood at the door.

'All tiny, these people,' said Wilshere, 'no bigger than fairies. Come from my wife's part of the country.'

He spoke in perfect Portuguese. The maid dipped and ducked in an attempted curtsy. Anne navigated the furniture to the door and followed the maid up the stairs and down a corridor to a room which would have been above the end of the living room. It was a corner room, with views of the sea and Estoril. There was a private bathroom which overlooked the terrace and, beyond some hedges, a grass tennis court, brown from the sun. The cast-iron bath had clawed feet holding on to small worlds. A shower rose the size of a frying pan stuck out from the wall. The maid left, closing the door. Anne waited for the footsteps to retreat, ran at the four-poster bed, flung herself at it wildly and writhed in luxury. She lay with her arms spread out, trying to encompass her new world.

She stripped, showered and changed into a pleated cotton skirt and a simple blouse which left her arms bare. She brushed out her hair, struck poses in the full-length mirror, pouting her mouth, flicking at her skirt, but still failed to match her surroundings.

She headed back down the corridor towards the stairs. A figure appeared at the far end of the gallery. A woman with a face whiter than her mother's and long grey hair down to the middle of her back. She wore a white nightdress. The woman faded into the darkness of a room, shut the door.

Mafalda the Mad, very Jane Eyre, she thought, and fled down the stairs.

Anne returned to the living room, which was empty. Wilshere was sitting on his own on the back terrace in front of a wrought-iron table with a cigarette box and the cut-glass tumbler, emptier. He had his boots up on an unoccupied chair opposite. She joined him.

'Ye-e-es,' he said, 'that's better.'

'What happened to Mr Cardew?'

'Sit down, sit down, won't you,' he said, pulling her down into a chair next to him, his palm rough on her bare arm. His green eyes stroked her all over and the hand held on to the soft part below her shoulder. His look was neither prurient nor penetrative, two other looks she'd had that day, but attentive, oddly intimate, as if they were old friends, or even stronger – lovers, maybe, who'd had a life together, parted and come back for another visit.

'Drink?'

How to play this? She'd been hoping to observe while Cardew talked but now she was in it. He likes a girl with spunk.

'Gin,' she said, 'and tonic.'

'Excellent,' he said, releasing her arm, calling a boy over, who Anne hadn't seen in the shade of the terrace.

Wilshere punched some words into him and drained his own glass which he handed over.

'Smoke?'

She took a cigarette which he lit for her. She blew the smoke out into the still, very hot evening. It smelled like burnt dung. The boy returned and laid out two tumblers and a small dish of black, shiny olives. They chinked glasses. The cold drink and the fizz of the tonic smacked into her system and she had to restrain herself from jutting her breasts.

'You'll probably want to go to the beach tomorrow,' said Wilshere, 'although I should warn you that our friendly dictator, Dr Salazar, does not agree with men and women disporting themselves semi-naked on the strand. There are police. An intimidating squad of fearless men whose job it is to maintain the moral rectitude of the country by sniffing out depravity at source. All those refugees, you see, brought their immoral ideas and fashions with them and the good Doctor's determined that it won't get out of hand. The three F's. Football, *Fado* and Fátima. The great man's solution to the evils of modern society.'

'*Fado*?'

'Singing. Very sad singing . . . wailing, in fact,' he said. 'Perhaps some of my Irishness has worn off in this sunshine. All that rain and terrible history, I should have a natural inclination for drink and melancholy thought, but I don't.'

'Drink?' asked Anne, archly, which earned a flash of white teeth.

'I've never felt the need to brood over things. They happen. They pass. I move on. Construct. I've never been one for sitting about, longing for previous states. States of what? Lost innocence? Simpler times? And I don't have much time for destiny or fate,

82

which is what *fado* means. People who believe in destiny are invariably justifying their own failure. Don't you think? Or am I a godless fellow?'

'I thought belief in fate was just a way of accepting life's inexplicability,' said Anne, 'and you still haven't told me how *fado* is supposed to stiffen moral fibre. How can fate or destiny be a social policy?'

Wilshere smiled. Cardew had been right about spunk.

'It's what they sing about in the *fado*. *Saudades* – which is longings. I've no time for it. You know where it comes from? This is a country with a magnificent past, a tremendously powerful empire with the world's wealth in their hands. Take the spice trade. The Portuguese controlled the trade that made food taste good . . . and then they lost it all and not only that . . . their capital was destroyed by a cataclysmic event.'

'The earthquake.'

'On All Souls' Day too,' he said. 'Most of the population were in church. Crushed by falling roofs. Then flood and fire. The perils of Egypt, minus the plague and locusts, were visited on them in a few hours. So that's where *fado* comes from. Dwelling in and on the past. There are other things too. Men putting out to sea in boats and not always coming back. The women left behind to fend for themselves and to sing them back into existence. Yes, it's a sad place, Lisbon, and *fado* provides the anthems. That's why I don't live there. Go there as little as possible. You have to have the right spirit for the city and it's not one that sits well with me. Pay no attention to *fado*. It's just Salazar's way of subduing the population. That and the miraculous sighting of the Virgin at Fátima . . . ye-e-e-s, Catholicism.'

'That must be hard work if they all died in church back in 1755.'

'Ah, well, you see, the good doctor's trained to be a priest, he's a monk *manqué* . . . he knows better than anybody how to control a population. You might have heard of the PVDE.'

'Not yet,' she lied.

'His secret police. His Inquisitors. They root out all non-believers, the heretics and the blasphemers, and break them on the wheel.'

She looked sceptical.

'I promise you, Anne, there's no difference except it's politics now and not religion.'

83

He beckoned the boy, who approached, whisky bottle in hand, and filled Wilshere's glass to within a quarter-inch of the brim. He took an olive, bit out the pit, and threw it unconsciously into the garden. He sucked the top off his drink, lit another cigarette and was surprised to find his old one still going in the ashtray. He crushed it out, flung a boot up on to the chair and missed. He looked at his watch as if someone had burnt his wrist.

'Better change for dinner. Didn't realize it was so late.'

Anne stood with him.

'No, no, you stay here,' he said, patting her arm. 'You'll do fine like that. Perfect. I still smell of horse.'

He did. And whisky. And something sour, which smelled the same as fear but wasn't.

'Will your wife be joining us?' Anne asked his retiring back.

'My *wife*?' he asked, turning on his boot heel, the whisky from his glass slopping on to his wrist.

'I thought I saw her . . .'

'What did you see?' he asked rapidly, drawing on his cigarette, which he then flicked away across the terrace.

'On the way down from my room. A woman in a nightdress . . . that was all. In the corridor upstairs.'

'What did Cardew say about my wife?' asked Wilshere, the savage edge to his voice even sharper.

'Only that he thought she was unwell, which was why I asked you . . .'

'Unwell?'

'. . . which was why I asked you whether she would be joining us for dinner, that's all,' finished Anne, holding her ground against Wilshere's sudden blast.

His top lip extended over the glass rim and sucked up an inch of whisky, the sweat from the alcohol in this heat standing out on his forehead in beads.

'Dinner's in fifteen minutes,' he said and turned through the french windows, clipping the door, which juddered in its frame.

Anne sat back down, a small tremble in the tip of her cigarette as she put it to her mouth. She sipped more gin, finished smoking and walked out on to the crepuscular lawn. Lights were on down in the town – rooms here and there in buildings, streets brought up in monochrome, the crowns of the gathered stone pines billowing like thick black smoke, the railway station with people waiting, mesmerized by the track or staring off down the rails of past and future. Normality, and next to this, the vast and threatening blackness of the unlit ocean.

Two squares of light came on in the house behind her. A figure came to one of the lit windows and looked down on her although, in the twilight, she wasn't sure if she was visible. She felt the drag, almost heard the sinister rattle of the pebbles as with the inevitability of tide she was being drawn into the complicated currents of other people's lives.

Chapter 9

Saturday, 15th July 1944, Wilshere's house, Estoril, near Lisbon.

The servant came out on to the lawn to get her, made her jump as she was lounging about in her own thoughts. She'd lost herself in the graininess where the town's light met the darkening air. She turned to the boy and found that the façade of the house was now lit by footlights as if it was a monument. It only came to her then. The freedom of artificial light. She hadn't thought about it looking down on the town. No blackout. This alarming country – free and yet forbidding.

She followed the boy. His thighs thumped out of the side of his trousers, massive as a weightlifter's. He walked her across the terrace, already cleared of her half-drunk gin and tonic, and on to the dining room halfway down the corridor. Three glass chandeliers hung over a table which had been shortened to fifteen feet for this, more intimate, occasion. Wilshere stood, almost at attention. He was dressed in a dinner jacket with a board-hard shirt front and black bow tie. He presented his wife, who was in a floor-length evening gown, breasts encased, waist pinched, skirts full of animal rustlings. Her hair was up and she wore a necklace of three large, set rubies. Her face still had the terrible pallor but it was not the alabaster whiteness of her mother's, more the ghastliness of unsuccessful junket.

Anne shook her hand which had been held out like a bishop's, waiting to be kissed. It was puffy, swollen by fluid retention, so that the knuckles were dimples. They sat. Anne, midway between their two ends, awkward in her informal dress. The light from the three chandeliers was surgically bright and harsh – operative.

A soup was served, greyish-green with a slice of sausage floating in the middle. White wine trickled into glasses. Mafalda refused the wine, placed her spoon in her soup and looked about. The wine tasted of cold metal with a fizz like the end of a battery. The soup was replaced by a plate of three fish each, their eyes cataracted by frying. Anne's intestines screamed for a break to the shattering silence but Wilshere, unmoved, holding his knife like a scalpel, dismantled his fish expertly, while Anne reduced hers to a pile of bony hash. Mafalda's knife and fork tinkered around the sea bass and subsided. The fish were taken away. Large chunks of indeterminate meat flecked with red were served, clamshells rattled on the plates.

Anne, desperate to communicate, found her thoughts crashing about her head like a late-night drunk looking for food in a hotel kitchen. Mafalda corralled her meat on one side of her plate, the clams on the other, and laid down her irons. Red wine jugged into different glasses. It smelled of damp socks but tasted as complex as a kiss. Wilshere swilled it in his mouth, his lips pursed to a smooch beneath his joyous moustache.

'Your husband was telling me about *fado* this evening,' gasped Anne, having two goes at it, finding not just a frog in her throat but a whole fat toad.

'I can't think why,' said Mafalda. 'He doesn't know anything about it. Loathes it. Runs – no, sprints – to turn it off when it comes on the radio.'

Wilshere's jaws chewed over the meat in his mouth, interminable as cud.

'He was saying,' Anne pressed on, 'he was saying that they're songs about longing, about dwelling . . .'

Mafalda just rattled the cutlery on the side of her monogrammed plate and Anne shut up.

'I like that new girl. Amália,' said Wilshere. 'Amália Rodrigues. Yes, she's rather good.'

'Her voice?' asked Mafalda on the end of a coal-black look.

'I didn't know there was anything else to *fado*,' said Wilshere, 'or were you asking me whether I thought she had the spirit, the soul, the *alma* of *fado*?'

A twitch had started up around Mafalda's left eye. She stroked it down with her little finger. Anne looked from one end of the table to the other – the idiot spectator.

'Of course, she has marvellous . . .' said Wilshere, and his search for a word set the air quivering, '. . . marvellous deportment.'

'De*portment*?' scoffed Mafalda. 'He means . . .'

She reined herself in. Her small puffy fist banging the edge of the linen tablecloth a light thump.

'Perhaps I should have chosen something less contentious,' said Wilshere. 'We were merely conversing about our good friend the great Doctor and, of course, the three "F"s came up. Perhaps we should have talked about history, but even that's a minefield. You'll be glad to know that I didn't make any mention of *O Encoberto*, the Hidden One, my dear.'

'The Hidden One?' asked Anne.

'Dom Sebastião,' said Wilshere. 'No, I didn't make any mention of him, my dear, I knew you'd rather tell Anne all about that yourself. My wife, you see, Anne, is a monarchist. A state that hasn't existed in this country for more than thirty years. She believes that the Hidden One, who was killed – ooooh, four hundred years ago, wasn't it? – on the battlefield of El Kebir in Morocco, will somehow return . . .'

Mafalda stood with some difficulty. Wilshere broke off. A servant was pulling back her chair and offering his shoulder for her to lean on.

'I'm not feeling so well,' she said. 'I'm afraid I will have to withdraw.'

She left the room without appearing to shift any of her weight on to the servant's shoulder, which she gripped in a fistful of material. She hadn't been that unsteady upstairs in her nightclothes. Mafalda gave Anne the shadow of a nod. The door closed with a brass click. Anne dropped back into the dent of her upholstered chair, traumatized. Her half-eaten meat was removed. Fruit salad appeared. Steps receded to the kitchen. They were left alone in the chandeliered glare, the red wine on a small silver tray in front of Wilshere.

'Words, words, words,' said Wilshere under his breath, 'it's only words.'

Earlier, out on the terrace Wilshere had been on his way up to drunkenness. The flash of anger at the mention of his wife had been a hiatus in the usual, uninterrupted progression. In the short fifteen minutes he'd taken to get changed he'd shot through drunkenness and regained sobriety, but with a difference. He was now capable of seamless transformations from belligerent to maudlin, from vindictive to self-pitying. Perhaps Cardew's estimation of the mental state of the occupants was the reverse. Mafalda was just unwell and the man drumming his stiff bib at the end of the table, contemplating the level of wine in his glass, was, if not mad, then close to it.

'Don't eat dessert myself,' he said. 'No sweet tooth.'

He chinked the edge of his plate with the spoon, drank the wine and poured the remains into his glass. The servants arrived with coffee. He told them to serve it out on the terrace. He finished the wine in a single draught as if compelled to drink it – condemned to death by poisoning.

On the terrace Wilshere forced a glass of port from another century on to Anne. This was no longer pleasurable drinking.

'Let's take a walk down to the casino,' said Wilshere after a prolonged silence in which his body became an impregnable fortification, behind which the man's mind had retreated to fight some internal battle. 'Run along and put your best party frock on.'

She put her only party frock on, one of her mother's from before the war. She looked down out of the bathroom window on to the terrace where Wilshere sat immobile. Refocusing on her own image in the glass she felt a crack of fear opening up. She remembered her training – the talk about mental stamina for the work – and breathed the panic back down.

She walked downstairs with her shoes in her hand, not wanting another confrontation with the spectral Mafalda. On the terrace she rejoined Wilshere, who was staring through the footlights into the wall of darkness. He jerked himself out of his chair, held her by the shoulders but not with the soft touch of her old piano teacher. His breath, an ammoniacal reek that could have blistered paintwork, made her blink. Sweat had appeared in the parted channel of his perky moustache. His mouth was no more than inches from her own. Everything in her body recoiled and a squeal moved up from her stomach. He let her go. Goose flesh flourished where his hands had been.

They walked through the curtain of light on to the lawn and round to the cobbled pathway that led down the garden. A half-moon lit the way. Not far from the bottom a path forked off to a summerhouse and a bower which had formed around some stone pillars providing a shelter of hanging fronds for a bench with a view out to the sea. It looked unused, as if the house's occupants had no need of such tranquillity but preferred the relentlessness of the dark halls and the corridors of their natural habitat.

They crossed the road under the dense darkness of the stone pines at the rear of the casino, a modern featureless building which knew that its attraction was not architectural. They joined the current of expensive-looking people going in – the rustle of taffeta, the sizzle of nylons and the crack of wads of freshly minted folding money.

Wilshere headed straight for the bar and ordered a whisky. Anne opted for a brandy and soda. As Wilshere lit her cigarette a meaty arm came around his shoulders. His slim body flinched.

'Wilshere!' said an expansive American voice, not looking at him but putting his head close as if about to touch cheeks. A hand stretched out towards Anne. 'Beecham Lazard.'

'The third,' said Wilshere, shrugging the American's arm off. 'This is Miss Anne Ashworth.'

Lazard was taller and wider than Wilshere. He was dressed in a dinner jacket too, but his was crammed full and bulging. He was younger than Wilshere by twenty years and had black hair with a precision-tooled side parting. His smile was faultless and his skin tone utterly consistent. There was something of waxwork perfection about him, both fascinating and repellent.

'We gotta talk,' said Lazard to the side of Wilshere's face.

Wilshere looked down his shirt front like a man on a high ledge.

'Anne is my new house guest,' he said. 'Flew in from London today. I was just showing her the wonderful place in which we live.'

'Sure thing,' said Lazard, releasing Anne's hand, which he'd been rubbing with a smoothing thumb. 'It's just about dates . . . a few seconds, that's all.'

Wilshere, annoyed, excused himself and backed off to the entrance of the bar where they talked, jostled by others streaming past them. Anne fiddled with her cigarette and felt juvenile in her outfit. *Haute couture* Paris had shifted to Lisbon and the clothes on the people around her made her feel as if she was waiting for the jellies to come out at a tea party. She smoked as a diversionary tactic and cast about to compensate. Even that proved difficult. Her idle, confident gaze was easily met by others' with stronger, more demanding eyes. Her head snapped back to the mirrors and glassware of the bar, which reflected a multiplication of eyes, some drunk, some sad, some hungry, some hard – but all wanting.

'Americans,' said Wilshere, back at her side. 'No idea of the time or the place.'

He took her over to a table and introduced her to four women and two men. The foreign names rushed past like a hunt in full cry, all titles and ancestry, fanfare and heraldry. They spoke to Wilshere in French and ignored her. All they needed to know of Anne was apparent in her dress – some skivvy that Wilshere was tupping. He detached himself from their imploring jewelled and knotted fingers, and bowed.

'Has to be done, I'm afraid,' he said to Anne's cheek. 'Ignore the Romanians at your peril. Frightful gossips.'

They headed for the *caixa* where Wilshere wrote a cheque for some chips and they wheeled through the swing doors into the gaming room. He gave Anne an inch of his chips and went straight to the baccarat table, took a seat next to another slumped player and lapsed into dense concentration. Anne hung at his back, suspended in layers of smoke. Cards were drawn from the slab. The players turned up the corners. Sometimes they asked to stand, other times to draw and rarely they declared a natural. It was tedious unless you were one of the rivet-eyed players, who clenched the air in fists, hissing at their losses and uncurling, but only for a second, at their wins.

Wilshere's transformation was instant. All vestiges of amusement and ennui had left him. His interest now was only calculable in percentages, his intelligence reduced to a wavering telepathy with numbered suits. Anne diverted herself by computing the bank's advantage in the game and started to yawn. The gambling had sucked out the oxygen in the air. She wandered the room, keen to get away from the joyless backs of the baccarat players. No straying eyes connected with hers, money more compelling than lust in here. The room was quiet, but prickling with anticipation and torment. The yards of green baize and acres of carpet added stealth to wealth and hushed any sudden collapse of funds.

She was drawn to roulette. There was noise in roulette, especially when an American was playing, and the clicking of the ivory ball, playing its own *fado*, was almost a sweet distraction after the murderous cards. She joined the crowd, found herself embraced by it, welcomed, offered a cigarette, crushed and, in this familiar, slaughter-yard jostle, confirmed what she had known from the moment those swing doors had batted shut behind her. She was being watched.

It would have been easy enough to turn, to look over the heads bowed in supplication to the green baize god. It would have been easy to find the only other face in the room uncomplicated by numbers, unconcerned by the concentration of avidity. But she couldn't do it. The tension set in her neck, her head began to tremble. An arm snaked around her shoulder and dragged her into a damp shirt.

'Ladies for luck,' roared the American. 'Come on. Let's hear it for number twenty-eight.'

The American gripped her tighter. The croupier terminated the betting, span the wheel and set the ball in motion. Girls squealed. The ball began its chatter. Anne was clenched to the American's chest, harder. His smell as strong as roast meat. The ball played the flibbertigibbet – coy, tantalizing, coquettish – jumping in and out of bed, over the numbers' brass divides. Anne's head was almost on the man's chest now, such was his determination, and into the corner of her eye, back from the crowd, just inside the spread of light, came the strap of neck muscle, the prominent jawline, the hollow cheek of the one she knew was watching her.

He dipped his head. The cheekbones high against the blue eyes, the vulnerable mouth, the dented chin, the throat like a small fist framed by the straining neck. Seeing the eyes complicated matters. It was impossible to understand the motive, to accurately translate the look. Her throat closed up, heat prickled up her neck. She wrestled her eyes back down to the table but not to the squares and numbers, not to the black and red diamonds but to the soft, green felt that was easy on the mind. Her head clicked back up, jerked on a nervous string. Still there. His intent as close as thunder. A roar went up.

'*Vingt-huit*,' said the croupier.

The American's fist punched the underbelly of the smoke above, cigar in the corner of his mouth. Anne, released from his grip, fell forward and saw another girl on his other side still in the man's hug, tiny, thrush-sized with pointy breasts and a sharp beak. He kissed the little bird's head. The croupier raked in the dead chips, leaving the American's bet. He made his calculation and pushed a New York skyline back. Anne backed out of the crowd, sucked on her cigarette and headed for the baccarat tables. She had to concentrate on her walking, as if she had someone else's legs and feet, ones that might run off on their own.

Wilshere's back was still buttressed against the baccarat table, but now Beecham Lazard was sitting next to him. She held back from their orbit. The dealer had his back to the two men, preparing new slabs of cards. The American looked left and swept a stack of high-denomination chips across to Wilshere, whose shoulders widened for a moment and collapsed back.

Anne had to get out of the room, get away from the suffocating quiet of money, the fierce addiction of the gamblers, and away from those blue eyes. She headed for the padded swing doors. The way out of the asylum. She heard music from the Wonderbar and headed for it. She hid in the darkness, away from the lighted dance floor and smoked the cigarette down to her nails.

'Surprised to see you out on your own on your first night,' said a voice from below her.

The band's drummer enjoyed a roll and thrashed his cymbals. Jim Wallis was sitting at a table a few feet to her left, with a spare chair next to him. Across the dance floor, the face from the gaming room appeared at the edge of the light, swept round and fell back into the dark. She took Wallis's offer of a cigarette and drank some of his whisky and soda, which clawed at her throat. Blood smacked into her cheeks.

'I seem to be being followed already,' she said through the music.

'Not surprised,' said Wallis, almost miserable.

'I thought nobody was supposed to know who I am.'

'They want to, though,' he said and leaned into her with his lighter.

'I don't know what you mean.'

'You're beautiful,' he said, the flame wavering in her face. 'Simple as that.'

'Jim,' she said, warning him.

'You asked a question.'

'What are *you* doing here?'

'Waiting and watching,' he said. 'Do you want to dance . . . pass the time?'

'Aren't you with someone?'

'She likes roulette,' said Wallis, holding open his hands to reveal a man with shallow means.

He led Anne to the dance floor. The music started slow. They danced close but formally. She told him about the summerhouse and the covered bower which would make a good place for a dead-letter drop. She'd check it out the next day. The band leader announced a dance number and the couples multiplied on the floor.

She danced for half an hour and went into the powder room when the band took a break. By the time she arrived back at the bar, Wilshere stood on his own with his back to her, foot up on the brass rail, his elbow turned out so that she knew he was still drinking. She told him she wanted to get back to bed. He finished his drink with small ceremony and held out his arm, which she took and they went out into a night that was no cooler.

'These nights . . .' said Wilshere, panting, but without offering anything more, weary of them she could tell.

Wilshere's pace slowed as they reached the edge of the stone pines near the entrance to the garden. She thought at first that he couldn't face going back to the house, that smell on him again, which wasn't fear but like it. He disengaged his arm and put it around her shoulder. They moved on, she supporting him.

The moonlight coaxed the darkness of the garden to blue and Wilshere was staggering and snatching at the fat leaves of the hedge. He was sobbing from such a depth that it came out as a retch, as if he was trying to sick up this thing inside him, some horror tormenting his innards. He hugged her tighter to him. The sharp edges of the jacket stuffed with casino chips cut into her ribs. Anne's heels ripped over the uneven edges of the cobbled steps. They careened off the path and crashed through the hedge and landed, humped on top of each other, in the soft earth on the other side. Wilshere lay on his back. His face was slack, his breathing regular. She pushed away from his limp embrace and started at the sound of wildlife, large and loud, coming through the foliage. A white shirt front flitted, cuffs reached down to the comatose Wilshere.

'You're going to have to help me,' said the voice in quiet, accented English.

She helped Wilshere over the stranger's shoulder, chips cascading down his legs. He backed out of the hedge and set off at a steady lope up the lawn. The lights were off inside and outside the house. They went in through the french windows by the terrace.

'Where does he sleep?'

'I don't . . . I think . . . just put him in there,' she said.

The stranger sidestepped into the sitting room, threw Wilshere down on the first sofa and pulled off his shoes. Wilshere struggled with himself and fell silent. She went to the window and opened the shutter which the servants had closed against the morning sunshine. By the time she'd turned back the stranger had gone. Back at the window she saw him cross the moonlit lawn at a calm night-watchman's pace. He turned at the top of the path to look back, his face obscure. He trotted down the steps, his leather soles pattering the cobbles to silence.

Chapter 10

In the heat of the morning Anne lay in bed, a crack of light across the foot of the bed warming her ankles. The night's events crawled through her mind and she understood how quickly adults' lives could complicate themselves – a compression of thought and action in time, of too much happening in a confined space, of daily need and greed, triumph and disappointment – and how interminably slow a child's life was, how long the summers used to be with nothing in them. Her mind worked cyclically, coming round to fix on the same single image which had disturbed her even more than Wilshere's behaviour; the man's face, his look, intense and intent – inscrutable, too – threatening or benevolent?

She replayed the night to a final tableau in the casino. As she collected Wilshere from the bar Jim Wallis was sitting at his table with a girl. The girl was the song thrush from under the American roulette-player's arm. She was pretty, in the way of a porcelain doll, if a face that gave out so little could be attractive. It was a hard face that promised but never rewarded. Wallis's good nature might break itself against that face.

Her dress on the back of the chair was filthy. She recalled the catastrophe in the bushes. Wilshere fighting his way into unconsciousness, desperate to stop living with whatever he had in his mind. She threw on some clothes and ran downstairs barefoot. There was no Wilshere in the silent drawing room where dust motes rolled in the single shaft of light from the one half-opened shutter.

She ran out of the house, across the lawn, hot and rough underfoot, to the cobbled path and down to the bushes which she crashed through to find the soil raked over. The neat furrows twitched with ants. She felt around with her feet and fingers and found a casino

96

chip of the highest denomination: five thousand escudos – fifty pounds. She crossed the path to the summerhouse and the pillared bower whose wooden crossbeams were overgrown with passion-flower, its exotic purple and white tropical discs hanging above the stone seat. She placed the casino chip on the top of the left pillar to test her dead-letter drop.

The sun was already grilling her shoulders as she went back up to the house. She broke into a run across the lawn, thudded over the empty terrace and up to the french windows where Wilshere caught her by the arms so suddenly that her feet dangled for a moment. He brushed his thumbs over her hot shoulders, ran his fingers down her arms and off at her elbows so that she shivered.

'Mafalda doesn't like running in the house,' he said, as if this was a rule he'd just made up.

He was dressed as she'd first seen him, in riding gear, and if she expected to see a man dishevelled by his hangover, she was disappointed. He was fresh, perhaps in a way that had taken some work – washing, boiling, starching and ironing – but he was not the man who'd tried to throw himself into hibernation the night before.

'D'you fancy a ride?' he asked.

'You don't look as if you mean a donkey on the beach.'

'No-o-o.'

'Well, that's just about the upper limit of my riding experience.'

'I see,' he said, teasing his moustache up to points with his fingers. 'It's a start, I suppose. At least you've been aboard an animal before.'

'I don't have any clothes ... or boots.'

'The maid's laid some things out for you on your bed. Try them on. They should fit.'

Back in her room the dirty evening dress had been removed and on the bed were britches, socks, a shirt, a jacket, and boots on the floor. Everything fitted, only the britches were a little short in the leg. She dressed, buttoning the shirt, looking out of the window, thinking that these were not Mafalda's clothes. They belonged to a young woman. Wilshere came striding back up the cobbled path, whacking his boot with his crop.

She turned, knowing she wasn't alone in the room. Mafalda stood in the doorway of the bathroom, hair down, wearing the nightdress again, her face shocked and taking in every inch of Anne as if she knew her and couldn't believe that she'd had the nerve to reappear in her house.

'I'm Anne, the English girl, Dona Mafalda,' she said. 'We met last night . . .'

The words didn't break the spell. Mafalda's head reared back, incredulous, and then she was away, the cotton nightdress wrapping itself around her thighs, her slippered feet striding the hem to full stretch. The floor in the corridor creaked as Mafalda disappeared in a sound of unfurling sailcloth. Anne pulled on the boots, a dark weight settled in her. If Sutherland thought that Cardew had successfully positioned her in this house without Wilshere's premeditation, he was wrong.

Wilshere was standing in the hall, nodding his approval as she came down the stairs and smoking.

'Perfect fit,' he said on the way to the car, a soft-top Bentley polished to new.

'Whose are they?

'A friend of Mafalda's,' he said.

'She seemed surprised to see me wearing them.'

'She saw you?'

'She was in my bathroom.'

'Mafalda?' he said, unconcerned. 'She's such a stickler for cleanliness. Always checking up on the maids. I tell you . . . you wouldn't want to be in service here.'

'She seemed to think I was someone else,' she said, pressing him.

'I can't think who that would be,' he said, smiling out of the corner of his face. 'You don't look like anybody else . . . that we know.'

They drove down to the seafront, turned right and along the new Marginal road to Cascais. Anne stared ahead, thinking of opening gambits to break through Wilshere's shiny, deflecting carapace. None came to her. They rounded the harbour, drove up past the block of the old fort and out to the west. The sea, with more swell in it than yesterday, pounded against the low cliffs and sent up towers of saltine spray through holes in the rock, which the light breeze carried across the road, prickling the skin.

'Boca do Inferno,' said Wilshere, almost to himself. 'Mouth of Hell. Don't see it like that myself, do you?'

'I only see hell how the nuns taught me to see hell.'

'Well, you're still young, Anne.'

'How do you see it?'

'Hell's a silent place, not . . .' he stopped, shifted again. 'I know it's Sunday but let's talk about something else, can we? Hell isn't my . . .'

He trailed off, put his foot down on the accelerator. The road broke through a clump of stone pines and continued along the coast to Guincho. The wind was stronger out here, blowing sand across the road, which corrugated to washboard, hammering at the suspension.

The hump of the Serra de Sintra appeared with the lighthouse at its point. The road climbed, twisted and turned back on itself – a grim chapel and fortification high above on a wind-blasted peak, naked of vegetation, looked out over the surf-fringed coast, now far below, tapering off into the Atlantic.

At the highest point the road turned north and into a thick bank of cloud. The vapour condensed on their faces and hair. The light sunk to an autumnal grey. Homesickness and gloom descended with it.

At the hamlet of Pé da Serra Wilshere turned right up a steep climb and on the first bend stopped outside some wooden gates flanked by two large terracotta urns. A servant opened the gates and they rolled into a cobbled yard in which vines had been trained to form a green canopy over a right-angled arcade. Piles of dung littered the stones and a Citroën was parked with its nose under one of the arches.

As the Bentley pulled up alongside, a man mounted on a black stallion came from behind the building. The horse stepped daintily around the piles of ordure, its hooves ringing on the damp satin cobbles. The rider, seeing Wilshere, turned his animal, the musculature in the horse's hindquarters straining to be out on the gallop. The horse snorted and tongued the bit. Wilshere shrugged into his jacket, introduced Anne to Major Luís da Cunha Almeida and tried to stroke the stallion's head, but the horse shook him off. The major was powerfully built, his shoulders as restless as the animal underneath him. His hands and wrists toiled with the reins while his thick knees and thighs gripped the horse's impatience. They exchanged a few words and the major turned his horse and trotted out of the yard.

The groom brought a large grey mare and a chestnut filly into the yard. Wilshere mounted the mare, took the reins of the filly and led it to some steps. The groom held the stirrup while Anne mounted. Wilshere arranged her reins for her, gave brief instructions, and they followed the major out on to the hills.

They walked the horses, climbing steadily through the pine on a sandy track through the forest. Wilshere retreated into himself, blended to the animal beneath him. Anne moved her body with the filly's strides, trying to think of a way into Wilshere, looking at the man in his silent place – his hell, he'd said. After three-quarters of an hour they arrived at a stone fountain and a low, miserable grey rock building, with a cross on the apex of its roof, which was submerged in the surrounding vegetation with the green streaks of damp clinging to its walls. Wilshere seemed surprised and annoyed to find himself at this spot.

'What is it?' asked Anne.

'Convento dos Capuchos,' said Wilshere, turning his horse. 'A monastery.'

'Shall we take a look?'

'No,' he said abruptly. 'I took the wrong road.'

'Why don't we take a look now that we're here?'

'I said no.'

Wilshere turned her horse and set her off back down the track. His own mare kept settling back on her hindquarters, raising her forelegs off the ground, apparently uncomfortable with the rider. They danced while Wilshere tried to wrestle her back down. Then he dug in his heels and let her have her head. They careered down the track, almost sideways, Wilshere bent over the horse's neck. They closed rapidly on the filly and, as they reached her, Wilshere leaned over and gave the animal a whack across the rump with his crop. Anne felt her horse start beneath her, tip back on its hind legs. Then the filly lunged forward, tearing the reins from her fingers and throwing Anne on to its neck so that the mane, coarse and bitter, was stuffed into her mouth.

The filly's fast hooves rattled over the dry stones and the hard-baked track ripped past underneath. Anne hung on to the mane with her cheek pressed to the smooth skin, felt the thick beam of muscle in the horse's neck, saw the animal's eye wild and white-edged with panic.

The track narrowed, the trees closed in. The filly's tongue was hanging out of its head as foam crept up her jaws. Branches snapped at their flanks, cracking against Anne's flattened back, whipping against the horse's chest, spurring it on. Adrenalin had burst into her system and yet she found herself detached – both on the horse and yet looking on, too.

They burst out of the trees and cloud into the brilliant sunshine, a rough brush underfoot. The wind crumpled in her ears. There was a clattering noise off to the right. A charging presence pursued by dust swirling in tight screws closed on her. The hot lathered flanks of the major's black stallion pulled alongside and a thick wrist gripped the strap of the bridle and the fractions crunched into each other to make slow seconds until they stopped altogether.

She pushed herself up straight against the major's arm, legs quivering.

'Where's Senhor Wilshere?' asked the major, in English.

'I don't know ... I ...' she ducked at the memory of him, crop raised, bearing down on her.

'Something frightened the horse?'

Anne, gulping at the air, working at the events in her brain, searched for any possible reason for Wilshere's bizarre action.

'Whose clothes are these?' she asked.

'I don't understand,' said the major, squinting at her.

'Mr Wilshere ... did he come riding here with someone ... before? Before me. Another woman?'

'You mean the American?'

'Yes, the American. What was her name?'

'Senhora Laverne,' he said. 'Senhora Judy Laverne.'

'What happened to her? What happened to Judy Laverne?'

'I don't know. I've been away some months. Perhaps she went back to America.'

'Without her clothes?'

'Her clothes?' he asked, confused.

'These clothes,' she said, slapping her thigh.

The major wiped sweat out of his eyebrow.

'How long have you known Senhor Wilshere?' he asked.

'I arrived in Portugal yesterday.'

'You didn't know him before?'

'Before what?'

'Before you arrived,' he said, solid, calm.

Anne filled her lungs with air, unbuttoned her jacket. The filly turned and put its head to the stallion's flank. High up on a ridge Wilshere appeared, white shirt against the blue sky, and waved at them. He worked the mare down through the brush and rocks and on to the path.

'I lost you,' said Wilshere, approaching them on the now subdued mare. As if that was all it had been.

'My horse bolted,' said Anne, not ready for confrontation, not in front of the major. 'The major rescued me.'

Consternation crossed Wilshere's face. It seemed so genuine that Anne almost accepted it, even though she'd seen he'd stripped off his jacket, which was strapped to the back of his saddle. Not the behaviour of an urgent man.

'Well, thank you, Major,' said Wilshere. 'You must be rattled, my dear. Perhaps we should head back.'

Anne eased the filly out from under the stallion's haunch. Wilshere gave the major a casual half-salute. They headed back down the path towards the dense cloud on the north side of the *serra*. The major stayed behind, motionless on his horse, solid as an equestrian statue in a city square.

They walked nose to tail back to the *quinta*, back into the gloom of the low cloud. Anne, mesmerized by the rhythm of the horses, replayed the incident; not Wilshere's madness, but the exhilaration of the adrenalin rush on the back of the runaway horse – fear had not been as frightening as she'd imagined. It seemed to tell her something about the faces in the gaming room of the casino, about the thrill and fear of gain and loss. Perhaps there was more thrill in losing – the morbid draw of possible catastrophe. She shuddered, which turned Wilshere in his saddle. She gave him a smile torn from a magazine.

They dismounted in the courtyard of the *quinta* and the groom led the horses away. Anne's buttocks and thighs felt like a cooling bronze's, the heat deep within, the surface set hard. The sweat in her hair was now cold, her muscles seizing as she followed Wilshere under the arches and into a rustic stone-flagged room with heavy wooden furniture, a dark family portrait and English hunting prints on the walls. Stags' horns pricked the palpable, mildewed air in the room. A macabre chandelier of antlers hung from the ceiling, unlit, over a refectory table set with plates of cheeses, *chouriços, presunto*, olives and bread. Wilshere poured himself a large tumbler of white wine from a clay jug and handed a clay goblet to Anne.

'Cheers,' he said. 'You'll need it after that.'

She was infuriated by his coolness and sank her wine. Questions backed up inside her. She wanted to find the join in his armour, prise it open, stick him with something sharp.

'Care for anything to eat?' he asked, diverting her, fluttering his hand over the food, not interested himself, gulping at the wine.

'Yes,' she said, 'I didn't eat breakfast.'

'Perhaps I shouldn't have dragged you out . . .'

'No, no, I was glad of it,' she said, facing off his mask of infallible politeness. 'I wanted to ask . . .'

'What?' he teased, an interruption to undermine her. 'What did you want to ask?'

'I wanted to ask about the major,' she said, not that interested in him, but he could be a lever, man against man. She took an olive from the table.

'What about him?'

'He seemed a very . . . ah . . . noble man,' she said, walking around to the opposite side of the table, grinding her teeth on the olive pit.

'Noble?' Wilshere asked himself. 'Noble. Yes, noble's . . . very apposite. He *is* a noble fellow.'

'Nobility sounds so old-fashioned these days,' said Anne, keeping her eye on Wilshere, who had come round to her side of the table.

'Something, perhaps, we associate with earlier conflicts,' he said.

'Except the major's not at war and yet he has . . .'

'Quite so, Anne, quite so. Perhaps because he was mounted on a horse, that made you think of nobility and other aspects of the chivalric code.'

'Other aspects?'

'Rescuing damsels in distress,' he said, blinking, almost batting his eyelids.

She peeled a length of skin off a slice of *chouriço*, Wilshere's presence close, unmistakably extortionate. He seemed like a small boy curious as to what would happen to a spider if he were to dismember it.

'I suppose if he'd had a red satin-lined cloak and a plumed tricorn hat . . .' she started, and Wilshere guffawed to the antler chandelier, reducing this little episode to some romantic nonsense. Anne gritted her teeth.

'Is that Mafalda's family up there?' she asked, pointing with her cup to the portrait of a group whose white faces stared out of the dark oil of the painting.

'Yes,' said Wilshere, without shifting his gaze from her. 'They used to come out here . . .'

'Hunting?'

'No, no, these trophies are from all over . . . Spain, France . . . I think there's even some Scottish ones up there . . . Yes, look, Glamis Castle. No. The family came out *here* to keep cool in the summer. Lisbon, you know, can get awfully torrid and the family seat is in the Alentejo, which is even more so.'

'And her family now?'

'Most of that lot are dead now. In fact her father died only last year. She took it very badly . . . been rather unwell as a result. Not good . . . as Cardew said . . .'

Anne paced the perimeter of the room. Below the antlers were photographs, hunting parties standing behind the day's slaughter, which in some cases was so considerable that the hunters were reduced to stick figures at the apex of thousands of rabbits, birds and some fewer deer and boar.

'Isn't that Mafalda,' asked Anne, surprised to see the woman young and smiling, gregarious amidst a group, 'with a gun?'

'Oh, yes,' said Wilshere, black against the grey light of the window, 'she's very handy with a twelve bore. Crack shot with a rifle too. I never saw it, mind, but her father told me she had quite an eye.'

'Mafalda,' said Anne, impressed.

She moved round to the portrait.

'Is she in this?'

'It's not that good, is it?' said Wilshere. 'She's third from the left, next to her brother.'

'And the brother?' asked Anne, face up to the two figures.

'Hunting accident . . . years ago, before I met Mafalda,' he said, almost confirming that he couldn't possibly have had anything to do with it. 'Tragic.'

'Mafalda must feel quite lonely now.'

Wilshere didn't answer.

Chapter 11

The heat steepened in the late afternoon, the Quinta da Águia slumped in silence. Anne's room on the west side of the house was hot, even with the shutters closed, and she couldn't sleep with the fan churning the stuffiness. She took her swimsuit, a robe and a towel and went down to the beach. Estoril was submerged in a haze, the sea blended into the sky.

There was no breeze in the gardens of the square. The palms hung their shredded heads in the heat. The cafés were empty. She crossed the road, the silver railway tracks, continued past the empty station and on to the beach. She woke up an attendant, who lay in the shade of one of the huts, gave him a coin and changed.

The beach looked empty at first, but as she walked down towards the sea a couple lying on the sand, arms linked, were given away by a dog digging at their feet. A woman in a white two-piece bathing costume stood up to reveal she'd been lying with someone in a dip in the sand. She wore white-framed sunglasses and was talking to a comatose man at her feet while smoking a cigarette in a short black holder. Anne sat on her towel twenty feet away from the woman, who whined loudly in an American accent.

'Hal,' she said.

'Yeah,' said Hal, drowsy, a straw hat over his eyes and a cigar burning out of the back of his hand which lay on his chest.

'I don't see why we have to be nice to Beecham Lazard.'

No answer. She toed him in the leg.

'Yeah, right. Beecham. Before you get going on Beecham, lemme ask you, what are we doin' here, Mary? What are we doin' in Lisbon?'

'Making money,' she said, bored to death.

'Right.'

'Except we ain't made none yet.'

'Right, too. Know why?'

''Cos you think Beecham Lazard's the key to success. Me . . . ?'

'Yeah, I know what you think . . . but he happens to be my only contact.'

She sat back on her heels and looked around. Anne studied the sand between her toes. Hal snored. Mary shook her head, stood and walked straight up to Anne.

'You speak English?'

'I *am* English.'

'Oh, great,' she said, and introduced herself as Mary Couples. 'I knew you had to be a foreigner . . . sitting on your own on the beach. Not a Portuguesey kinda thing to do.'

'No?'

'Not yet. The girls have shaken off their chaperones but they haven't quite got the idea of going some place on their own. You ever seen a Portuguese woman in a bar without a man?'

'I haven't . . .'

'Exactly,' she said, and removed the smoked cigarette from her holder.

Hal snorted, growled and continued snoring louder.

'That's my husband, Hal . . . over there . . . making all the noise,' she said, and looked at him, sadly, as if he was permanently crippled. 'He got stewed lunchtime. He got stewed last night in the casino. He was playing roulette. He won. He always gets stewed when he wins. He always gets stewed, period.'

'I was in the casino last night,' said Anne. 'I didn't see you.'

'I stay at home when he plays roulette.'

'Where's that?' Anne asked, being polite.

'A little place in Cascais. You?'

'I'm staying with the Wilsheres here in Estoril.'

'Oh yeah, nice place. Hal and I are going up there tonight for the cocktail party. You gonna be there?'

'I suppose so,' said Anne, digging a hole in the sand with her heel. 'Do you know many of the Americans round here? I heard you talking about Beecham Lazard.'

'Sure . . . he's not my favourite out of all of them . . .'

'Did you know a woman called Judy Laverne?'

106

'I heard about her. She was before my time. Hal and I have only been here a couple of months.'

'But you know what happened to her?'

There was a fraction of silence, a half-beat, before Mary replied.

'I think she was deported. Some confusion with her visa. She went to the PVDE, like you have to every three months, and they wouldn't renew it. She had three days to leave. I think that was it. Judy Laverne . . . ?' She repeated the name to herself, shook her head.

'You don't know why?'

'The PVDE don't have to give explanations. They're the secret police. They do what the hell they like and a lot of it's not nice. I mean, it's OK for foreigners, the worst that can happen is they deport you . . . no, that's not true, the worst that can happen is they stick you in jail and then deport you . . . but they don't *do* anything to you.'

'*Do* anything to you?'

'Torture is something they do to their own people,' she said, putting a new cigarette into the holder. 'Like Hal says, it's all palm trees and the casino on the surface and . . . You haven't been here very long, have you?'

'Didn't Judy Laverne work for somebody? Wasn't there anybody who could help her?'

Mary weighed that for a few moments.

'You mentioned Beecham Lazard,' she said.

'I was introduced to him last night . . . in the casino,' said Anne. 'She used to work for him?'

Mary turned down the corners of her heavily lipsticked mouth.

'If *he* couldn't keep her in the country, nobody could.'

'And what does Beecham Lazard do?'

'If you want to do business in this town – with anybody, with the government, with the Allies, with the Nazis, anybody – you gotta go through Beecham Lazard . . . that's what Hal says, anyway.'

'You don't like him . . . I heard you earlier.'

'Only because he likes to touch and I consider myself a bit of a museum piece these days . . . you can look and that's it,' she said, pushing the sunglasses up over her head and squeezing the bridge of her nose.

Mary Couples was no longer stunning. She *had* been, but the green eyes under her dark hair didn't shine any more. They had the matt finish of someone who saw things a little more clearly. She was in her thirties and, although intact on the outside, the mind had been working from the inside and the first signs of that weariness, from the long years of holding things together, had crept into her face and started making a bed.

'So why couldn't Beecham Lazard help her?'

'What's your interest in Judy Laverne?' asked Mary, nailing Anne with a direct look.

'I found myself wearing her riding clothes this morning,' she said. 'I was with Patrick Wilshere out on the *serra*. I was just wondering why.'

'Welcome to Estoril,' said Mary, and the sunglasses dropped over her eyes.

'Does that mean Wilshere was having an affair with her?'

Mary nodded.

'And somebody arranged for her to be deported?'

'I don't know,' she said, irritated now. 'Ask Beecham Lazard. One of his pals is the Director of the PVDE, Captain Lourenço.'

'Are you saying that *he* got rid of her?'

Mary froze and then in a nervous reaction started checking herself for a lighter which was still lying next to Hal's heaving body.

'Gotta get a light,' she said, and staggered back to her husband, whose cigar was still trailing acrid smoke into the late afternoon.

A figure ran and plunged into the sea and set off in an explosive burst of crawl.

'The PVDE,' said Mary, handing her a cigarette, lighting it, 'is a state within a state. Nobody tells them what to do ... Did you tell me your name?'

'No, I didn't. It's Anne. Anne Ashworth.'

'You working out here?'

'I work for Shell. I'm a secretary. My boss is a friend of Patrick Wilshere ... which is why he offered me a room.'

'Who's your boss?'

'Cardew. Meredith Cardew,' said Anne, her insides congealing as Mary turned the talk around.

'Merry,' she said, 'that's what Hal calls him, which I suppose is fair. He's always smiling. Saying nothing, but smiling.'

'Yes, well, he's my boss.'

'You wouldn't have thought those two would have much in common,' said Mary. 'Merry and Pat. The oil executive and the ... maverick.'

'What's he being a maverick at?'

'That, Anne, is the nature of the maverick,' she said, drawing a large heart in the sand with her finger. 'Who knows?'

They smoked. Anne wanted to be out in the ocean, away from the American woman and her brass accent, away from the information exchange, away from what could be a knowledge debt.

'If I was you,' said Mary, scrubbing out the heart she'd drawn, 'I wouldn't get involved. Stick to the surface ... the palm trees and the casino. It's nicer that way.'

'Hey!' roared Hal, jerking awake, flinging the cigar off into the sand.

'Hal gets his fingers burned,' said Mary, to herself. 'Over here, Hal!'

Hal got to his feet, blew on his hand. Anne recognized him as the American who'd hugged her to his chest at the roulette table, the one with Wallis's songbird under his other arm. Mary introduced them. Hal acknowledged her, looked at his watch, told her they had to go. Anne watched them leave, knowing that Mary was filling Hal in on everything because Hal was looking back at her, either nervous, or as if he wished he'd done more than wave his burnt fingers at her.

Anne threw off her robe and walked down to the sea. She scanned the surface, which was empty. She tied her hair back, stuffed it into a cap. She waded in and threw herself on to the water and swam with quick strokes, hands knifing into the slow sea. She swam unconsciously, letting the complications slide off her body into her roiling wake, listening to the air and water ruckling in the hollows of her clavicles, feeling the brilliant coolness on her forehead. She hit a rhythm, her body rolled smooth as a sculling shell as she sucked in air from under her shoulder.

Her head came up just before impact. An intuitive radar. Bone hit bone. Her face slipped over his shoulder which caught her across the throat. Her arms flailed in a morass of sea and sunlight. She rolled off a man's hard shoulder, bubbles shooting out of her mouth. The light dimmed as she receded into the blue, his legs kicked in the frothing chaos above.

The peace was surprising, a slow noiseless calm, a place where panic couldn't reach. Even when her mother's face slipped through the gate of her memory, the burning house, and Rawlinson's leg, the nuns and $x = \frac{-b \pm \sqrt{(b^2 - 4ac)}}{2a}$ and the wheel turning and the ivory ball jumping, and Mary . . .

The hands in her armpits were an intrusion, the light coming down to meet her unwelcome, the air and water slashing into her lungs, brutal. She heaved and coughed out a ghastly hot acid liquor. She struggled and struggled as if it was all too new and real. She felt the lips on the back of her neck, heard quiet words against her skin, moving over her scalp. Her head rocked back and they were moving, the steady kick of his legs underneath her, his arm across her chest, the blue sky passing overhead and the notion of lying in a pram in the garden in Clapham.

He lifted her out of the water and lay her face-down on the sand. Sea water streamed out of her head in clear rivulets. She put a sand-coated hand to her head and pressed the fleshy protuberance on her temple. She puked without raising her head. The sand darkened into a continental archipelago.

Dead . . . and twice in one day, came the bizarre thought. Is this what happened when you left home? Was the world beyond parental guidance really this dangerous?

The man was talking to her distantly, the sound hollow, faint and echoing as if her head was under a bell jar. It was the same voice as last night. A face with prominent bones, bones so close to the surface they looked painful, the skin covering them too thin. Blue eyes. Blond hair. The cleft chin. An ambiguous face – strong and vulnerable, naïve and shrewd. There was a tightness round her throat again.

'Who are you?' she asked, scared now, eyes blinking, dropping from his neck to his small shrivelled nipples.

'Karl Voss.'

Chapter 12

She woke up lying on top of the bed, the counterpane rough against her cheek, a burning disc on her temple and her knees almost up to her chin. The window was open and the air was no longer thick with heat. Her back felt cool. The walls of the room were tinted to rose-water by the evening light. She rolled over to see a vast pink funnel of cloud taking up a segment of the light blue dome of the sky.

Her pillow was wet, an ear bunged with water and a low roar. She sat up, shook her head. Hot water trickled from her ear down her jaw. She stared between her splayed knees as snatches of dialogue emerged in the sloppy horizons of her mind.

'You're German, aren't you?' she'd asked, panting into the sand.

'Yes, I'm the military attaché at the German Legation in Lapa.'

Nobody's here for a holiday.

'Do I know you?'

'Not yet.'

'You're familiar.'

'I don't mean to be,' he said. 'I carried your friend up to the house last night.'

'Were you following me?'

'Your friend was drunk. I knew you were going to need some help.'

'I saw you before . . . you were in the casino, watching the roulette.'

'No, not watching the roulette.'

The changing hut. Getting dressed in the hot wood smell, the sand rasping underfoot, the splintery planks furred at the edges. Him . . . Karl, sitting on the platform outside in khaki trousers and a white open-necked shirt, plimsolls, no socks. Walking back with him across the railway tracks and up through the gardens. No words. Nothing coming to her at all. His arm hanging next to hers, so close on a few occasions that the down on her forearm rose. At the garden gate behind the casino she could think of nothing else to do but hold out her hand.

'I didn't thank you.'

He shook his head, not necessary.

'And we had the whole Atlantic to swim in,' he said.

She walked back up the long steps to the house thinking 'not watching the roulette'.

She fell back on the bed, folded her hands over her stomach, the pink funnel in the sky reshaped itself into something like a Jewish candelabra. She thought about people not saying anything – the internal scream of silence inside Dona Mafalda, the black, empty lift-shaft behind Wilshere's impeccable manners and the complicated calm of Karl Voss.

Cars arrived outside the house, the drubbing of the tyres on cobbles as they rounded the fountain below. Doors slammed and opened the stopcock of gaiety. Hysterical, deadly vivacity sheared through the wistaria-clad walls below her window. The façade lights of the house came on, tearing the pink light out of the room and throwing yellow artificial bars and squares up on the ceiling.

Over the chair at the end of the bed was an evening gown, not her own, and a suspender belt and stockings. Without thinking, she stepped into the dress, leaving the more intimate wear. It was a modern cut of midnight-blue satin with a neckline that plunged. It matched a pair of satin evening slippers. A long, narrow box on the table with a faded gold name on the back contained a string of pearls. She put them on automatically. They were luminous against her skin, which had darkened in the couple of hours she'd spent in the sun. More cars arrived, more glass laughter shattered around the fountain.

'Henrique!' cried a girl.

'Françoise,' came the reply, '*la déesse de Lisbonne.*'

'*Dieter, wo ist meine Handtasche?*'

'*Ich weiss es nicht. Hast du im Wagen nachgeschaut?*'

And then an ironic voice over the top of the crowd.

'Oi! Myrtle! Weren't you who with me on the ships at Mylae!'

'Pipe down, Julian . . . you're drunk already.'

'Has that corpse you planted in your garden sprouted yet?'

'You're not even saying it right.'

'Bugger it.'

Anne's palms moistened as she looked down on the shining metal of the cars, the men in dark suits, the women in their jewels waiting for an arm. She brushed out her hair, pinned it up, smoothed her fingers over the collision point on her temple whose swelling had gone down. She applied lipstick, tried to look into herself beyond the black shining pupils. The dress made her feel confident, brought back that feeling of the actress in her as when she'd first arrived.

She walked down the corridor, but held back from the explosive laughter shooting up from the stairwell. Voices came from a room to her left whose door was ajar. The room was empty, not even a bed. The voices came from the fireplace. She counted off the rooms. She was above what must be Wilshere's study. She'd caught a glimpse of the book-lined walls, the desk and safe earlier in the day. She knelt by the mantelpiece, listened.

There were three men in the room below. Wilshere, Beecham Lazard and one other who spoke English with a heavy, guttural accent. Occasionally this voice and Wilshere's would lapse into German to clarify a point and Beecham's would cut in hard and fast: 'What was that? What did you say?'

It was clear, though, from what followed, that Lazard, far from being excluded from the conversation, was in fact joining with the German to apply pressure on Wilshere, who felt he had no need to step down from his position of strength.

'Say what you like,' said Wilshere, 'but I'm not going to release the goods until the Swiss have notified me that the funds have arrived.'

'Have we ever failed you, my friend?' said the German.

'No, but you know that's not the point.'

'Maybe you think that because of the Allied invasion of France we might be diverting funds away from this kind of activity.'

'That's your business. My business is to make sure that the goods are paid for. And as you know, they are not only my goods. I am representing a number of vendors . . . this is not a regular piece of business . . . not a parcel of this size and quality.'

'All I know is that there's a flight leaving for Dakar on Tuesday evening, which will connect perfectly with the Rio flight on

Wednesday morning,' said Lazard, 'and I want the stones on board.'

'Why so urgent?'

'We have a buyer lined up in New York.'

'And he's going to go away?'

'What's being sold might go to others.'

Silence for some time. Party murmurs. More cars arrived.

'The Russians?' asked Wilshere.

No response.

'When can the funds be in Zurich?'

'Friday.'

'Well, I can see that this is very different from the other business we've done,' said Wilshere. 'Is there anything you can give me that would help the people I'm representing to understand the unusual circumstances?'

'What do you mean?' asked the German brutally.

'Are you talking about a bonus?' Lazard nudged, the percentage man.

'Perhaps we could agree a bonus,' said the German, 'if we could see the goods.'

'Now it's my turn,' said Wilshere, gathering himself. 'Have I ever failed you?'

'Come on, Paddy,' said Lazard.

'Have I?' he asked. 'No. I haven't. I've followed your instructions to the letter. There's nothing under thirty carats in the parcel.'

'It's the value per carat that concerns us,' said the German. 'These are not the usual industrial quality. And whilst the last parcel we bought from the Congo was not entirely satisfactory, and we have confidence in your Angolan product, it does not mean that we're afraid to go back to Léopoldville.'

'But *my* goods are here . . . now,' said Wilshere. 'Ready to go to Dakar as soon as . . .'

'How much?' asked the German, the two words coming down with guillotine weight.

'What can you give me . . . in advance? To show your good intentions.'

'Escudos,' said Lazard.

'I don't want escudos, but . . . perhaps that commodity you use to buy your escudos?'

'Gold? That's all accounted for at the Bank of Portugal, it would be impossible . . .'

'Is it?' Wilshere cut in. 'I've heard there have been some interesting diversions since June the sixth.'

Silence. Brittle, frost hard, silence. Anne stared into the grate where a single dry fir cone lay on its side, its scales open, brown and black seeds showing. A floorboard creaked in the corridor. Her head turned slowly, her heart fighting between the two sacs of her lungs. A patch of nightdress flitted past the crack in the door.

She slipped out of her shoes, went to the door. Some strange wiring in her head reminded her of the luminous pearls against her skin and she covered them with her hand.

Mafalda stood on the threshold of Anne's room, looking back down towards the unlit stairwell. More neurotic night strolling?

'What are you talking about, Paddy?' asked Lazard, from down below.

Anne clenched her fists as Mafalda went into her room.

'A coincidence. The Allies invade Normandy. Salazar puts an embargo on wolfram exports.'

'Well, he's done that before.'

'But this time the embargo's effective. He's not worried about being invaded now. He's playing with the winners. My three mines up in the Beira have been closed down . . . officially. Boarded up. There's an Englishman roaming the countryside making sure of it. And yet . . . and yet . . .'

'Spit it out, Paddy.'

'The gold keeps coming in. Two consignments last month. If the price of tinned sardines had gone up that much, I think I would have heard about it and been in there.'

Silence again as the German digested Wilshere's perfect intelligence. Anne's neck shook with the tension. She padded down to her room, which was light and bursting with noise coming up through the open windows. Mafalda had the sheets peeled back. She was sniffing them like a dog over ground recently stained by a bitch.

Anne switched on the light. Mafalda stood between the bed and the window, blinking and bewildered. Anne stepped back in mock surprise.

'What are you *doing* here?' asked Mafalda.

'Isn't this my room?'

'Why have you come back?'

'Do you know who I am, Dona Mafalda?'

The older woman moved into the middle of the room, her breasts and the flesh of her thighs quivering against the cotton nightdress.

'If you young girls had any sense of honour, you'd know when to stay away.'

'My name is Anne Ashworth. I am English. I am *not* Judy Laverne.'

Mafalda winced at the name and her hands came up as if to cover her ears, except she'd already heard the offending name. She made for the door, brushed past Anne and fluttered down the corridor like a moth looking for another light source to baffle against.

Anne checked the corridors and went back to the empty room. Someone was resuming their seat in the room below. Wilshere and Lazard were alone.

'How did you know about those consignments going into the Banco de Oceano e Rocha?'

'Why? Didn't you?'

'Sure I did,' bluffed Lazard.

'Probably the same source then,' said Wilshere. 'The question is, do you know what the diamonds are going to buy in New York?'

'Dollars,' said Lazard, happy to oblige.

'And with the dollars . . . ?' said Wilshere.

'You're not feeling guilty are you, Paddy?'

'I know you like "Paddy", but I prefer "Patrick", is that all right, Beecham?'

'Sure, Patrick.'

'And what do I have to feel guilty about?' said Wilshere, to the sound of a striking match. 'I'm merely curious as to the raised tension, the established urgency to this particular deal. And, of course, the very specific requirements as to the quality of the goods, which are clearly designed to produce a market value of around one million dollars.'

'The answer is, I don't know,' said Lazard.

'*You* don't know?'

'That's what I said.'

'Then nobody knows,' said Wilshere, 'not even your old friends at American IG.'

'Maybe . . . have you thought about *this*, Patrick? Maybe it's information we shouldn't know about.'

'The age of innocence, Beecham, is long gone.'

Anne went downstairs into the dark hall and along the unlit corridor to the back terrace where the cocktail party hummed in the yellow light coming up from the lawn. Cardew waved from some way off. She stepped into the crush of dinner-jacketed bodies, swiped a saucer of champagne from a passing tray and found her elbow cupped from the side. She turned into the white shirt and loose dark jacket of Hal Couples.

'You were talking to my wife on the beach,' he said, more friendly now.

'I've been even closer than that, Mr Couples.'

'Hal,' he said, mystified. 'Call me Hal.'

'Is your wife here?'

'She's in there somewhere,' he said, dismissing her, and produced a packet of Lucky Strike.

They smoked, sipped their drinks, sizing each other.

'You work for Shell. Mary told me.'

'That's right . . . she didn't say what you did, apart from having to be nice to Beecham Lazard.'

'I work for a company called Ozalid. We sell machines that reproduce blueprints, you know, architectural drawings, that kinda thing. Lisbon's going through a construction boom so we figure we should be here selling our equipment . . . a-a-a-nd waiting until they finish fighting in the rest of Europe and then moving in there . . . making a lot of money on the way.'

'Interesting.'

'I'll be honest with you, Anne, and tell you . . . it's not. But it *is* a living and when Ike gets to Berlin . . . even more of a living. The state of that place . . .' he said, shaking his head at the possibilities.

'You know I'm English?'

'You *are*?' he said, not that surprised but feeling he had to be.

'You know something about the English? We spent hundreds of years building our empire and in that time we made lots of money and yet – this is the strange thing – we're not allowed to talk about it. It's funny that . . . We've been taught to think it's rude.'

'Hey, Anne, I'm sorry.'

'No need to apologize to me. It's just something I've noticed

117

about Americans. You talk about it, we don't. I think it's because
. . . well, my mother would call it showing off, drawing attention
to yourself, which is nearly a criminal offence in England.'

'It is?'

She remembered another rule from training – no irony with
Americans.

'It's the only reason we've kept the death sentence.'

'Tell your mother from me,' said Hal conspiratorially over his
glass, 'it's *all* about making money and if you don't talk about it
. . . you don't make it. I don't know how you limeys ever fall in
love.'

It made her wonder about her mother broaching the subject
with Rawlinson, helping him off with his wooden leg. Some things
just weren't meant to be thought about.

'I don't know,' she said, suddenly made lame by the idea.

'Stiff upper lip,' said Hal, showing her one.

'I don't think we like to look that stupid.'

Hal was looking at her differently now. She glanced around the
crowd and had a rush of freedom. Nobody knew her. She knew
nobody. She could be whoever she liked . . . as long as it was Anne
Ashworth.

'Do you play roulette?' asked Hal.

'We already did.'

'Did we?'

'Last night. I was on the other side from your *petite grive*.'

'My *petite* what?'

'Song thrush,' said Anne. 'And I wouldn't play roulette, Hal.
The odds are terrible.'

'Yeah, I guessed as much. You don't look the type.'

'You two finally met,' said Mary, coming between them.

'Yeah,' said Hal, dubious now, shifting on to his back foot to
see which way this would go.

'I was going to persuade Hal to give up roulette,' said Anne.
'Talk him through the odds.'

'I'd *love* you to do that.'

Beecham Lazard appeared at the french windows. Hal put his
arm around Mary and steered her away.

'Excuse us, Anne. Honey, there's Beecham, let's go talk to him,'
he said. 'See you later, Anne.'

118

'Bye, Hal.'

Mary rolled her eyes. They reached Lazard, who put his arm around Mary, buffed her shoulder. Anne finished her cigarette, socked back the tepid champagne, pleased with herself. A hand took the empty glass and replaced it with a full one.

'The bump's gone down,' said Karl Voss.

'I slept. I'm fine now,' she said, the social fluency she'd experienced with Hal freezing up inside her.

They stood shoulder to shoulder at the edge of the terrace looking at the party.

'I wanted to ask you something earlier, but I didn't want to appear . . . callous.'

'You mean, when in fact you *are* callous,' she said, the line coming out wrong – rude, not funny.

He laughed – both of them nervous.

'I mean it would have seemed . . . ah . . . scientific to have asked the question . . . or clinical.'

'Which was?'

'Whether while drowning you saw your life flash before you. It's what everybody says.'

'Does that mean old people take longer to drown?' she asked. 'All those reels to get through.'

'I hadn't thought of it like that.'

'I did see some things, but it's not what I would have called a whole life . . . more of a newsreel. Quite a dull one too. What would yours be like?'

'Well, not *Gone with the Wind*, if that's what you mean.'

'I haven't seen the film.'

'Lisbon is the only city in Europe where you can see it, maybe . . .' He stopped himself, remembered at the last minute where he was, who he was and who he was talking to. 'Maybe when life is less complicated . . .'

'Does life get any less complicated?'

'Possibly not,' he said, 'but there are good complications and bad ones.'

'We have a choice?'

'No, but to seize the good ones when they come along, that's the thing . . . like this afternoon.'

'That was an accident, wasn't it?' she said to the ground.

'Was it?' he asked, and turned to face the façade lights on the lawn.

Insects swirled high above their heads. The light took his face down to monochrome, white with black lines and grey cross-hatching. An artist's view. A geometrician's. She looked at him now, stared at him wide-eyed as a child, until she remembered in some ridiculous corner of her brain that it was rude to stare, and rude to point and rude to talk about money or food and rude to get down from the table without asking. The rules of rudeness. How could there be so many?

'What are you thinking?' he asked, turning his face to hers.

She reeled her mind in, ransacked it for some intelligent thought.

'About fate,' she lied, 'seeing as you brought it up.'

'I'm not sure there can be any fate in wartime,' he said. 'It's as if God's lost control of the game and the children have taken over ... naughty children. Don't you think...? We're in the hands of...'

'Ah, Voss, you haven't introduced me to your charming companion.'

The voice belonged to the German she'd heard in Wilshere's study, a voice as clipped as a shod hoof on cobbles. Voss held out his hand towards her, his brain frantically riffling the pages of memory. All blanks. He opened his other hand to the man next to him, who was tall, balding and held a pince-nez to his fattish face, which was broken up by a goatee beard, giving him the look of an academic, an art historian perhaps.

'General Reinhardt Wolters, may I present...' He turned back to her, his mind unjogged.

'Anne Ashworth,' she said. 'I'm staying here with the Wilsheres.'

'A beautiful house,' said Wolters, which it wasn't, 'a magnificent evening. Are you English, Miss Ashworth?'

'Yes, I am,' she said, bringing her defiance under control.

'Forgive me for asking. You sound it but don't look it.'

'I've been in the sun,' she said.

'I think you are new here ... no? You must be quite surprised, coming from England into this...' He spread his hand out in front of him at nothing in particular.

'You mean the lights?'

'The lights,' he agreed, 'and the level of ... fraternization with the enemy. We can all be friends in Lisbon.'

Wolters smiled with teeth gone yellow and a gap next to a canine. He was wrong. She didn't like being this close to the enemy, or at least this version of the enemy, but then Voss was the enemy, too.

'You're right, Mr Wolters, but it doesn't feel like war here,' she said. 'Perhaps if bombs were falling on us we'd feel differently about each other. As it is . . .'

She dipped her mouth to the champagne glass.

'Quite so, quite so,' said Wolters. 'Captain Voss, a word with you, please.'

Voss and the general nodded to her and they stepped off the terrace and walked beyond the façade lights into the matt black of the garden. She fingered the bump on her head thinking that this could be a hard school. She hadn't expected the lines to be so blurred. She hadn't expected someone like Karl Voss, military attaché to the German Legation, whom she knew even now she was looking for and waiting to come back.

'Some people are staying for dinner,' said Wilshere, touching her on the shoulder with two fingers. Always touching. 'You'll join us, won't you?'

He didn't wait for her reply because he was set upon by the pack of women Anne remembered collectively as the Romanians. She backed down the steps and retreated into the darkness. The party was already dispersing.

'*Je vous remercies infinement*' – she heard a woman's voice pitched hard against the soft night – '*mais on étés invités de diner par le roi d'Italie.*'

She turned her back, let her eyes grow used to the dark. There was no one on the lawn. She headed for the bushes, towards human noises which, as she neared them, made her veer suddenly away. Grunting, panting, the slap of skin. She stood in the lee of the bushes, confused. The noises stopped. Moments later Beecham Lazard appeared in a gap in the hedge, combing his hair back into its imperturbable shape, stretching his neck out of his collar. He loped back towards the house. A minute later, Mary Couples materialized in the same gap. She lifted the hem of her dress and brushed her knees. She threw her head back and shoved life into her hair.

Chapter 13

Anne hoped there would be someone English at dinner, Cardew and his wife perhaps, she'd seen him wave at the beginning of the party but only got to him at the end. She'd had time to pass on her dead-letter drop site and nothing more and they'd left for a dinner with a Spanish trade delegation. Now she looked down the table at two Portuguese couples, an Argentinian and a Spanish couple, Wolters from the German Legation, Beecham Lazard and, the only other single woman, an Italian contessa of some age and faded beauty.

Anne was seated between an Argentinian and Lazard on the window side. She was opposite a small Portuguese woman with hair curled tight to her head, who was wearing a dress made for someone more elegant. Wilshere sat at one end. His wife's chair was empty. Nobody asked after her.

A thick, smooth yellow soup was served from large silver tureens. Its only taste was faint and pewtery, perhaps from the ladle. Throughout this course Lazard kept his left leg pressed against her thigh while he spoke scrap-metal Portuguese to the woman on his right. She replied in perfect English, but Lazard's determination was unbreachable.

The fish course arrived, which was a tacit signal for all the men to start conversing with the woman on their other side. Lazard turned on Anne, looking her over like a complicated dessert, contemplating which bit to eat first.

'I met Hal and Mary Couples today,' she said, to divert him. 'Two of your fellow Americans.'

'Ah, yes, Hal,' he said, as if he were a distant relative, rather than the man whose wife he'd been tussling with in the bushes. 'I bet he talked to you about business. That's what Hal likes to do.'

'And roulette . . . and songbirds. A passion of his.'

'I wouldn't have believed it,' said Lazard. 'And what's your passion, Anne? I hope you're not going to say typing and shorthand.'

She opened up her fish, imitating Lazard, slitting it along the bone and levering the flesh away. She was glad of the distraction. What was her passion, now that she was Anne Ashworth? Not mathematics.

'Maybe I'm an old-fashioned good-time girl, but one who hasn't had a lot of practice. England hasn't been a good-time place these last few years.'

'Maybe I should take you out . . . show you the fleshpots of Lisbon.'

'Are there any?'

'Sure, we could have dinner in the Negresco, go to the Miami dancing bar, take a look in the Olimpia Club. They're all classy joints.'

He lifted away the bone and head of his fish, parted the white meat below.

'There was a riot yesterday in the middle of Lisbon just before my flight arrived. Somebody told me it was a food riot. Sawdust in the *chouriços*.'

'Communists,' said Lazard, as if they were a terminal disease. 'There's a lot of different worlds down there in the city, Anne, but roughly speaking they break down into two groups. The "haves" and the "have nots". You're a "have" and you'll have to get used to the "have nots" or stay out here in Estoril, where there's nothing but "haves".'

He put his knife and fork together over the skeleton of his fish and gulped down the remainder of his glass of white wine, which was instantly refilled. The plates were removed and, in the quiet while the meat course was served, the contessa made her first contribution of the evening, from one end of the table to the other.

'Now that Cherbourg has been lost, Herr Wolters, and the Allies are marching on Paris, what do you think your Herr Schickelgruber's going to do next?'

'Her again,' said Lazard, into his napkin.

Wolters took the insult face on, holding his glass by the stem and looking into the wine as if for some prescience. He pursed his goatee.

'The Führer, madam, is calm,' he said, batting back her rudeness, 'and as for marching on Paris, it may look a short distance on the map but be assured the Allies will meet with the fiercest resistance.'

'And the Russians?' she asked, without missing a beat.

Wolters gripped the edge of the table, shifted his buttocks on the brocade upholstery of his seat. All heads tuned in for some special intelligence. Only the clatter of the servants' spoons, dishing out the rice and vegetables, disturbed the quiet. Wolters looked as if he was tempted to turn the table up and over this venal bunch. He surveyed them in turn, apart from the English girl and the threadbare Milanese contessa, silently accusing them of getting fat from selling whatever they could lay their hands on to the Reich.

'It's true. The Russians have been enjoying some success,' he said, unruffled, measured, 'but don't believe for a moment that one hectare of Ger— ... of French soil will be given up without the most bitter fighting the world has ever seen. There will be no surrender.'

His cold-blooded certainty shook nerves around the table, except for Wilshere's. He seemed amused at the fanaticism on display.

'You don't think they'll get rid of him ...' started the contessa.

'*They?*' asked Wolters.

'Germans who would like there still to be a Germany after this business is all finished.'

'There will *always* be a Germany,' said Wolters, who'd never reached the cold, windy passage of this type of thinking.

'You still believe in miracles, I see.'

'We have ruled out nothing,' said Wolters who, suddenly aware that those words might appear ridiculous, added, 'Perhaps you are unaware of our unmanned rockets dropping on London.'

Eyes switched to Anne momentarily. They all knew by now she was English, from London.

'*This,*' he said, holding up a stiff finger, 'this is merely practice.'

The cutlery hovered over the china.

'We've been hearing about these miracle weapons from the German press for years,' said Lazard. 'Are they ready now?'

Wolters didn't reply but stabbed into his meat and ate wolfishly, as if the dish were Europe and he had plenty of appetite for it.

After dinner the women went into the sitting room to smoke cigarettes and drink coffee, the men filed into a room off the dining room where cigars and port had been laid on. Wolters joined shoulders with Wilshere as he rounded the dining table.

'Who was *she*?' he asked, loudly.

'La Contessa della Trecata,' said Wilshere, smiling.

'Is she a Jew?'

The Italian woman caught hold of Anne's arm as they walked down the corridor, her hand gripped and regripped the firm flesh.

'I am, of course,' she said, in her paper-thin voice.

'What?'

'Jewish. I insulted him too much . . . him and his Herr Schickelgruber,' she said. 'But then . . . you're English, aren't you?'

'Yes, I'm staying here while I work in Lisbon.'

'What do you think of your Mr Moseley?'

'I think he is mistaken.'

'Yes,' she said, 'maybe I should learn something from you about choice of words. Mistaken. Needless to say, we are the only non-fascists here. The Argentines are *Peronistas*, the Spaniards are *Francophilos*, the Portuguese are *Salazaristocratos* and the German, well, you know what the German is.'

'And Mr Lazard?'

'*Capitalista*,' she said, dismissing him with a snort.

'And Mr Wilshere?'

'Unpredictable Irish blood. He is supposed to be neutral like Salazar, if you see what I mean. A man who admires one party whilst making money out of both. In Wilshere's case I think he *dislikes* one party while making money out of both.'

'So . . . not a fascist.'

The women sat around the empty fireplace, the two Portuguese fitting cigarettes into ostentatious holders. The contessa smoked hers straight, offering one to Anne. A maid poured the coffee.

'Has anyone seen Mafalda?' asked one of the Portuguese.

'I understand she's unwell,' said the contessa.

'For some time now,' said the Spaniard.

'We've been in the north,' said the other Portuguese. 'We're out of touch.'

'I've seen her,' said Anne.

'Well?'

'But I only arrived yesterday.'

'But you've seen her.'

'Yes.'

'Well, tell us.'

'It's just that . . .'

'We are all *friends* of Mafalda here,' said the Spaniard, which sounded threatening.

'Let the girl speak,' said the contessa.

'She seems to be confused,' Anne said, guarded.

'Confused. What's confused?'

'She seems to think I'm somebody else.'

'Mafalda? This is nonsense.'

'I told you,' said one Portuguese to the other in her own language. 'Didn't I tell you about the dress?'

'Whose dress is that?' asked the Argentine in English.

All eyes fell on Anne, except the contessa's – she stood at the fireplace smoking with her chin raised, the gossip well beneath her contempt.

'That's not your dress, is it?' asked the first Portuguese.

'If you let the girl draw breath, she'll tell you,' said the contessa.

'No, it is not my dress. Mine is being cleaned. This was left for me in my room while I was sleeping.'

'I knew it. It's come straight from that Parisienne's scissors in the Chiado. She's cut one for me.'

'Not the one you're wearing, I hope,' said the contessa.

'I think this dress and some riding clothes I wore this morning belonged to an American woman . . . and Dona Mafalda seems to thinks so, too. She has us confused.'

'Hoody Laberna,' said the Spaniard, throwing up her hands, triumphant.

The Argentinian's coffee cup flipped in its saucer.

'Hoody who?'

'Judy Laverne,' said Anne. 'I was told she was deported some months ago.'

'Who told you that?'

'Another American – Mary Couples.'

'What does *she* know?' said the Portuguese.

'The little *puta* wasn't even here,' confirmed the Spaniard, and her Argentinian friend laughed.

'Judy Laverne died in a car accident,' said the contessa, '*before* she was deported.'

'If you've been riding up on the *serra* you'll know the road,' said the Portuguese. 'She was on her way back to Cascais and she came off on that tight bend, just after the Azoia junction. There's a very steep drop. It was a terrible thing. The car exploded. She didn't stand a chance.'

'They say she'd been drinking,' said the other Portuguese.

'I don't know how they would know that,' said the contessa. 'The body was completely burnt.'

The string of pearls around Anne's throat felt suddenly tight. She pushed a finger up underneath them. How could Mary Couples not have heard about this?

'But why am I wearing Judy Laverne's clothes?' she asked.

'They were left, I suppose . . .' said the Portuguese. 'If you've come from England I imagine you don't have much of a wardrobe.'

Their eyes dropped away from her, swapped knowing looks amongst themselves. Anne felt hemmed in by the dress, these people and their society. The Argentinian with her hair scraped back so tight her eyebrows were up to her hairline. The Spaniard and her sexual suspicions, her tittering disdain for Mary Couples. The Portuguese and their gossip, sitting on their plump behinds, smoking out of their ridiculous holders. All of them desperate to show how much they knew about absolutely nothing. The contessa seemed to be the only decent person in the room.

'I hope none of you are suffering from the same confusion as Dona Mafalda,' said Anne. 'I might be wearing her clothes, but I'm *not* Judy Laverne.'

'Of course not, dear,' said the Portuguese, voice oozing. 'Whoever said you were?'

The condescension incensed her further and she knew she was going to overstep the mark.

'You all knew that Judy Laverne was Mr Wilshere's mistress and you've all made the assumption that because I've stepped into her shoes that *I'll* be his mistress too. Well, I'm not and I won't be, and never will.'

She should have stormed out then but two things stopped her. She knew how complicated it was to work around all the furniture in the room and . . . damn them. The contessa patted her on the arm. Anne wasn't sure whether it was reassurance or some friendly advice to leave it at that.

The air had stiffened up around the fireplace. Cigarettes and holders were stuck in the silence.

'Who do you think will get to Berlin first?' asked the contessa.

The question shot through the gathering and thudded into the wall like a flaming arrow. Everyone ignored it. The Argentinian and the Spaniard started talking about horse racing, the Portuguese went into an important name exchange. The house could have burnt down before they got round to responding.

Anne was left with the contessa. She asked her how she came to be in Portugal. The contessa told her she was on her own, living in a small *pensão* in Cascais. Her family had shipped her across to Spain in 1942 with the explanation that the war was getting closer. It was on the boat and the subsequent train journey to Madrid that she found out from other refugees why her family had done this. It was the first she'd heard of the Jews being rounded up all over Europe. There'd been no word from her family since.

'I think they have gone underground,' she said. 'They couldn't expect me to live like that at my age so they sent me away. In a few months this will be over and they will send for me. I am patient.'

As the contessa spoke her face roamed the objects in the room. The words came out detached from another mental process, which was working on her eyes and jaw. The words forced belief, while the subconscious battled against the unimaginable certainty that she was now alone. The clothes, the hairstyles, the painted lips, the eager teeth behind them, the soft fleshy tongues rooted in the hollow mouths, the incessant chatter in the room suddenly grated on Anne's ears like a steel butcher's saw ripping through bone.

A servant came to tell them the cars were ready. Anne supported the contessa to the door, put her into a car. As she was about to close the door, the contessa leaned forward, took her hand.

'Be careful with Senhor Wilshere,' she said, 'or Mafalda will have you deported, just like she did Judy Laverne.'

She let go of her hand. Anne closed the door. The car moved off after the others. The contessa's tired half-lit face didn't turn – the night, her friend, took her in for a few more hours until the start of another interminable, brilliant summer's day.

Anne left Wilshere saying goodbye to his guests and retreated to the back terrace, where she smoked in the uncomfortable light, all these lives suddenly pressing in on her own. The last car pulled away and the façade lights drowned in the darkness, dowsed to orange filaments that glowed like night insects. The smell of cigar smoke preceded a red coal crowded with ash. Wilshere sat down across the table from her, crossed his legs. Faint light from the house caught the rim of his glass as it went up to his lips.

'Another long day in paradise gone,' he said, the man stuffed full of its cloying sweetness.

She didn't respond, still thinking about the gross happenings of the day, trying to make them net, trying to see the profit, if there was any. Too much had happened. There was too much to be considered. That was the adult state. You might start swimming against the torrent of events and exchanges but then, after a while, you tired and let it all rush over you, until finally, like the contessa, it wore you away however hard the rock you were made of.

'Thinking anything interesting?' asked Wilshere.

'I was thinking,' she said, stopping her foot from nodding with the irritation building inside her, 'I was asking myself, why do you keep dressing me up as Judy Laverne?'

The words came out with their hard edges and she watched them in amazement as the points and corners of the toppling letters delivered their little blows to the dark face of the man opposite.

There was a long silence, filled only by the softest whistling of the crickets, in which Wilshere's presence intensified, his cigar glowing redder as he drew on the smoke.

'I miss her,' he said.

'What happened to her?' she asked, but not softly, still angry, and when he didn't immediately reply, she added: 'There seems to be some doubt. This afternoon I was told she was deported, this evening that she died in a car accident.'

'No doubt,' he said, something catching in his throat, the harsh smoke or the brute emotion. 'She died . . . in a car accident.'

Darkness and the descent of the night's cathedral cool brought the confessional to the table. A nightingale started up with hollow bars of song from the high vaulted trees and Wilshere's glass resettled on the table. The cigar seemed screwed into the night.

'We'd argued,' he said. 'We were up at the house in Pé da Serra. We'd been riding all afternoon and afterwards we started drinking. I was on the whisky, she, as always, drank brandy. The alcohol went to our heads and we started arguing . . . I can't remember what it was about even. She'd driven up in her own car so, when she stormed out, she just drove off. I followed her. She was a good driver normally. I let her drive the Bentley whenever. But, you see, she was angry, angry *and* drunk. She drove too fast for the road. She went into a tight bend, couldn't hold it and the car shot over the edge. It's a terrible drop there, a terrible drop. Even if the petrol tank hadn't caught she'd have been . . .'

'When was this?'

'Some months ago. Early May,' he said, and the nightingale stopped. 'I fell for her, you see, fell all the way, Anne. Never happened to me before, and at my age, too.'

The way he said it, his reaching for the glass, made her think that perhaps the argument had been that Judy Laverne had not fallen in the same way or to the same extent as he.

'That argument . . .' she started, but Wilshere leapt to his feet, shook his head and arms, panic-struck, as if he'd felt himself slipping away somewhere to forget who and where he was. The cigar coal rolled to a corner of the terrace.

Wilshere turned his back on the lawn, let his head rock back to release himself from the thoughts he did not want. Anne was gripping her chair arms with her elbows and didn't see what Wilshere saw in the window above – Mafalda's white nightdress, her palms pressed against the glass.

Wilshere drew Anne up to her feet.

'I'm going to bed,' he said, and kissed her, the corner of his mouth connecting with hers so that her organs flinched.

Anne wasn't tired, too restless with aggregate knowledge. She took a couple of cigarettes from the box and some matches from a glass holder. She kicked her shoes off and walked across the lawn to the path and down to the summerhouse and the bower. She sat under the hanging fronds of the passionflower, pulled her heels up on to the edge of the seat and fitted a cigarette into her mouth, chin resting on her knees. She slashed a match across the stone seat and started in the flare of light. Sitting in the corner, ankles crossed, arms folded, was Karl Voss.

'You can frighten people like that, Mr Voss.'

'But not you.'

She lit the cigarette, shook the match dead, eased her back against the tiled panel behind.

'Is the military attaché from the German Legation watching this house?'

'Not particularly the house.'

'The people *in* the house, then?'

'Not all of them.'

A thin silver thread tugged her stomach tight.

'So what's going to happen this time?'

'I can't think what you mean.'

'You have a way of being on hand, Mr Voss.'

'On hand?'

'Around when you're needed, for carrying and life-saving, for instance.'

'I seem to have my uses,' he said. 'What for this time . . . who knows?'

He followed the tip of her cigarette. Her lips, nose and cheek glowed as she drew on it, burning that facial fragment on to his retina. He searched himself for words, like a man who's put a ticket in too safe a place.

'How well do you know Mr Wilshere?' she asked.

'Well enough.'

'Is that well enough to carry him home when he's drunk or well enough that you don't want to get to know him better?'

'I've done business with him. He seems honest. That's all I've needed to know about him so far.'

'Did you ever see him with his mistress . . . Judy Laverne?'

'A few times . . . they weren't hiding . . . at least not when they were in Lisbon. They used to go to nightspots and bars quite openly.'

'How did they look together?'

A long silence, long enough for Anne to finish the cigarette and crush it out on the underside of the stone seat.

'I didn't mean the question to be that hard,' she said.

'In love,' he said, 'that's how they looked.'

'But you had to think about it,' she said. 'Do you think it was two-way?'

'Yes, but what does anybody know from just looking?'

She liked that. It showed an understanding of unspoken languages.

'I've a cigarette, only one, if you want to share,' she offered.

He had his own in his pocket but he came and sat next to her. She found his hand with hers, put the cigarette into it. The match rasped and ignited between them. He held the back of her hand just as she had imagined somebody would. He drew a knee up and rested his cigarette hand on it.

'Why are you asking me these things about Wilshere?'

'I've been billeted with a man who dresses me up in his ex-lover's – no, his *late* lover's clothes. I don't know what that means except that it upsets his wife. He told me tonight that he missed her . . . the lover.'

'That could be true.'

'But you, as a man, you don't think that's strange?'

'He wishes that she wasn't dead. He's playing a trick on his mind.'

'Why should he do that?'

'There were things he left unsaid, maybe.'

'Or he feels guilty?'

'Probably.'

She slid the cigarette out of his hand, drew on it and eased it back between his fingers, feeling bolder with him now. Kissing by proxy.

'Did you hear about the accident?' she asked.

'Yes . . . I also heard that she was leaving.'

'Deported.'

'So they said.'

'You mean she might not have been? She might have *wanted* to leave.'

'I didn't know her,' he said, and shrugged. 'I couldn't say.'

They smoked again, fingers touching.

'Could you kill someone if they didn't love you?' she asked.

'That might depend on some things.'

'Like what?'

'How far I'd fallen. How jealous I was . . .'

'But you *could* kill . . . ?'

He didn't shoot the answer back. It took some ruminative smoking.

'I don't think so,' he replied. 'No.'

'That was the right answer, Mr Voss,' she said, and they both laughed.

He crushed the cigarette out with his foot. They sat in silence and when their heads turned to each other there was only inches between them. He kissed her. His lips changed physiognomies with a touch, fear and desire became indistinguishable. She had to wrench herself away, get to her feet.

'Tomorrow night,' he said to her back. 'I'll be here.'

She was already running.

She ran back up the path, sprinted to the back terrace and collapsed on the chair panting, acid in her lungs, her heart walloping in her throat. She slumped back, looked up at the stars, fought her heart back down behind her ribs, thinking stupid girl, that's all I am, a stupid little girl. The memory of the slash of her mother's white hand across her face in the garden in Clapham sat her up straight.

Fraternizing with the enemy, Wolters had called it. Fraternizing. Brothering. This was more than that. This was crazy and dangerous. She could feel herself coming off the silver tracks. She bent over, gripped her forehead with her fingertips. Why him? Why not Jim Wallis? Why not anybody else but him?

She picked up her shoes, exhausted now by her behaviour, no better than a heroine from a slushy romance. She went into the house, up the corridor into the hall, thinking how else do we learn about these things? Not from mothers. The clay figurines in their cabinet caught her eye, one in particular. She turned on the light, opened the glass doors. The figurine was one of several, not the same exactly, but developments on the theme. It was of a woman blindfolded. She turned it over, looking for some clue as to its meaning. On the bottom was the maker's name, nothing more. A blur closed in, a face sharpened as it appeared on the other side of the glass door. The skin on her scalp crawled and tightened.

Mafalda reached round the door and snatched the figurine from her hands.

'I just wanted to know what it meant,' said Anne.

'*Amor é cego*,' said Mafalda, replacing the figurine, closing the glass doors. 'Love is blind.'

Chapter 14

Meredith Cardew was writing in pencil on single sheets of paper directly on to his highly polished desktop. Anne was fascinated by the work, which seemed more like brush strokes, Chinese calligraphy, than handwriting. Nothing touched the page apart from the anchor point of his palm, protected by a handkerchief, and the lead of the pencil which he sharpened between bouts. His script was not legible even the right way up and looked Cyrillic or hieroglyphic rather than English. He only wrote on one side of the paper and only drew new sheets from a particular pad in the third drawer down on the right of his desk. Occasionally he lifted the sheet and brushed his handkerchief over the desk's polished surface. Was this eccentricity or security?

The debrief was long, more than three hours, because Cardew went over all the conversations at least twice and, in the case of the three-way discussion between Wilshere, Lazard and Wolters, five or six times. The word that seemed to bother him most was 'Russians' and he wanted to be certain that it was Wilshere who'd said it, that it had been interrogative and that there'd been no reply.

'Is that it, my dear?' asked Cardew, as his clock ticked round to midday and the heat outside finally caused him to remove his suit jacket.

'Isn't that enough, sir?' she asked, desperate not to fail at her first debrief.

'No, no, it's fine. It's very good. A very good weekend's work. You'll be coming into the office for a rest. No, excellent. I just wanted to be sure that we'd left nothing out.'

We? thought Anne and then the name Karl Voss, who'd been mentioned in passing on the beach and having a word with Wolters at the cocktail party but not, never, reappearing later that night down by the summerhouse. None of that exchange had found its way into the report.

'We've left nothing out, sir.'

'Well, now,' said Cardew, laying down his pencil, counting off the sheets and then clawing tobacco into his pipe, 'we might be about to see a very rare thing.'

Cardew swung round in his chair to face the window and its view of the heat cramming down on the red rooftops of Lisbon.

'We might be about to see Sutherland in a state of excitement,' he said.

The meeting was set for 4.00 p.m. in a safe house in Rua de Madres in the Madragoa district of Lisbon. Anne was to report to the PVDE in Rua António Maria Cardoso after lunch to confirm her residency and receive her work permit. From there she would go to Rua Garrett and buy cakes at the Jerónimo Martims cake shop and then walk to Rua de Madres where she would ring the bell to number 11 three times. To whoever came to the door she was to say:

'I've come to see Senhora Maria Santos Ribeira.'

If the housekeeper said that Senhora Ribeira was out, Anne was to reply with the line: '*Come what come may, / Time and the hour runs through the roughest day.*'

The housekeeper would then tell her she could come in and wait. Anne relished the absurdity.

Shortly after 4.00 p.m. *Macbeth* had been recited and Anne was sitting on a hard wooden chair in a shuttered room that was initially so dark Sutherland was not immediately apparent. He was sitting in a soft chair with wooden arms in a corner furthest from the window. Tea was laid out in front of him with an empty plate for the cakes. Behind him a crack had worked its way up the wall and finished in an estuary of lath at the ceiling. Sutherland volunteered to be mother, which she learned later from Wallis meant that he was pleased with her.

'Lemon?' he asked. 'Milk's a little complicated in this heat, although there might be some powder. Not the same, though, is it?'

'Lemon,' she said.

'No problems with lemons in this country,' he said, and sat back with his legs crossed, cup and saucer in hand, cake on the side. His first question was surprising but, she realized with more experience, typical.

'Wilshere . . . whacking your horse like that . . . what do you think that was all about?'

'Judy Laverne . . . I was wearing her riding clothes at the time.'

'According to Cardew's notes, or rather Rose's reading of Cardew's notes, because I still can't read a damned word of what that man writes, you didn't ask Wilshere what the hell he was up to, hitting your horse out of the blue, so to speak.'

'No, sir.'

'Any reason?'

'First of all I didn't want there to be any confrontation in front of the major and secondly, if he knew what he was doing . . .'

'You mean if he was conscious of what he was doing . . . ?'

'He would have apologized with an excuse, invented an accident.'

'Unless he *wanted* a reaction from you.'

'Of course, if he *wasn't* conscious then we are dealing with somebody who has a mental problem and he would have to be handled accordingly. I decided to bide my time . . . see what else happened.'

'You didn't think that perhaps he was testing your cover?'

The words cooled her innards, which with the heat stuffed into the room as thick as wadding, made her light-headed.

'I know this is a difficult situation, the sociability of the environment, but didn't you think of that?' he said, nibbling his cake.

'Yes, but I was thinking more about Judy Laverne . . . I'd been unsettled by Wilshere's wife's reaction to the riding clothes . . .'

'I think you should bring it up. Sooner rather than later,' said Sutherland. 'Make it plausible. You know . . . you didn't want to bring it up in front of Major Almeida, been thinking about it a couple of days . . . that sort of thing. Give him chance to apologize and make his excuses.'

'And if he doesn't?'

'You mean if it *was* an unconscious act? Well, then it would appear that whatever happened between Wilshere and Judy Laverne has made him a somewhat unpredictable entity.'

'And who was this Judy Laverne, sir?'

'Ah, yes,' he said. 'A mess. A terrible mess. I don't know whether we'll ever get the full story on her. She used to be a secretary at American IG.'

'What's American IG?'

'The American sister company of IG Farben, the German chemical conglomerate,' said Sutherland. 'And, as *you* know from what you overheard in Wilshere's study, Lazard had been an executive with American IG too. As far as I can make out, Judy Laverne had lost her job with them back in America and Lazard invited her over here to work for him.'

'So, she wasn't working for the Americans.'

'In intelligence? The Office of Strategic Studies, you mean? Another one of their brilliant euphemisms, I must say. No, no, I don't think she was, although there seems to be some confusion here. It seems that they were trying to get her to do some work for them but she was very loyal to Lazard, and enjoying herself with Wilshere, so didn't want any part of it. We don't know what they were after from Lazard, still don't. Totally obsessive about secrecy, these Yanks – and this even after D-day, which, Christ Almighty, must . . .' Sutherland reined himself in, pinched the bridge of his nose, screwed the tiredness up in his fist and threw it on the floor.

'Do we know that she died in a car accident?' asked Anne. 'There was some confusion about deportation.'

'Her visa renewal had been turned down by the PVDE, *that* was true. She had three days to leave, true as well. And she did meet her death in a car that came off the road around the Azoia junction . . .'

'You don't know why she was being deported?'

'No, nor did the Americans. In retrospect we thought they might have arranged it, pulled her out when she wouldn't play ball, but they deny it. They say it was as much a surprise for them as it was for Judy Laverne.'

'The Italian contessa said that Mafalda arranged for her deportation.'

'You can take that with a pinch of salt,' he said. 'Beecham Lazard is very close to the PVDE director, Captain Lourenço. He'd have found out.'

'Do you think Lazard suspected that she was being approached by the OSS?'

'Possibly.'

'Do you think his suspicion might have been stronger than that?'

'If he thought she was *working* for the OSS I don't think he'd have just arranged for her deportation.'

'You mean he'd have killed her?' asked Anne. 'Well, she did die.'

'In a car accident.'

'You're satisfied with that?'

'The PVDE came down on it hard and fast, wrapped it up in a matter of hours – don't like a song and dance over foreigners' deaths. They sent a full report to the American consulate. The Americans accepted it, or at least they didn't react. More tea?'

She drank the first cup down. He poured more. The air became breathable again.

'So, you don't think my position is vulnerable.'

'As long as you maintain your cover, no,' said Sutherland. 'We didn't exactly position you, remember. We took advantage of an opportunity given to Cardew by Wilshere as a result of their relationship. The background to it is strong. Cardew's secretary getting pregnant, wanting to leave . . . all that. But *you* tell me . . . what's your worst fear?'

'That Judy Laverne *was* working for the OSS, her cover was blown and Wilshere or Lazard killed her.'

'Do you think Wilshere could have killed her?' he asked, suddenly following the crack in the wall up to the lath estuary. 'You say he loved her. Our reports of them being seen together in Lisbon indicate the same.'

What does anybody know from just looking, she thought. Voss's words, which she'd so admired, suddenly began to create doubts in her own mind about his interest in her.

'How would you feel,' she said, 'if you found that the woman you loved was a spy, was spying on you? You'd start thinking that her love was part of the cover, wouldn't you? And that would make you very angry, I'd have thought . . . that your trust had been so completely abused.'

'*If* she was an agent, which she wasn't.'

'You asked me for my worst fear.'

'And I say it has no basis in fact and that even if it did I doubt Wilshere could have killed her . . . Lazard, on the other hand . . .'

'*That* makes me feel safe.'

Sutherland writhed in his seat, exasperated by what he saw as nothing but an irrelevance to the real intelligence operation.

'You have to stop thinking about Judy Laverne,' he said. 'She has nothing to do with your assignment.'

'But she could have a bearing, surely,' she insisted.

'We've examined the possibility of Wilshere positioning you so that he can control the flow of information or disinformation going out. We have decided that it was a game he didn't need to play, so why, when there is so much at stake, play it?'

'He's a gambler. Cardew said.'

'Yes,' said Sutherland, taking out the chip which had found its way back to him from the dead-letter drop. 'What is this?'

'One of the many chips that Lazard swept over to Wilshere in the casino.'

'But, you see, to me this is not a man who is gambling. This is a man who sat at a baccarat table and took a pay-off. He is someone who is playing certainties.'

Anne blushed at her own stupidity. She was losing this. Her mind was not concentrated on the information at hand. She'd been distracted by what she thought Sutherland would probably have called emotional nonsense. And not just Judy Laverne's.

'One other question . . . the man who helped you up to the house with Wilshere?' asked Sutherland. 'You didn't say . . .'

'He didn't make himself known.'

'But clearly someone who was following you.'

'It wasn't Jim Wallis.'

'Yes, well, I'd asked him to keep an eye on you but not to get too close. If he humped Wilshere up to the house that is what I would call . . .'

'Then we have a mystery man.'

'They're all mystery men,' said Sutherland.

'Except for Beecham Lazard.'

'Yes, he seems quite straightforwardly venal . . . although I was surprised by this business with Mary Couples.'

'Perhaps the Couples are more desperate than we think.'

'Well, now, here's something interesting. You say he worked for Ozalid?'

'That's what he told me.'

'We were talking about American IG earlier,' said Sutherland. 'Among the companies they own are General Aniline & Film, Agfa,

139

Ansco and . . . Ozalid. GAF supplied khaki and dyes for military uniforms, which gave their salesmen access to every military installation in the United States. All military training films were developed in Agfa/Ansco labs. All blueprints of military installations were made by Ozalid.'

'And all that information found its way back to Berlin?'

'It was a phenomenal breach of security, but it all changed in 1942 after Pearl Harbor,' said Sutherland. 'They had a spring clean . . . as they say.'

'And one of the people swept out was Beecham Lazard?'

'Which was why he came here . . . but as a free agent. He doesn't work exclusively for the Germans, but he has those high-level contacts, he's trusted by them . . .'

'And by the Americans.'

'It seems so,' said Sutherland.

'So, given that they worked for connected companies, it's possible that Hal Couples and Beecham Lazard already knew each other?'

'We're not sure.'

'Do you know when Couples started working for Ozalid?'

'We've asked for more information from the Americans. It takes time.'

'What would Hal Couples have for sale that could possibly be of interest to the Germans on a continent thousands of miles away?'

'Quite. The dogs are on their doorstep, why should they want to know the state of the kennels?' said Sutherland, sucking on his empty pipe, desperate for a smoke. 'Now look, let's not jump to conclusions about Couples. The Americans will come back in their own time. From our side we'll be watching all the Lisbon/Dakar flights. Your next task is to get into Wilshere's study and find any information you can about the provenance of these diamonds, where they're being held, how this business is going to work . . . anything. If Wilshere *is* holding these diamonds you work out a system with Wallis to let him know if and when the gems leave the house.

'Now, personalities . . . Wolters you know about. I think he revealed himself sufficiently at the dinner. To give you an idea, he took up this post at the beginning of the year as an SS Colonel. When the head of the Abwehr, Admiral Canaris, was removed from office he was promoted. He is now an SS General. He is effectively running the German Legation. Who else? The Contessa della Trecata. I notice you gave her a very sympathetic review. Do not talk to her. She is dangerous for the very reason that she elicits sympathy. The others, well ... you know, I think.'

'You haven't mentioned Karl Voss.'

'The military attaché is an Abwehr man. He reports directly to Wolters,' said Sutherland, stopping in the middle of the room, on the brink of offering additional material but deciding against it.

'Major Almeida?'

'Portuguese Army officer. Don't know which side his bread is buttered, so steer clear,' he said. 'That's it, isn't it?'

If there were other things, Anne couldn't think of them. What she thought, at first, was the stress coming from Sutherland seemed to have pushed everything else out of the room. It was only later, as she made her way down to the station, that she realized it could have been something else – ambition. This could be Sutherland's big moment of the war.

Karl Voss was happy, although he didn't quite know it yet. He was at that stage of happiness where his behaviour could still be classified as normal – no unconscious outbursts of laughter, no running skips in the street, no profligacy to beggars – but a change had taken place. His insides were weightless, his step was light on the uneven cobbles, he hopped off pavements, trotted over tramlines, made way for struggling ladies, even in the dire heat he couldn't put a foot wrong. He looked up and out too. He noticed things in an unintelligent way for the first time in years. Façades of buildings, panels of tiles, shop fronts, railings, dogs flaked out in the square, a girl hanging out washing from a high window, dust on the leaves of the trees, and the blue sky, even the blue sky beyond the skeletal arches of the Igreja do Carmo, destroyed in the earthquake and left as a monument to Lisbon's dead. He was at that stage of happiness where he no longer looked down or inwards. He wasn't thinking about his situation any more.

He broke into a run as he saw people coming across the metal walkway. The *elevador* had just arrived. He made it to the lift, which descended to the Baixa. He took the steps down to the Rua do Ouro two at a time and headed towards the river at a fast walk. He crossed the road to the building of the Banco de Oceano e Rocha which at this time of the day was closed. He looked up and down the street for the car he'd arranged to meet him outside the bank. He didn't mind the five-minute wait, which was unusual for him. The car arrived, he rang the bell to the offices on the first floor. Fifteen minutes later he was sitting in the back of the car with a small but heavy case beside him.

Chapter 15

Monday, 17th July 1944, outside Lisbon.

Anne sat in a railway carriage opposite a Portuguese couple in their sixties with a dog at their feet, which had legs too short for its body and bulging eyes. The man had a goitre the size of a cantaloupe hanging from his neck. The woman was so small her feet didn't touch the floor and her left leg was swollen to twice its normal size. Anne didn't want to look at them but each time she turned away from the view out to sea, of a three-funnelled ship pumping black smudges into the bleached sky, their eyes were on her, even the dog's. It was only on the third occasion, as she let her gaze drop from thyroid to dog, that she noticed the couple's hands were clasped between them, resting on the seat.

She leaned her forehead against the window. The silver train curved out in front, reflecting the ocean in its glass panels. A sandbank surfaced outside the Tagus estuary, the surf peeling back from its brown hump. She had an irrational desire to be out there, alone, simple, offshore from the complexities of the city. She glanced back over her seat. Jim Wallis had his head down in the *Diário de Notícias*. He looked up but not at her. They'd spoken earlier about the diamonds – how she would signal if the gems left the house. She turned back to the sea. Her mind circled back to the same spot – Karl Voss, Abwehr.

She would have to stop this . . . this what? What was it she had to stop with Karl Voss? A kiss. Was that anything? She told herself not to think. The Rawlinson gambit – the *danger*'s in the thinking. Just finish it. Simplify the equation. Reduce the variables.

Forget Judy Laverne. Let her into the bracket and she was the quickest route to a blown cover.

Sutherland wanting her to break into Wilshere's study. Was that the right thing to do? Was that an unnecessary risk? Surely the Americans were right, Lazard was the man to watch. He was the go-between.

She was leaning forward, her eyes were unconsciously drilling into the soft neck of the woman in front of her. She eased back. The train braked with a screech of metal as they came into Paço de Arcos station. The old couple got up and left the carriage, the woman on the man's arm, the dog shuffling behind.

The image of Karl Voss returned, stronger now.

They hadn't said anything to each other. They'd smoked a cigarette. Touched lips. Nothing had happened but everything had changed. They didn't know each other and would never know anything of each other, except what was allowed to be known, and none of that was true. But then how much do we want to know about each other? Everything? Everything except that which sustains our interest – the mystery. To know that is to kill it.

Her thoughts multiplied. Squared. Cubed. Ramified to the nth.

She walked up through the square in Estoril. The heat was still terrible but a dying heat now, one that was slumped against the buildings, sagging in the stillness of the palm trees. She felt drowsy, needed to lie down after a long day, after long hours spent running around in her head.

The path up to the house seemed longer. She stumbled across the lawn and went into the house through the french windows at the back. There were voices in the drawing room. She put her head in. The Contessa della Trecata and Mafalda stopped talking. Sutherland hadn't mentioned Mafalda, probably written her off as a sad case. The contessa patted the sofa.

'Come and tell us about the real world,' she said.

Mafalda, in a blue tea gown, was wearing the plaster cast of her own face – white, still and void.

'The real world of dictation and typing has not been very interesting today.'

She tried to excuse herself but the contessa insisted. She sat on the sofa.

'Don't they let you out?'

'I went to the PVDE for my papers, that was all.'

'But lunch, you have to have lunch.'

'Mr Cardew is very demanding.'

'I'm surprised a young girl like you should want to come to a backwater like Lisbon . . . to be a secretary.'

'I tried to join the WRENS. They wouldn't have me. Medical. Lungs.'

'You seem to be running around here all right,' said Mafalda, as if this was the kind of cat-house behaviour she'd had to get used to.

'In London I can hardly get to the end of the street without . . .'

'Those peasoupers,' said the contessa. 'Shocking.'

'My mother thought it was the bombing.'

'Yes, well that would fit, wouldn't it?' said Mafalda, as if it was meant to but didn't, not in her mind. 'Nerves can do strange things.'

'What does your father have to say on the matter?'

From nowhere came the image of her mother sitting on her like a bully girl at school.

'My father? I don't have . . .' She checked herself, the image of her real mother had crowded out her surrogate parents. 'I don't have the faintest idea. He doesn't have an opinion.'

'Most odd,' said Mafalda. 'My father was always inquiring after our health. Probably should have been a doctor.'

'I never knew my father,' said the contessa.

'You've never mentioned him,' confirmed Mafalda.

'He was overseeing the loading of one of his ships in Genoa. A piece of cargo swept him overboard. He drowned before they got to him. My mother never recovered from it. It made her a very bitter, difficult woman. Nothing ever came up to standard in her view. She survived to a great age on the strength of it.'

'My mother's a very difficult woman too,' said Anne, the words out before her teeth could clamp down on them.

'Well, I'm sure there was some sadness in her life which has made her like that.'

'Does your mother do anything with herself?' asked Mafalda.

She lost it. The thread was just plucked out of her hand. She couldn't think what her mother did. Even her name had gone. Ashworth, yes, but her first name.

'She does what everybody's doing these days,' she said slowly, waiting for the jog which never came. 'She works for the government.'

That wasn't it. It would have to do. She would have to relearn that. Why couldn't she think of her name? It was like forgetting the most famous person in the world at the moment. Retrain the mind. *Gone with the Wind*, lead actress . . . Clark Gable was the lead man and the lead actress was . . . Scarlett O'Hara . . . come on, think.

'Are you all right, dear?' said the contessa. 'This heat today has been . . .'

'I'm sorry, did you ask something? It *has* been a long day. I should really . . .'

Why has this happened? This has never happened before. Your role is Miss Ashworth. You play the part. The lines are . . .

But reality had crept back in. All she saw was the audience. There were no lines. In her head there was only panic.

'Mafalda just asked about your father, that was all. Is he in the fighting?'

'No,' she said, trying to swallow but not being able to, her mind even forgetting the motor reflexes.

'No?' asked the contessa, both women riveted to Anne's crisis.

'No,' she reiterated, tears coming now, tears of frustration. She couldn't think of his name either, nor his profession. The only name that arrived in her head was Joaquim Reis Leitão. 'He's dead.'

'Not in the bombing?' said Mafalda, appalled.

'You're upset,' said the contessa, 'perhaps you should lie down.'

'No, not in the bombing,' said Anne, buying herself seconds, waiting, hoping for the part to come back to her. She looked down at Mafalda's feet, exactly where the prompter would have been in the theatre.

All I need is a name and it will all fit again.

'So what happened, dear girl?' asked the contessa, insistent, interested.

A car pulled up outside, the radiator grille visible at the corner of the window. Mafalda announced her husband's return.

'This heat,' said Anne, getting to her feet. 'Will you excuse me.'

She staggered from the room, set off down the corridor at a half run, a whining in her ears, a whining buzz like a reel paying out line to a sounding fish. She ran past Wilshere coming through the front door, swung up the stairs, felt his eyes rippling on her through the mahogany bannisters. She got to the bedroom door, shut it behind her. Sick. Had she thrown it away? She collapsed on the bed. The breathing came back. The swallowing, too. How had she become this fragile? She took stock, an egg count. Cracks only. No omelette. She drank some warm water from the jug at her bedside.

The simplest cover story known to man . . . but who knows it? She undressed, ran a thumb down her wet spine, held her dress up to the window. A dark patch ran down the centre of the back. Nobody knows. She stood under the tepid shower, soaped herself, rinsed off the sweat. Nobody knows. She towelled herself dry, lay naked on the bed with just the towel over her. The PVDE knows. She wrote it on their form. Graham Ashworth. Accountant. But not deceased. It had all come back. Finally. The simplest cover story ever.

Another car arrived. She levered herself off the bed, wrapped herself in the towel, went to the window. Just who she didn't want to see. Karl Voss got out of the driver's seat, went round to the passenger side and pulled out a briefcase which hung heavily on his arm. Her stomach tightened. The silver thread tugged again. He stopped in front of the door. Anne pressed her eye to the glass to see him at that acute angle to the house. He ran a hand over his bony features, preparing a new face.

She dressed and went down the corridor to the empty bedroom over the study. Voss's voice came up the stairwell. She sat at the fireplace. Small talk, the clink of bottles on glass, the gush of soda. She imagined his lips on the thin rim of the crystal.

'Another brutally hot day in Lisbon?' said Wilshere.

'There's more to come . . . so they say.'

'When it's like this I think of Ireland and the soft rain falling endlessly.'

'And when you're in Ireland . . . ?'

'Exactly, Herr Voss. It's only variety we're after.'

'I never think of Berlin,' he said.

'There's a different rain falling over there.'

'My mother's moved out to relatives in Dresden. She was in Schlachtensee. All the bombers flew over her on their way to Neukölln and . . . perhaps you don't know this, but air bombing is a very inaccurate science. She had three land in the garden. Unexploded, fortunately.'

'I didn't know that about air bombing.'

'But if you bomb enough . . .' Voss trailed off. 'Tell me something, Mr Wilshere. What do you think of the idea of a single bomb that could completely annihilate a whole city? People, buildings, trees, parks, monuments . . . all life and the product of life?'

Silence. The wood ticked. A huff of breeze shambled through the exhausted trees outside. A cigarette was offered and accepted. Chairs creaked.

'I wouldn't think it possible,' said Wilshere.

'Wouldn't you?' asked Voss. 'But if you look at history it's the only logical conclusion. In the last century we were standing in formation, blasting each other with inaccurate muskets. By the beginning of this century we were cutting each other down with very precise machine-gun fire and shelling each other from miles away. Twenty years later we have thousand bomber raids, tanks crash through countries bringing them to heel in a matter of weeks, unmanned rockets fall on cities hundreds of miles away. It stands to reason, given man's creativity for destruction, that someone will invent the ultimately destructive device. Believe me, it's going to happen. My only question is . . . what does it mean?'

'Perhaps it will mean the end of war.'

'A good thing then?'

'Yes . . . in the long run.'

'A good observation, Mr Wilshere. It's the short run that's the problem, isn't it? In the short run there would have to be a demonstration of the power of the device and, of course, a demonstration of the ruthlessness to use it, too. So it's possible that before the end of this war, depending on which side has the device, Berlin, Moscow or London could cease to exist.'

'That's a terrible thought,' said Wilshere, without conveying it.

'But the only logical one. I'm predicting that this war generation will invent what H. G. Wells said they would invent at the end of the last century.'

'I've never read H. G. Wells.'

'He called them atomic bombs.'

'You've taken an interest in this.'

'I studied physics at Heidelberg University before the war. I keep up with the journals.'

It was difficult to judge the silence that followed, whether awkward or ruminative. Voss broke it.

'Still, this is nothing to worry us here in Lisbon, where the sun shines whether we like it or not. I have brought your gold. It has been weighed at the bank as you will see from their receipt, but if you wish to verify that . . .'

'That won't be necessary,' said Wilshere, moving across the room. 'I'll want you to count these to confirm that you've received one hundred and sixty-eight stones.'

'We've arranged for the quality to be checked tomorrow morning.'

'I'm sure there won't be any problem but I'll be here all day tomorrow if there is.'

The trickling of metal slipping against metal as Wilshere dialled in the combination to his safe. Silence while Voss counted the diamonds and Wilshere paced the room. A signature was applied to paper. The door opened. Voices entered the hall. Anne went back to her room and hung her wet towel out of the window. Her sign to Wallis.

Voss drove back to Lisbon, followed by Wallis. He went straight to Lapa and the German Legation where he presented Wolters with the receipt and the stones, watched him count them out and put them in the safe.

Voss walked back in the darkening evening to his one-roomed apartment overlooking the Estrela Gardens and basilica. He showered and lay on his bed smoking and sinking into a drowsy sensuality. He wanted to bring her here, not that it was Lisbon's best apartment, but it was a place to be alone, away from the eyes, a place where the moment wouldn't have to be snatched. There would be time for . . . there would be time and intimacy. He ran his hand up his stomach and chest, drew on the thick white end of the cigarette, felt the blood rush, the prickle and the brain smoothing out into the warm evening.

'I am not alone,' he said, out loud, conscious of being absurdly dramatic – the melodrama of the Berlin cabaret singer to a bored audience.

He laughed at his insanity and ramped his head up on his elbow. With no warning the faces of his father and brother came to him. His eyes filled, blurring the room, and the long hot day drew to a close.

Chapter 16

At 9.30 p.m. Voss got up, dressed, picked up a newspaper, drank a coffee at the corner café and went to his customary bench in the Estrela Gardens. He sat with the newspaper on his lap. People walked under the trees. There was a sense of relief after the brutal heat of the day. Most of the women were well dressed – in expensive silks if they could afford it or high-quality cottons if they couldn't. The men, if they were Portuguese, wore dark suits and hats. If they were foreigners, the richer ones were dressed in linen, the poorer in material too thick for the weather. Money had filtered through Lisbon.

Voss blinked, saw the scene through a different lens, saw the other people in the gardens. These were not men and women enjoying an evening stroll. These were the sweat of the city. They oozed out of the dark, polluted buildings, seeped out of the cheap *pensões*, which stank of the drains, leaked out of the stuffy attics in rinsed underwear dried crisp in the sun. They were looking for the odd escudo to weigh down the damp pockets creeping up their thighs. They were the watchers, the listeners, the whisperers, the fabricators, the rumourmongers – the liars, the cheats, the conmen and the crows.

One of this number sat on Voss's bench. He was small, emaciated, unshaven and toothless with black eyebrows that sprouted an inch from his head. Voss tapped the bench with his newspaper and some of the man's sour smell wafted towards him. His name was Rui.

'Your Frenchman hasn't been out of his room for three days,' said Rui.

'Is he dead?' asked Voss.

'No, no, I mean he's only been out for coffee.'

'And he drank that on his own?'

'Yes. He bought some bread and tinned sardines too,' added Rui.

'Did he speak to anyone?'

'He's scared, this one. I haven't seen anyone so scared. He'd turn on his own shadow and kick at it in the street.'

You would too, thought Voss. Olivier Mesnel had come from Paris where he had only one enemy, to Lisbon where he has two, the Germans and the PVDE. Who'd be a French communist here?

'Has he made any more trips to the outskirts of town?'

'Those trips to Monsanto, they seem to drain him too much. This is a man who has few reserves left . . . not for what he's doing.'

'Tell me when he does something. You know the form,' said Voss, getting up and leaving the newspaper, which Rui started flicking though to find the twenty-escudo note slipped between the sports pages.

Voss left the gardens at the exit closest to the basilica and headed for the Bairro Alto down the Calçada da Estrela, looking behind him for a taxi but also checking that there was no *bufos* on him. A cab pulled up and he let it take him to the Largo do Chiado. He thought about Mesnel. He worried about him. Always the same worries. Why would the Russians choose such a man for intelligence work? The hopeless loner, the seedy neurotic, the unwashed loser, the . . . the liver fluke, the mattress flea.

Voss left the cab and walked at pace up through the grid of the battered cobbled streets of the Bairro Alto to a *tasca* where they where grilling horse mackerel outside. He took a seat in the darkest corner with views out of two doors. He ordered the mackerel and a small jug of white wine. He ate with no enthusiasm and washed it back with the wine, fast so that he couldn't taste its sharpness. Nobody showed at the two doors. He ordered a *bagaço*. He wanted that ferocity of the pure, colourless alcohol in is throat. He smoked. The cigarette stuck to the sweat between his fingers.

Anne tried the study door. It was unlocked and empty. She moved on to the sitting room. Dark. On the back terrace Wilshere sat alone at the small table smoking and drinking undiluted whisky from a tumbler. She sat. He didn't seem to notice her but kept up

151

his silent vigil on the empty lawn, while moving the heavy, dark furniture of his doubts and concerns around in his head.

She was trying to work out how she was going to fit Sutherland's orders into her strange relationship with Wilshere. She had no ease with the man. Whatever charm Cardew said he possessed must be reserved for men. With her he was either disconcertingly intimate or unfathomably distant. Either stroking her, kissing the corner of her mouth or thrashing the hide off her horse. The man's wealth had insulated him from ordinary mortals, it was always a job to think how to tease his brain towards interest.

'Dinner ready?' he asked, exhausted by the notion.

'I don't know, I've been upstairs.'

'Drink?'

'I'm all right, thank you.'

'Smoke?'

He lit her cigarette, tossed his own and lit another.

'I will have that drink, after all,' she decided.

'João?' called Wilshere, to no response. 'I thought it was awfully quiet. You know, I don't know whether we're going to get any dinner tonight.'

He fixed Anne a brandy and soda from the tray.

'I'm not hungry,' she said.

'They *should* give us something. Mafalda confuses them sometimes, I think.'

'When we were riding yesterday,' said Anne, deciding on a frontal assault, 'why did you hit my horse?'

'Hit your horse?' he said, sitting slowly.

'You remember my horse bolted?'

'Yes,' he said, but careful now, uncertain of other things, 'she did bolt.'

'It was because you hit her with your crop as you rode past.'

'I did,' he said, a statement, but on the edge of a question.

'Why was that? I didn't want to bring it up in front of the major. I was thinking that it might have had something to do with this girl Judy Laverne. I've been worrying about it.'

'Worrying?'

'Yes,' she said, realizing now that she'd drawn a blank.

His eyes turned furtive in his head. It scared her. Sutherland had been wrong. This had not been the right thing to do.

'I thought it was . . . I thought it was maybe my mare that had spooked the filly, coming up on you so fast like that.'

She had the image of him clear in her head – half standing out of the saddle, crop arm raised, intent on damage.

'Perhaps that was it,' she said, grasping at anything conciliatory. 'Was Judy Laverne a good horsewoman?'

'No,' he said, close to vehement now, 'she was a *brilliant* horsewoman. Fearless, too.'

He socked back the whisky, drew savagely on the cigarette and bit his thumbnail, staring through her, wild for a moment.

'I think I'll go and see what's happened to dinner,' he said.

The lawn darkened another degree. She gulped her brandy. Her confidence in Sutherland had evaporated. Whatever this was, her presence here, it was *all* to do with Judy Laverne.

Voss left a few coins on the table, the meal costing so little it was difficult to imagine the lives of those providing it. He walked back down to the statue of Luís de Camões, did a circuit under the trees of the people sitting on the stone seats who were not interested in him. He headed down the Rua do Alecrim to the railway station at Cais do Sodré and bought a ticket to Estoril. He sat in one of the middle carriages of the almost empty train. Just before the train was due to pull out he left the carriage and walked back up the platform. There was nobody following him. The guard blew his whistle. He stepped into the first carriage of the moving train.

In Estoril he walked up through the gardens to the Hotel Parque. He watched the cars and people from under the palm trees, waited until the pavements were clear and crossed the road. He walked towards the casino and, in a single movement, opened a car door and swung in behind the wheel. He started the car, drove behind the casino and down the other side of the square. He headed west, through Cascais and out to Guincho, where the long stretches of straight road showed him that he was not being followed.

The road climbed up the Serra de Sintra past Malveira, past the bend in the road where the American woman had come off, past the Azoia junction, through Pé da Serra, down to Colares and then back up the north side of the *serra*, past a dark village, some unlit *quintas*. After some kilometres he pulled off the road and parked the car deep in some trees. He crossed the road, went through an iron gate and down a cobbled track into the gardens of Monserrate.

Twenty yards down the track he was joined by a man behind and a man in front, who shone a torch in his face.

'Good evening, sir,' said an English voice. *'What is the worst of woes that wait on age?'*

The man with the torch spurted laughter, while the one at Voss's rear whispered softly in his ear.

'What stamps the wrinkle deeper on the brow?'

Voss sighed but remembered his lines:

'To view each loved one blotted from life's page,
And be alone on earth, as I am now.'

'It's not as bad as all that, sir. We're all friends here, as you know.'

The English and their sense of humour, thought Voss. This was Richard Rose's work, the writer. He had the whole of the Lisbon station spouting the classics.

'Learn while you work,' he'd said. 'It's our way of handling the serious business.'

The three men walked down to the unlit building in the centre of the gardens. The first time Rose had met Voss here he'd told him that the gardens had originally been landscaped by an eighteenth-century English aesthete called William Beckford, who'd had to leave England in a hurry or face the noose.

'What had he done?' Voss had asked, innocent.

'Buggered little boys, Voss,' said Rose, eyes shining and alive to the possibilities. 'The love that dare not speak its name.'

He'd confirmed it in German too, just to make sure Voss understood, to see how straight the tracks were that Voss was running on.

They arrived at the strange palace built in the middle of the last century by another English eccentric. The lead escort pointed with his torch down the Moorish colonnade to some open glass doors at the far end. Voss was relieved to see Sutherland there with Rose, the two men sitting on wooden chairs in the deserted room with the light from a hurricane lamp shuddering up the walls.

'Ah!' said Rose, standing up to greet Voss, *'the wandering outlaw of his own dark mind.'*

'I'm not sure I understand you very well,' said Voss, blank, unamused by Rose.

'It's nothing, Voss, old chap, nothing,' said Rose. 'Just a line from the poem that provides your codename . . . *Childe Harold*. Did you know that was written just down the road in Sintra?'

Voss didn't respond. They sat, lit cigarettes. Sutherland sucked on his empty pipe. Rose removed three small metal goblets from a leather holder and half-filled them from a hip flask.

'We've never thanked you properly for the information on the rockets,' said Sutherland, raising his cup to Voss, striking the note he wanted for this meeting, steering away from Rose's more reckless style.

'Didn't stop them falling, of course,' said Rose, arm over the back of his chair, 'but cheers, anyway.'

'At least you were prepared,' said Voss. 'And you tested the craters?'

'We tested the craters.'

'And I assume you found that what I said was true.'

'No evidence of radiation,' said Sutherland. 'Conventional explosives. But it doesn't mean we're no longer concerned.'

'We're of the opinion that they were test flights,' said Rose.

'Given the seriousness of the situation in Italy, France and the East, do you think the Führer is of the temperament to spend his time in testing?' said Voss.

'The flight path of the rockets?' asked Rose. 'Yes, we do . . . until such time as Heisenberg has developed the atomic pile to create the Ekarhenium, as you call it.'

'We've been through this before. Heisenberg and Hahn have been explicit. There is no atomic bomb programme.'

'Heisenberg wasn't explicit to Niels Bohr, and Niels Bohr is with the Americans now and he, along with others, has convinced them that Germany's made serious advances, you're damned close.'

Voss closed his eyes which were sore in his head. Some smoking ensued.

'We know you didn't bring us all the way out here just to talk us through that one again, Voss,' said Sutherland. 'You're never going to convince us . . . and even if you did, we wouldn't be able to convince the Americans, what with all the evidence they've been accumulating.'

'There's probably only twenty scientists in the world who know what any of this is about,' said Rose. 'Even you with your years of physics at Heidelberg University wouldn't understand what it entails. You might have grasped some theory but don't tell us that you, here in Lisbon, could have the first idea of the practicalities. This is innovative science. Brilliant men see things differently. Short cuts can be made. Heisenberg and Hahn are two such men. It would take a lot more than your word to send us back to London telling our people not to worry.'

'I have something else for you,' said Voss, sick of this endless battering and getting nowhere – intelligence services the world over only believe what they want to believe, or what their leadership wants them to believe.

Sutherland leaned forward to hide his excitement. Rose cupped his knee in the stirrup of his hands, tilted his head.

'We have completed some negotiations and are now in possession of a number of diamonds, which are not of industrial quality. They have a value in excess of one million dollars. These diamonds, which I have just delivered to the German Legation in Lapa, will be handed over to Beecham Lazard, who will be travelling tomorrow via Dakar and Rio to New York. I understand he will be acquiring something with the proceeds of the diamond sales which could advance or lead to the acquisition of a secret weapon programme for Germany. I don't know what exactly he is buying or from whom, or even whether it is in New York.'

'You said "secret weapon" – how do you know that much?'

'I am reporting to you what has been heard in Germany, that there is talk of a secret weapon in Berlin and this has now reached the Führer. The best confirmation of this that I can offer is that, at the moment, we have insufficient funds in Switzerland to buy the diamonds outright and to make up the shortfall we had to take a loan of some gold from the Banco de Oceano e Rocha. That gold would not have been released without the highest authority from Berlin. I would suggest that it is worth following Lazard to New York.'

'We'll tail him from Lisbon.'

'I wouldn't put anybody on the flight,' said Voss. 'He's a very cautious man. Even our own agents won't make contact until he arrives in Rio.'

'We'll check him on and check him off,' said Sutherland. 'Can I have a word, Richard?'

The two Englishmen went out on to the colonnade and as they went down some steps and on to a steep lawn out of sight Voss heard their opening exchange:

'You can't put this to him now,' said Sutherland.

'On the contrary,' said Rose, 'I think the timing is perfect.'

Voss pressed the sweat out of his eyebrows with the edge of his thumb. Five minutes and the two men were back. Sutherland was, as usual, grave and Rose's reliable levity was turned off. They'd gone out English and come back very serious men. Voss felt something turning in his bowels.

'We're going to make a communication with Wolters through our usual channels,' said Sutherland.

'Your usual channels?' asked Voss. 'I'm not sure what that means.'

'We have a way of letting Wolters know about intelligence we want him to hear.'

'Real intelligence?'

'Yes, the real thing.'

'You mean threats?'

'Sometimes.'

'And you're going to tell me first . . . to see how I react?'

'Not exactly,' said Rose. 'We know how you'll react. It's just that we think the information you've given us makes you a member of our club.'

'I don't like clubs,' said Voss, suddenly revealing things about himself. 'I'm not a member of any.'

'It's also important that you know that this message to Wolters has nothing to do with the intelligence you've just given us.'

'The communiqué that will be given to Wolters tomorrow will be as follows,' said Sutherland, his voice so low that the other two had to lean in to him: 'If we do not have an unconditional surrender from Germany by the 15th August, by the end of that month an atomic device will be dropped on the city of Dresden.'

Voss lost the ability to swallow. It was as if what his mind was refusing to accept was also being rejected by his body. The sweat, which had gathered in his hair and eyebrows from the hot night and the heat of the hurricane lamp, now broke and flowed over the taut skin of his drawn features, so that he had to wipe his cheeks as if he was crying. He thought of his mother.

157

'Are there any other circumstances, apart from unconditional surrender, in which this could be prevented from happening?'

The two men opposite him thought about the meaning of unconditional surrender.

'Well, I suppose . . . Hitler's death might do it . . . as long as Himmler didn't take over, or anyone like him,' said Rose.

'If we got cast-iron proof that there was no atomic bomb programme, or we had the exact location of any laboratories and the crucial scientists involved in the programme – Heisenberg, Hahn, Weizsäcker – so that they can be destroyed . . . then possibly the action could be . . .' said Sutherland.

'It would save a great number of lives,' said Rose.

'But not many of them in Dresden,' said Voss.

The two Englishmen stood. Voss felt broken in the middle, his legs not operational. As they left, Rose, not a normally demonstrative man, patted him on the back. Voss sat alone for a quarter of an hour until his motor responses normalized. He picked up the hurricane lamp, went out of the room and handed it to the remaining agent, who stood at the edge of shadow under the Moorish arches of the colonnade.

'A beautiful evening, sir,' said the agent, dowsing the lamp.

Voss's legs didn't work the pedals very well on the way back. He scared himself taking hairpin bends with one foot flooring the clutch and the other still on the accelerator. The tyres had squealed, the engine howled, and the steering wheel slithered through his wet hands. He found himself thinking of Judy Laverne coming off the same road and wondered whether this was what had happened. Something terrible had been said to her, some terrible revelation and she'd given up, thrown herself away, exhausted by man's capacity for inflicting horror.

He took a walk on the beach at Guincho for twenty minutes to stop his legs shaking, to see if the Atlantic rollers could thump out the dark empty space in his chest and guts. But all he'd felt was the ground trembling beneath him and its reverberation through the cast of his body. He'd thought about something Rose had quoted to him in a previous meeting. Something about hollow men. He couldn't remember it precisely, but Rose's first words, as they'd met that evening, came back to him. *The wandering outlaw of his own dark mind.* Yes, that was what he'd become. Alone out here, between the earth and the sea. Nobody. He was nobody any more. Modelled. Fabricated. Moulded. Cast. And with no way back to the old Karl Voss. The one that . . . the one that used to what? Believe in things? Admire people? The Führer? Pah! He was lost. That Rose. He says these words and then: 'Nothing, Voss, old chap, nothing.' It *is* nothing. He's right. Karl Voss is nothing but a hunted man. Hunted by himself.

He'd been drawn back to the car, winched to it. He sat behind the wheel, held his head out of the window, rested his chin on the ledge and smoked, staring at the ground. He drifted deeper into his dark mind, retreated until, panic-struck by his wanderings over that empty landscape, he started the car and headed back to Estoril.

Voss parked up somewhere between the Hotel Parque and the casino. Smoking was all that was holding him together. He lit one cigarette from another. He strode up towards the casino. He wasn't thinking any more. He was doing. He was desperate. He walked past Jim Wallis in his car without noticing. He went straight into Wilshere's garden without checking his rear. Wallis had to run to catch up with him and even then he only just saw Voss's back disappearing into the bower next to the summerhouse. Wallis slowed, eased back into the hedge, waited.

Chapter 17

It was 2.00 a.m. Anne lay on the bed, pinned to it, absorbed by the ceiling, waiting for time to shift. She wasn't thinking about what she had to do – search the study. She was floating in and out of fantasy and reality, between Judy Laverne and Wilshere, Karl Voss and herself.

Wilshere said he missed Judy Laverne, said he'd fallen. They appeared to be in love according to Voss and others. Now Wilshere was using her to remind himself of Judy Laverne. To torment his wife? To torment himself? He *had* struck the filly. He'd been angry, deranged by the vision of her. He'd wanted to drive her away, to banish her from his thoughts.

Did Karl Voss know what she was? Was he on an operation or did he, in the heart of the paranoid city, see this as one of hers? Would it ever be possible to know what was real? She decided that she wouldn't see him again or rather that she wasn't going to put herself in that position. There would be no visit to the bottom of the garden tonight. There was too much that was unknowable. The equation would never simplify. The variables would mount. The additional logic would defeat itself. She didn't have the tools to prove any part of the solution. In the end the silver thread would stop tugging.

It was time to go to work. She walked the dark corridor, her shoulder brushing the wall. She waited at the gallery above the hall. The wood in the house groaned after a day spent straining against the heat. Moonlight lay in a blue rhombus across the chequered tiles. She went down the stairs, stepped around the moonlight, past the cases of Mafalda's silent figurines. *Amor é cego.* She walked the length of the house and unlocked the french windows to the back terrace in case she had to get back in that way after escaping out

160

of the window. She went back to the study, let herself in, closed the door behind her.

She crossed the room, opened the window behind the desk and moved a plant on the window sill three inches to the right. She lifted her nightdress and took a torch from the waistband of her knickers. She sat in Wilshere's chair and surveyed the night-lit room.

The books in neat, leather-bound collections filled the walls. Two paintings on either side of the door, one of men in Arab dress on camels in a desert scene, the other of a fishing boat dragged up on a mist-filled beach. Ireland, perhaps. One corner was African, with three masks mounted on the wall, the one at the apex maybe three-foot long with inch slits for eyes and mouth, the mask never more than six inches across through its entire length. Hair, a kind of rough hemp, sprouted from the top. The mouth even appeared to have teeth.

She listened again to the settling house and painted the desktop with her torch beam. A blotter, two old newspapers, a pen and ink tray, tidy. She opened the central drawer. One block of clean paper and beside it a single sheet with a four-line stanza accompanied by jottings in the margins, the odd word crossed out and the replacement word connected by a line. The stanza seemed to read:

> Crow black in the middle night
> Around the marchers come for another fight.
> No boots, but claws scratching through the dust,
> No armour, but shells blistered with rust.

That was how it stood at the moment, but it looked as if there were more drafts to be done and even then it would find its way to the bin. The wastepaper basket was empty. She drummed her chin with her fingers and shuddered. If that was what Wilshere had teeming through his mind of a night – ghostly, dark, restless, seething with ugly energy – maybe he *was* going mad. She had a memory flash, a story of her mother's when she'd visited a cave in India – alone but with the sense of not being alone. Above her, covering every inch of the roof of the cave, were hanging, sleeping bats. The sight of the dormant army, their jostling folded wings, had turned

161

her mother and sent her out in a crouched sprint into the sunlight. Was that the inside of Wilshere's cranium?

She opened all the desk drawers; some were empty, most of little interest. The bottom one was locked. She shifted books in the bookcase, she lifted pictures, she checked the fireplace. To the left of the fireplace in the darkest corner of the room was the cabinet where Wilshere kept his safe with a combination dial lock. She went back to the desk. She listened. Hands moist now. First nerves creeping in. House noises growing into something else in her mind. Footsteps on a stair. Stop breathing. Sweat under her breasts. She stood up. Remembered her training: never leave a warm chair. She opened all the drawers again, checked the roofs and sides. Central drawer, at the back, stuck with something resinous, a key.

It opened the bottom drawer; inside was a single thick book bound in very soft untooled leather, its plain unlined pages covered in the same handwriting as the stanza of poetry. There were dates. A diary, which at a quick glance she could tell was personal. Day after day with no mention of business. Started 1st January 1944. The initial entries were rarely more than a couple of lines long – observations such as: '*4th January. A rare frost. The lawn quite white. The low sun turns it back to green in a matter of moments. Not what you'd call an Irish frost. It would be quite something to have real foot-stamping weather for once.*' '*23rd January. Heavy storm out at sea. Drove out to Cabo da Roca, walked the coast to Praia Adraga. The rain driven off the ocean, lacerating. Waves clawed at the rocks and shot up the cliff faces. Rollers on the beach like I've never seen. Thunderous. Had to run to stay out of their clutches.*'

A man overwhelmed by tedium or positively reflective? Hard to tell. The first entry of more than a few lines came on 3rd February and coincided with Beecham Lazard introducing his new assistant, Judy Laverne. '*I've never seen such a mouth. So wide and what lips! The bottom one so plump I just wanted to put my finger to it, feel its soft cushion. And bright red lipstick which rings all her cigarette stubs, which I've kept.*' Infatuated from the first moment. Karl Voss shuttled through her brain.

She skimmed the pages. They ride almost every day, in invigorating rain, in sunshine that was never so brilliant, under magnificent turbulent skies. There's no such thing as bad weather now. They sleep together in the house at Pé da Serra. Wilshere has fallen. He can't keep the pen off the page. Her blue-black hair, her marble breasts, her hard, pink, shilling-sized nipples, her jet strip, not triangle, of pubic hair. It was embarrassing, it was touching, it was so private it made the sweat trickle down Anne's ribs. Until the end of April.

'*25th April. Lazard has lost his head. He spends too much time in Lisbon. He's reading bizarre things into normal everyday life. That's what happens if you spend too much time in that city – everybody watching each other – anyone's bound to look odd eventually. Why shouldn't Judy meet another American? She's American. She wants to talk to her own people. So what if they go for a walk through the Igreja do Carmo. It's something to do. Were they holding hands? No. I don't see what he's getting at . . .*'

The tirade continued to the bottom of the page, by which time Lazard's words had wormed their way into his mind and laid their eggs. The parasites proliferated. Doubt scuttled from page to page, a black spider against the white paper, desperate for the dark safety of the book's spine. The lyricism vanished. Wilshere's open, flowing italics tightened, his hand cramped on the page. Lazard reported another meeting in *A Brasileira* café with a different American. He has them followed to the Pensão Londres where they stayed for an hour. Jealousy took root, spreading, ravaging like couch grass. Wilshere was in a torment. Lazard haunted the pages, as reliable as any Iago. Then in early May Judy Laverne announced that the PVDE had refused to extend her visa. She was going to have to leave. Wilshere was sick. He wrote things. Terrible things. Things that should never have been written down, in language that shouldn't be known, couldn't be known by anybody outside hell. The page was spattered with ink dried to a coppery blood, the paper had been torn up by the blade of the dry, frustrated nib. Anne turned the pages, the empty pages, pages that could have been full and ripe, to the end of the book where, on the inside of the back cover, were six sets of numbers and letters – R12, R6, L4, R8, L13, R1.

This time the creak of the wooden stair was followed by the slap of a leather slipper on the tiled floor of the hall. Anne wiped the diary clean with her sleeve, replaced it in the drawer, shut it, turned the key. Light from the corridor appeared in a line at the foot of the door. She found the resin in the central drawer, restuck the key, straightened the chair, stepped on to the sill and out of the window, pulled the plant across, shut the window. The door opened. The light came on in the study. She crouched, her back was as cold as cod, her nightdress soaked through. Wilshere drew up his chair, sat down. She ran across the lawn and down the path to the summerhouse.

In the study, Wilshere leaned back in his chair rubbing his fingers. He sniffed the air. Wisteria. He stood and pushed the unfastened window open, rubbed his fingers again. He looked below the window ledge and then up at his shadow reaching out across the empty lawn.

Anne slowed at the bottom of the path. Her heart rattled against her ribs. Her throat was tight, constricted, as if the neckline of the nightdress was strangling her. She pulled up the hem and wiped her face, pushed the torch into her knickers. She looked back up the path, shook herself out and went into the bower. Voss lay on his back on the stone seat, asleep. She started to turn. He sat up, ran his hand down his face.

'I'd given up on you,' he said.

Her breasts were still heaving under the cotton.

'I didn't think you were going to come,' said Voss, pinching the sleep out of his eyes.

'I didn't intend to,' she said, moving into the darkest corner behind him.

He swivelled on the seat.

'You didn't *intend* to,' he repeated.

'No.'

'You're scared,' he said. 'I can see.'

'And why shouldn't I be?' she said, the blade of her mother's voice in her own.

'Of me?'

'We're enemies, aren't we?'

'Out there,' he said, and his hand caught the edge of the moonlight.

'There's more of out there than there is in here.'

'True ... but what's in here is ours.'

'Is it?' she asked. 'Do you think that? How am I to know that?'

164

'Because we're talking like this.'

'We can talk, but I still don't know if you're . . . honourable.'

'Which is why you didn't intend to come,' he said. 'So why did you?'

'I ran out of cigarettes.'

He laughed. Her organs went back to their places. Spies in love. Bloody hopeless. Would they ever tell each other anything? He offered a cigarette.

'You're probably a spy, Mr Military Attaché,' she said, taking one. 'I work for Shell, the oil company. A sensitive economic commodity.'

'Everybody's a spy,' said Voss, searching himself for a lighter.

'In Lisbon, maybe.'

'Anywhere,' he said, lighting their cigarettes. 'We all have our secrets.'

'Spies have even more.'

'It's just their job and they're dull secrets.'

'You seem to know.'

'It's wartime and I work in the German Legation; there are secrets all over.'

'Which is the problem. Where does the job end?'

'So you think, for instance, that attraction is easy to act,' he said. 'Love, too?'

She sucked on the cigarette, her cheeks sinking in sharply, drawing in the smoke to disguise the race around her heart, the fast blood standing the hairs up on her arms, itching around her teeth.

'It depends,' she said, flicking her ash, dizzy now from the nicotine rush.

'I'm listening,' he said.

'It depends, say, if the object of your affection is predisposed to that kind of attention.'

'That sounds like experience.'

'Not personal.'

'How did you find out?'

'I read it in a book.'

'Is that the sum total of your experience?'

'There's nothing wrong with learning from people who write books.'

'My mother told me that in affairs of the heart no rules apply.

165

No one's love is the same as anybody else's. Comparisons don't work. Even love between two people can't be relied on to stay the same,' said Voss.

'Your *mother* told you that?'

'I was *her* child. My elder brother was my father's.'

'Do you know what she meant?'

'Probably that loving my father was hard work. She did it, but he never made it easy for her,' said Voss.

Silence, Anne waiting for him to continue, praying for him to continue. Voss, staring into the ground, prepared himself to tell it for the first time.

'In the beginning,' he said, as if this was now legend, 'my father was an exciting man, an army officer, my mother . . . a beautiful . . . well, girl, I suppose. She was sixteen and she thought she'd found true romantic love until one day he told her that there'd been someone else. A girl he'd loved, who'd died. Those few words wrung out all the romance from their so-called "true love". But what was she to do? Suddenly not love him when she knew she did? They married the next year in 1910. Four years later he went to war and for four years she hardly saw him. He had some leave . . . enough to create my brother and then me but when he did come back home in 1918, on the losing side, he was a different man. Damaged. He wasn't exciting any more. My mother said he was like a house with the windows bricked in. So she had to find a different way of loving him, and she made it work for twenty-odd years . . . until the next war.

'My father was a principled man – one of those generals who spoke out against some of the orders given to the army before the Russian campaign – it cost him his job. They retired him, sent him home. Now he was a man who was not only no longer exciting, but bitter, too. Then my brother was killed at Stalingrad and that was the end for my father. He shot himself, because as far as he was concerned he'd lost everything. He didn't say it, but my mother was not enough. That was how I found out. In a letter he asked me to spread his ashes over the first woman's grave and my mother, who *still* loved him, made sure that I did it.'

Silence while Voss turned that over, reploughed it into his mind.

'That, I think, is what she meant,' he said. 'Are you still scared of me?'

166

'Not of you.'

'By me?'

'No.'

'Someone's scared you.'

'Patrick Wilshere.'

'Why?'

'I read his diary tonight,' she said, drawn in by the intimacy.

'Like I said, we're all spies.'

'I find his behaviour . . . threatening. I wanted to know what he was thinking.'

'And now?'

'More so. It wasn't a relaxing read.'

'What did the diary say?'

'That he was madly in love with Judy Laverne until Lazard told him he'd seen her in Lisbon with other men. He became insanely jealous and, although it wasn't actually in the diary, there were things written that would suggest that he would have happily seen her dead.'

'I don't see what bearing this has on you.'

'I don't know what I'm doing here. I don't know why he has invited me into his house but I'm certain that it wasn't to give a secretary somewhere to sleep.'

'Tell me.'

She told him about the riding incident on the *serra* and the subsequent conversation with Wilshere. He lit two more cigarettes from the coal of his own, handed her one.

'And when you confronted him he did not appear to have been aware of his actions,' Voss repeated. 'So now you think that Wilshere is deranged, has drawn another woman into his orbit to punish her for the crimes, real or imagined, committed by the first. No, I don't think so.'

That annoyed her. Dismissing the silly girl.

'What does the omniscient Military Attaché think, then?'

'Sorry,' he said, 'I wasn't being patronizing. I don't disbelieve you. I just think there is more to it. Wilshere is a complicated individual. He wouldn't position you simply to satisfy his need for vengeance, although sexual jealousy is a very potent force. No. He has seen an opportunity in having you there. By confronting him with the riding incident you have revealed a weakness to him. He can no longer rely on himself. He is . . . leaking. It *could* make him more dangerous.'

'And everything had been going so well,' said Anne.

'It's strange that the English don't have a word for *sang froid*, and yet the French, who rarely exhibit it, do.'

'If you take things too seriously it could feed your inclination to give up.'

'We Germans take everything seriously.'

'But unfortunately it doesn't seem to work with you.'

Voss's laugh was barely a grunt. He hadn't expected to find anything funny after what he'd been told.

They sat in the accumulative silence of a moment when life goes one way or the other. Two people who knew that words would not continue the thing. A move was needed, possibly two. Then the words could restart but in a different light, in a light that others wouldn't be able to see and would shake their heads at, mystified.

He threw his cigarette on the floor, hers went after it, the coals smouldered on the black floor, smoke strayed into the moonlight. Their lips searched the dark. Touched. It was not a tender moment. There was too much desperation. And just as she'd thought she would let him have her there, on the stone seat, at the edge of moonlight, she remembered the torch in her knickers and other small details fell in afterwards so that she knew there would have to be another time and place.

He told her to come to his apartment after work the following afternoon. He would leave the downstairs door open for her. She stroked the bones in his face with her hands, like a blind person wanting to remember.

She went back up to the house, adrenalin slick in her system. Her feet found the steps of the back terrace, her nose the smell of cigar smoke. She stepped into a sudden funnel of torchlight.

'What are you doing?' asked Wilshere, voice liquid, floating between inquiry and menace.

'It was too hot to sleep. I've been walking in the garden,' she said. 'And you?'

His slippers clapped his heels as the beam of light compressed between them. She put a hand up to shield her face.

'I wasn't tired,' he said. 'I was lying in bed thinking too much.'

He snapped off the torch, slipped it into his pocket, tossed his cigar.

'You look cold now,' he said.

'No,' she replied, her skin tight as blubber, 'not cold.'

He held her arms and kissed her. Tobacco bitter. Whisky sour.

'Forgive me,' he said in a voice that wasn't asking. 'You were irresistible.'

She unwelded her feet from the stone floor.

'I'll lead the way,' he said almost gaily, and set off torch in hand through the french windows, the beam swaggering from wall to wall. She followed him up the protesting stairs, revulsion seething in her chest.

As she entered her room, Wilshere blew her a kiss.

On the other side of the gallery, Mafalda's door shut.

Voss arrived back in Lisbon close to 4.00 a.m. He was beyond tiredness. He parked outside his apartment and checked his dead-letter drop in the gardens. Although he checked it regularly this particular one was used infrequently and he was surprised to find something in it. A coded message asking him to go, whatever the time, to an address in Madragoa which belonged to a colonel of the Free Poles. He walked down the Calçada da Estrela and turned right into the narrow streets of Madragoa.

He found Rua Garcia da Horta and went into the building, which was always open, and up the narrow stairs to the first floor. He knocked on the door twice, then three times, then twice again. The door opened a crack and then all the way. He went into the dark apartment, following the colonel, who didn't speak but pointed to the open windows where he spent most of the night trying to get cool. Still not used to the heat after a lifetime in Warsaw.

Even without being able to see the man in the room clearly, he knew that sitting in a chair to the side of the window was the same man he'd spoken to in the Hotel Lutecia in Paris at the end of January.

'Drink?' he asked, holding up a bottle.

'What is it?' asked Voss.

'I don't know what the colonel called it,' he said, 'but it's rough.'

He poured him a measure into a wine glass.

'How is it going with the British?' he asked.

'Very badly,' said Voss. 'They don't believe a word I say except, of course, after it has happened. Then they thank me and tell me how much they have suffered and follow that up with threats.'

'Threats?'

'They're threatening to drop an atomic device on Dresden in mid August unless they get an unconditional German surrender.'

'Doesn't that sound like bluff?'

'They're very nervous about our nonexistent bomb programme. The Americans even more so.'

'What more do they want?'

'Nothing much,' said Voss, scathing. 'The deaths of all our major scientists – Heisenberg, Hahn, Weizsäcker, the lot. The location of all our research laboratories so that they can be bombed to rubble, and the death of the Führer, as long as he's not replaced by another National Socialist leader.'

Silence while the man turned his head and lit a cigarette.

'You have been alone a long time, I know. It has been very hard. The British are making what they see as necessarily cruel demands. But they are the only ones we can rely on. We have to tell them everything we can in the hope that they will relent,' he said. 'You will tell them about the V2 rockets. You can tell them they can bomb the laboratories in Berlin-Dahlem to dust if that will make them feel better. And you may tell them that the Führer will be assassinated around midday Berlin time in his bunker in the *Wolfsschanze* on 20th July.'

Voss was stunned. The alcohol trembled in his glass. He drank it automatically. The man continued in his quiet voice.

'Your job, once you've received the signal that Operation Valkyrie has started, will be to take control of the German Legation here in Lisbon. It may require strong methods. If SS General Wolters does not obey your orders you will shoot him without hesitation. Do you have a gun?'

'Only one from the legation which I have to sign in and out.'

'The colonel will provide you with a firearm.'

'Is this certain?'

'We have been close several times but have been frustrated at the last moment by changes in schedule. This time the Führer is fixed at the *Wolfsschanze* and *we* are going to *him*. This is the most certain we have ever been, which is why you are being informed and can pass it on to the British. I hope this means you won't be alone for much longer,' he said. 'One last thing before you go. Olivier Mesnel?'

'Olivier Mesnel, as far as I am informed, does nothing except have occasional, unspeakable assignations with gypsy boys in the caves on the outskirts of the city.'

'The colonel has found that he's making contact with a communist courier who visits him in the Pensão Silva on Rua Braancamp. The colonel believes that whatever Mesnel is giving him will find its way back to the Russians.'

'I don't know what he *can* be giving him. He never goes out.'

'Then perhaps he's receiving instructions. The point is that whatever he's involved in could help us with the British. If we can show that the Russians are not to be trusted it will help our cause.'

Chapter 18

The man in the dark suit sat with his hands clasped and jammed between his knees. He was tense and the natural hunch his occupation had given him gave the impression that he was about to sustain a series of blows across the shoulders. His hat sat on the table in front of him. A black homburg. The drag of the heavy bags under his eyes made his long face longer, his sadness sadder.

'Couldn't you find anyone else?' asked Voss, looking at him through the glass panel of the door. 'In all those jewellery stores off the Rossio? There must have been someone local, surely.'

Hein, one of Voss's subordinates, didn't say anything but let his hand do the talking. They were too gabby down there.

'Where did you find him?'

'The Jewish Refugee Commission.'

'Did he volunteer?'

'Kempf said he'd find out about his family for him.'

'And did he?'

Hein gave Voss a diagonal look and shrugged.

'Well, he won't talk, that's for sure,' said Voss. 'Where's he from?'

'Antwerp. Worked a lot with Belgian Congo product.'

'Keep Wolters away from him.'

'That's probably your job, isn't it, sir?'

'What's his name?'

'Hirschfeld ... er ... Samuel Hirschfeld,' said Hein, morose now.

Voss went in, shook hands with the man and told him to set up his equipment. The man, wordless, opened a wooden case and lifted out his scales, weights, tweezers, eyeglass and a square of worn dark velvet.

Voss knocked on Wolters' door, waited the customary beat, announced the diamond assessor.

'Bring him in, Voss, bring him in.'

'I've just told him to set up in the other room.'

'Each stone individually weighed and valued.'

'Yes, sir.'

'And someone in the room with him at all times.'

'Yes, sir.'

Wolters lobbed him the bag as if it was nothing more than a sack of marbles. Voss went back to the Belgian, who declined his offer of a cigarette and went to work.

Jim Wallis had filed his report at 8.00 a.m. and gone home to bed. Sutherland read it shortly afterwards and smoked a whole pipe bowl thinking about it. At 9.30 a.m. Cardew sent a coded message to the embassy and an hour later Sutherland and Rose were in a safe house just off the Largo do Rato with Anne sitting, knees pressed together, handbag on top, just like the virgin Sutherland had imagined her to be.

She took them through last night's business. Sutherland whistled through the now empty pipe, annoying her. He checked the numbers she gave him from Wilshere's diary. They talked about the safe, its make, whether there was a key as well as a combination. He told her Cardew would arrange for her instruction on how to open the safe. Anne continued the story, same as she had for Cardew. How Wilshere had surprised her in the study, how she had left via the window, how she wandered the garden and the final incident on the back terrace. Sutherland nodded her through it.

'Your report is incomplete,' said Sutherland.

'I don't think so, sir.'

'Perhaps you've forgotten something.'

'No, I'm sure I haven't.'

She was sweating in the close, curtained room. The light from the single overhead bulb was jaundiced after the fierce brightness of the street. Nausea turned in her stomach.

Sutherland bared his teeth where they were gnawing into his pipe stem.

'Your angel,' Rose prompted.

173

She blinked. Jim Wallis. She *had* forgotten about Jim Wallis, who they'd sent to keep an eye on her. Free-fall sweat.

The mournful notes of a knife-grinder's flute sounded in the street below.

'From the beginning,' said Sutherland, drilling her.

She told him about Karl Voss. The casino. The man who carried Wilshere back to the house. The beach. The cocktail party. The first and accidental meeting and the second, observed by Wallis, the unintentional one.

'You may recall that I told you that Voss was with the Abwehr,' said Sutherland.

'Yes, sir.'

'Have you spoken to him about any of our business?'

'No, sir, I haven't. He thinks I'm a secretary at Shell.'

'Karl Voss is an experienced officer,' said Sutherland. 'He's been with military intelligence in Zeitzler's team in Rastenburg. He's worked at the Zossen headquarters in Berlin, Avenue Foch in Paris and now here in Lisbon. Do you for one moment think he doesn't know how to play the . . . toy with the romantic illusions of a young woman?'

'All I can tell you, sir, is that I haven't told – '

'Have you . . .' Rose interrupted bluntly. 'Have you had a *physical* relationship with Voss?'

'No, sir.'

'That's something,' said Rose. 'He's a charismatic man, Voss. Very successful with the ladies. You wouldn't have been the first and you most definitely wouldn't have been the last.'

Rose's toxic words entered her intravenously. They went straight through her heart and into her head where the virus multiplied into a fever. Anger came first, a torrential rage, followed by cold, hard jealousy. They ran a circuit in her head, chasing, chasing but never catching up with the words, which remained intact, clear, defined as in the first moment that they were spoken.

'Can I make a suggestion?' said Sutherland, not looking for an affirmative. 'That you leave Captain Voss to his womanizing and concentrate on your job.'

Her handbag hung from her grip like a bad puppy as she went over to Sutherland, put him in her shadow.

'I did not have sex with him,' she said firmly. 'I have not spoken to him about our business.'

'If you had, my dear, you'd be on the first plane back to London,' he said, those blackberry smudges under his eyes swollen with insomnia. 'Dismissed.'

By the time the Contessa della Trecata arrived at the German Legation at 11.00 a.m. the shade temperature was in the low nineties and the British agents were settled into their routine, watching from apartments at the side and rear. Sutherland had put additional men in cars in the backstreets, while their paid *ardinas* – the newspaper boys – walked the hot *calçada* barefoot, ready to flag them and set Operation Dragnet in motion.

The contessa, wearing a petrol-blue silk dress cut to the mid calf of her still excellent but unsteady legs, climbed the few steps into the legation, eyed the swastika flag hanging dead over the doorway and fluttered her fan under her chin. She was taken upstairs to a gilded chair outside Wolters' office where she sat, fanning herself, in the still corridor. Voss watched her through the door from behind the hunched diamond assessor.

She was called into Wolters' office. They didn't shake hands. No contact was an understood part of their arrangement. Wolters puffed his cigar heavily as if fumigating his office.

'I know you see it as part of your cover, but could you be a little . . . a lot less rude when we're in company?' said Wolters.

'I'm sorry to have overplayed my part.'

'I can only think you used to be on the stage.'

The contessa accepted this small humiliation.

'What do you have for me?' asked Wolters.

The contessa set off in French, their common language, and the usual, baroque elaborations began to scroll the thick air of the room. Wolters slumped in his seat, fitted his cigar into the side of his mouth, between the gap in his teeth. He was used to the contessa's embellishments, the magnificent constructions of stylish detail which were the accompaniment to the tiny morsels of intelligence she brought. For him it was like tugging aside four hundred petticoats until ah! – yes, the ankle. But not today. He banged the edge of the table, which sent the contessa's fan off under her chin.

'Tell me,' he ordered.

'The British girl staying at the Wilsheres' house is a spy.'

'Evidence?'

'Dona Mafalda's seen her wandering the house at all hours and she's lied on her residency form to the PVDE about her father. To them she has said that he is an accountant and alive, to me that he is dead.'

'Is that all?'

The contessa wanted to round it out, give it body and depth, to disguise what in fact she was doing. She attempted to fill the silence. Wolters snapped her shut. He stood to drive her out. Her head ducked and trembled as she became the cringing bitch.

'My family,' she asked, 'have they been found yet?'

Wolters dropped his eyes to her. What was it to be today? Hope or no hope? He felt good.

'They've been found,' he said. 'We'll be moving them shortly. They were in Poland.'

'In Poland?'

'I am busy,' he said, and pointed to the door.

Voss glanced up from the diamond assessor as the contessa left. Samuel Hirschfeld signed a receipt for the small sum he'd been paid for the work.

'I'll go now,' said Hirschfeld, wiping the palms of his hands on his knees.

'Pack your things but wait for one moment.'

Hirschfeld tried to sit back in his seat but couldn't, his acid stomach churned around his ancient ulcers and tipped him forward. Voss took the diamonds and Hirschfeld's calculations across to Wolters, who was standing at his window looking down on the nonchalant but significant activity in the Rua do Sacramento à Lapa.

'Isn't this unusual?' asked Wolters, taking the paper from Voss, pointing to the street. 'I mean they watch us, we watch them, but this . . . this is excessive.'

'They're on to something, sir.'

'Or somebody's told them something,' said Wolters, no vaude-ville menace but quiet, with weight.

'What did the contessa have to say?' asked Voss. 'She was quick today.'

'Yes,' said Wolters, 'I kept her on the leash this time.'

Voss frowned behind Wolters' shoulder.

'It was the usual thing,' said Wolters. 'Telling me things I already know. A baroque recital for a crumb of the obvious. Ach! These revolting people. They lick the hand that beats as eagerly as the one that feeds.'

He shook his hand as if saliva still clung to it.

Voss preferred Wolters in this mood. The man who knew, the man who was in total command of the multiplicity of strands that only his iron fist could hold.

'Today's treat?' said Wolters, over his shoulder. 'Today's smear of caviar on toast?'

'Yes?' said Voss, letting Wolters dangle it in front of him.

'The English girl in Wilshere's house is a spy. Really? Does that Milanese strumpet think we are fools?'

'Clearly,' said Voss, his head crammed full.

'And now this –' said Wolters, nodding at the street, shaking with false mirth. 'Ants.'

He turned his back to the window, a silhouette against the brightness of the day. He threw himself into his chair, stamped his foot.

'We will crush them.'

'The parcel came out at close to one million one hundred thousand dollars,' said Voss.

'That should do it, don't you think?'

'As I'm sure you're aware, you and I haven't discussed anything beyond Lazard flying with these stones to Rio and on to New York, sir,' said Voss. 'Should I know what will happen there?'

'I don't want Lazard to be bothered by any of your people in Dakar,' snapped Wolters. 'Don't have him tailed, he's nervous enough as it is. Doesn't know who's who any more. Let him get to Rio in peace and we'll pick him up there and make sure he gets to New York.'

'And the return journey?'

'That depends on the success of the negotiations.'

'Very good, sir,' said Voss, getting to his feet, hoping to lure Wolters out by his own reticence.

Wolters was disappointed with Voss's deference. He burned with the brilliance of his plan. He wanted Voss to try harder, to work on him, to tease more out of him.

'I understand the need for secrecy, sir,' said Voss, making for the door. 'I can only offer my help.'

'Of course, Voss,' said Wolters. 'Thank you. Yes. This . . . *this* will be the single most important intelligence event of the war and you will have been a part of it. *Heil Hitler.*'

Voss matched Wolters' salute and left with some of what he'd wanted, which was confirmation of his assumption of the day before, that the diamonds were involved in the purchase of the Führer's 'secret weapon'.

Kempf handed Voss the extracts from their dead-letter boxes. Voss read them through. Kempf stood at ease, hands behind back, eyes forward as if on parade.

'What's going on, sir?'

'What do you mean, Kempf?'

'It's like Piccadilly Circus out there, sir. They'll be driving on the left-hand side of the road by the end of the day.'

'I don't doubt it.'

'Beg your pardon, sir?'

'We're getting a little more attention than usual.'

'It's "Ring a ring of roses" out there, sir.'

'What was that, Kempf?'

'It's an English nursery game, sir.'

'You're very knowledgeable, Kempf.'

'Had an English girlfriend before the war, sir. She was the nanny from across the road. They were the only games she knew, apart from . . . but we won't go into that, sir.'

Kempf drifted into a momentary blissful state. Voss smiled.

'I can't tell you anything, Kempf. I'm in the dark myself.'

'The Jew's still waiting, sir. The stone man.'

'Damn,' said Voss. 'I forgot about him. Hein said you made him a promise.'

'You know how it is, sir,' said Kempf. 'I'll move him along then, shall I?'

'I'll go, Kempf. I'll go.'

Hirschfeld was a little wild in the eye by this stage. Voss released him. His little feet clattered down the stairs and didn't stop running until they were beyond the gates in Rua do Pau de Bandeira.

Voss sat in Hirschfeld's vacated warm, damp chair, tapped his lips with a finger. One of the dead-letter drops had revealed that Olivier Mesnel had made a move and not to the caves of Monsanto to perform any of his ghastly acts. He'd gone to an address in Rua da Arrábida off the Largo do Rato.

Voss left the legation. Kempf had been right, the *ardinas* were as good as selling *The Times*. He bought a *Diário de Notícias* and headed downhill, down the cobbled, stepped streets and into the Rua das Janelas Verdes. He turned into the dark, stone steps of the Pensão Rocha and climbed slowly up to the courtyard writing down the address and pushing it inside the newspaper with a twenty-escudo note. He took a seat at a table. The clientele, exclusively men, eyed him over and around their own newspapers, not all of them today's. The waiter, a boy, stood next to him, barefoot, trousers tied up with string.

'Bring me Paco,' said Voss.

The boy walked through the tables, watched by the printed pages of the newspapers. He went into the *pensão* and did not return. Paco appeared some minutes later, a short, dark Spaniard from Galicia, with no forehead between hair and eyebrows and sunken cheeks that had known hunger from birth. He sat at Voss's table, cheap suit, shirt buttoned to the throat, no tie and the faint smell of urine.

'Are you sick?' asked Voss.

'I'm all right.'

'Looking for work?'

He shrugged, looked away, desperate for work.

'I bought you this newspaper. There's an address. I want to know how it's used. Don't take any friends.'

Paco closed his eyes once. One of the newspapers behind him folded, upped and left.

'Any new faces?' asked Voss.

'Not here.'

'In Lisbon?'

'There's been talk of an English girl.'

'Anything?'

'She's a secretary for Shell,' he said, eyes dead, heading towards sleep. 'Lives in a big house in Estoril.'

'Is that it?' asked Voss, putting two packets of cigarettes on the newspaper.

'She's working,' he said, economic.

'How do you know?'

'I've been watching Wallis,' he said, shifting a shoulder. 'I think he's looking after her.'

'Be quick,' said Voss, and got out of there.

Back at the legation there were four cars in the short driveway between the gate and the steps up to the building. Voss went upstairs and stood in one of the front windows overlooking the intersection of Rua do Pau de Bandeira and Rua do Sacramento à Lapa. It was lunchtime and from underneath him people began to pour out of the legation building, an unusual number at once. Some got into the cars, others headed for the gates, which were now fully open. The cars all left in different directions. The streets were suddenly crowded, the *ardinas* flagging left and right in the confusion. In moments there was a traffic jam and people streamed off the pavements in between the cars. Men who had been walking like extras in a movie were now in a farce, looking up and down the four possible exits in complete indecision. Voss walked through the empty building and down the stairs. Wolters met him on the way up, grinning.

'We finally gave them something to do,' he said.

Beecham Lazard leaned against the ship's rail of the small trans-Tagus ferry. There were four cars on board and over seventy passengers. He'd seen his man come on at the ferry terminal at Cais do Sodré and had worked around him from several angles to make sure he was clean. The ferry was crossing to Cacilhas and everyone was on deck to catch the cooler air on the water. The ferry made slow going through the crowded river of cargo boats and liners waiting to dock and the low, muscular tug boats looking for work. Black smoke from a ship's funnel joined the haze on the river, scarfing the high sun. The colonnade of the huge square of the Praça do Comércio behind them was soon vague behind a humid gauze.

Lazard completed another circuit of the ferry and walked into a gap on the ship's rail next to his contact man, who'd been one of the crowd coming out of the legation for lunch. They knew each other by sight. They switched identical briefcases and parted,

Lazard now with the diamonds. Fifteen minutes later Lazard stepped off the ferry and walked to the Cacilhas bus terminal, where he took a ride along the south bank of the Tagus to the village of Caparica and then down to the ferry station at Porto Brandão. He waited there for half an hour until the ferry arrived and took him back across the river to Belém and the old 1940 Expo site. He checked his back walking around the docks, and crossed the railway tracks through the Belém train station. He took a short walk up to a house on the Rua Embaixador.

He'd rented a small apartment on the first floor. He took off his dark grey suit and put on a light blue one. He took a white hat with a dark band out of the wardrobe and laid it on the bed. He closed the other suit and briefcase into the now empty wardrobe. He checked the empty street, picked up the telephone and dialled a Lisbon number. He spoke to a man with a Brazilian accent.

'Did you pick up my laundry?' asked Lazard.

'Yes,' he said, words from a wooden actor, 'and it had all been ironed.'

Lazard hung up, annoyed, and checked his watch. He was running early. Hours to go before check-in. He took off his jacket, moved the hat to one side and lay down. Important thoughts hung in his brain like large harbour fish. His mind drifted through them until he came across something that would help pass the time. Mary Couples kneeling at the foot of the hedge with her dress bunched up around her waist, her underwear stretched between her thighs, the dark crease through her white bottom, the tan lines from her bathing costume, his thumbs hooked around the two straps of her suspender belt, her shoulders lunging forward with each of his thrusts.

Why had she done it? He was quite used to having the lewd suggestions he made to her pearl-studded lobes turned down. Why had she acquiesced suddenly and degraded herself in such a fashion? He was sure she didn't even like him.

From there it was a short hop to the thought that Mary didn't like Hal much, either, and probably not herself too. These thoughts excited him. Could she be pushed further? He entertained himself by making unacceptable proposals to Mary Couples. His hand stroked the seam of his fly as his mind dropped further into his cold, dark world.

181

At 4.30 p.m. he swung his legs off the bed, straightened his trousers, put on his jacket, the white hat and a pair of sunglasses. He picked up a suitcase and briefcase in matching caramel leather, both monogrammed BL in dark red lettering. He walked down to the taxi rank and asked to be taken to the airport where he checked in his suitcase. He sipped coffee in the lounge and picked out the British and German agents loitering in and around the airport building.

At 5.45 p.m. he went to the toilets, urinated, washed his hands until the room was empty and took the cubicle closest to the wall in which there was yesterday's sports newspaper *A Bola* on the cistern. He locked the door, removed his hat and sunglasses and passed them under the cubicle wall with his briefcase. He removed his suit and red tie and the brown English brogues which followed the hat which was still sitting on the floor. His eyes widened. He checked the newspaper. It was the right one. He had a sudden hysterical vision of a stranger staring at a hat, briefcase and a bundle of clothes, puzzled and then affronted, followed by an interview with the GNR in his stockinged feet.

A dark suit appeared under the cubicle wall. A black hat, a dark blue tie, a pair of black Oxfords, no briefcase. Lazard dressed, left the toilets and walked directly out of the building to the taxi rank and took a cab into the centre of town and a train from Cais do Sodré to Belém.

At 6.20 p.m. a man in a light blue suit, white hat and sunglasses, carrying a caramel briefcase with BL in red on the side, boarded the evening flight to Dakar. As the plane took off the exhausted agents from both sides made their reports.

Sutherland, still shaking at the morning's catastrophe, slumped in his chair, beckoning tobacco into his pipe. Rose let himself into the office, leaned over the desk.

'We seem to have clawed something back from that fiasco outside the legation this morning.'

'Lazard's on the plane?'

'Let's hope Voss's intelligence is correct and he has the diamonds with him.'

'Voss has asked for another meeting.'

'Already?' asked Sutherland.

182

'He's rated it even higher priority than last night.'

Voss, having made his dead-letter drop to the British on the way back from the legation, sat in the Estrela Gardens waiting for Paco. He tapped his knee with yet another newspaper, thinking this business was an editor's dream. When this war was over there'd be a circulation drop of a thousand because one thing nobody ever did was *read* the newspapers, which were heavily censored. There was also the question of the Portuguese journalistic style, which was not dissimilar to Wolters' description of the contessa's intelligence reports, except there were the four hundred petticoats and then, damn, no ankle.

Paco dropped on to the bench. He smelt worse, as if he was sweating some disease out of his system – something bad like yellow fever or plague. In fact, Paco had a black rim to his lips on the inside of his mouth, reminding Voss of yellow fever's common name – black vomit.

'Are you sure you're not sick?' asked Voss.

'No sicker than I was at lunchtime.'

'You said you were all right then.'

'I'd been lying down,' he said, resting his knees on his elbows, hunched forward as if constipated.

'So what's the matter?'

'I don't know. I'm always sick. So was my mother and she lived to be ninety-four.'

'Go and see a doctor.'

'Doctors. Doctors . . . they just say: "Paco, with you the good Lord should have started again." Then they charge some money. I don't go to doctors.'

'What about the address?'

'It's a communist safe house.'

'How do you know?'

'They're not careful. The PVDE will find that place in no time.'

'Give it a few days, Paco.'

'*I* won't tell them. Those Reds,' he said, shaking his head, 'they'll advertise it in their magazine, *Avante*, on the property rentals page.'

Paco's face strained into the closest expression he could get to a laugh but only managed to look as if he was passing a belligerent stool.

Voss walked up to his apartment with the uneasy feeling that he could catch something from Paco. That Paco could be the death of him.

Chapter 19

Voss was sitting on the back of his sofa, looking out of the dormer window of his top-floor apartment over the Estrela Gardens and the square in front of the basilica. Anne had already come out of the gardens and he'd recognized Wallis leaning against the railings, reading the predictable newspaper. He was interested to see how she would deal with Wallis, who glanced up as she crossed the square and entered the basilica. Wallis took up a position in the shade by the entrance, lit a cigarette, rested a foot behind him against the wall. Pigeons took off from one of the basilica's towers, performed a circuit, relanded. A nun mounted the steps, brushing past Wallis. Two boys with shaved heads, filthy shirts and bare feet sprinted out of the gardens pursued by a policeman with his truncheon out. His cap came off, bounced off his back. Voss put his hand into the cold, wet towel sling he had hanging from the bolt of the window, testing the cool of the wine bottle. He smoked, flicked ash down the tiles in front of the window.

'How much time do you spend looking out of that window waiting for your girlfriends?'

He twisted and fell back awkwardly on to the sofa. She was sitting in a wooden armchair with her feet out of her shoes. Her face was set hard, not lovely, not how he remembered it in the kind flicker of a match flame. He smiled. This is what he liked about her – always challenging. He started forward but came up against some unseen field which repelled him, pushed him back on to the sofa.

'Where do I fit in?' she asked. 'Which shift?'

He smoked hard, thinking, glancing up at her.

'You can throw one of those across,' she said.

He got up again.

'Throw it.'

He threw the packet, which she caught one-handed. She picked up a book of matches from the table, read the cover. She lit her cigarette.

'The Negresco,' she said. 'You know, Beecham Lazard offered to take me there one night. He said it was *the* place to be seen in Lisbon for elegant couples ... people like, for instance, Judy Laverne and Patrick Wilshere, I should think. Is that where you take yours?'

'My what?'

'Of course, *I* don't even get to see the inside of the Negresco,' she said. 'I get a glass of lukewarm white wine, and then what? I suppose it's bed.'

She glanced at the bed visible through the door to the bedroom, a single, ascetic, hard-looking anchorite's cot, rather than a Lothario's empire bed, decked in shot silk and notched with conquests. She dragged on the cigarette.

'Is this an English thing?' he asked. 'One of those humorous things that we Germans don't understand.'

Her glare was fierce, oxyacetylene harsh. Voss didn't take his eyes off her in case she threw something. He crushed out his cigarette in the ashtray on the table between them. Drew back, slow movements as if with a wild animal. He wasn't sure how to proceed now, like a comedian who's tipped his audience over into tragedy and can't get them back. Her eyes shifted to the bedroom again and then around the living room, taking in the shelf with three books and a family photograph, two landscapes on the wall, the bottle of wine in the towel, the carpets beaten and clean, the dark red sofa with two dents, neat.

'I don't like to be one of a crowd,' she said.

He nodded, taking it in, not understanding. He checked the room, as she had, to see if there were answers amongst his few possessions.

'Are you an honourable man, Mr Voss?'

'I've never been to the Negresco, if that helps.'

She flung the book of matches at him. They fluttered and landed in no man's land.

'I know,' he said, 'but I've never been there. They were given to me.'

186

'Who by?'

'Er, Kempf, I think.'

'*Mein Kempf*, no doubt,' she said.

He studied her, the small, silly, throwaway pun taking its time to work through the confusion of the initial minutes. He blurted a laugh, then a wheezing chuckle, followed by an open-mouthed belly roar and finally silent hysteria, which was fuelled by Anne's maintenance of the steel line of her unsmiling lips. She held it for a minute until Voss's madness filled the room and the thought occurred to her that this was a man who must be kept very short of decent jokes, which set her off. 'I bought some wine,' he said, wiping tears out of the corner of his eyes with the knuckle of his thumb.

'And glasses?'

He left the room, came back with two tumblers. She watched his movements, his face. Boyish. Eager to please. Tenderness, which had been tied up outside the door, managed to creep in and settle under the table.

'I'm thinking,' he said, 'that somebody has told you something about me.'

'That you're a womanizer.'

'Funny,' he said, 'I don't know anybody in Shell. Oh, except Cardew, I know Cardew to say hello to . . . but not to exchange my private life with him . . . and he's married, he wouldn't go to the Negresco, couldn't possibly have seen me even if I had been there.'

They drank the first glass of wine quickly and Voss repoured, Anne with her eyes on him, not letting him go for a second – Sutherland's words gone now, her day on the rack forgotten.

'So you *are*,' she said.

'A womanizer? To be honest, Anne . . . and honourable with you . . . there's been the opportunity here in Lisbon, but not the inclination. I work and I sleep. There's little time in between. Whoever told you . . .'

'They had their reasons,' she said.

'They?' he said. 'A collective attack. It seems one can make enemies in Lisbon without even trying.'

'*He* was being protective.'

'You know what I'd like?' said Voss, looking at the door. 'That in here it's just us.'

There was a pause while all the unwanted guests got out. Anne walked over to where he was sitting on the sofa on trembling legs. She threw her cigarette out of the window and put a hand through his hair while she drained the glass of wine. She kissed him and he groaned as if something had snapped inside him. He pulled her on to the sofa, her neck rested on the back, her hair spread out all over. They kissed madly, knowing that the kissing wasn't going to be enough. Her tumbler rolled across the floor.

Voss pulled away, rested his neck on the back of the sofa, held her hand. Her eyes drifted around the room taking in the softening light, the warm air. She knew that everything was going to happen here, that her whole life was going to take place in this room. He kissed her knuckles, turned to her, spanned her slim waist with his hand, moved it up her ribcage, felt her shivering underneath. She rolled towards him, held his face, searched the fragile contours. He ran a hand down her spine so that she pushed her hips to him. She pulled at the knot of his tie, inexpert, reduced it to a hard nut. He pulled the tie off over his head, tossed it away and found the hem of her dress, the warm, smooth skin of her leg. He watched as she undid his shirt buttons, better with those. She tugged the shirt out of his trousers, pushed her hands up his body. He bent down, kissed her knee, her thigh, each touch of his lips welding him to her. She undid the buttons of her dress so that it fell open. He kissed her stomach, her breasts still encased in their bra. She peeled his shirt back off his shoulders, down his arms, cuffing his hands behind him. He wrestled with himself, like a madman in a straitjacket. She shrugged off her dress, unhooked her bra. He hopped about, tearing off his shoes and socks, threw his trousers, showering money, keys and coins. He pulled her away from the dress which was left open on the sofa, ravaged.

He walked her to the bedroom, took off his shorts and sat on the narrow bed. He kissed her stomach, drew her knickers down her long legs. Their bodies tensed as they touched in full-length nakedness. He kissed her all over, each individual rib, the tiny, hard, brown nipples, while her hands found every bone and muscle in his back.

They looked into each other's faces as he eased into her, the pain twitching around her eyes. She loved his bony hardness, the trace of hair that joined his nipples, the ridges of his stomach straining under the thin, stretched layer of skin. She looked down his body to the dark join and wanted all of him. She brought her knees up and dug her heels into the dents in the sides of his buttocks, spurring him on.

She woke up with her lips on his skin, her head on his chest rising and falling. Beyond the cliff of his ribs, down the flat landscape of his stomach, his penis slept. She reached for it, examined it, played with it, almost politely, until it enlarged and she became more strenuous. Her tongue flickered over the salty skin on his ribs. The tendons in his feet surfaced as his toes curled away from the end of the bed. His thighs twitched, his stomach quivered. She turned to his creased face, his closed eyes, his open mouth straining against the sweet agony so that she had to kiss him, lightly on the lip, while in her hand he leapt.

He rolled and looked through the bedroom door. She was kneeling on the sofa, naked, her elbows up on the window ledge, her face to the evening light, birds sweeping across the square of sky in the frame. His eyes traced the cello of her body. He went to her. She glanced at him over her shoulder and then back to the sky. He put his hands on either side of her elbows on the window ledge, kissed her back, each individual vertebra from bottom to neck, until she trembled. She reached behind, pulled him in to her, rested her chin on her arms, felt her nipples harden against the cracked paint of the window ledge. His hands held her at the cello's waist, the hardness of his thighs feathering against the back of her legs, and the bells started up for evening Mass. He took it as some sort of signal and began in earnest. She braced herself against the window, threw her head back laughing at the profanity of it, the bells so loud they could both shout at the reddening sky and not be heard.

Naked, they sat at either end of the sofa, her knees between his, a single glass of wine on top and a shared cigarette, no light in the room. He'd asked about her family and she was talking about her mother, her real mother, and Rawlinson – but not by name – with his wooden leg. How her mother had got her the job because she didn't want her daughter to hear her with her peg-leg *beau*, helping him off with it at night, leaning it up against the wall and finding her waxing and polishing it in the mornings for him before he went to work. Voss was laughing, shaking his head at the irreverence, never heard a woman speak like this before. He asked about the father, who was dead, nothing more, but she wouldn't look at him.

'I want to get dressed and go for a walk,' she said, 'with you. Like lovers would . . . afterwards.'

'It's not safe here,' he said. 'The city's different. Everybody's watching . . . As you said, oil is sensitive.'

'Oil,' she repeated, eyes wandering.

'It's all right to meet at a cocktail party, Anne, but . . .'

'I want you to call me Andrea,' she said.

'Andrea?'

'Not a question . . . a name.'

Voss stood up and looked out of the window, surveyed the square and what he could see of the gardens. He knelt back down, said the words into her mouth.

'I was interested to see how you'd lose him . . . Wallis.'

'You knew it . . .' she said, their eyes locked.

'I saw you go into the basilica.'

'There's always more than one way out of a church,' she said. 'How long have you known?'

'The contessa gave a report to Wolters,' he said, sad at how work had come back into the room like an engine starting up, ruining silence. 'And others have noticed you.'

'I didn't last very long.'

'Everybody knows everybody in Lisbon by now,' he said, and then as an afterthought, striding ahead: 'All we have to do is hang on, survive, until the end.'

He wiped the thoughts of Beecham Lazard on a plane to Dakar, of another plane that could fly over Dresden just as the leaves were turning red and gold.

'It's already dark,' she said. 'We'll walk. I'll hold on to your arm. I want to show you something.'

'We can't leave together,' he said and gave her directions to a small church in the Bairro Alto.

Olivier Mesnel had spent the afternoon and evening stretched out on the floor. His room was like a furnace, his mattress thin and stuffed with something horrible like half-ground bonemeal, so it was always more comfortable lying on the floor on the strip of frayed carpet. His mind wouldn't leave him alone, wouldn't stop questioning him like some ghastly inquisitor off in the dark. Why had the Russians chosen him for this? How could they possibly think he was capable of such an act?

His stomach was shot, completely burnt away, a rag of threadbare tripe. He would never be the same, digestion was something that had happened to him as distant as learning biology at school. He couldn't remember his last solid motion, he would check the bowl to make sure he hadn't given birth to his innards. He was carcass. Carcass with a mind that scribbled inside, like the mosquitoes at night close to his ear.

He stood on his thin, shaking legs in the ludicrous sleeves of his pants, his buckled chest panting in a dishcloth vest. He stepped into his trousers whose waistband still had residual damp from the morning walk to Rua da Arrábida. Traffic gushed on the Rua Braancamp. He pulled on a shirt and jacket, a dark tie. He dabbed the sweat out of his moustache. He sat on the edge of the torture bed, his pelvis painful to his fleshless buttocks. The revolver which he'd taken delivery of that morning from the local communists lay under the pillow. He slid it out and reminded himself of its workings, checked the chambers, four bullets only. Enough.

'Russians,' he said to himself, a snippet from the tape of his thoughts. 'Why have the Russians chosen *me* to be an assassin? I'm an intellectual. I study literature. And now I fire bullets into people.'

At 9.30 p.m. he found himself sweat-slicked on the edge of the city so unable to control his fear and apprehension that he'd taken to walking backwards for several paces at a time until the inevitable had happened and now one side of him was covered in street dust, his left arm dead below the elbow and an imprint of the revolver on his flank.

Rui and his partner were following Voss's orders and shadowing him from behind and in front, used to the man's problems after all these months. They were bored. They knew, as always, where he was heading. It was a hot night and they didn't want to be out in it, especially not following the Frenchman. When they arrived at the Monsanto hills they let Mesnel get ahead so that he could perform his usual disgusting business with the gypsy boys in the

191

caves. They lay down in the burnt, dry grass and talked about cigarettes which neither of them had.

Mesnel waited for his two shadows as he had done on a number of occasions before when he'd come to these meetings. He satisfied himself that they weren't following, turned away from the caves and began the brutal ascent to the Alto da Serafina and the viewpoint high above the western end of Lisbon. He sat exhausted on a rock and stared open-mouthed at the aura over the city, its dark-crowded edges pricked with light, a view of a different galaxy. Sweat dripped off his chin. He wanted away from this. He wanted Paris. A Paris that would be free in months, maybe weeks. He would have survived the occupation but . . . the Russians had asked him to do this thing. For the Party.

'You can't see the mulberry trees this time of night,' said the American voice behind him, soft, a presence that had been there all the time watching him.

'The worm turns it to silk,' said Mesnel, to identify himself.

'You alone?'

'You know I'm alone. My apostles are down there, as usual, lying in the grass talking about football. Benfica. Sporting.'

The American moved around him, stepped on to his rock and then in front of him, his face not visible.

'So what did you get for me?'

Mesnel sighed. A hot breeze blew from the city bringing stink and pollution.

'You did see your guys?' asked the voice. 'I told you this was the last chance.'

'As you know it's not so easy without a Russian mission in Lisbon.'

'We been through that a few times already.'

'But I did see them, yes.'

'So what did they offer for the opportunity not just to become an atomic power but to prevent the Germans from becoming one, too?'

'They didn't,' said Mesnel, shifting his position, his hand easing over towards the hardness on his left hipbone.

'They didn't?' said the American. 'Do they understand what we've been talking about? That this is a unique opportunity to get on even terms with the United States in the production of an atomic

192

bomb. Did they really understand that? I know you're a university man, but did you tell them right?'

'I told them correctly . . . as you told me. They understand,' said Mesnel, 'but they're not interested.'

'How long have we been talking, Monsieur O?'

'Some months.'

'Some months? It's been nearly five months. And it's after five months that they decide they're not interested?'

'Monsieur, you can't just pick up the phone in Paris and call Moscow. We haven't even been able to call London for four years. Imagine what it's like. It all goes by courier . . .'

'You're boring me.'

Mesnel moved his hand again.

'And don't move.'

'I only want to wipe my face. It's a hot night, monsieur.'

The American, who'd had his hand in his pocket, released the safety catch on his revolver, took it out of his pocket and rested it on Mesnel's forehead.

'What is this?' said Mesnel, bowels liquefying as his own hand closed over the butt sticking out of his waistband. He heard the hammer click back.

'It's a Smith & Wesson revolver, Monsieur O.'

'I'm only the messenger,' said Mesnel.

'Are you?' said the American. 'I don't know who you are any more, but you're not the guy who's brought me a Russian offer which I've been waiting for very patiently for five months.'

'They've seen your sample drawings of the structure of the pile, just as you gave them to me. They had better intelligence themselves from inside the American project. That is all. There is nothing to be gained from shooting me . . .'

'They have better?'

'That's what they said. They have their own people in America.'

The revolver slipped on Mesnel's greasy forehead. He fell to one side. The American fired, grazing Mesnel's head. Mesnel tore out his own revolver but the American was on him. The revolver back in his face, on his eye, jammed into the socket with anger.

'Just the messenger, Monsieur O?'

'Not now, monsieur, please,' said Mesnel, close to tears. 'It's nearly the end of all this. Paris will be liberated in weeks. Please, monsieur, it's nearly all over.'

'I know,' said the American, nearly kind. 'It's just policy.'

A second shot and the whining finally stopped in Mesnel's head.

Rui and Luís had heard the first shot, it brought them to their feet.

'What was that?' asked Rui.

'Don't be an idiot, *homem*.'

'What do you think?'

The second shot.

'I think that the boys in the caves don't have guns.'

They ran down the hill, split up and walked back into the safety of the well-lighted city.

Voss was waiting for her in the shadows of the church in Largo de Jesus. They came together as if they'd been a week apart. She as excited as a child, wrapped her arms around his neck, crushed the tendons. He held her, nearly paternal. She kissed him, moulded herself to him.

'Now can we walk,' she said.

They went behind the church, through the back alleys, across the Rua do Século and into the narrow streets of the Bairro Alto. Relief had come for the people of the Bairro with the cool of the night. Their windows and shutters were open and there was the smell of fried onions and garlic, the grilling of fish. Families murmured on the other side of lace curtains and the tentative plucking of the strings of a Portuguese mandolin joined the rattling of feet on the cobbles.

A woman's voice started up, sang a single tremulous phrase and stopped, as did the people in the street. Women appeared in doorways, dark women, dark as dates, feet bare under their colossal skirts hiding ranks of children. The lovers leaned back against a flaking wall to listen. Another phrase, a wail to silence, the words not discernible, comprehensible only as a terrible sense of loss or the pity of it. The voice rose again. They listened, despite having found what this voice had lost. All love born with an innate understanding of its fragility.

They pushed through the streets, always walking across the steep slope, until they broke out into the Rua São Pedro de Alcântara.

They walked up the hill following the silver threads of the tramlines until they reached the boarding stage of the funicular. They crossed the road and drifted under the dark trees and along the railings of a small park as the lighted carriage of the funicular began its groaning descent.

They were alone. The lights of Lisbon were spread out before them across the Baixa below and up to the medina of the Alfama and the Castelo de São Jorge. She leaned against the railings, dragged him to her by the lapels, wanted to squeeze him into her.

'Is this completely normal?' she asked.

'I don't know,' he said. 'I've only been in love once.'

'Who with?' she asked, those few words opening up an abyss.

'You,' he said, 'crazy.'

She laughed, relief flooding the momentary chasm, and realized the absurd frailty of any commitment. It all hung by threads and words could sabre through them.

They talked, lover's talk. Talk unbearable to the ears of normal mortals with jobs and attic rooms and small coins for the rest of the week. Talk that married people might hear in small snatches in cafés and bars and shake their heads. Talk that might make a wife look at a husband and try to remember if he'd ever said things like that. Talk that was so interesting that Anne forgot there was a world with cigarettes until Karl produced a crumpled packet and they held on to the bars of the railings and smoked.

The Baixa below them began to fill with mist drifting up from the river. Buildings blurred, their lights diffused. The castle glowed in grainy luminescence. Anne leaned back into him, fists clamped to the railings below his.

Karl looked at his watch.

They walked back through the Bairro, the streets and doorways still full of people, Voss nervous now, looking for faces he knew, who knew him. They split up and took different routes back to the Estrela Gardens. Voss ran back up to his apartment and found the gun given to him by the colonel from the Free Poles. He wanted it with him now at all times. He wasn't just protecting himself any more. He put the gun in its cloth back in the tool box in the boot. He picked her up from a dark street by the gardens and took her back to Estoril, the glare of the headlights butting against the sea mist that hung just off the coast. The air cool on that side. He dropped her in a street away from the casino, crushed a kiss on to her lips and took his usual long roundabout route to the gardens of Monserrate.

Chapter 20

There'd been a bad scene in the kitchen at Hal and Mary Couples' small house in Cascais in the late morning. The heat had just worked its way under the roof and there seemed to be nowhere in the house where the distance between them could be described as comfortable. So they stood on either side of the kitchen table, holding on to the chair backs, shouting at each other over a pair of soiled and crumpled knickers.

'Maybe you should ask yourself,' screamed Mary, 'maybe you should ask yourself what you're doing going through my dirty laundry.'

'But I'm not,' said Hal, 'because that was not the crime.'

'Crime? Since when has it been a crime? Maybe that says more about you, Hal Couples, than it does about me.'

'I'm just asking you, who you did it with and why. You tell me and it's finished. We'll work it out and move on from there.'

She leaned over the chair back, heavy breasts. His eyes flickered from her face to her cleavage and back up.

'Beecham Lazard,' she said, a whisper over the crumple of white cotton on the table.

His face twitched on one side as if she'd slapped it.

'You *slept* with Beecham Lazard?' he said, the words coming out piecemeal from his perplexed mind.

'Not *slept* exactly,' she said, straightening up.

'When?' he asked, sharp as a hatchet.

'At the cocktail party.'

'You went upstairs at Wilshere's cocktail party?'

'Not upstairs. We found someplace in the garden.'

Hal squeezed his eyes shut with his fingers and thumb, gripped the flesh over the bridge of his nose.

'I don't get it,' he said to himself. 'I thought you hated Beecham Lazard.'

Mary was unnerved. She'd expected, wanted, a different reaction, more explosive, more physical. If there'd been a crime, there should be punishment. But not this, not reason, because there was no reason, not one that had surfaced in her mind.

'We've been living a long time like this,' she said.

Hal's guts went cold. He reached for the half-smoked cigar in the ashtray, plugged in its chewed end, relit it.

'There's been some pressure,' he said, to get some thinking time, to keep at bay what was coming out in the room.

'The man and wife bit,' she said, and pushed her arms together so her cleavage swelled, 'you know . . . but not.'

Hal puffed hard. What is this? He stared at the underwear, blinked at it. She's cracking up. For Christ's sake, push back the stuffing, doll, we've only got twenty-four more hours of this to go.

'Maybe you should go and pick up the mail,' he said.

She nodded, backed away from the table, turned into the hall. She checked herself in the mirror, applied lipstick. She left the house. He watched her hips walk down the street. He picked up the under-wear, went back to the bathroom and laid it on the lid of the laundry basket where he'd found it. Women don't leave their underwear lying around like that, he thought, and tipped the lid over.

Hal Couples – Harald Koppels – had been an Ozalid salesman in Los Angeles for twelve years when the FBI came to him one night in early 1942 and gave him two options: jail on a spying charge or work for the government. He was divorced and living alone and he could see that this could be the undramatic end to what had been a short life. He took their offer, turned Ozalid inside out for them and GAF and Agfa, too. Handed them all the names of anybody of whom he had the slightest suspicion of spying. He did his bit, but they kept that hook stuck in his gullet and wouldn't let him off. One last job, they said. You're going to Lisbon to look up an old friend. This is your new wife, her name's Mary, she's going to keep an eye on you. What they didn't say was: Don't go to bed with Mary, it makes her nuts. He went to bed with her, but it wasn't what he wanted, so he slept in the spare room and took his fun where he could find it. Mary started to go nuts.

*   *   *

198

Now it was night and they were sitting in the living room, Mary with her feet up on the sofa, reading a fashion magazine, fanning herself with the pages. She hadn't eaten all day, had a stomach full of olive sticks and could have used the dry martinis to go with them. She wanted to talk to him but he'd been in professional mode all afternoon, preparing his product, the strips of microfilm with the plans, the dots with the building specs. He fed film into the seams of the buff envelope, attached microdots to the documents to go inside. She clapped her heel with her shoe, the foot nodding in the corner of his eye, the beat in his ear. He didn't look up.

'Oh, Hal,' she said, back in her wifey voice, 'I can't wait 'til we get back.'

He nodded. She flicked the pages, sighed.

'I'll meet him on my own if you want,' he said, a vague hope.

'It's not what he's expecting,' she said, her voice grating, as if this was a trip to a difficult in-law.

Maybe he should let her have the drink. That might help. He went into the kitchen, fixed two Tom Collins with lots of ice. They drank, but it didn't smooth him out. He finished the work.

'You ready?' he asked.

'As I'll ever be, Hal.'

He put a dark jacket on over his dark shirt, ran a comb through his hair.

'You look nice, Hal.'

He fixed her with a look. She unpinned it, went over to him and brushed off his shoulders, straightened his lapels, made the hair on the back of his neck stand up.

'It was only sex, Hal,' she said from behind him. 'Nothing important.'

'Yeah, but it wasn't part of the brief,' he said. 'We don't know what it means when we get up there. How it's going to affect the deal we're doing with him.'

'It won't mean anything, Hal,' she said. 'Now that I know.'

There it was again.

'Mary,' he said, 'I'm not sure who you are any more – what you want.'

199

'I'm your wife, Hal,' she said, and that worried him. 'All I want is a little kiss and let's get going.'

He went to kiss her forehead but she tilted her head back and fastened her lips on to his, they were wet and cool from the ice, they were sucking, penetrating and their teeth clashed. It was like eating a mollusc on the half-shell.

She brushed past him into the hall. He followed her dark blouse, black skirt, stockings and soft leather pumps. They got into the car and started driving out of Cascais, heading west on the Guincho road. He checked the rear view and her all the way.

He'd tried to make the OSS pull her out, but she was their agent. He'd insisted that her behaviour could threaten the assignment, but of course, when she was with them, she was always fine. 'It's too important for personal considerations,' they'd said. Now look. The woman's mind unravelling like bad knitting.

'We'll be all right,' she said, 'you'll see. After this we'll get back together and it'll just be you and me.'

She rested a hand on his thigh, kneaded the muscle, and Hal's sole inspiration for getting through the night was a decision to just go along with it.

'Florida,' he said.

'The Keys,' she said. 'You ever been to the Keys?'

'Fishing,' he said, and her hand moved higher and the little finger strayed over his fly.

He removed her hand from his crotch, kissed the back of it, held it on his knee and rubbed it with his thumb.

'They run rum up from Cuba,' she said. 'We could do that.'

'I thought you were talking about a holiday.'

'I was . . . but maybe we could live there, you know . . . the two of us on an island.'

He'd have been pushed to spend ten minutes with her in New York City, let alone a lifetime on a Florida Key. She slipped down the leather seat of the car, rested her neck on the back and let her head loll, wanting him to look. Her skirt had ridden up her thighs to the stocking tops. She stretched her legs out and drew her heels back up but this time with her knees open.

'We'll get tight on our rum,' she said. 'Drink all the profit.'

She laughed and took his hand off the steering wheel and put it on the inside of her thigh, part on the stocking top, part on the

200

hot skin. He swallowed. Christ, this is what happens when you go with it.

'We'll do it on the beach in the open air and it won't matter, not like it does here, with all the bathing suit police.'

She drew the hand up to the apex. He yanked it away as if he'd touched red-hot iron.

'Jesus Christ, Mary, where's your goddamn underwear?'

'You know I don't like blasphemy, Hal.'

'Where is it, for God . . . where is it?'

'I don't have any clean.'

'You can't . . .'

'Nobody's going to know.'

He rubbed the side of his little finger which had come into contact with her damp sex. It itched. The car climbed up through the pine trees of the *serra*.

'This is business, Mary,' he said. 'This is the work, now.'

Her face hardened. She sat up, pushed the skirt back down. The one eye Hal could see had a nasty determination to it. They turned away from Malveira and headed towards Azoia.

'Did I ever tell you about Judy Laverne?' asked Mary.

'No,' he said flatly. He didn't want to hear about her from Mary. He'd liked Judy Laverne. She was one of the few people in American IG who'd been spotless, but it hadn't mattered, she was linked to Lazard, the OSS made sure she was fired.

'That's where she came off the road,' said Mary, as they rounded the bend.

Hal changed gear, turned hard right up a dirt track, doubling back on himself. Mary looked down on the old crash site. Hal slowed and dowsed the lights.

'There were no skid marks in the road,' she said. 'The guys from the OSS said that if the car had been moving at speed the impact point would have been much further down the hill.'

'What are you saying, Mary?'

'I'm saying her car was rolled off.'

Hal was driving with his face up close to the windscreen, the darkness impenetrable amongst the pine trees. They crawled along the ridge.

'By who?' he asked.

'Who do you think?'

'Maybe she wasn't moving that fast.'

'Anyway, it's kinda sad, don't you think?'

'What?'

'That she wasn't even working for us. She'd turned us down and they didn't have anything on her, not like they had with you.'

'So why did they roll her off, Mary?'

'It's a mystery, Hal,' she said. 'A sad mystery. She was crazy about Wilshere. Crazy about him.'

Hal stuck his head out of the open window to see if the visibility was any better and because he didn't want to hear Mary any more, not when she was talking about people being crazy about each other.

They connected with another track, turned right and began a slow descent into the back end of the village of Malveira. The first building they came to was a partially built villa which overlooked the rest of the village on the main road below. The house had a roof and walls but the windows were boarded up, the land around full of builder's detritus, not much evidence of recent work.

They took hurricane lamps from the boot and a flashlight. Mary walked on ahead with the envelope containing all the microfilmed plans. Hal pocketed a small revolver which he'd hidden earlier in the tool box and followed her. They let themselves in with a key, which Hal knew where to find. They lit the lamps, put them on a table made of a board supported by bricks. Hal sat on a column of stacked bricks. Mary paced the room. There was some threat in the way she moved, the careful placement of each foot. He tried to think of some small talk to smooth her out but none came to mind in the heat and smell of cement. At 11.30 p.m. a car pulled up outside. Mary went to one of the boarded-up windows, peered through the crack.

'It's Lazard,' she said.

Mary was applying lipstick, using a hand mirror with the torch balanced in a niche in the wall. Hal and Lazard made the usual identifying exchanges and Hal opened the door.

'Hi, Beech,' said Mary.

'Hal . . . Mary,' said Lazard, shaking hands, except Mary kissed him on the cheek, too. He was sweating and she wiped her lips afterwards.

'Hot night,' said Hal.

'I thought it'd be cooler up here.'

They stood around for a moment, uncertain as to how this business should be conducted.

'I don't have much time,' said Lazard, knowing the flight was due to land in Dakar in an hour.

'Give him the envelope, Hal.'

Hal wanted to hit her, keep her mouth shut. Lazard noted the palpable friction, handed over the diamonds.

'I'm just going to have to check these over quickly,' said Hal.

'Sure,' said Lazard, calmer by the second.

'This your place, Beech?' asked Mary.

Lazard nodded.

'Whyn't you show me around while *Hal* does his work,' she said, and wiggled the flashlight, whose beam happened to be on Lazard's thigh. Hal wouldn't have minded breaking her teeth. Lazard shrugged. Hal went to the table, laid a piece of velvet on the board and poured the diamonds on to it. Mary took Lazard by the arm and went off into the house. Hal watched them leave, the torch beam bouncing around the walls, their voices echoing in the distant rooms. He went to work. Minutes passed.

'We're just going upstairs, Hal,' Mary called, sing-song, from deep in the house.

Back to the stones, Hal counting them, making the basic visual tests as he'd been taught, just to make sure he wasn't getting glass. A noise stopped him. A noise over the loud whistling of the cicadas in the hot, still night. Was that grunting? He didn't believe it. He stood up. Mary's voice, loud and clear. Oh! Yes!

She thinks she's goading me . . . Jesus.

He sat down, shaking his head. Only minutes and it'll all be over. Mary's voice cut through, almost a shriek this time, overplaying the pleasure. She never liked it that much. Hal knew.

Silence. A tense, rock-hard silence. Then a crash, bodies upsetting something, falling into or over . . . He took the gun out of his pocket, moved through the ground-floor rooms to the bottom of the stairs. Not a sound inside the walls . . . only mosquitoes or tinnitus.

Hal walked sideways up the stairs, back to the wall, no bannister on the open side. On to the landing, cracks of light around the boarded window on the far wall. The moon up high now outside. Light came from a doorless room, low light, floor height. He stepped into it. The flashlight lay on the wooden boards. He put the gun into the room first. Against the wall, to the right, Mary lay on her front, the wooden board of a workman's table underneath her, the bricks toppled. She had a length of hemp rope wrapped around her neck so tight that her eyes were halfway out of her head. Her skirt was up over her buttocks, black suspenders, disappearing tracks. A black smear from the crack of her bottom that ran down the back of her thigh to her stockings. Blood.

Hal swallowed hard against the gristle of his Adam's apple, acid rising from his stomach. Nobody had mentioned this kind of thing in any of the briefings. The muzzle of Lazard's revolver screwed itself into his neck.

'Oh, Christ,' said Hal, the horizontals going in his mind.

'Kneel down, just there, behind her,' said Lazard. 'I'll take the gun as you go down.'

Hal's legs shook so much he dropped to the floor as if he'd been rabbit-punched. Lazard slipped the gun out of his wet grip and took hold of Hal's jacket collar to keep him steady.

'Now crawl over to her feet.'

The sweat ran off Hal, sweat and tears because he knew this was it. He'd survived, made it through to the last minute and instead of the new beginning, it was the end of everything. Wasted years. Holy Christ. His head was shaking from side to side as he inched towards Mary's fallen heels.

'Drop your pants.'

He undid his trousers.

'And your undershorts.'

He pushed them down and saw, now, what Lazard had done, what he'd done as he held her by the reins of his garrotte. He wanted to vomit.

Lazard put the gun to Hal's temple, pulled the trigger, the noise thunderous and ringing in the room. He let Hal fall forward. He came to rest with his face in the middle of her back, his groin on her buttocks.

Lazard put the gun into Hal's slack hand and took the front-door key from the dead man's pocket.

Downstairs he poured the diamonds back into the bag, cleared the velvet and Hal's eyeglass. He knocked one of the boards out of a downstairs window, locked the house up, got into his car and drove up into the pine forest of the *serra*.

Chapter 21

Tuesday, 18th July 1944, Monserrate Gardens, Serra de Sintra.

Just before midnight Sutherland, Rose and Voss were in the Moorish pavilion sitting on their usual chairs, smoking, apart from Sutherland, and drinking from Rose's steel tumblers.

'Two nights in a row,' said Rose. 'I hope it's worth it. It's no small operation to secure this place.'

Rose always had his difficulties.

Voss was preparing his words, small words which could accumulate to mean a future for Germany and an end to destruction or the bleak possibility of life under the Russian knout.

'Did you make your communiqué to Wolters?' asked Voss.

'You haven't spoken to him?' asked Sutherland.

'Not since that fiasco outside the German Legation this morning, no.'

'Yes,' said Rose, 'what was that all about?'

'Incompetence on a large scale,' said Voss, 'rather than the usual small-scale idiocies, which are an everyday occurrence in the intelligence world. I assumed you thought my services dispensable. What do you think Wolters made of it? He actually said to me that somebody must have told them something.'

Rose and Sutherland stared at the chequered floor. Voss remembered postal games with his father. Chess. Strong central pawn.

'You said last night that there were two possibilities for Germany to achieve a conditional surrender.'

'Did we?' asked Rose. 'I thought we said that we wouldn't drop an atomic device on Dresden if you would give us the means to destroy your bomb programme or you disposed of your leadership. That's not an offer of conditional surrender.'

'Does that mean,' said Voss, getting to his feet, 'that even if we fulfil those conditions you will not open negotiations?'

Silence, as they watched him move towards the door. There was the smell of sea and pine in the room, clean, as if it might have been possible for things to work out after all.

'It would strengthen your position.'

'That doesn't sound like a "yes".'

'But it's not a "no" either, Voss.'

'I have information about a secret weapons programme. I have the locations of our research laboratories. I have very important intelligence about the German leadership. However, before I give you any of this I must have some assurances. Assurances which, after months of us talking and me giving the highest quality information, have still not been given.'

'We're not just British any more, Voss,' said Sutherland. 'We're Allies.'

'I know, but what do I have to show after months of giving you intelligence? No assurances, only an appalling threat.'

'You told us about the V1 rockets,' said Rose. 'You were right. They came. They fell.'

'With conventional explosives. I told you that, too.'

'One of your ... compatriots told us, months ago now, that Hitler would be assassinated,' said Rose.

'Still nothing,' said Sutherland.

'We told you about the U-boats,' said Voss. 'We pushed your false intelligence about the June landings in the Pas de Calais to the German leadership. Every day I receive reams of intelligence from your man sitting in his attic room in Lisbon, concocting his stories about British defences and aerodromes and God knows what rubbish, and I pass it on, as if it's the genuine article, not a word out of place ...'

'Yes, yes, and yes,' said Sutherland, 'but, of that, what has been persuasive enough for us to break agreements with our Allies?'

'Let's be *more* specific,' said Rose. 'With an ally who has so far sacrificed millions of his countrymen to repel an invading army, which in turn has given *us* the opportunity to take the advantage on the western front. If we turn on the Russians now I doubt there'll be peace in Europe for a hundred years.'

'You'll see what'll happen,' said Voss. 'You'll end up with your friends, the Bolsheviks, on your doorstep and you know how it is with them, with Stalin. You can't talk to the man. He'll give you nothing except the cold wind from the steppes.'

'He hasn't failed us yet,' said Rose. 'It would be impossible for us to . . .'

'Tell us, Voss,' said Sutherland, scything through the world politics on which none of them would have the remotest effect. 'By telling us, you at least give yourself a chance.'

Voss had retaken his seat and found that he was now crouched over his knees as if racked by some terrible colic. He sat up and back, drew on his cigarette, drank his drink. That other world came to him, that distant planet less than fifty kilometres away where there had been certainties – a trembling ribcage in his hands and, beyond the bars, the railings, some kind of hope, the faintest possibility.

'You all right, Voss, old man?' asked Rose.

Voss stood up again, another attempt to get away from this, to leave this dried husk, this slough of skin, the knotted nerves and stupid bones underneath.

'Drop of whisky, perhaps, would that help?' said Rose, leaning over with the flask, chugging the spirit in so that it splashed cold on Voss's hand. Voss licked it, found the taste of her in the web between thumb and forefinger and gnawed at it.

'You still there, old man?'

'I look forward,' said Voss, thinking she would be proud of him, 'to seeing you kiss Stalin on his red, moustachioed lips.'

'Now look here, Voss,' said Rose, and Voss did, daring him, thinking where's your sense of humour now, Richard *verdammt* Rose?

Sutherland held up his hand between the two men.

'We are Lisbon station, Voss. That is who and all we are. We communicate everything back to London. We are not able to make political decisions or offers. We can only do what we are told. London is very appreciative of your intelligence . . .'

'We are helping you win the war,' said Voss. 'A war that is nearly over, that will see Europe change, that could see – if you persist with your romantic attachment to the East – half of it sheafed under the scythe and beaten with the hammer. Is that what you want?'

'Very poetic,' said Rose, deadpan.

'It's not our decision,' said Sutherland. 'We put your case, believe me. We put your case very strongly.'

'And my reward?' asked Voss, holding out his hands. 'An atomic device will be dropped on Dresden. I thank you for it.'

'Long night ahead of us, you know, Voss,' said Rose, walking behind Sutherland to the fireplace.

'What we *can* do,' said Sutherland, 'is look after *you*.'

'Look after *me*?'

'Here in Lisbon,' said Rose. 'You know how it is when you start losing a war. Start spit-roasting the traitors.'

'For God's sake, Richard,' said Sutherland.

Rose crossed his legs at the ankle, made a suave Noël Coward gesture with his cigarette hand. 'It's true, isn't it?'

'You could be comfortable in Lisbon,' said Sutherland.

'As long as you like your women *morena*,' said Rose, staring into him.

Their argument twitched in Voss's mind. They know something. Wallis must have seen something. But when?

'Do you think my personal safety has been an issue in any of this?' asked Voss. 'Do you think I play this game to save my own skin?'

Sutherland felt instantly shabby, disgusted. Rose, not so.

'It's an option,' said Rose, light as duck down.

These men are no better than SS Colonel Weiss at Rastenburg, thought Voss. Not only is there never any credit with them, but they're paid . . . they're paid not so much to open the chink into the light, but more to find the slimy crevice into the sweaty cavern of men's shameful needs.

'What he means,' said Sutherland, nauseated by Rose himself, 'is that we will make sure you don't go down. If they're closing in on you and we hear about it, we'll get you out.'

'But that is not why I am here. I thought you understood that,' said Voss, directly to Sutherland. 'I'm here . . . I'm here . . .'

'Yes?' said Rose.

Why was he here? What was his motive? He'd never examined it to be put into words. He'd only assumed it. His country? No, that wasn't right. That wasn't precise.

'Why *are* you here?' pressed Rose, taking delight in Voss's discomfiture.

'I'm here because of my father,' said Voss, and nearly wept at the thought of it. 'I'm here because of my brother.'

Sutherland looked mortified. Rose had hoped for something more kitsch – I'm here to save my country from the Russian bear – that would have satisfied. That could have been punctured.

Voss resumed his seat, looked around the room, felt the quality of their silence. Rose? Damn him. Sutherland. He'd tell Sutherland.

'A new type of rocket will be launched at the end of next month,' said Voss, speaking before he was even aware of it himself. 'It's long range and, unlike the V1, which I understand has been named the doodlebug, it is totally silent. It also weighs fourteen tons.'

'Fourteen tons!' said Sutherland.

'Now come on, Voss,' said Rose. 'What's going to be the payload on something like that? Don't tell us . . .'

'I *am* telling you, if you're prepared to listen. It is these rockets that Hitler is calling his miracle weapons, *but*,' he said, raising a finger, 'they will still be carrying conventional explosives.'

'Where are the rockets?' asked Sutherland, cutting Rose dead.

'Underground. They're in the Harz mountains, not far from Buchenwald. They'll be nearly impossible to destroy from the air.'

'I can't believe . . .' started Rose.

'You'll *have* to believe me.'

'So what is Wolters buying from Lazard?' asked Rose. 'Don't tell us Lazard's coming back with a million dollars' worth of TNT.'

'Lazard is out of our hands now. You'll only find that out when you pick him up in New York. I doubt, if he has any sense, that he'll be wandering about with a case of atomic material.'

'It's an interesting coincidence, though,' said Rose. 'The new, bigger rocket and Lazard's trip.'

'That's why you have to be careful . . . not to lose Lazard,' said Voss. 'Either way you might like to bomb the research laboratories in Berlin-Dahlem. It will give you small satisfaction. I've told you again and again, and you must know from your own research, that the industrial activity to produce the substance of an atomic bomb would be enormous. Unmissable. Germany has neither the money nor the material.'

'But you have Hahn and Heisenberg.'

'They are scientists, not wizards. They are just like Dornberger and von Braun.'

'The rocket men?'

'The difference with Dornberger and von Braun, though, is that *they* have the necessary materials to build rockets. The other two men only have a small half-working cyclotron, a little heavy water left from Rjukan. Even their precious uranium will be thrown at the enemy now that the wolfram supply has been closed off.'

Sutherland checked his watch.

'You said something about the leadership.'

'What time is it?' asked Voss.

'Past midnight.'

'Tomorrow on 20th July some time before midday, Hitler will be assassinated by a bomb planted in the situation room at his headquarters in Rastenburg,' said Voss, calmer about it now, but still expecting to make a big impression.

'How many times did we hear that from Otto John in March?' jeered Rose.

'But not from me . . . now,' said Voss. 'The assassination will launch Operation Valkyrie. I will arrest or shoot SS General Wolters and any other SS men in the legation. At that point, gentlemen, I hope and presume we will be able to start our proper negotiations.'

'And if the assassination attempt fails?' asked Sutherland.

There was a knock on the glass of the door. One of the agents under the colonnade asked permission to interrupt. Rose went outside, talked to the man behind the closed door.

'To answer your question,' said Voss. 'Few of us, if any, will survive but it will be a deliv—'

Rose wrenched the door open, slammed it shut behind him. The glass rattled in the frame.

'Lazard wasn't on the plane when it landed in Dakar,' he said.

Chapter 22

Anne walked the warm, quiet streets until she came out into the casino square. She skirted the parking area, keeping to the deeper shadow beneath the dark spread of the trees. She was looking for Jim Wallis but he wasn't there, not sitting in any of the cars. She went into Wilshere's garden, through the gate. Waited. Still no Wallis. She knew she should go back up to the house and get some sleep before working on the safe in the early hours of the morning but she didn't want to see Wilshere. She went down to a café in the square, straightened herself out in the ladies room and looked for Wallis, expecting to see him in the bar looking after her again. She found an empty table, ordered a brandy and soda. Still no Wallis, but people. She needed to be amongst people. She stayed there until the waiters started turning up the chairs. She walked back up to the house and sat in the darkness of the bower until 1.00 a.m.

She took the shoes off her aching feet and went back up to the house whose windows were dark. She thought about the safe, wondered if she should just go straight in now and open it, but exhaustion hit her as she tripped across the lawn and she stood for a moment rolling her head on her shoulders, thinking of Voss and the room over the Estrela Gardens. Her eyes were half-closed ready for sleep when she went up on to the back terrace, nudged into a piece of the garden furniture which jabbed her thigh.

'Ah,' said Wilshere, as if he'd been waiting all evening, relief in his voice. 'Been working late?'

She was irritated to find him there, sitting at one end of a bench with bottle and glass in front of him, two packets of cigarettes piled on the table.

'I went out with someone from work.'

'Where did you go?'

'The Negresco,' she said. 'I'm tired.'

'Shell must be paying well these days,' he said, and patted the bench beside him. 'Have a seat.'

'I've had a long day.'

'Drink?' he asked.

'I just want to go to bed.'

'Just a quick one. Keep an old man company on a long, hot night.'

She dropped her shoes, sat on automatic, yawning.

'Nothing complicated, if you don't mind,' he said. 'Have to get it myself. Servants really are off tonight.'

'All of them?'

'Like to be alone sometimes,' he said. 'You don't know what a strain it is to be with people all the time. Never have the place to yourself. Never . . . private. So . . . every so often . . . we pack them off. They've all got families around here. Bit of peace and quiet. Remind myself how to make a sandwich.'

He made her a brandy and soda, which she didn't really want. He lit cigarettes, sat on the bench with his arm along the back.

'They say the weather's going to break,' he said.

'There was a fog in Lisbon.'

'Yes, that's supposed to mean something but I can't remember what.'

His finger came to rest on her shoulder. She glanced at it, set her jaw. She shifted her shoulder while crossing her legs and looked him in the eye, so that he'd know that these invasions were not allowed any more. It signalled something to him. He held her look, returning her cold, hard stare with a slack, expressionless face. The sexual confidence she had to stare him down vanished, and was replaced by undiluted panic. It wasn't her life she was afraid of losing so much as everything that had just started. To be nothing now, to cease to exist after the beginning of something new would be terrible. She turned away from him.

'Why am I here?' she asked, taking a large slug of the brandy, needing a bottle to see this one out. 'Why did you invite me to come and stay at your house?'

'To spy on me,' he said, quite calm.

Her breathing shallowed, the blood drained out of her lips, how cold they went. She put the cigarette to them knowing from her short study of the history of spying that nobody says something like that without having drastic intentions.

'Spy?' she said, a lame effort at denial.

'Cardew's an amateur. Most of the rest of them think they're not. Rose, Sutherland, all the people they've sent to my door. Do you think I could have supplied Germany with diamonds throughout the war without knowing who's who in the SIS and all their stupid tricks? Amateurs, the lot of them. The local drama group could do better.'

It was so still, not even the smoke moved off. Her brain crashed through the possibilities. All she'd heard in this house had been gifted to her. Parcelled. Not one piece of unconsidered information. Lazard. The diamonds. New York. If that was so, there were no variables left. She worked out the equation. Lazard – American IG – Ozalid. Lazard had known Hal Couples before. Hal Couples, still working for Ozalid, had picked something up and was now selling it for the diamonds supplied by Wilshere.

'Hal Couples,' she said.

'Bravo,' he said and clapped, a slow sardonic clap. All he could manage for the local drama group.

'What does he have that's worth that sort of money?'

'Nuclear know-how,' he said. 'The core to the atomic apple. Don't ask me the ins and outs.'

'You'd let Lazard sell that to the Germans?'

'You're too involved with your own game to see what's happening on the other pitch.'

'What other pitch?'

'Anything the Germans do to bring closer a united Ireland is fine by me,' said Wilshere. 'They can reduce London to ashes and we'll run the dogs out of the north.'

She needed to talk. That would extend things. She had to unbalance Wilshere but even then, no Wallis, no back-up.

And why me? That was another thought that was not helping her.

Wilshere moved down the bench, put his arm all the way around her, his warm dry palm cupped her shoulder – no sex, avuncular now. The only idea that came up in her head and wouldn't go away was Judy Laverne, Wilshere's weakness.

Why not play out her theory? What had been her greatest fear had probably been Wilshere's too. Keep twisting the blade stuck in his ribs, see what happens when steel grates against bone.

'There was somebody, wasn't there, who got through?' she said.

'None of them . . . they were all hopeless.'

'You're forgetting Judy Laverne. She was a professional. When did you find out about her?' she said, and Wilshere's arm flinched.

'Find out what?' he asked.

'That Lazard wasn't quite telling you the truth.'

'Lazard?' he said, more intrigued.

'He tried to persuade you that she was seeing other men, didn't he?' she said, dredging up the diary. 'He must have known she was a spy, though. Why do you think he'd do a thing like that? Or maybe you know already.'

She could almost hear him blinking. He gripped her arm hard, squeezed the flesh.

'You wouldn't have thought that someone like Beecham Lazard would bother with Shakespeare.'

'Shakespeare?' he said, confused.

'*Othello*,' she said. 'He doesn't seem the cultured type, does he? I think it must have just been an innate understanding of the . . . of the manipulative power of jealousy. I suppose if he'd done it the other way round – told you that she was a spy first – he wouldn't have had the same measure of control over you, would he? And that's what Lazard's after in all his dealings, isn't it? Control. Whose idea was it to get me to come and stay, yours or his?'

'I know what you're doing,' he said.

'*You* are hurting my arm,' she said, feeling stronger now.

He stopped squeezing, stroked instead.

'What's going to happen to you has already been planned,' he said, 'but keep talking, you're amusing me.'

'But you don't answer, do you?' she said. 'I don't think you're being fair.'

She reached for her drink. He grabbed at her arm, then let her pick up the glass, put it down for her. They smoked.

'I was relieved at first,' said Wilshere.

'That she was a spy?'

'It explained everything,' he said, and Wilshere's confirmation spooled out the ramifications.

215

'Except one thing, surely.'

'Ye-e-es,' he said, and never had the affirmative been so despairing.

'How did it come out . . . that she was working?'

'Beecham caught her. She got careless one day, disturbed things on his desk, which made him watchful. So eventually he left the office and came back suddenly to find her . . . *in flagrante.*'

'What was she looking for?'

'The diamond trail. There're two ways to stop rockets falling on London. One is to bomb the launch sites, except that bombing isn't accurate and rebuilding the damage is comparatively easy. The other way is to stop the rockets being built in the first place. Cut off the diamond supply, no more precision tools . . . end of rocket programme.'

'How did the Americans know that Lazard was the broker between you and the Germans?'

He seemed on the brink of an automatic answer but then stopped to think. Maybe it wasn't so obvious.

'They knew about him from when he was an executive at American IG.'

'I mean specifically diamonds?'

'I suppose it must have just . . . They knew he was handling a lot of business for the Germans . . . so they put her in there.'

'But who told you she was after the diamond trail?'

'Lazard, of course.'

'But how did she get to you? I'm sure Lazard doesn't leave notes around his office saying four hundred carats of diamonds from Wilshere received 20th May 1944, does he?'

'I think . . . I think what it was . . . it was that she saw Lazard and I together in the casino.'

'One of your little transactions with the high-denomination chips?'

'Yes.'

'And the only way she could think of getting close to you was to fall in love with you?'

Wilshere's cigarette travelled to his lips on trembling fingers. He drank heavily from his glass, topped it up again from the bottle.

'Lazard caught her, as I said. She talked her way out of it brilli-

216

antly. She was so . . . charming . . . so vivacious. It was impossible not to believe every word she said. Lazard accepted her cover story and that night came to see me. He said . . .' Wilshere swallowed hard, 'he said she had to be . . . what were his words? Neutralized, that was it . . . she had to be neutralized before she could be pulled out. I was vehemently against it. I didn't . . . I couldn't believe it . . . And, I mean, why kill her? What did she really know, after all? Let her go, I said. But Lazard said that it wasn't the way things worked, that he had to know what she knew, and what the Americans knew about his operation, so that he could protect his business. I still couldn't accept it. He said: "You'll see, Paddy, she'll be here tomorrow telling you she's got to go . . . mother's dying or something, and that'll be it. We'll be exposed." What else did he say? Yes . . . that was it: "I know you're sweet on her, Paddy," he said, "but she's a spy. Whatever there is between you and her isn't real, not from her side anyway. We're going to have to cut her out." My God, as if she were a cancer or something.

'I saw her that night. We met in the casino. We danced, played cards, some roulette, had a few drinks. I walked her home. We made love in her single bed and, you know, she wasn't just calm . . . she was serene. She was serene and appeared deeply happy. Lazard was wrong, I thought. He just had to be wrong.'

Wilshere hugged Anne to his chest. Smoked the cigarette down to his fingers, which were steadier now that the story was coming out. He lit another and drank more. Anne was silent, her desperate thoughts being interfered with now by Karl Voss and whether that was 'real' and how do you know what's true about anybody anyway? Karl Voss hadn't known about his father's first love. Throwing his ashes on a stranger's grave. And, unbidden, like a piece of dream from the night before that suddenly becomes clear, the image of Mafalda appeared, taking the clay figurine out of her hands, the blindfolded woman – *Amor é cego*. Love is blind.

'The next day Lazard called to say that Judy's visa had not been renewed by the PVDE. She had two or three days to leave. We both called Captain Lourenço but he claimed it was out of his hands. There was nothing he could do. Lazard went to see him, offered money . . . nothing. We knew then it was political. Lazard offered Lourenço money just to tell him why she wasn't getting a visa. He said one word – *Americanos*. It was as Lazard had said . . .

217

they were pulling her out. Later Lazard found out there was a petrol contract attached to the deal. I was sick. I did actually vomit. Lazard said we had to act. He told me to get her to drive up in her own car to Pé da Serra . . . that it would be our last day's riding out on the *serra* or something like that. He met us there.'

Wilshere stopped for a moment, his eyes fixed on something so far away that it had to be in the middle of his mind. His grip tightened again on Anne's shoulder. Anne needed the support. Terrible things were happening to her. There was no part of her body that wasn't reacting to the appalling realization of what had happened, that only she, at this moment, understood. Her flesh stood away from her, the body's covering repelled by the calculations of the mind. Air was hard to come by, or she couldn't get the necessary oxygen from it. Wilshere ploughed on, unmoved.

'I spoke to Judy first. She denied everything. She was very convincing, but as soon as I started the questions I saw the fear in her. And she did everything she could, everything. She told me how much she loved me, how I should come with her to America, how different it would be over there, away from the war. And . . . and . . . I didn't believe a word of it. Her fear in that first instant. It was something terrible. I'd reached the pinnacle, the zenith of . . . total love and in that moment it was all dust.

'Lazard took over. He took her off to the stables. He said I shouldn't go. I didn't go. I couldn't watch that. He had to find out what he had to. He tied her up, beat her. I didn't . . .'

He shook his head, denying it all. The part that hadn't happened. Anne was shaking, her heart pattered fast and tight, fingers on a hard drum skin. Wilshere consoled her, rubbing her arm, feeling the goose flesh.

'Lazard put her in the car. She was barely conscious. He forced brandy down her. He drove her to the Azoia junction. I followed in Lazard's car. Lazard pushed me to help him drag her across into the driving seat. I couldn't bring myself to touch her. He sent me back to the car to get the jerry can he had in the boot. He told me cars don't burst into flames on their own. He poured the petrol in all over her. She was slumped over the wheel, the back of her dress all torn and bloody. The petrol fumes brought her round and she flung herself back and it splashed over her face and hair. She started coughing and spluttering and I didn't hear it at first. But even then she was saying . . . she was saying: "But I love you, Patrick. I love you.'"

His voice cracked, and he coughed against the emotion in his chest.

'We pushed the car to the edge. Lazard gave me the matches. He was holding the steering wheel. I lit the match and as the wheels went over I tossed it in. I tell you – it went up like a bomb.

'We drove back to Pé da Serra. I got drunk. I got so drunk I woke up in the stables, lying on the cobbled floor in the morning fog and I didn't know who or where I was.'

Anne started to struggle but Wilshere crushed her to him so that she thought her chest wall would collapse under the pressure. She went limp. Fell across him. He kissed her temple, stroked her hair. She sobbed into his shirt.

'Why are you crying?' he asked.

She couldn't speak. She held on to him and wept. He cradled her, strangely . . . paternally.

'Lazard will be here soon,' he said.

Anne sat up, still choking. She drank the brandy down in two gulps, wiped her face with the back of her hands.

'Don't run away,' said Wilshere, who got up and brought the brandy bottle over.

He poured her a large measure.

'No soda,' she said, and lit one of his cigarettes.

Wilshere put the bottle on the table, breathed in the still night with a sense of relief, as if he'd come to terms with something. The brandy glass rattled against her teeth. He took it from her. She brought her heels up on to the edge of the bench and hugged her knees.

'I'm going to tell you something now,' said Anne. 'I'm going to tell you something you won't believe.'

'Then why tell it?'

'Because it's the truth and it's something you should know, even though you might find it hard . . . you might find it unbearable.'

'Believe me, Anne, when I tell you that I can bear anything now. Anything. Nothing is unbearable to me.'

'But not this,' she said. 'Not this.'

'Tell me.'

'The report I made to Sutherland on Monday afternoon about

my first weekend in your house ... the first part of it ... was all about Judy Laverne. You know why. You knew what you were doing. I was very worried about the significance of your actions. I thought I was vulnerable. Sutherland, to try and calm me down, told me what he knew about Judy Laverne. He said that she used to work for American IG where Lazard was an executive until after Pearl Harbour. The OSS decided that the company represented a security risk because of its German connections and had to be cleared of all spies and vetted. Judy Laverne subsequently lost her job, probably because of her link with Lazard, who'd been asked to leave on suspicion of dealing for the Germans. When Lazard heard, he invited her over to Portugal to work for him.'

She stopped. Wilshere had drawn up a chair and was sitting opposite her, staring into her as if she was a prophet and every word counted towards his salvation.

'Go on,' he said, desperate to hear more about Laverne. 'Go on.'

'She arrived in Lisbon, started working for Lazard, and the OSS made an approach. They asked her if she would pass on information about Lazard's business dealings. She refused point-blank. She was totally loyal to Lazard, who'd helped her out with a new job. The OSS didn't have anything on her. They left her alone. I asked Sutherland about her deportation order. He said the Americans categorically denied that they had anything to do with it. The first time I met the contessa, you remember I helped her to the car, and as I closed the door for her she said: "Be careful with Senhor Wilshere or Mafalda will have you deported, just like she did Judy Laverne."'

Wilshere's chair shot back away from him. He stood holding on to his head. Anne was not sure whether he was trying to stop hearing what she was saying or whether he was trying to wrench out what he'd just heard. The lines of his face deepened in his agony, as if he'd felt that first tightening in his chest, a prelude to what could only possibly mean death.

'How conclusive was Lazard's proof to you that she was a spy?' asked Anne. 'From what you've told me, you accepted *his* word on everything. But did he actually *show* you anything and did she ever, even in her direst moment, even as Lazard beat her in the stables, even as she went over the edge soaked in petrol, did she ever admit anything that would lead you to believe that she was a spy?'

Wilshere was staring at her through the bars of his fingers, a man caged by his own torment.

'Did he?'

If he did, Wilshere couldn't think of it, didn't have to think of it. He knew.

'You said that it was her fear when you finally questioned her that made you believe in what Lazard had told you, that changed your love to dust. Wouldn't *you* be scared if your lover suddenly made these accusations, wouldn't *you* find that the most terrifying experience, that the man you love more than yourself is questioning your trust? It would be like a dagger in my breast,' she said, 'it would be like seeing the life flowing out of a mortal wound.'

'Shut up!' he said, almost a hiss from behind his hands.

'*Amor é cego,*' she whispered. 'Lazard at least knew that.'

Wilshere didn't seem to know where to put himself, like a man with barbed wire insides, every inch of life was a writhing torment. He dropped to his knees, crawled to the table as if he was remembering the benefits of prayer from a religion he'd dropped decades before. His face came out from behind his hands. He looked like one of Dante's heroes.

'But why?' he said. 'Why?'

Anne barely had to think. Her day on the rack after she'd been told of Voss's womanizing came back to her. The moment that he'd said he'd only been in love once. There was only one answer.

'Because Lazard was in love with her himself.'

No other words could have had that effect. They were so evidently true that they had a calming influence on Wilshere. He stood up, dusted his trousers down, drank a finger of scotch and looked at her, looked through her.

'I don't have any proof of that, Mr Wilshere,' she said, feeling stupid using his name formally like that when they'd just been so close, closer even than lovers could ever hope to get. 'How could I?'

'Of course not,' he said. 'I see that. Nobody could have known that . . . except me.'

'Did Judy Laverne say something?'

He smoothed his moustache with thumb and forefinger, madly, obsessively until all amusement from those turned-up points had been ironed out of it. Throughout this exercise he nodded, as if he had a tic in his mind. Then his face relaxed, his head turned away from her and a smile wandered across his lips.

Beecham Lazard walked up the steps on to the terrace. He was carrying a briefcase and a jacket. He was sweating, but the machine-tooled parting was still in place.

'You look hot, Beecham,' said Wilshere. 'I'm afraid we don't have any ice out here. Can I get you a drink?'

'You know what I'd really like, Paddy,' he said, without bothering to correct himself, using the name Wilshere didn't like. 'I'd really like a bourbon. But I guess that's out of the question, so I'll take a scotch and . . . be generous, Paddy, we're celebrating. I got the plans.'

Lazard waved an envelope as Wilshere handed him the drink. They all stood. The men touched glasses, ignored Anne.

'Let's go to the study,' said Wilshere. 'We'll finish the business there. You'll have to come too, my dear. Can't have you slipping away.'

They carried their glasses up the corridor, filed into the study, Anne in the middle, Lazard prodding her in the back with his finger so that she turned on him.

'You're not my problem,' he said quietly, just between the two of them.

'Problem?'

'I was never wild about the idea of using you,' he said, 'although . . . you're prettier than Voss.'

'Voss?'

Lazard and Anne sat in chairs in front of the desk. Wilshere leaned against it, stared intently at Lazard, who'd put the briefcase on the floor, settled with his jacket and the envelope across his lap, and was sipping scotch unaware of Wilshere's attention. A floorboard creaked above their heads without concerning either man.

'I figured we didn't need two lines of communication to the boys at Lisbon station,' Lazard said to Anne. 'Voss was enough, but Paddy wanted you, didn't you, Paddy?'

'Voss is with the Abwehr,' said Anne.

'Don't tell me you didn't know he was a double?' said Lazard, laughing. 'That's how the limeys operate, isn't it, Paddy? Nobody knows what anybody else is doing. It makes life easier for people like us.'

'Why did you need me as well?' Anne asked Wilshere.

'Because,' said Lazard, leaning over the arm of his chair, 'he was very disappointed by somebody else and he thought the Allies should be made to pay for that.'

'I was having a very interesting conversation with Anne, here, before you arrived, Beecham.'

'Oh yeah, what was that about?' he asked, uninterested.

'Well, naturally she was concerned about her future so she was doing a lot of thinking and talking in the hope that she would be able to persuade me that it wasn't going to be necessary for her to be ... what's that word you use again, Beecham? It always escapes me.'

'Neutralized.'

'Yes, neutralized. Nobody likes to be neutralized. Made neutral. Neutered. I suppose all those words come from the same ... Latin *ne ... uter* ... not either.'

'I don't know what you're getting at, Paddy.'

Nor did Anne.

'We got to talking about somebody else, whom we'd had to neutralize ... because she'd proved herself untrustworthy,' said Wilshere. 'My disappointment, you call her.'

'You know, time is not on our side, Paddy.'

'Anne told me it wasn't the Americans who arranged for Judy's visa not to be renewed. It was Mafalda. And you know, come to think of it, she'd be one of the few people with influence who could ... yes, family's very important here, Beecham. Your name gets you a long way, even with people like Captain Lourenço – *especially* with people like Lourenço ...'

'I really have to move now, Paddy.'

'You've got nothing to say to that ... Beech?'

'Look, I just came by to tell you we're celebrating ...'

'Is that the only reason you came by ... Beech?' asked Wilshere. 'It's something I've been thinking about. Why does Beecham Lazard have to come and see me tonight, his last night in Portugal? Is it to celebrate and say goodbye? Just that?'

223

'Apart from a few little things we gotta tie up, yeah, I think that's it.'

'Are you sure it's not because you had to take one last look at your masterpiece?'

Wilshere was being very strange. Lazard saw it, too.

'I don't collect art,' said Lazard.

'*I* am your masterpiece,' said Wilshere, and Anne's skin came alive – the scalp clung to her head, the hair straining against it.

Lazard's face went dead, only his eyes darted around the room, from Anne, to Wilshere, to the safe. His waxy cheeks twitched out a laugh.

'I asked Anne this question,' said Wilshere " 'What sort of a man would tell another that his lover was seeing other men, then tell him that she was spying on him, and when her visa is not renewed tell him that it was her spymasters pulling her and then not just make him complicit in the murder of his lover but actually get him to light the match, to burn her alive? What sort of a man would do that? *Why* would he do that?" And you know what she said?'

'Paddy, you just *told* me this girl has been trying to get herself off the hook . . .'

'Listen to this line, Beecham, the words . . . are you ready? She said: "Because he was in love with her himself." How does that sound to you?'

Wilshere was standing over him now, tall, wild, as if he'd been out riding on a blasted heath all night.

'Are you OK, Paddy?'

'No, I'm not,' he said, dropping his hands on to the arms of the chair, pushing his face up close to Lazard's. 'You know what Judy Laverne said to me after the third or fourth time we made love? No, you don't, because she would never have said it to you, she could never have been that blunt. She said: "Beecham's got a crush on me . . . he's kind of in love with me, but . . ." '

Wilshere coughed, wretched, gasped. Lazard's arm had shot out and buried itself in Wilshere's crotch – in it was the Smith & Wesson revolver. Wilshere staggered back, thumped against the desk, dropped to his knees holding on to himself.

'Want to be neutered, Paddy?' said Lazard. ' "Not either"? Is that what you want?'

Lazard locked the door, put the key in his pocket. Wilshere was doubled up. Lazard kicked him hard in the leg and toppled him over.

'Get over to that safe, Paddy,' said Lazard, and kicked him again. 'Go on, Paddy.'

He laid into him with his feet, both feet, and then he trampled on him, jamming his heels down into the inert body, strutting and jabbing as if he was a ram asserting his mating rights. Anne rushed at Lazard. He grabbed hold of her front – dress, bra and breast – flung her across the room.

He hauled Wilshere across to the safe.

'Open it, Paddy. Open the safe.'

'She said ... she said ...' Wilshere struggled to get the breath to talk, 'she said, "I like Beecham, I like him a lot. He's been very good to me, but physically ..." Are you listening to this? "But physically ... he disgusts me." Did you get that, Beecham? "He disgusts me."'

Lazard raised the revolver.

'You hit or shoot me and you'll never get this safe open,' said Wilshere.

Lazard strode across the room, sheafed Anne's hair, wrapped it around his fist and dragged her to the safe.

'Was that what you couldn't bear, Beech? That there she was with me, a man more than twice her age, and it wasn't you and it would never be you.'

Lazard tore a bottle of brandy out of the cabinet above the safe and poured it over Anne's head.

'Do you want to see this again, Paddy? Do you? Do you want to watch another one of your beauties burn?'

He took a Zippo lighter out of his pocket, flicked it open and swiped it across his leg. The flame came up a lazy yellow.

'That's enough, Beecham, I'm opening the safe. Put out the light,' roared Wilshere. 'I said, put out the light!'

Lazard waved the flame, the brandy was vaporizing quickly in the heat. Anne was paralysed, the smell strong as ammonia in her nostrils. He clicked the Zippo shut, threw Anne down, across the floor in front of him. Wilshere pulled himself up to the safe, entered the combination into the dial. Lazard brushed the muzzle of the revolver up and down Anne's leg, pushing the hem of the dress up further each time.

'Look at this, Paddy,' said Lazard.

Wilshere opened the safe, tugging on the heavy door. He reached in and closed his hand around the revolver he kept in there, thumbed back the hammer. There were no further questions he had for Lazard. He turned. Lazard looked up from Anne's exposed leg. The bullet, which should have gone through his head, tore Lazard's throat out. He fell back, dropping his gun, applying both hands to the massive black haemorrhage where his Adam's apple used to be. A gargling, coughing noise broke from Lazard's body as his hands panicked around his throat, trying to stem the gouts of blood.

'Get the door key,' said Wilshere, grim as winter.

Anne crawled over to Lazard, searched his pockets, the body now in some terrible state of spasm as life clung on, or struggled away.

'Open the door,' said Wilshere. 'We're going to finish this all now.'

He grabbed Anne's wrist and dragged her past the figurines, *amor é cego*, across the hall and up the wooden stairs, the panelled wall, Anne hardly able to keep her feet, until he suddenly stopped.

Mafalda stood at the top of the stairs in her nightdress. She had a leather cartridge belt slung over her shoulder and a twelve-bore shotgun in her hands. After the shot and what she'd heard coming up through the fireplace, she'd known who was going to be next. Anne took one look at her and decided that nothing was up for discussion. She twisted her wrist out of Wilshere's grip, hurled herself over the bannister into the hall, as Mafalda pulled both triggers. Wilshere took the double quantities of shot in the chest. It ripped him open, tore everything out. Everything that had ever troubled him.

Mafalda didn't pause. She broke the gun, the spent cartridges popped out. She reloaded, turned her shoulder and put both barrels into the ceiling. The massive wrought-iron chandelier, fixed to the ceiling by a metal plate, parted from the splintered wood. A quarter of a ton of chandelier headed for the floor. Anne scrabbled across the chequered squares. The chandelier crashed into the tiled floor, sending out shrapnel of black and white chippings. Mafalda reloaded, walked down the stairs, calm, professional, work to be done. Anne hobbled down the corridor to the french windows, which she now saw were shut. Had Lazard locked them? The seconds it would take to try might be vital. Mafalda skirted the fallen chandelier, saw Anne sidestep into the drawing room, slowed down, checked her weapon, triggered the triggers, proceeded.

Chapter 23

Voss sat alone in the dark palace. Rose and Sutherland had run for their cars and headed back into Lisbon. The agent from the colonnade came in, lowered the flame on the lamp and picked it up. He waited while Voss applied his fingertips to his temples, trying to force in the energy to think.

After a minute of the agent swinging the lamp and watching the effect on their shadows, Voss stood. The agent led him up through the trees to his car. Voss stared at the steering wheel, the agent looked in on him.

'You have to put the key in the ignition, and turn it, sir,' said the agent. 'That way the motor starts. Good night, sir.'

Voss pulled out and drove back to Sintra, past the palace of Seteais, blue and silent in the moonlight. He took the high road above Sintra town and drove through the unlit village of São Pedro heading south to Estoril. Check Wilshere first, he thought, there was a chance that Lazard would go there if they were in this together, and check Anne, too. Then go back to Lisbon.

In the open country between the *serra* and the coast he pulled off the road under some pines trees. Another thought: whatever Lazard was doing had been a carefully planned operation; Voss would represent a threat to that plan. He went to the boot and lifted out the tool box. From the cloth bag he removed the Walther PPK, well-oiled and loaded. He checked it, laid it on the passenger seat and drove into Estoril from the north, heading down to the sea and the casino square.

He walked up the garden, the night air full of barking dogs that had been set off by Wilshere's shot. He heard Mafalda put both barrels into Wilshere. He was running by the time the next two

228

barrels were emptied into the ceiling. He hit the lawn at a sprint and slowed, checking the windows of the house. Light in the study only, then light in the drawing room and Mafalda holding the twelve bore with the cartridge belt still over her shoulder, sweeping the room like a hunter in a copse.

He ducked, ran across the lawn and hit the wall close to the last window. Mafalda had got up on a coffee table and was looking amongst the furniture.

'Judy,' she said in a little voice, coaxing a kitten. 'Judy.'

Now he could see Anne hiding behind the sofa at the far end of the room, crouched with a dark stain around the neck and shoulders of her dress. He ran to the back terrace, eased open the doors of the french windows and stood in the doorway of the sitting room. Mafalda had her back to him. He raised the Walther PPK.

'Put the gun down, Dona Mafalda.'

Mafalda turned slowly, the twelve bore at her hip.

'Put it down, slowly,' said Voss, checking her face.

He stepped behind the corridor wall as the shot crashed through the open doorway and ravaged the plaster beyond. Voss stepped back into the frame as a large vase hurled from the far end of the room shattered on the edge of the table on which Mafalda was standing. She lost her balance, fell, the gun slipped off her hip, the stock thudded into the floor. The blast ripped into her nightdress, rolled her off the table – a crack as she hit the floor. Voss was on her in a second, pulled open the shredded nightdress, her left breast gone, the blood – thick, arterial, important – flooded into her ragged lungs, drained out.

Anne crashed across the room. Voss tucked his gun into his waistband. Outside, the ringing bell of a police car started up in the distance. Anne, oddly calm, seeing everything slowly now, walked quickly back into the study. She opened Lazard's briefcase, slapped the envelope on top of the velvet bag of high-quality gems, scraped the contents of the safe into it, which included a few white paper sachets of other diamonds and some documents, shut the briefcase and left the safe open with the gold bars still in it. Headlights flashed through the front door into the hall. She and Voss ran out on to the back terrace and on through the hedge to the perimeter wall at the back of the property. Over the wall they walked briskly downhill and back towards the casino, which they avoided because a crowd had gathered outside. The town dogs were still barking and howling into the night.

They drove down the Marginal without exchanging a word. Voss hung on to the wheel as if it was a cliff face, Anne pulled her heels up on to the seat, jammed herself into a corner and hugged her knees, shaking. Lisbon was fogbound and strangely cool. They went to Estrela, parked and walked up to the apartment. He ran a bath, lit cigarettes, poured out some harsh *bagaço* he kept in the kitchen. He took her into the bathroom, stripped off her dress and put it in the basin to soak. He bathed her as he would a child and towelled her dry. He put her into bed, where she cried for an hour; the images of the burning woman, the innocent burning woman with love and petrol in her throat in the furnace car, refused to go out. He washed her dress, hung it up by the window. He stripped, got into bed behind her, pulled her back to his chest. They stared into the dark corner of the room. She told him everything that had happened.

Dawn came early with a faint mist by the window and woke them up out of short, deep sleep and back into hard fact. Her forehead was pressed against his back, her arm over his chest. His hand was resting on her hip. She knew he was awake, could hear his brain ticking.

'Lazard and Wilshere knew you were a double,' she said, the words reverberating up his spine. 'Lazard told me last night. Does that mean Wolters knows?'

He didn't reply but brushed his thumb over her hip bone, back and forward. He was staring at the briefcase under the table. He imagined Colonel Claus Schenk von Stauffenberg going into the *Wolfsschanze* situation room (or would it be in the new bunker, whose five-metre thick walls he'd never seen), positioning his brief-case, being called out to the telephone, the explosion and then the end of all this and a return to real life – which, of course, would not be possible, to go back, to return. There was only one direction in this life and that was relentlessly forward, away from old states of comparative innocence and on to new states, the images collecting in the brain to be shown in one horrific flash should you be unfortunate enough to drown.

'Did you hear me?' she asked. 'You can't go back.'

'Back?' he asked, momentarily confused.

'To the legation,' she said. 'They know you're a double.'

'I have no choice,' he said. 'I have to go back.'

'If you come with me now to the embassy . . .'

'I can't. I have my duty.'

'What duty?'

'With any luck, tomorrow will be the beginning of the end and I have to be there for it. I have my part to play.'

'Take the case,' she said. 'It's got everything in it . . . the diamonds . . . the envelope with the plans, everything you need to survive.'

'I can't take the case. I can't do that. If Wolters gets those plans, everything I've worked for will have been for nothing.'

'Then take the case and leave me the envelope. At least you'll salvage the diamonds.'

'If I take the case I place myself at the scene. They will know I was at the house. There are three dead bodies there including Lazard, who was supposedly brokering a deal for us. It will be difficult.'

'You invent something. If you go back empty-handed I don't know how you'll be able to survive. You'll have nothing to bargain with. Nothing that proves you're not a double.'

'It won't make any difference. My only chance to hold Wolters off, if he knows I'm a double, would be if I gave the briefcase to him complete and saved his intelligence coup from disaster. I won't do that.'

He got up, made coffee which they drank without sugar because he hadn't picked up his ration. They shared a dry biscuit. It felt like the spare meal of a condemned man who no longer had an appetite for life. Voss looked at his watch and then out of the window.

'The sun will burn this off in no time.'

'When do I see you?' she said, suddenly made desperate by his insouciance.

'That will be difficult. You're going to be in trouble, too. There'll be a lot of explaining. I'll be here in the evenings, if you can come . . . come, but not tomorrow. I will be here at five thirty on Friday. If something happens . . . if I'm not here . . . call this number and ask for Le Père Goriot. He'll tell you.'

He gave her a number and the lines of code. She didn't want to hear them. They made her feel dark, cavernous. He gave her keys to his apartment. They kissed, a brushing of the lips, and he handed her the briefcase. He followed her out of the room, watched her go down the stairs, looking up at him as she went, until her face disappeared in the dark well.

He went to the window and waited for her. She walked up the short hill behind the basilica and at the top she turned and waved, one straight arm salute, which he returned.

She went straight to work and a one-hour debrief with Cardew, who pushed her to tell him everything not just about the débâcle in the Wilsheres' house but about Voss as well. Once Wallis had lost her, Rose and Sutherland had been on to him, and now he wanted to give them as full a picture as possible about her movements. He was annoyed.

At 9.30 a.m. she was sitting in the room of the safe house in Rua de Madres in Madragoa. Rose and Sutherland were there and two Americans, OSS men from the American consulate.

The men took up their positions around the room, Sutherland and Rose in the chairs, the Americans standing by the walls. No explanation was given for the Americans' presence.

They asked for her story, the same story she'd given Cardew, from the moment she left the Shell building the previous afternoon. It meant she had to start where she didn't want to – with Karl Voss. Sutherland was still annoyed after receiving Cardew's report. Rose was prurient. The Americans were baffled.

'How long were you with him?' asked Sutherland.

'Five hours or so.'

'Where?'

'Part of the time in his apartment but we went for a walk in the Bairro Alto, too. Then he drove me back to Estoril.'

'How long were you in the apartment?'

'Two to three hours.'

Silence while the Americans' boredom settled. This was not why they were here.

'Did you have . . . relations?' asked Rose.

'Yes, sir,' she said, bold now, and one of the Americans raised his eyebrows, smirked, straightened his tie. 'We *are* lovers, sir,' she added.

'Was that all it was?' asked Sutherland.

'What else could it have been, sir?' asked Anne.

They moved on to Estoril. They went through what had happened in Wilshere's house four or five times until the Americans were satisfied and got to their feet.

'Do you mind?' asked one of them to no one in particular.

He opened the briefcase, removed the envelope, looked it over and tapped it on his fingernail.

'Pity,' he said, and the two Americans left the room.

Rose took the empty chair, played a quick piece up and down the arms, not chopsticks, more Mozart. It annoyed Sutherland.

'Pity?' asked Anne.

'The OSS were running an operation without telling us,' said Sutherland, more drained than ever before. 'When I heard Lazard wasn't on the Dakar flight I contacted them. By then they had permission to talk to us about Hal and Mary Couples. They asked what you were doing and I told them that you were an observer. Their only comment was that you should "maintain that status".'

'And what were the Couples doing?' she asked.

'Hal Couples worked for Ozalid. He was spying on military installations while selling them Ozalid machines. The OSS turned him and he cleaned out the American IG stable for them. This was his last job. They put one of their agents with him and sent him to Lisbon with a set of plans. I think I told you that Bohr was being debriefed by the Americans about the German atomic programme. He had with him a sketch that Heisenberg had given him the year before. He thought it was an atomic bomb. The American scientists saw something different – not a bomb but an atomic pile . . . something that could make fissionable material for use in a bomb in quantity.'

'Wilshere called it the core to the atomic apple.'

'Artistic mind, that Wilshere,' said Rose.

'The Americans have been worried by the quality of the physics coming out of Germany in the last five years. After debriefing Bohr they were concerned about Heisenberg's loyalties. Was it to physics or the Führer? They decided that, although he might not be a fanatical Nazi, he was sufficiently drawn to the excitement of

233

progress that he might be developing a bomb. With the German rocket capability this became a somewhat worrying prospect.'

'So if the Couples were working for the OSS, what did they have for sale?'

'Some cleverly constructed plans that would have built a very dangerous atomic pile. The intelligence the Americans would get back after the documents were received would have given them a clear indication of how close the Germans were to including unconventional explosives in their rockets.'

'You mean Karl Voss could have taken the case, he could have given General Wolters the envelope, that was what the Americans wanted, that would have been the perfect solution?'

Sutherland and Rose said nothing. Anne's eyes filled with tears which rolled down her face, bit into the corners of her mouth and dripped off her jaw on to her still damp dress, silent as soft rain off the eaves.

Voss had been right. By the time he arrived at the legation the sun had burnt off the mist and the temperature was already in the high twenties centigrade. He called Dakar airport and asked them for a report on the Rio flight. It still hadn't taken off. He went straight in to see Wolters with this diversionary piece of information and was astonished to find him cheerful and expansive.

'So maybe it will be a little cooler today, Voss,' he said.

'I don't know about that, sir,' he said. 'Just to let you know, sir, the Dakar/Rio flight still hasn't taken off.'

'Thank you, Voss, I had that checked. I hope that wasn't a report you received.'

'No, sir, I cleared all our men away from the airport.'

'Keep it that way.'

Voss was dismissed. He went to his office light on his feet again, threw himself into his chair. Happy.

'You in love, sir?' asked Kempf.

Voss whipped round, hadn't seen him there in the corner of the room, leaning up against the window.

'Just had a good night's sleep, that's all, Kempf. First cool night in weeks. You?'

'What, sir? Sleeping well?'

'Or in love?'

'Not that sort of love, sir. Not the sort that makes you happy.'

'What sort, Kempf?'

'The sort that makes the first piss of the morning absolute agony, sir. Think I've got myself a dose.'

'Take the morning off, Kempf.'

'Thank you, sir.'

Voss lit a cigarette, stretched his feet out and saw the cello of Anne's body at the window and the thick black sash of her hair over one shoulder. The phone rang. He listened, hung up and left the legation, buying his usual newspaper as he went.

He walked down to the Pensão Rocha with nothing on his mind apart from the blue Tagus in front of him and ships easing past, visible though the gaps in the buildings heading for the Atlantic.

He took his usual table in the courtyard, laid the newspaper in front of him, saw a small item at the foot of the front page. The PVDE announced that a communist cell had been captured in a safe house in Rua da Arrábida. The same place where Mesnel had been visiting and he'd sent Paco to check. Paco, thought Voss. You have to be careful of Paco. He has only one loyalty – money. A few minutes later Rui lowered himself into the chair opposite.

'Your Frenchman was shot last night. Dead,' said Rui.

'Tell me.'

'We followed him to the caves, as usual. He went off to do his business and we left him to it, except we heard a shot, two shots. We went back up there this morning. Somebody found the body around six o'clock. The PVDE were up there because he was a foreigner, so I didn't get too close. He'd been shot in the head at the viewpoint of the Alto da Serafina.'

'That's it?'

'I heard he was found with a gun on him,' he said, 'and some PVDE men were talking about a triple killing up in a big house in Estoril. Two foreigners and a Portuguese woman from a big family.'

Voss drummed the tabletop, gave Rui a cigarette which he pocketed without thinking.

'Do we do anything?' asked Rui.

'You wait,' said Voss, and left the newspaper on the table.

The PVDE had been hard at it since they arrived at Quinta da Águia at close to 2.15 a.m. They were working conscientiously to hide the fact that they had been unimpressively late on the scene. The first phone call about gunshot noise from the Wilsheres' house had come in around 1.50 a.m. and had been discounted as carpet beating. By 2.00 a.m., however, there'd been another four calls, each reporting the same thing, gunshots – one quite loud, followed by two very loud and then two not so loud – and so it was that two PVDE men and two GNR men reluctantly got into a car and drove up to the Quinta da Águia with the bell on, just so that everyone in the neighbourhood would be woken up and they could feel important.

At 6.00 a.m., because of the names of the dead found in the house, Captain Lourenço was informed and once he took a personal interest in the investigation the servants were rounded up and later in the morning a search began for the Englishwoman, whose address on her visa application was given as Quinta da Águia. They were waiting for her at the Shell building when she came back from Rua de Madres. They put her into a car and drove her to the PVDE headquarters on Rua António Maria Cardoso where there was intense activity as the reports of three other murders were being filed.

Sutherland and Rose had gone through Anne's story and come up against a serious difficulty – the hours spent in the café after Voss had dropped her placed her in Estoril. They had hoped to be able to hide her at the Cardews' house – dinner and then too tired to go home, stayed the night. The time at the café made this impossible. They toyed with the idea of the truth, omitting her presence at the Wilsheres' house but confirming that she spent the night with Voss – but it would compromise Voss. They'd hammered away at the problem until Anne put the idea of Wallis.

Jim Wallis was found. He'd spent the night alone. A story was plugged into him – that Anne had dined with the Cardews, been dropped at the *quinta*, gone to the café, waited and waited for him, left, met him outside and gone back to his apartment in Lisbon. There were some shaky elements, not least of which was that Anne had never been to Wallis's apartment and Wallis had a landlady. Anne was instructed to play her interrogation coy and reticent until the murders were disclosed and then, well, natural instincts would prevail. As she walked to the Shell building she elaborated the germ of the lie until it was an infection of perfect reality in her mind.

She was desperate for it to work, her fear being that they would keep her locked up without charge for as long as they wanted to.

The PVDE worked on her throughout the morning as more and more information came in. The Frenchman, Mesnel, whose revolver had not been fired, had been shot twice, grazed once and mortally wounded the second time. The bullet in Mesnel's body matched that of the Smith & Wesson lying near Lazard's body, with his fingerprints on it, in the Wilsheres' house. The sides and underside of Lazard's car, found outside the casino, were covered in cement powder and sand, and the tyre tracks matched those left at the site of the half-built villa belonging to Lazard where the bodies of the Couples had been discovered. The PVDE inspector was not convinced, by the way the bodies lay, that Hal Couples had done this unspeakable thing to his wife, strangled her and then shot himself in the head. As a scenario he didn't believe it, and he said as much in his initial report to Lourenço, who had the benefit of an autopsy on Lazard which revealed blood on his penis and undershorts.

By the end of the morning Lourenço saw it like this: Lazard had shot Mesnel in Monsanto, driven to Malveira, raped and strangled Mary Couples, shot Hal Couples with the man's own gun. He had then driven to Estoril where there had been a disagreement, resulting in Wilshere shooting him with a gun probably kept in the safe. Wilshere had then been shot by Mafalda on the stairs and Mafalda had apparently shot herself by accident in the sitting room. There were some questions. Why did Mafalda put both barrels into the ceiling? Had she first attempted to kill her husband by dropping the chandelier on him? It seemed unlikely. Why was there the stink of brandy in the study, an empty bottle, a stain on the floor, but no stains on any of the bodies? Why, if the motive was robbery, was the safe open with four bars of gold in it? It wasn't long before Lourenço was convinced that there was somebody missing from the scene.

None of this information filtered down to Anne, who was in Room 3 with a single interrogator who asked a lot of questions and took copious notes. She told him how she had dined with the Cardews (tomato soup, mutton stew and cheese), gone to a café for a drink and then gone back to the Wilsheres' where she'd overslept in the morning, taken the train to Lisbon and walked to work, arriving late. He drew the story out of her again, chipping away at her for more detail and getting it, masses of it. What she wore in bed, her dreams, whether she heard anything in the night (no), breakfast with Mr Wilshere (Dona Mafalda rarely attends), the walk to the station, the beauty of the morning sunshine coming through the mist, the cool after the terrible days of swelter. It was only after she was asked for a third rendering that Anne began to appear concerned.

The PVDE man gathered the copious notes and left the room. She was there on her own for an hour (early lunch for the interrogators) and she developed some worry, which was not hard to do.

At 12.15 two men came in and it was immediately different. They had strong alcohol and coffee on their breath and the words that came out on the back of it were ugly – liar, thief, murderer. She asked for a cigarette. They hit the table with their fists. They stood on either side of her, each with one hand on the back of her chair and the other on the table in front. They hemmed her in, breathed on her and told her what had happened at the Quinta da Águia the night before. She winced, shrank, paled and looked down into her hands, her shoulders shaking, her back shuddering under the implacable eyes of the two PVDE men.

They gave her a cigarette, pulled their chairs around to the side of the table and smoked with her. One gave her his handkerchief and it was to him that she revealed her affair with Jim Wallis. Two *agentes* were dispatched. They picked up Wallis within the hour. During that hour Lourenço received a report in which he was informed that officially Lazard had left the country from Lisbon airport on a flight to Dakar the previous afternoon. This complicating development had the effect of clarifying everything to the PVDE chief, who treated this detail as confirmation that only foreign intelligence services could possibly have made such a fantastic mess.

Voss returned to the legation and put a call in to his contact at the PVDE who told him the names of the three murdered people in the Quinta da Águia. He went straight across to Wolters' office and asked to see him urgently. They sat in the darkened office, shutters closed to the high sun, only cracks of intense light around the edges.

'I've had some disturbing news which I don't fully understand,' said Voss. 'One of the agents I've been using to follow the French communist Olivier Mesnel reported to me that he was shot last night. The agent went up to Monsanto in the morning to where the body was found and overheard two PVDE men discussing a triple murder in a big house in Estoril. I've just contacted the PVDE who've confirmed the names of the three dead as follows: Mr Patrick Wilshere, Senhora Mafalda de Carmo Wilshere and Mr Beecham Lazard.'

Wolters' face was perfectly still, the only movement in the room was the cigar smoke trailing from his fingers. The phone rang, more urgent than usual to Voss's mind, and he sat back to admire Wolters' collapsing world.

The call was from Captain Lourenço demanding to see a representative from the German Legation in his office in Rua António Maria Cardoso. This was how Voss came to be sitting at the hottest point of the day staring at the PVDE chief's back as he stood looking out of the unshuttered window in the vague direction of the São Carlos theatre. Voss was still thinking about Wolters, convinced that the general was as stunned by Lazard's murder here, in Portugal, as he was himself.

'It's been very hot these past few days,' said Lourenço. 'I've been glad my office faces east . . . not that it makes that much difference. In Lisbon, you see, it's the humidity that throttles.'

'You should get out of the city more, sir,' said Voss.

'I would. I'd love to . . . if people would give me the time.'

'Surely . . .'

'People like yourself, Senhor Voss.'

'Me, Captain?'

'What's going on, Senhor Voss?'

'You've confused me now, sir.'

'I don't think so, Senhor Voss. You don't strike me as a man who confuses easily,' said Lourenço. 'I'm looking at six murders, five of them foreigners. I'm quite certain that that is a record for one night in Lisbon and it is one record I am not proud of holding.'

'Were any of them German?' asked Voss. 'Is that why . . . ?'

'No, none of them were German. That is why you're here,' said Lourenço. 'I find it interesting that the military attaché has been sent, don't you?'

'I was sent because I was on hand,' said Voss, wondering how long his dumb show could continue.

'This *is* an intelligence matter, Senhor Voss,' he said, settling behind his desk, smoothing his moustache with his fingertips. 'So, please, let's not walk around each other for an hour.'

'We are as shocked by last night's . . .'

'Yes, yes . . . please, Senhor Voss, the point.'

'We were expecting some goods from Senhor Lazard, that is true,' said Voss. 'But we were expecting him to leave the country in order to procure them. In fact, we *know* he left the country and we were very surprised to find him still here and even more –'

'What were the goods?'

'Well, I say "goods" . . . what I mean is that he left with diamonds in order to buy dollars. We have a hard currency problem in Europe.'

'So he should have had some diamonds on him?'

'I don't know about on him, but they should have been in his possession, unless they were being carried by the man who boarded the Dakar flight impersonating Mr Lazard.'

'Don't try to confuse the issue, Senhor Voss. It's very clear in my mind. All I want to know is why Lazard should shoot a Frenchman in Monsanto, drive to the Serra de Sintra to rape and strangle Senhora Couples, shoot Senhor Couples and then go on to Estoril where I am sure he was about to shoot Senhor Wilshere.'

'I'd like to propose the theory that Senhor Lazard was operating in his own interests,' said Voss. 'Have the Allies been forthcoming about Senhor and Senhora Couples?'

Lourenço's dark eyes didn't leave Voss's face as they lit up with his first idea of the afternoon.

'Ah, yes, now I see . . . is it possible he was using your diamonds to buy something from Senhor and Senhora Couples? Then, having got what he wanted, he killed them. The only problem is that Senhor Couples, according to the American consulate, is a salesman for a company which makes printing machines for use in the construction industry . . . she was his wife. There's been gossip that she was having an affair with Senhor Lazard, which I find hard to believe. What was the value of the diamonds?'

'Why?'

'I would like to know, Senhor Voss.'

'I meant why do you find it hard to believe that Senhor Lazard would be having an affair with Senhora Couples?'

'The details of her death were not pleasant ... You will have noticed that I used the word rape ... that was ... I was being ... ach! ... the man was an animal,' said Lourenço, throwing his hand away. 'And who is this Frenchman? That's another thing.'

Voss dipped his head, sorry that he was unable to enlighten.

'Have you spoken to the English girl who was staying at the house, she must ... ?' said Voss.

'She knows nothing. She wasn't there,' he said. 'She said she was there. She said she had breakfast with Wilshere in the morning and went to work, but the reality ... I don't know ... foreigners.'

'Foreigners?'

'She was off with her English boyfriend somewhere in Lisbon ... These women ... she only arrived here on Saturday. I should have been born ...'

Lourenço trailed off. Voss survived the jolt, which had started out as fear, turned into a wild, irrational jealousy and finished as happiness. He lost Lourenço's words as he stared across the street at the sun blinding the windows of the building opposite.

Wolters listened to Voss's report of the interview with Lourenço in hard silence, his eyes blinking once a minute as if that was part of the process of taking in the disaster. A million dollars lost, the most valuable supplier of industrial diamonds dead, the plans, which would have taken them a step nearer to a secret weapon, well, where were they? Did they ever exist?

'What do we know about this?' asked Wolters, the process of shifting blame already starting in his head.

'What we know is useless to us,' said Voss, relishing this moment, wanting to be able to share it with someone – this was what happened when the SS took over Abwehr intelligence operations.

'But we do know something?' he asked, clutching.

'We know that someone calling himself Beecham Lazard boarded the Lisbon/Dakar flight. According to Immigration in Dakar he arrived safely but nobody of that name was on the Dakar/Rio flight which has now taken off ...'

'Yes, yes ... I know these things.'

Voss studied him, looking for confirmation of his theory, but

241

Wolters was expressionless. There was nothing in his face to show whether he knew what Lazard had been doing, whether this had been part of the game – a bluff to the SIS and the OSS to focus their attention outside Portugal. Whatever. It had gone wrong.

'*I* will write the report of this matter,' said Wolters. '*I* will send the report personally to Berlin. Is that understood?'

Voss waited until evening to see whether a report came out of Wolters' office. Only Wolters himself came out and that was to leave the legation for a cocktail party at the Hotel Aviz and then dinner at the Negresco afterwards.

Voss left the building at 7.00 p.m. and went back to his apartment where he knelt at the window smoking, drinking his preferred rubbing alcohol and watching the square, waiting, waiting for tomorrow to finally arrive.

Because he never took cabs it had been a long walk for Paco to the small park above the Santa Clara market in the Alfama district. He had been told that the information he was going to be given would certainly be worth the very long walk from Lapa across the city. He sat under the trees with a view over the church of Santa Engrácia, wondering whether this was a dangerous place to be. Behind him, watching him, was someone else who was also reflecting on the same building, which was still incomplete after 262 years' work. Paco sat back and tried to enjoy the warm night air of the empty park and watched the lights of small craft inching their way across the Tagus which was as big as a small sea at this point.

The voice that came to Paco from behind him was not Portuguese. He had heard this kind of voice before. It was a voice incapable of relaxing. It was an English voice and only capable of speaking barely comprehensible Portuguese. The park was so dark that even when he turned round he couldn't see who was speaking. He didn't like this voice. Paco didn't *like* anybody. But he especially didn't like this voice because it belonged to someone who wouldn't make themselves known, the type who would always be on the edge of light, just in the shadows.

'Ah yes, Paco. Beautiful up here, isn't it? Especially at night. Very quiet. Hardly aware of the city.'

Paco didn't reply. These were just some of the things that Englishmen said.

'I have something for you, Paco. A piece of information. Something that you could use at the right moment. I can't tell you when that moment will be. It might be tomorrow or the next day. You will listen and watch as you always do and you will decide the correct moment for you to go with this piece of information to the man who will pay you well.'

'Who is the man who will pay me well?'

'This isn't anything that should go to the PVDE.'

'*They* do not pay me well.'

'Then that is good,' said the English voice. 'The man who will pay you well is SS General Reinhardt Wolters of the German Legation.'

'He will never see me. Why should such a man want to see Paco Gomez?'

'There is no doubt that he will want to see you with this piece of information.'

'Tell me.'

'You will tell him that last night you saw his military attaché, Captain Karl Voss . . . you do know who I mean, don't you, Paco?'

'Certainly.'

'You will tell him you saw Captain Karl Voss with the English girl . . .'

'The English girl who works for Shell, who lives in the house of Senhor Wilshere?'

'Yes, that girl. You will tell him that you saw them walking together in the Bairro Alto last night,' said the English voice, 'and that they are lovers. That is all.'

Chapter 24

Thursday, 20th July 1944, PVDE Headquarters, Rua António Maria Cardoso, Lisbon.

Anne was released in the morning at 9.00 a.m. She was met by Cardew who took her straight off to his home in Carcavelos, where she showered and changed into some clothes borrowed from his wife. Anne insisted on going into work. She needed to be occupied, she said. She didn't say that she needed to be in Lisbon with a chance of seeing Voss.

They drove back into Lisbon. She typed for the rest of the morning and then began translating articles on physics from the *Naturwissenschafen* journal. She looked at the clock constantly, so frequently that the hands stopped moving.

Voss sat in his office looking at the clock giving Berlin time which, because of the Führer's insistence that all parts of the Third Reich should operate on German time, meant that he was also looking at Rastenburg time, *Wolfsschanze* time. It was midday and in a matter of minutes Colonel Claus Schenk von Stauffenberg would be positioning his briefcase, maybe he had already positioned his briefcase and was waiting to be called to the telephone, praying to be called to the telephone in the *Wolfsschanze* signals room. Voss tried the bottom drawer of his desk, which was locked. It contained the Walther PPK given to him by the Free Poles colonel which he'd brought into the building that morning and was going to be used to take control of the German Legation.

'You all right, sir?' asked Kempf.

'Yes, yes, just stretching my back, Kempf,' said Voss. 'You better?'

'Not better exactly, sir.'

'You should stick to English nannies, Kempf.'

'Thank you for the advice, sir. I'll try to remember that the next time I'm drunk, down at the Santos docks surrounded by sailors,' said Kempf. 'I'll put out the call for an English nanny . . .'

'Point taken, Kempf.'

'If you're trying to get into that drawer, sir, I'd . . .'

'No, no, Kempf. Just stretching.'

'I was going to say, a good kick will sort it out. I know that desk.'

'No, no, no, Kempf. It's just a way of bracing myself, that's all. Let's go through the mail. You have brought the mail with you?'

Kempf stalled.

'Go and get the mail, Kempf.'

Voss sat back, his whole body in a lather.

Paco lay on his bed curled in a tight ball, with his kneecaps pressed into his eye sockets, tears leaking out at the excruciating pain in his stomach. After the Englishman had given him his intelligence gift he had also pushed a hundred-escudo note into his pocket and with this Paco had gone back through the Alfama district where he'd stopped and eaten his first meal of the day. He had been stupid to choose the pork. Pork in this heat . . . and you never knew how long they'd kept it there, rotting in their kitchens, these filthy people. As soon as he'd tasted that sharpness he should have stopped. It was the sharpness of vinegar which they used to disguise the age of the meat. He'd spent the whole night crouched over the stinking toilet, vomiting between his knees, while his innards streamed out of his backside. When he was empty, when he was no more than a dry, flattened bladder, he'd crawled to his room and dry-retched until dawn, while a fever wrung out the little moisture left in him, so that the yellowing bedsheets were soaked through. The boy had come and made him drink water and the wire spring of his abdomen had contracted, doubled him over so that his vertebrae stuck out of his back under his paper-thin skin. Only at midday did his stomach release him, let him stretch out and fall into a prickly sleep, from which he would jolt awake at the strange and ghastly images that surfaced in his mind.

At lunchtime Anne went to the Estrela Gardens, sat on a bench and watched people, checking if she was being followed. She went into the basilica and out again and up the wooden stairs to Voss's apartment. She let herself in, he wasn't there. She wandered about the rooms, tested the sofa, sat on his bed and looked at his family photograph, the three men in it. The father and Julius looked alike, broad, strong men with dark hair and eyebrows, handsome, sporty. They were in uniform. Voss was wearing a suit and a student scarf. He had the same fair looks as his mother and, it seemed to her, the same light-coloured eyes and vulnerable bone structure. She held the image of the mother up to her eye to see if any of that sadness she must have felt, that disappointment at not being the love of her husband's life, was evident. It wasn't, she looked happy.

She put the photograph down on the bed, went to the dresser, rummaged amongst his clothes in the drawers and found a small package of letters tied with ribbon. She read the letters, the need for a sense of his presence was too strong for her to consider privacy. The letters were in date order and most of them consisted of a few lines from his father finishing with a chess move. She flipped through them in a state of vague contentment until she reached Julius's letter, dated New Year's Day 1943. She found herself crying, half blind with tears, not seeing the deserving end of an invading army but the unfolding of a family tragedy – a father's desperation, a brother presenting Julius with his terrible choice and then the final letter from the unknown lieutenant. She retied the ribbon, tucked the letters back in the drawer and took some of his hairs out of his brush and comb. She went to the bathroom even hungrier for him now and fingered his shaving gear, thumbed the badger brush, sniffed the razor to see if there was something of him on it. Nothing. She had to go, yet she wanted to leave something of herself for him but nothing legible, or personal so that it could be traced back to her. She went to the dresser, plucked a hair from her own head and wove it amongst the bristles and hairs in the brush.

Voss watched the Berlin clock move around to 5.00 p.m. The hour at which it would be certain that Stauffenberg would be back in Berlin after the three-hour flight from Rastenburg. Still nothing. Voss forced himself to stay still, sitting at his desk he went through papers again and again, reading nothing, taking in nothing, being nothing.

Wolters had kept his secretary working late and now she was leaving the building, her heels clopping on the tiled hall, skipping down the stone steps to the driveway and into the hot evening of the city. Voss sat back in his chair, elbow up on the arm, thumb supporting his chin, forefinger sweeping over his lips back and forth, eyes blinking once a minute in the thickening silence. Wolters stirred out of his office. Voss tracked the creaking leather of the man's shoes until they reached his door. The handle turned.

'Ah, Voss,' said Wolters, 'working late?'

'Thinking late, sir.'

'Would you care to join me for a drink? I've just taken delivery of some rather fine cognac.'

Voss followed him back to his office where Wolters laid out the glasses and poured the brandy.

'What were you thinking about, Voss?'

Lines sprinted through Voss's mind, none of them usable. Wolters' lips hovered over the rim of his glass, waiting. Alternatives did not immediately present themselves to Voss. His head was too full of what should be happening now in Berlin.

'It was nothing important,' he said.

'Tell me.'

'I was wondering why Mesnel was armed. Had I been running him, I would not have used him for assassination work. That was all.'

Wolters' face darkened. He stuck two fingers into his collar, pulled at it to let some of the blood drain into his body. Voss raised his glass. They drank. The alcohol smoothed Wolters out. He lit a cigar.

'I have been thinking about something, too,' said Wolters. 'I have spoken to Captain Lourenço myself now. It seems that he is under the impression that there were two people who left Quinta da Águia alive on that Tuesday night.'

'Why two people?'

'The situation in the drawing room where they found the body of Dona Mafalda.'

'What was that?'

'A vase had been thrown the length of the room. The vase was one of a pair that belonged on the mantelpiece.'

'Yes.'

'And there was evidence of shot having peppered the wall of the corridor beyond the living-room door,' said Wolters. 'Captain Lourenço thinks that Dona Mafalda was shooting at someone in the doorway and that another person, at the far end of the room, either wanted to distract her or hit her with the vase. The vase smashed, startling Dona Mafalda, who lost her footing and accidentally shot herself as she fell. Captain Lourenço doesn't think that the person who was shot at in the doorway could be the same as the one who threw the vase from the other end of the room, which is why he now thinks that there are two people unaccounted for. I have been thinking, Captain Voss . . .'

'Yes, sir.'

'I have been thinking that I would very much like to talk to those two people and that what they took from the Quinta da Águia that night could be very interesting to us.'

'Yes, sir.'

'I want you to use your considerable intelligence resources to find those two people.'

The phone rang, jolting the two men in the smoke-layered stillness. Wolters picked up the phone and Voss heard the urgent voice of the switchboard operator, a corporal in the telegraph room. Von Ribbentrop, the Reichsminister for Foreign Affairs, was on the line. Wolters checked his watch, just after 8.00 p.m. He asked Voss to leave the office for a moment, take his glass. Voss paced the corridor for some minutes and then collapsed behind his desk, suddenly exhausted, nerves shot, knowing that von Ribbentrop calling Lisbon at this hour was not a good sign. He gulped the brandy, which slipped down like burning silk. He lit a cigarette, watched his trembling fingers until they stilled, then sat back and smoked. Did they delay again? But von Ribbentrop calling on the evening of such a day. They must have failed. The gun. He must get the gun out of the building. If a gun is found in his desk he will be finished. Now they will be looking at everyone, especially the ex-Abwehr men.

Wolters left his office, his shoes smacked down the corridor in triumphant strides. He flung open the door. Voss found himself looking up, hunched over his cigarette like a prisoner in his cell.

'A attempt was made on the Führer's life this afternoon,' Wolters announced, excitedly. 'A bomb was placed in the situation room in the *Wolfsschanze*. It exploded right underneath the Führer's feet but ... it must be a sign, it must be some sort of a turning point ... he has only been lightly wounded. An incredible thing. The Reichsminister said that, had they been in the new bunker, nobody would have survived ... as it was, they were in Reichsminister Speer's blockhouse, the bomb blew out the sides, releasing the blast, eleven people were injured, four of them seriously. Reichsminister von Ribbentrop is uncertain but he thinks that Colonel Brandt and General Schmundt have not survived their injuries. The Führer has a slight concussion, burst eardrums, damage to his elbow and splinters from the table have been blown into his legs, but he has assured everyone that he will be back at work tomorrow. The coup has been defeated. The terrorists are being rounded up in Berlin as we speak. It is a great day for the Führer, a great day for the Third Reich, a terrible day for our enemies and a great day for us, Captain Voss. *Heil Hitler.*'

Wolters clicked his heels and shot his arm out. Voss stood and responded in kind. They went back to Wolters' study, replenished their glasses and toasted the survival of the right, the victory of justice, the defeat of terrorism, death to the conspirators and many more until the bottle was finished and Voss reeled out of the office drunk, desperate and clammy with fear. He went sweating back to his desk, removed the gun from its drawer and jammed it down his trousers where it stuck into his groin, but he was numb to pain. He picked up his briefcase, crammed his head into his hat and left the building in the tunnel of his own mind. His eyes, pricked by the heat, were glassy as an old man's and as he walked from Lapa to Estrela he stumbled over the *calçada* of the pavements and cobbled streets, his cheeks wet with tears – drained from rejoicing with Wolters, released from the tension of the past weeks and bleak with his vision of the future.

At the top of the Rua de São Domingos à Lapa he looked back down the hill at the limp Union Jack outside the British Embassy. A tram rumbled past, people stared out at him, looking without seeing, two boys hanging off the back yelled, seemed to be beckoning him. Anne's words spoken into his back that morning came to him and he took two steps down the hill, saw himself knocking on the British Embassy door, his welcome into the sanctuary and then a terrible settling. The emptiness of defeat, the end of his cause while others, unbent by setbacks, endangered by his resignation, continued their struggle, his struggle.

He crossed the street, turned right down Rua de Buenos Aires, which was hot and stinking with the remains of a dead dog in the gutter. He dithered over the carcass, the bared teeth in the snout fierce in death, the intestines strewn and flattened across the road. He bared his own teeth at the thought of Wolters swaggering away from his costly intelligence fiasco into a new age of anti-conspiracy zeal, a place where his kind could shine, deflecting all critical scrutiny. Voss walked on at pace towards the back of the basilica, the brandy, hot and acidic, rising in his gullet.

Anne lay in bed in Cardew's house listening to the excited whispered chatter of his daughters next door. Her empty stomach had been unable to accept any dinner, she'd redesigned the landscape of her plate consuming nothing, as Dona Mafalda used to do. The ghastly images marched across her unclosed eyes of the innocent Judy Laverne, tearing down into the ravine in a cage of flame, Wilshere's clawed fingers trying to prohibit entry of the worst possible truth into his mind, Lazard trampling the tortured Wilshere, Lazard's torn throat after the ear-splitting blast from the gun from the safe, Wilshere's ruptured chest as he fell back down the stairs and Mafalda's missing left breast, the dark hole filled with black, central blood, the pallor of her life-drained face, the uncoloured lips. War in the living room. No different to the bombs that had fallen into her piano teacher's house on the corner of Lydon Road in that other life that she'd lived, except this had been so personal.

She could feel her mind restructuring. These were sights, sounds, smells and emotions which could not be accommodated in the soft, pliable naïveté of her life of just last week. They'd been gulped, forced, packed in, rammed down her gullet, so that she thought she could never be hungry again, so that her mind would never lack for this terrible nourishment which trembled her fingers, shuddered her insides, crawled over her skin to the top point of her scalp. She knew then, lying under the open window in the vague, indirect moonlight, how much Voss mattered. He was the only one who knew. He was the only one who could comprehend. He would be her salvation, the one who could order this fresh chaos and make it sad, documentary reading.

She was living for 5.30 p.m. Friday 21st July 1944. As long as there was this one last time everything else would work out. It would be like the clue, the code, the recipe for an equation which would give her the unknown value of x.

Her thoughts sped like silver fish out of the light into the darkness of sleep and she dreamt for the first time the dream which would be hers for years. She was running through the streets of an unknown city – buildings, monuments that were all foreign to her. It was hot. She was dressed in a slip but there was snow on the ground and her breath was visible. She was heading for somewhere where she knew she would find him and she found the door in an unlit alley. There was yellow light coming from the door, painting the cobbles gold. She ran up the wooden stairs and she found she knew the stairs and that her heart and mind were full of hope, that she knew she was going to see him, that he would be waiting for her in the room at the top, their room. She was running faster and faster up the stairs, more landings . . . more landings than she could remember, so many landings and new flights that she began to worry that this wasn't the stair, the right house, the correct street, the real city. But then the door appeared, the right door, behind which she would find him, and she hung exhausted on to the handle, preparing herself for the sight of his face, the bones pushing up under his skin in the way that made his face unique, and she threw open the door, and there was nothing, there was no floor, there was no room, there was only a hot, dry wind over the frozen city and she was falling into the dark.

She woke in a flash of light on a black horizon. Dawn had settled into the room, comfortable as a pet. Her scalp was drenched in sweat, her heart thumping between the walls of her chest like a hard ball thrashed by a madman. Was this it? Was this the mind's new régime?

She got dressed like an old person, consciously putting each foot through the leg hole of her knickers, drawing them up to her waist. She harnessed herself in her bra. Her dress hung off her differently. The hairbrush bit into her scalp as it had never done. The mirror showed her someone who was so nearly her that she had to lean forward to see what was missing from her face. It was all there, all in the right order, no anagram but a nuance. That was something unbearable to a mathematician, because a nuance meant that

251

something was just slightly wrong, the logic had foundered and thrown up, not an error, but just the *nuance* of one, something that was deep in the logic, perhaps a small line somewhere in a mass of equations, something that would be immensely difficult to find and root out, something that might mean you'd have to start all over again ... from scratch. But there was no starting again for her. This was it for the rest of time. A change that would have to be accepted, housed, hidden from view. And for no reason at all her mother came to mind.

She had breakfast. She let coffee trickle down her throat, no solids. Family conversation careered around the table, vectors that never reached her. Cardew drove her to work beside a sea so blue it made her ache.

Dawn came up in Sutherland's office gradually painting him into a corner of his room in the embassy where he'd sat all night after hearing news of the failed assassination attempt, smoking bowl after bowl of tobacco in his pipe. The empty pouch now lay on the floor along with loose strands of shag and dead matches from the overflowing ashtray on the arm of the chair. He'd been thinking about everything, everything that had ever happened to him, including the one thought that he'd never allowed, from the moment he'd received the letter back in 1940 telling him that she'd died in an air raid. How had he dealt with that? Everyone had someone who'd died in an air raid, he was no different. And now here he was, exhausted, completely shattered, the tiredness so profound that it had gone through all his organs and leaked into his bones, sucking on the marrow.

The responsibilities which Richard Rose wore like a summer suit hung off Sutherland's shoulders like a yoke of full pails. The losses from various operations stacked up in his mind, like coffins in a carpenter's yard. This time, though, he would not make the same mistake. He would pull Karl Voss, codename Childe Harold. He would get him out. The man had been right about everything and now, with the failure of the assassination attempt and what Anne had told them, he was in terrible danger, his identity as the military attaché in the German Legation held in place by paper walls. As soon as Rose came in he would announce the operation. Voss would be on his way to London and taking a debrief by evening.

Rose announced himself with a roll of knuckles on the door at 9.00 a.m. He walked in to what he thought was an empty room, not seeing Sutherland still in his chair behind the door.

'We're pulling Voss out today, Richard,' said Sutherland.

'Good morning, old boy,' said Rose, spinning on his heel. 'Just came to talk to you about these decodes.'

'After the failed coup he's sitting in a house of cards ... one breath from the wrong direction and the whole lot'll come down around him.'

'To be frank, I'm surprised he's not here. He must have heard hours before we did ... should have come knocking straight away, if he could.'

Sutherland was unbalanced. For some reason he'd expected resistance from Rose. Rose always hated losing sources. The battles they'd had.

'Checked his whereabouts, old man?' asked Rose.

'Not yet.'

'Well, if he's gone to work that should give us some idea of how he feels about the situation himself.'

'We pull him, Richard. I won't tolerate ...'

'Of course we do, but we can't drive up Rua do Pau de Bandeira calling for him to come out, can we, old chap?'

Old boy, old man, old chap ... just call me Sutherland, he thought, raising himself out of his chair, his arm curiously tingling, his left foot dead.

'Are you all right? Look damned pale to me.'

'Been up all night,' he said, trying to shake life back into his foot.

'Steady on.'

Sutherland was suddenly seeing the world at floor height, a landscape of carpet and furniture legs, with an atmosphere of dust motes and broken sunlight. He didn't understand it and he couldn't articulate his inability to comprehend. His mind ticked like a gramophone needle stuck in a groove.

At 10.00 a.m. the ambassador assembled everyone in the German Legation and gave the same announcement that Wolters had made to Voss the night before. The opening of the speech that followed was about betrayal, treason and terrorism. Wolters, the disciplinarian at the headmaster's side, surveyed the room with the eyes of a bird of prey, so that everyone glued their looks to the picture of the Führer above the dignitaries' heads. The ambassador finally asked them to rejoice in the tragedy averted and led them into an exultant *Heil Hitler!* which rattled the windows. They went back to their offices like chastened schoolchildren after assembly. The world was no different as they streamed back to their desks, only now there was an undertow which was black and uncertain. An undertow that would be random in its search for a scapegoat.

Voss sat at his desk in the legation, sweat at the back of his knees trickling down his calf muscles to his sock tops. He had woken at 5.00 a.m. on the sofa with his tie still up to his neck. He'd clawed it down to his chest, popped the stud at his throat, gulped in air that was at its coolest now but only for an hour. He'd stripped, gone to the bed and found the photograph face-up on the pillow. He put it on the shelf, laid down and found the faintest smell of her on his pillow, sunk his face into it and then looked up through the bars of the bedhead at the plaster beyond and those words came to him again:

'Lazard and Wilshere knew you were a double. Lazard told me last night. Does that mean Wolters knows?'

He'd showered, shaved and walked naked to the chest of drawers to find the top one open a crack and his brush in a different position. He turned it over and saw the single long black thread of hair, doubled back four times through his own.

Now he was giving Hein and Kempf a solid good morning. Cheerful. All black thoughts banished to the black metal trunk with the white stencilling at the back of his mind. Now he thought of fields of buttercup. Shadows of clouds blown across the face of the sun moving over the flowers at summer's speed. He briefed Kempf and Hein about the two people who were presumed by Lourenço to have been in the Quinta da Águia but were still unaccounted for. He sent them out to put the word on the streets and told them that all reports must come to him first and none of them must be written. This would be a verbal operation. Kempf and Hein looked at each other. There was no such thing.

'These are direct orders from SS General Wolters,' said Voss.

'Nothing written?'

'That's what he said. He will make the written report to Berlin when the matter has been resolved.'

Kempf and Hein left the legation and drifted into the cafés and dark bars, where the occupants took their time to develop after the fierce light of the street and who, on hearing the word from the legation's men, downed their tumblers of wine and waded out into the crushing heat.

Voss stayed in his office, smoked and took some small comfort from moving his thumb up and down, nose to hairline. It had to be that only Lazard and Wilshere had known that he was a double. That Wolters' knowledge stopped at Anne as the informer positioned by Wilshere to send the British chasing after the wrong Beecham Lazard. How else could he be surviving this débâcle? Nobody knew that he'd been in the house. Lourenço had bought Anne's story. He was surviving. The next hours were critical, but what would come back from the street? Had anyone seen him and Anne walking in the Bairro Alto? The cigarette trembled in his mouth. He drew too hard and burnt his lips.

That morning, when the sweat of the city oozed out of their attics, their threadbare *pensões*, their stuffy rooms and dark bars they found the streets zipping with the new blood of fresh news. They sucked it in, this strange tribe, like cannibals who have to eat it to make something their own. They regurgitated it into the mouths of others, with new morsels added from their own inventive minds. The rumours grew and then multiplied when an ambulance reversed into the gateway of the British Embassy, stayed for five minutes and sped out, bell ringing, heading for the Hospital São José. The city ran a fever until lunchtime when those who'd made their small piece piled their olive pits, ate their fish and chewed their bread.

Except Paco.

Paco woke up at three in the afternoon, still dry-retching. He told the boy to bring him a jug of lemon water with salt dissolved into it. He drank it, forcing it down his throat, crying at its sourness. It revived him instantly. He went downstairs on shaky legs and sat, like a patient, under a shade in the sunlit courtyard. He found a half-smoked cigarette in his pocket which, when the boy bought him a herbal tea, he lit for him. He spoke to the boy, and because he was the only one who ever spoke to the boy with consideration, the boy told him things, told him everything that had happened whilst he'd been sick. Paco sat back and knew that his time had come, knew that this was the moment the Englishman had spoken about. Now it was only a question of timing and money.

The tea made him sweat and he thought he should go back upstairs and lie down, but then a Portuguese lowered himself on to the wooden chair opposite.

'I didn't see you this morning,' said Rui.

'I was sick.'

'You missed it all.'

'I don't think so.'

'You could have made your piece.'

'There's time.'

'So you do know something,' said Rui. 'I knew if there was anybody who would know something it would be Paco.'

'What do I know?' asked Paco.

The Portuguese sat back from the table to size up the state of Paco's mind, see if there was anything written on his face. He offered Paco a cigarette, a generosity which in Paco's experience was unusual.

'You heard about the murders?' asked the Portuguese.

'I heard there were six deaths. I don't know how many of them were murders.'

'Three people died in Estoril.'

'In the Quinta da Águia ... where they had the robbery.'

'The husband killed the American. The wife killed the husband. But who killed the wife?'

'I thought it was an accident,' said Paco.

'Nearly.'

'Who got the loot?'

'Exactly.'

'Haven't they asked the English girl who was staying at the house?'

'She wasn't there ... off fucking her boyfriend ... that Englishman you see down at the docks ... what's his name?'

'Wallis,' said Paco, screwing his fist on to his chin so that, for the first time, Rui knew with certainty that Paco held cards.

'There's money in this, Paco.'

'From whom, and how much?'

'The Germans, and that depends.'

'Not the PVDE.'

'No.'

'Is it interesting for them to know that the *inglesa* is lying?' asked Paco, and Rui went very still. 'That her lover is *not* Jim Wallis?'

'I don't know.'

'What do they want to know?'

'The identities of two people who left the Quinta da Águia on the night of the killings.'

'I can tell them something from which they will be able to draw their own conclusions.'

'How much?'

'But I will only talk to General Reinhardt Wolters . . . nobody else.'

'How much?'

'Fifty thousand escudos.'

'You're crazy.'

Paco closed his eyes, dismissing the notion. Rui nodded in sudden comprehension.

'You think it's all over?' he asked. 'Time to get out?'

'For me,' said Paco. 'You belong here.'

'Buy yourself some land, is that what you're thinking?'

Paco shrugged. Exactly that. Back to Galicia. No more selling water in the Alfama as he'd done in the years before the war. His own piece.

The Portuguese told him not to move and ran down the steps and back up Rua das Janelas Verdes, leaping up the *calçada* steps towards the British Embassy and swinging left to the German Legation, arriving at the gate with his lungs in rags. He babbled to the gate man and the very correct woman in reception. He dripped on the floor by her desk as he watched the muscles stand out in the backs of her bare legs as she climbed the stairs. She was back in seconds and didn't bother coming all the way down but beckoned him to follow her. He held his hat over his groin as he told Wolters the news, saw his eyebrows rise when he said the *inglesa* was lying, heard the explosion as he gave the price.

'Fifty thousand to know why the Englishwoman was lying,' roared Wolters. 'How much are you taking?'

'Nothing. I swear to you. Nothing.'
'Bring him.'

Voss had felt something different. There was something distinctive about urgency in forty degrees Centigrade. He opened his door a crack, saw the receptionist scuttle out of Wolters' office and down the stairs. She came back up with Rui dripping with sweat. He waited. Rui came back out, rattled down the stairs. Voss crossed to the window, watched him swing on the gate post and sprint down Rua do Pau de Bandeira. As far as Voss knew, this was a man who never ran. He put an eye to the crack of the door. Wolters crossed the corridor to the safe room, returned with blocks of escudo notes. Expenses.

Voss went back to the window and smoked hard, so hard that the nicotine closed the walls in around him. He waited for a lifetime, which in normal currency was only twenty minutes. The Portuguese came back down Rua Pau da Bandeira, trying to make Paco walk faster, but Paco, as Voss knew, had only one pace.

As they came up the stairs, Voss leaned against the door jamb, half in the corridor. Rui knocked on Wolters' door, holding Paco by the arm. Very valuable merchandise. Paco glanced over his shoulder at Voss and in one shameful lowering of his eyelids communicated everything Voss needed to know.

Voss didn't go back into his office. He walked straight down the stairs and out into the barbaric heat, forcing his legs down the driveway in casual strides. He slipped out of the gates with a nod to the gateman and as his foot hit the cobbles of the street he heard the first shout. There was no need to look back. He leaned into the thick air and ran.

He sprinted down Rua do Sacramento à Lapa; the sun at his back needled straight through his jacket and shirt. Sweat popped fatly in his hair. He heard the boots on the cobbles behind him, put his head down, lifted his knees and stamped his feet harder into the pavement. A tram thudded across the entrance to the street, heading downhill towards the British Embassy. He hit the corner fast, coming out into the street and swinging wide and right in behind the tram. He ran between the silver rails, gaining on the tram as its brakes bit and the wheels screeched. The Union Jack appeared blue/red/white high in the corner of his eye. Then he saw the group who'd come out of the legation and run the other way, down Rua Pau da Bandeira, up Rua do Prior and were aiming to cut him off at the embassy gates, which they could because no gateman alive would understand such urgency in this heat. He closed on the tram, where two barefoot boys were hanging off the back, looking at the foreigner in amazement. Voss lashed out at the rail, once, twice, caught it. His feet flailed wildly until they found the ledge. He pressed his streaming face to the glass, a woman inside stepped back, nudged her companion, who turned and looked affronted. Voss worked his way round to the blind side of the tram and it wasn't until it slowed into the left-hand bend that he heard the group behind him roaring at the other pursuers to change direction. The tram picked up speed downhill. One of the runners fell over himself and brought down others in his wake, a few continued down the hill but quickly gave up.

Cardew told Anne he'd bring the car around to the front of the Shell office building. He was looking after her, she knew it, keeping her close. The news of Sutherland's collapse had shaken them both, but the feeling of Rose's new hands on the helm had been immediate. She was on the leash now, not exactly mistrusted but a variable that Rose did not like having in his calculations. She went into the ladies powder room and left, via the back of the building, and headed straight for Estrela and the basilica. She let herself into Voss's apartment, saw the photograph back on its shelf, inspected the brush to find her strand of hair missing. She sat on the back of the sofa, drew her dress up to her thighs to keep cool and smoked out of the window while looking down into the square between the gardens and the church. It was a few minutes past five o'clock.

The tram came to a halt on Calçada Ribeiro Santos just on the other side of Avenida 24 Julho from Santos station and Voss leapt off and on to the pavement. The liners and cargo ships in the docks beyond seemed, at first, an interesting place to lose himself, stow away even, but the risk of being picked up by the port police and taken to the PVDE was too high. He preferred the idea of getting into the maze of streets around the Alfama and disappearing until nightfall, when he could make contact with Sutherland.

The tram seemed to be stationary for a long time and Voss

looked around for cabs, which were rare now in this part of Lisbon with the fuel shortages. His shirt had become a second sodden skin under his suit. He emptied the jacket pockets into his trousers, keeping his eye on the road back up to Lapa from where he was expecting his pursuers. He tried to remember if there'd been any legation cars around. There'd been none in the driveway. At that moment the tram slowly pulled away again just as he heard the sound of a set of tyres squealing and thudding over hot cobbles. Voss hopped on to the ledge at the rear doorway of the tram, pressed himself against the folding door. A black legation Citröen, two chevrons on its grille, the windscreen crowded with faces, drove down Calçada Ribeiro Santos with two wheels up on the pavement.

The tram was painfully slow as it moved away from Santos, as if the electricity in the overhead cables was suddenly draining away into the Tagus. The legation Citroën overtook, with two men leaning out of the windows, straining to see into the tram. Voss crouched. The tram's speed increased suddenly as it moved out of Madragoa into the Bairro Alto. If he could stay with this tram until Cais do Sodré he knew he could get a cab from there into the old medina of the Alfama district and they'd never find him in there, with all the alleys and staircases, the *tascas* and shops, the crowds and chaos of the early evening.

The Citroën pulled up and parked across the tramlines in the Rua da Boa Vista – the bonnet was up but nobody was looking in the engine. A man stood forward from the car with his hand up to stop the tram. Voss worked his way around to the back and came off at a run and kept his momentum up some *calçada* steps. He saw Kempf's big fist reach out, the finger pointing, and heard the crack of leather soles on cobbles as three men gave chase. He wasn't worried about Kempf – heavy, and his system riddled with pox, he wasn't going to last in this terrain and heat – but the young men behind him were fit and fired up with Wolters' zeal. Voss cut through a small *largo*, sprinted up *travessas*, and got into his stride down the Rua do Poço dos Negros. The tram he wanted was just ahead of him, one that would take him through the Baixa and up into the Alfama. He felt oddly unpursued. There was no sound of running behind him. He glanced back at an empty street and he suddenly thought that he was going to get there, that he'd lost them. He tore off his jacket and hurled it into an open doorway and ran, taking big strides, feeling strong, feeling elated. He put his head back and stared up at the light sky above the canyon of the narrow street and his running thoughts suddenly met stationary ones. His knees juddered as he came to a halt. He looked at his watch. It was 5.15 p.m. He'd stopped between the silver threads of the tram tracks. He looked back down the empty street, dropped his hands to his knees, hung his head and knew that he was lost.

Anne would be in his apartment.

They would go to his apartment. They would find her and they wouldn't just kill her.

He stopped a cab going in the opposite direction and directed the driver to the rear of the Estrela Gardens. He sat in the back, a stripe of sun across his thighs, and felt himself suddenly on the other side of the impossible knot. He rolled up his shirtsleeves as the cab pulled in by the roundabout at the bottom of Avenida Álvares Cabral. He paid the driver and went into the gardens, heading for the basilica. He walked, a brisk walk through still, hot, empty gardens – the shade, the sun, the black, the white. He felt a strange exhilaration and in other times he would have stopped to examine it in his head, but this time he knew. He was happy. My God, he was happy. And he remembered Julius writing from the *Kessel* at Stalingrad and knew now what he'd meant. He was free.

He stepped out of the gardens, through the iron railings and looked up and she was there at the window, waiting for him just as he'd expected. At that instant he knew that out there in the blinding sunlight of the square, in the whirling hub of the paranoid city, he was not alone and that nothing else mattered.

She saw him as soon as he stepped out of the gardens and threw her cigarette down the slope of the tiled roof. She leaned out of the window, kneeling on the back of the sofa. She was going to wave at him, but now she saw he was in shirtsleeves and that he'd raised his arms above his head, a strange thing to do. They came at him, running across the square and from left and right. A car appeared from nowhere. He was making no attempt to run. He stood like a sporting hero, expecting adulation from the crowd. He let one arm fall by his side, leaving the right arm raised in a salute. He swiped the air above him and with that gesture said it all – goodbye and get out.

The car pulled up in front of him. They scrummed him in. Anne ran for the apartment door, heard boots thundering up the wooden stairs. She turned back to the dresser and grabbed the package of letters and the Voss family photograph. She climbed out on to the roof, up and over the dormer window and lay there under the brutal sun while they crashed about in the room beneath her, chiselling and hacking at the air with their German voices.

Above her the sky was rediscovering itself in an aching blue after the slow bleaching of the long afternoon. A flight of pigeons took off from the bell towers of the basilica, the first of the evening strollers arrived in the fading gardens and a knife-grinder played on his sad pipes in the street below.

Chapter 25

30th July 1944.

This is not a diary. I am not allowed to write a diary. I think it must be rule number one of spycraft. I know that if I'm to survive this, with my mind intact and my nerves not so close to the surface that I bristle like a cat at the slightest movement, I must find a way of getting, if not all, then at least a part of it out of me. A release of pressure . . . is that what I mean? At the moment it is like a tumour which, because it is of the body, even if it is cell structure gone mad, it is treasured and nurtured by my biology. I can't do anything about it. More blood supply attaches to it. It grows bigger, sucking from all corners like some beastly embryo. I've tried to contain it. I've tried to cordon it off. I've tried to shut it away in an attic room like a crazed aunt. But I can't get the lid down, it broke through the ropes, it's rampaging around the house breaking everything it can lay its hands on.

I've tried to breathe it out of me, speak it out of me, even vomit it out of me, anything to stop what it's doing, which is taking me over. I lie on my back at night, the package of his letters and the Voss family photograph on my chest with only the grainy ceiling in my vision. I breathe very shallowly. The breath coming out in an ooze like bad air from a swamp and through this ooze I say the words, the words that are a part of it. 'Are you alive or dead?' I couldn't keep this up for long because it didn't seem to be a question any more about KV's continuing existence. I began to take it personally. There . . . I've smiled, nearly laughed reading that back. This could be working, except that even now I can see what I'm doing. I'm describing it and what it does to me but I'm not writing what it is.

What has happened to me? Nothing. I have sustained no physical injury apart from a bump on the head. I have only seen and felt things. This is how my brain works. Rationally. Logically. I am only two weeks older than when I left London. I am still the same height and weight. There is only one physical difference. I am no longer a virgin. But what was that? A hymen. An unseen membrane. There was hardly any pain, perhaps a little blood – I didn't inspect the sheets. No, what I've come to realize is that the difference between now and then is that rather than living in a state of expectation, I am living in hope. Why am I hoping? Why am I desperately hoping?

All that time ago, in that different age, that first night in the casino, Voss was just a presence, nothing more. When he carried Wilshere up to the house he was just a body, mechanically useful. We didn't meet until we clashed in the sea and we hardly spoke afterwards. How is it that in nearly drowning me he came to take responsibility for my life? I saw him again at the party. What did we talk about then? Nothing much. Fate . . . that was it, what else would we have talked about? What did he say? 'It's as if God's lost control of the game and the children have taken over . . . naughty children.' He said something else but down at the bottom of the garden, something about Wilshere and Judy. 'What does anybody know from just looking?' A spy's words, or maybe not. He said something else along those lines too. 'Everybody's a spy . . . we all have our secrets.' His parents and theirs. Mine. What do I know about mine? We are formed by our secrets. They enter us like bullets. No, that's not it. Like diseases. Bullets are a sweet release if they kill you, crippling if they don't. Disease is more like it. One moment you are healthy, the next you are ill. You have caught something. Secrets are an emotional disease. You cope with it or you don't. Stubbornness helps. My mother is a stubborn woman. Am I? What is my disease?

The next time we met was in his flat. I was so angry. I've never known anger like that. Hot rage. With my mother I'm like ice. A sentence from Rose and I was mad. A few lines from KV and I wasn't. Tender and making love and then the walk. The walk. I'm crying now. Why am I crying about the walk? Yes, it was on the walk that he said, 'I've only been in love once.' I died at that moment, until he said, 'With you, crazy.' When the world dropped away from me then, I saw how anything could happen. How Lazard could have infected Wilshere's mind. How he would believe Lazard over the veracity of his own heart. I know because I'd been falling into the ravine until he said those words: 'You . . . crazy.' How could that be? *Amor é cego.* Mad Mafalda's blindfolded doll.

The last time. Not the very last time. The last time to touch. After the horror. He took charge of me again. He bathed me, towelled me dry, put me to bed as if I was a child. That's what a lover is. Everything. Father, brother, friend, lover. Then lying there with the importance of it all in the briefcase, in the room. That first time he'd said something about 'when we're in here I want it to be just us', and it was, but only that once. The other times we always had our terrible guests.

He made the decision, the important, noble decision, the only one a man like that could make. Wolters will not get his hands on those plans. And for what? All for nothing. Some trick by the Americans. Is that my disease? That he put himself in terrible danger for somebody else's idiotic game, which probably wouldn't have worked anyway. He would have been a hero to both sides if he hadn't been so damned noble. No. That's not it. That's just the world's disease. What's mine? What am I going to have to grow around?

The last time, only to see, not to touch. The irony is in the brevity of the moment. Voss's economy has produced the heaviest burden of all. That fearless walk from out of the dark gardens into the fierce heat and sunlight, his hands up, telling me he was caught. The salute, like my own when I left him that morning with the briefcase in my hand. Love and admiration in one. And the warning. Swiping the air as they came for him. Get out. I was the only one who would have understood him. Get out, Andrea.

I know things now that I didn't know then. Rose and Sutherland were having their first planning meeting about how to get Voss out of Lisbon when Sutherland collapsed. Rose has told me that the PVDE were looking for two people whom they believed had left the Quinta da Águia alive that night. Wallis told me that one of the *bufos* from the Pensão Rocha had seen Voss and I together in the Bairro Alto. The *bufo*, a Galician, had been seen going into the German Legation on that last afternoon. Voss had got out of the legation. He was on the run but he'd come back. It was thought that he'd left something in his flat, something vital to the Allied cause. That could have been the only reason why he would do such a foolish thing as to go back. Nobody knew. But I knew.

This is my disease. But can I write it? I wish it were as impersonal as an equation, all algebra meaning something else. My disease is that I made him go for a walk in the Bairro Alto and we were seen. My disease is that he came back to get me out of his flat. To save me . . . again. My disease is that I have almost nothing of him and yet he has left me with everything.

This is my hope. This is my desperate hope. Not a cure. The cure is to have him back. This is a remission. How many times have I counted the days? How many times have I gone back to 30th June and counted. I was due the day before yesterday and I'm never late.

Chapter 26

Anne burnt the crumpled pages in the grate, including the blank pages underneath, all the way down to the first undented sheet. She lit a cigarette with the same match and drew on it, knowing that these would be her friends for life. The writing of her disease, her assessment of it, her diagnosis of it was consumed in a green flame until only the blackened negative remained, the copper of the ink still legible. She beat it with her shoe until it had all broken up and showered in flakes and specks on to the swept stone below the grate.

There had been only fractions of seconds when her thoughts had not been full of Voss. Even the lighting of a cigarette brought thoughts of his unwavering hand in the darkness of the garden. Nothing else came to her. Numbers didn't matter any more. Her work was automatic. Every thought, however disconnected, found its way back to Voss or a reference to him.

Now there was a difference. The written confession had brought about some containment. Her mind no longer galloped away from her, which it had done when she'd heard that Voss had been smuggled out of Portugal and back to Germany for interrogation. During those days she'd found herself amongst terrible imaginings of dark, sobbing cells punctuated by bright, searing light and questions, endless questions. Questions to which there were no answers, and questions to which all possible answers would be inadequate. She'd been told about torture, and the detail, which had been at a manageable distance in a rainy springtime lecture theatre in Oxford, could now make her writhe in the morning sunshine.

She crushed out the cigarette and for the first time in a week lay down on her bed and slept six straight hours, no dreams. She woke up without the normal electrical jolt as her mind hit the thousand-volt reality. She was on top of the bed. The room warm and glowing pink from the setting sun. Her body felt languorous, as if she'd been walking all day. An exquisite lassitude seeped through her muscles. She stretched to full length like a cat with all day on its mind and had a memory flash so vivid she rolled over to check that the room was empty.

She was six years old, her mother was sitting by her on the bed, cigarettes and cocktails mingled with her perfume, which was different for parties – spiky, exotic. She had her hand on Anne's shoulder, who had been sleeping. The material of her dress wasn't making the usual quiet rustlings but was racked with creaks and convulsive friction. Anne had seen through the slits of her eyes that her mother was crying and not quiet tears. She had been too sleepy, too overwhelmed by the weight of slumber to even put a finger to her mother's knee. In the morning her mother had returned to her usual cool strictness and Anne had forgotten the moment.

A thought unravelled itself. Rawlinson and his missing leg. An odd notion about the integrity of integers, the missing fraction ruining the completeness. What about the invisible missing fraction or the unseen additional one? The structure altered, the equation would never work out. Mad thoughts manipulating maths to emotions, and yet there was such a thing as a nuance.

The Cardew children were already in bed. Anne went down for dinner which was eaten late in high summer and, this evening, out in the garden under the liquid yellow light from Cardew's hurricane lamps. There was a crowd. A chair was pulled out for her and, when the face of the man who had helped her re-entered the light, she saw that it was Major Luís da Cunha Almeida, the man who'd stopped her horse from bolting.

They ate cheese, *presunto* and olives with fresh bread. Cardew poured wine brought by the major from his family estate in the Alentejo. Mrs Cardew served the fresh seafood while the servants went to the village bread oven to collect the lamb, which the cook believed tasted better having been slow-roasted since the middle of the afternoon.

They all ate the lamb, even the servants in the dimly lit kitchen. The potatoes, which were glued to the bottom and sides of the clay roasting tray, were sticky with meat juice and pungent from the garlic and rosemary. The meal returned Anne to her tribe like a rider, horseless on the open plain, who'd made it back to civilization.

At the end of the evening the major asked her if she would like to go out for a drive with him one evening the following week. She didn't say no. He settled on Wednesday.

As she went up to bed, Cardew intercepted her at the bottom of the stairs. He patted her shoulder, gripped it.

'Glad to see you've pulled through, Anne,' he said. 'Terrible shock, I imagine . . . but good show.'

In bed she thought that this was what it was like to be English. This is how we handle things. We're natural spies. We never wear anything on the outside. Napoleon was wrong, we were not *une nation de boutiquiers* but a nation of secretkeepers. We all know you can't say a word with a stiff upper lip.

Richard Rose agreed to see her on Monday afternoon. A positive psychological report must have made its way to him because until now he'd refused to see her. They'd said he was busy, but Wallis had told her that, unlike Sutherland, Rose preferred to keep his distance. He wasn't going to risk discomfort in front of an emotional woman. Rose into women didn't go. They were indivisible.

It was the last day of July and there'd been no relenting of the heat. Rose sat behind Sutherland's desk in the room shuttered against the sun which hammered that side of the embassy building in the afternoons. She sat in the hot gloom, an indistinct, ignorable figure, while Rose read through papers, signed them off. He rubbed his bare elbows as if they were sore from desk work. He muttered excuses. She didn't respond. She knew she wasn't a welcome presence. Sutherland's secretary had been replaced by someone called Douggie who didn't look up when he was spoken to but pointed with his pen. Rose spoke while stacking his papers.

'How d'you fancy staying with Cardew?'

'As his secretary?'

'Thinks a lot of you, he does,' said Rose. 'You'd still be doing the translation work, of course. Very important work, that.'

'I thought that was just my cover.'

'It was, yes. But you can't work as an agent any more, can you? Not here in Lisbon. And given the flap on at the moment we're going to have a job to replace you immediately. London don't want to move you yet. Cautious buggers. They'll have a file on you by now . . . in Berlin.'

That word 'Berlin' shot past her like a bird in the room.

'If you think that's the best use of my abilities . . .'

'We do,' he said, too quickly, '. . . for the moment.'

'You know that I do want to continue with the Company, sir.'

'Of course.'

'If my involvement in the last operation is going to have any bearing on my future . . .'

'Your *involvement*?' he said, pinching his lips, looking her in the eye for the first time.

'That my actions resulted in the loss of a valuable double agent.'

'You shouldn't blame yourself for that, you know,' he said, his face bearing an approximation of pity. 'You were inexperienced. Voss . . . yes . . . he should have known better. A terrible risk he took. Madness, really, for such an old hand.'

'Has there been any news?' she asked, matter of fact, wringing the pathos out of her voice.

'What do you know?'

'Only that he was taken back to Germany.'

'There were two others on the same plane. Men who'd been kidnapped off the streets of Lisbon just like Voss. One of them, Count von Treuberg, has since been released. He told us that Voss had been packed in a trunk for the flight. They were all taken from Tempelhof to the Gestapo HQ in Prinz Albrechtstrasse in the back of a van. Von Treuberg spoke to Voss, who was not in good shape. He saw him once more on the day he was released.'

Rose fell silent. Anne stared into the floor. Her head weighed heavily on the cords of muscle in her neck.

'Voss had undergone three days of intensive interrogation. Von Treuberg was shocked.'

Anne's insides froze and her breathing shallowed.

'Are you sure you want to hear this?'

'I want to know *everything*,' she said with vehemence.

Rose fetched a thick file from the grey metal cabinets that now lined the room.

'The operation you were involved in with Voss took place at a very sensitive moment for the Third Reich.'

'The coup attempt, you mean?'

'SS General Wolters was running an intelligence operation which he hoped was going to be one of the great successes of the war. It's in the nature of the losing team to believe that they can suddenly turn things around with a miracle. His operation was a disaster. He's lost a lot of money and one of the main pipelines for diamonds to the Reich. Voss is his scapegoat. Taken by itself, the botched operation might earn Voss a reprimand and a nasty transfer, but in the light of the 20th July assassination attempt it becomes more serious, which is better for Wolters. Wolters will want to implicate him in the coup attempt, which, at this distance, you might think is improbable except that *we* know that Voss knew what was going to happen. He gave us notice, so it was clear he was involved. Given that he's an old Abwehr man, the only one left out here, we're of the opinion that his part was to take control of the legation in Lisbon. If that is the case and there's a single strand of evidence pointing to that sort of level of involvement . . .'

Rose let his sentence drift, lit himself a cigarette.

'Then what, sir?'

He opened the file, picked the pages apart with his nail and turned them as if they were ancient scriptures.

'The investigation of senior Wehrmacht officers is being carried out by the head of the Reich Main Security Office, SS General Ernst Kaltenbrunner. He's a lawyer, which you might think is a good sign until you've seen a photograph of him. Sinister-looking brute. Total fanatic . . . intensely loyal. He will . . . he hasn't shirked his duties. Thousands of people have been rounded up. Men, women, children . . . anybody with a family connection or otherwise to any of the known conspirators has been brought in for questioning. All other suspects are being interrogated by an SS Colonel Bruno Weiss. He used to be head of security at the *Wolfsschanze*, Hitler's Rastenburg HQ in East Prussia. If he were younger he could be taken for Kaltenbrunner's son. I don't know where they breed them.

'I have no doubt that these men will find something amongst the thousands of depositions because it is in the nature of ordinary people to write things down when they shouldn't, say things that should never be said and babble uncontrollably when they're scared. Voss's chances are not good. If he is charged he will appear in the so-called People's Court presided over by the most disgraceful

271

judge ever to find his way into the law, Roland Freisler, where, if the evidence is even vaguely positive, he will be sentenced to be executed, and if it's not, he will certainly end up in a concentration camp where he's very unlikely to survive.'

Rose flicked through the file. Anne sat rigid in the chair.

'Apart from what we've heard from von Treuberg there is no other news,' said Rose, more concerned with his file. 'If I were you, Miss Ashworth, I'd forget about him. Live your life. It's the nature of war.'

Anne stood on shaking legs, on knees that unless she locked them straight would buckle. She turned to the door.

'You'll continue with Cardew, then?' he said to the back of her head.

'Yes, sir,' she replied, and staggered out of the room into the corridor.

Anne worked with an intensity that unnerved Cardew. She rarely looked up and took no more than a quarter of an hour for lunch. On Wednesday evening she went out with Major Luís Almeida. They drove to Cascais and ate a fish meal. She didn't recall what fish. She remembered the way the major didn't take his eyes off her throughout the meal and even when he was driving, so that she had to brace herself occasionally to get him to look ahead. She knew then that she would be all right because she didn't want to die. She feared death, which she hadn't a week ago. She began to orbit nearer to the outer edges of normality as each day passed and another onion skin of insulation wrapped itself around her disease, her growth, which had been rendered benign now by the absence of any trace of menstrual blood.

The major, on holiday for the whole of August, intensified his campaign and took her out nearly every night. She never turned him down. She only refused to ride horses. His presence was a comfort, his attention close to avuncular. Their talk was formal, inquisitive without being intimate. She preferred that. She could retreat into herself while she was with him and he wouldn't pressure her. She knew that she was changing and that it was for her own protection. It was making her different and she couldn't help that difference materializing into distance. She would find herself in a crowd at a lunch, never aloof but always alone. Society took her in

272

and she let herself become a part of its edifice, not as a brick in its wall but more of a gargoyle spouting out of a corner.

On a mid August Saturday night Anne sat with the major outside a café in the main square in Estoril. He'd tried to persuade her into the casino but she wasn't ready for that yet, if ever. It was eleven o'clock and still hot. She had no appetite for food or drink. She proposed a walk along the front, away from the holiday bustle, the family scenes, the fractious palm trees. The major was glad to stretch his legs.

They walked the promenade above the beach. There was a little light from a crescent moon, no wind and the air was soft. Waves came in as phosphorescent ripples, collapsing on to the beach and running up to merge into the sand. She took his arm. Her heels made the only sound above the muted ocean.

She stopped to breathe it in and the major put his arm around her and she realized that he'd misinterpreted her motives. It wasn't as if she hadn't expected it. It was just that she'd never managed to think any further than it happening. She turned to him and put her hands up on his chest to keep him at bay but he wasn't tentative like Voss. He crushed her to him and kissed her on the mouth for the first time, long and hard, so that she was struggling for breath and completely unmoved.

His staidness vanished. His manner, which was normally governed by a stronger gravitational pull than that on most humans, giving him his granite-like dependability and solidity, broke its moorings and he became all ardour and expression. She was stunned by the transformation. He held her face in his hands and told her over and over how much he loved her, so that the words lost their meaning and she didn't listen to them, but began to think whether this was perhaps a Portuguese trait – to be hermetically sealed receptacles for mad passion.

He was breathing the words into her mouth, as if trying to make her say them back to him, and she was remembering his profound enjoyment of food, how eating one meal would remind him of the wonder of another. Wine to him was like a favourite piece of music. He drank it with his eyes closed, let it flow through him as if it was Grand Premier Cru Mozart. The flowers he bought for her he seemed to enjoy more himself – plucking a bloom, he wouldn't just sniff it, he would inhale it. It struck her that he was a sensualist and she'd hardly been aware of it because he had no talent for conversation but only physical pleasure.

He snapped her back into reality. He was holding her by the shoulders and willing her to respond, his forearms trembling as if he was restraining himself from crushing her. He was demanding that she marry him, but she couldn't find any words to begin to explain the complexity of her situation.

'Will you? Will you?' he asked, again and again, his English heavily accented so that each demand came from deeper and deeper down his throat like a man drowning in a well.

'You're hurting me, Luís,' she said.

He let her go, running his hands down her arms, hanging his head, suddenly ashamed.

'It's not so easy,' she said.

'It *is* easy,' he replied. 'It is *very* easy. You only have to say one word. Yes. That's it. It is the easiest "yes" you will ever say.'

'There are complications.'

'Then I am happy.'

'How can you be happy?'

'Complications are surmountable. I will talk to anybody. I will talk to the British Ambassador. I will talk to the Chairman of Shell. I will talk to your parents. I will . . .'

'My mother. I only have a mother.'

'I will talk to your mother.'

'Stop, Luís. You must stop and let me think for a moment.'

'I will only let you think if it is to overcome these complications, if it is to see that complications . . .' he said, running out of words for a second until he announced, 'Complications mean nothing to me. There is no complication that I cannot . . . that I cannot . . . *Raios*! . . . what is the word?'

'I don't know what you want to say . . . overleap?'

'Overleap!' he roared in agreement. 'No, no, not overleap. Overleap means that it is still there . . . behind you maybe, but still there. Vanquish. There is no complication that I cannot vanquish.'

She laughed at a vision of Luís with sword and shield flashing in the sun, blinding the complications.

'I can't answer you,' she said.

'I am *still* happy.'

'You can't still be happy, Luís. I haven't said anything.'

'I am happy,' he repeated, and he knew why, but he didn't want to say that it was because she hadn't given him the alternative, perhaps even easier, reply.

She crawled into bed at two in the morning. Luís wouldn't let her go home. His earlier boldness had given him new fuel to burn and he couldn't stop. He took her into Lisbon and they danced at the Dancing Bar Cristal. Luís had never been so animated and she realized that he could only speak when he was doing something else. As soon as they went back to the table for a rest he would fall back into silent contemplation of unknown complications until he could bear it no longer and he'd drag her back on to the floor. There he talked as if he knew something she didn't. His family, their estate outside Estremoz in the rural Alentejo, 150 miles east of Lisbon, his work, the barracks he was posted to, which luckily was in Estremoz, and all was related to how their life would be together, how she would fit into his world.

Anne slept and dreamt her dream and woke in a panic with the certainty that she would not be able to survive this pace. Like a fallen rider with a foot still trapped in the stirrup, dragged along at the whim of the horse, she needed a release, she needed control, but she could not bring her intelligence to bear down on the complications. The different strands knotted too quickly.

She asked herself a question. Why shouldn't she marry Luís? She didn't love him was not an answer, it was the reason she wanted to be with him. That she was still in love with Voss did not make any sense. Richard Rose had been brutal in his prognosis. The whole point of her involvement with Luís was to survive her guilt. That she was carrying Voss's embryo was the impediment, which, as soon as the thought occurred, was dispatched. It scared her, not in shivers of panic, they were surface qualms. This was core fear, a deep moral fear. Only religion did this to you, she thought. All that stuff the nuns had crammed into her head about guilt and evil, it shook her up, disorientated her. She paced the room to confirm the ground under her feet, to calm herself, to tether herself to what she now understood, which was that she *had* to marry Luís *because* she was carrying Voss's child.

She sat on the bed inspecting her hands. She had been young. She had been green and whippy, but now she could feel the brittleness of age creeping in and the breakability that came with it. Alone on her single bed, in the high August heat, with the cells multiplying inside her, she shivered in the cold shadows of society, the Church, her mother. She made her decision and even while making it the Catholic inside her knew that there would be some cost, some bloody awful price to pay later on. She would marry Luís da Cunha Almeida and her secret would sit with her other one, they would be joined like Siamese twins, individual but dependent on each other.

The morning light had a new clarity. The thick heat of the last few days and nights had been cut by a fresh, saltine zest from the Atlantic. The sun still shone in a clear sky but bodies felt less like carcasses. The Serra de Sintra was no longer vague in the haze and the palm trees applauded in the square. Out from under the close doom of night, Anne saw things differently. There was hope of a solution. She would talk to Dorothy Cardew. The women, between them, would get things out on the table where they could be examined.

The maid took the Cardew girls to the beach mid-morning and Anne found Dorothy on her own, sitting with her sewing box in the living room. She was working on a sampler, tackling the 'e' of 'Home'. Meredith was outside reading in the garden, his pipe signalling his enjoyment. Anne moved around the room, circling before landing, waiting for a way in. The needlepoint was badly at odds with what she had trampling through her mind. Dorothy Cardew eyed her, made mistakes in the sampler, gave up on it.

'Luís has asked me to marry him,' said Anne, which knocked Dorothy back into the cushions.

Anne registered the total relief in Dorothy's face. Good news after all.

'That's marvellous,' she said. 'Wonderful news . . . such a good man, Luís.'

And that was the end of it. This was not a day for trouble. The clear air, the breeze in the pines, the birds talking up the day so that anything other than good news would seem ill-mannered.

'Yes,' said Anne, the word dropping out of her like a drunk from a bar.

'You must let me tell Meredith.'

The scene developed, transformed from the one Anne had inside her head. Dorothy skipped to the french windows and called for her husband, hopping up on to one leg as she did so.

'Good news, darling,' she called.

Meredith slammed his book shut and scrambled like a fighter pilot. He joined his wife at the french windows, breathless, eager.

'Luís has asked Anne to marry him.'

A flicker of disappointment. Hitler hadn't surrendered after all.

'Congratulations!' he roared. 'Terrific chap, Luís.'

'Yes,' said Anne, another brawler ejected into the street.

A quizzical look from Cardew. Had he seen something? Had he sensed something other than spoken words in the room?

'Have you said anything to anyone?'

'Not yet.'

'Best talk to Richard first . . . could be complicated.'

'Yes.'

'Marvellous news, though . . . couldn't hope for a better chap than Luís. Terrific horseman, too,' he finished, as if that could be an enormous help in a marriage.

Anne's smile creaked into position. This was the future – words taken from her and put into a common language, the language of the receiver, never her own. It pricked her eyeballs because that was one of Voss's talents – an understanding of many languages but more especially the silent ones.

The following Tuesday Anne sat in the Estrela Gardens watching children, waiting for time to pass before heading into Lapa for her meeting with Rose. The children ran over the thousand changing shapes on the ground as the breeze rippled the sunlight through the trees. The pace was slowing at last. The relentlessness was still there but that breathless speed had gone. Now there was the sense of large forces manoeuvring, something perhaps to do with what was happening in Europe as the Russian, American and British armies bore down on the rubble of the Reich.

She walked to the gates opposite the basilica and looked up to the room where she'd been waiting only a few weeks ago. A maid was cleaning the window, a disembodied hand appeared and flicked a cigarette out. At her feet the silver tramlines embedded in the cobbles headed off down the hill of the Calçada da Estrela towards São Bento and the Bairro Alto where they would cross and connect with other rails but would never deviate from their dedicated path. What on one night had seemed like an exquisite thread tugging her to a hopeful future, now appeared as a terrible certainty from which the only way out was derailment and disaster.

She sat in front of Richard Rose again, who was not ignoring her but, because it was after lunch, was lounging back in his chair with a cigarette in his hand and either smoke in his eye or contempt tempered only by shrewdness.

'Cardew told me your news,' he said.

My news, thought Anne, dissociated from it already, a messenger for someone else.

Rose waved his match at her, tossed it into the ashtray. It enraged her, God knows why.

'When we trained you as an . . .'

'With all due respect, sir, you did not train me as a translator. I arrived with that ability on board.'

'When we trained you as an *agent* and the subsequent assessment of your training arrived here in Lisbon, I . . . *we* didn't perceive you as an emotional character. Everything pointed towards you being logical, rational, even clinical. That was why we liked you.'

'*Liked* me?'

'On paper you were perfect for the assignment,' he said, sitting back, flourishing his cigarette, stabbing the smoking end in her direction, goading her. 'You were female, very intelligent, excellent at role-play, of . . . beguiling looks, but also determined, clear-headed, detached . . . in short, perfect for the work.'

Silence while Rose inspected his cigarette box, seeing if that had been enough to elicit more reaction.

'You arrived,' he continued, 'and we were immediately impressed by the way you entered into your role. Good information. Strong social involvement. Excellent handling of some difficult personalities. Everything going swimmingly until . . .'

Rose blew out smoke in an exasperated jet.

'Even logical, rational, clinical people can fall in love,' said Anne.

'*Twice*?' asked Rose.

The cold, cutting edge of the word sliced into her. Its unjustness pushed her on to the defensive.

'It was you who told me to forget about Voss,' she said, 'that there was no hope for him.'

'I did, but . . .' he said, and let that hang with the smoke, accusatory, before dismissing it with a flick of his fingers. 'So, now you'd like to marry Major Luís da Cunha Almeida?'

'He has asked me. I want to know if it's possible,' said Anne. 'I don't intend to allow it to affect my work . . . the work which you indicated that I would be doing in the . . . until further notice.'

'There is the small question of identity,' said Rose. 'If you want to get married I don't see why you shouldn't, it's just that you will have to marry under your cover name and you won't be able to have any member of your family present. As far as the Portuguese are concerned you are Anne Ashworth and will have to remain so.'

'My name changes anyway.'

'Quite.'

'You should know that I broke my cover story.'

'How?'

'I was emotionally . . .'

'Just tell me how.'

'I told Dona Mafalda and the contessa that my father was dead.'

'I doubt that will be a problem. If it is we'll say that you were emotionally distraught, that your father died very recently in an air raid and you've been unable to accept it. On application forms you always put him down as alive but he is in fact dead. We'll arrange a death certificate. Finish.'

And that was the end of the matter. The end of Andrea Aspinall too. She stood and shook hands, headed for the door.

'We've had news of Voss, by the way. Not good,' he said to the back of her head. 'Our sources tell us that he was shot at dawn in Plötzensee prison last Friday with seven others.'

She slipped through the door without looking back. The corridor rocked like a ship's in a heavy sea. She concentrated on each stair going down to the street, nothing automatic, nothing certain. She breathed in the clear air, hoping it would somehow dislodge the obstruction in her chest, this fishbone, this piece of shrapnel, this sharp chunk of crystalline ice. She screwed up her face, doubled over and ran up the hill towards Estrela. It felt like a heart attack

279

and, when she reached the gardens, she found that she could think of nothing else but crossing the road to the basilica and hiding herself in the darkest corner.

Inside, she crossed herself and collapsed on to her knees, face in the crook of her elbow and the word 'never' repeating itself in her mind. She was never going to see Voss again, never going to be herself again, never going to be the same again. The pain loosened itself from the wall of her chest and moved up to her throat. She started crying, but not crying as she'd ever cried before, not bawling like a child, because this pain was pain that could not be articulated. It had no human sound. Her mouth was wide open, her eyes were creased shut. She wanted her agony to find some superhuman screech so that she could get it out of herself but there was nothing, it wasn't on her scale. Scalding tears coursed down her cheeks, acid streaks to the corner of her mouth. Snot and saliva poured out of her, hung in quivering skeins from her mouth and chin. She seemed to be crying for everything, not just herself but Karl Voss, her dead father, her distant mother, Patrick Wilshere, Judy Laverne, Dona Mafalda. She didn't think she would be able to recover from such crying, until a nun put a hand on her shoulder and that jerked her upright. She wasn't ready for nuns, nor the dark sweat box of the confessional.

'*Não falo Português,*' she said, smearing her face around with a ball of sodden handkerchief. She crashed through the pew into the aisle and ran for the door. Out in the sun, the breeze was still blowing. It went clean through her louvred ribs.

Book Two

The Secret Ministry of Frost

Chapter 27

16th August 1968, Luís and Anne Almeida's rented house in Estoril, near Lisbon.

The night before her flight to London Anne had another running dream. Almost every night since coming back from the vicious fighting in the Mozambique war she'd had running dreams. Sometimes she would be running in daylight, but most of the time it was twilight. This time it was dark and enclosed. She was running down a tunnel, a rough tunnel like an old mine. She had a torch in her hand which was picking up the black shiny walls and the uneven floor, showing the imprint of some old tracks, narrow gauge. She was running away from something and she would occasionally look over her shoulder to see only the blackness she'd left behind her. But there was also the sense of running towards something. She didn't know what it was and she could see nothing beyond the hole of light made by her torch.

She ran desperately. Her heart pounded and her lungs felt pierced. The torchlight began to waver. The beam flickered and yellowed. She shook the torch but it dimmed further and she found herself looking into the fading filament of the bulb, her breath suddenly visible as if it was cold. Finally it was totally black. No source of ambient light presented itself. Fear crawled up her throat and she tried to scream but nothing would come. She came awake with Luís holding her in his arms and she was crying as she hadn't cried in over twenty years.

'It's all right, it's only a dream,' he said, the obvious surprisingly comforting. 'She'll be all right. You'll be all right. We'll all be all right.'

She nodded into his chest, unable to speak, knowing it was more than that but going along with him. It had been a turning point. That subterranean river, which snatched people's lives and drove them harder and faster over the quick rocks, through the boiling water, down the chutes and cataracts, had just grabbed her again. The strong current was wrenching her away from her quiet past, slow at the moment, but the pace was gathering beneath her.

She didn't go back to sleep but lay on her side looking at her husband's broad back, blocking the sound of his violent snoring with thoughts that hadn't occurred to her in more than two decades. The news of her mother's illness had saved them from a formal separation after she'd refused to accompany him to yet another African war but, having arrived at the brink, she now found herself picking over her life, re-examining it in the new light of an uncertain future. One which was sending her back to London and her husband and son, colonel and lieutenant, fighting together in the same regiment in another independence war in Guiné in West Africa.

That other new beginning, twenty-four years ago, came back to her like biography, an objective fascination with another person's more interestingly led life but, somehow, subjectively dull. She saw herself on her wedding day on a belting hot morning in Estremoz. How she was able to appear happy because she was glad that Luís had been so desperate to marry her, he'd rushed her into the ceremony giving her no time to think of the complications she was carrying inside her down that aisle. It had also meant that when her baby arrived three weeks late there was no suspicious discrepancy in the dates between her wedding night and the birth of *their* son on the 6th May 1945.

That had been unforgivable. She still felt the pang of guilt as fresh as on the day she'd announced her pregnancy to Luís. The happiness he radiated, the tenderness with which he held her, cut through to her terrible twin secrets, jabbed them awake so that as Luís's joy grew sweeter, hers could only sour. It was then that she understood the true nature of the spy. The work she'd been doing for Rose and Sutherland hadn't been anything like spying. What she'd done to Luís was spying. Watching him believe in her, admire her, love her, while she silently betrayed him every moment of every day. It was why, she supposed, the punishment meted out to spies throughout the ages had always been cruel and swift.

So much had happened after they were married that she couldn't understand when looking back on it, especially that first year, why

284

it all seemed so flat. All the decisions she'd made – those lonely nights spent in the confines of her mind – had determined the following decades and yet they came back to her with such rational clarity, devoid of excitement, mere measures for the continuation of her existence.

The long weekend of the wedding had seen the beginning of a seismic shift in her view of the world. Snapshots entered her head of Luís's family, the Almeidas, and how they ran their estate in the depths of the rural Alentejo on principles she'd come across when studying the Middle Ages under the nuns. On the morning after the wedding, driving around the estate in a small cart with Luís, they'd come across workers of all ages, even small children, clothed from head to foot against the dry, unbearable heat, reaping corn by hand. She saw them again later sitting under a cork oak, eating the meagre rations provided by the estate and wincing with disgust at the barely edible food. She recognized some of the men who'd been brought in to sing at the wedding feast – slow, beautiful, melancholy songs, which had all the Almeidas, even the men, in tears.

She'd taken Luís to task about the treatment of these people and he hadn't answered her. It had always been like this. She was about to importune Luís's sister, hoping for a more sympathetic response, until the sister, showing her around the kitchens, described, almost with glee, how they pickled the olives with swathes of broom to make them more bitter so the farmworkers wouldn't eat too many. As she'd travelled back to work in Lisbon on the train, an action regarded as treachery by the Almeidas, who thought she should remain with her new family, she found ideas forming in her head, new ideas about a fairer way of life. Ideas which would mean that she wouldn't have to think too much about herself.

She rolled on to her back, turned away from Luís and his animal gruntings. She'd been lying in this same bed twenty-four years earlier with the baby growing inside her as rapidly as her guilt with all its Catholic foundations and she'd known then that there would have to be some payment for what she was doing. A heavy sum would be extracted and she'd hoped then, as she did now, that her unpredictable God would see fit to confine His punishment to her alone.

Her eyelids became impossibly heavy, even against her horror

285

of re-entering the dark tunnels of her dreams, and she slept until Luís, at his morning toilet, woke her.

If her mother hadn't been seriously ill she would have given up at the airport and gone to Guiné with them. She made a fool of herself outside the departures lounge. Luís had to prise her arms from around Julião. She wept in the toilet until her flight was called. As she flew she didn't eat but drank gin and tonics and sat at the back, smoking on her own. She couldn't seem to propel her thoughts forward. Like last night all they wanted to do was drift back listlessly over the past. This time it was her son, Julião, who occupied the foreground of her mind. How she'd failed him and he in turn had failed her.

She'd learned something about genetics on the day he was born. Looking into his face, screwed up against the harsh hospital light, she knew instantly that this child's personality was neither hers nor Karl Voss's and she hadn't been so astonished when Luís, the proud father, had picked him up and said:

'He's me, isn't he?'

In that moment the Voss family photograph came into her mind – the father and his eldest son, Julius, who'd died at Stalingrad – and she knew that this was who Luís was holding.

'I think we should call him Julião,' she said, and Luís had been jubilant that she'd chosen his grandfather's name.

It had been so poignant when they left the hospital two days later on VE day. They drove down the hill from the Hospital São José into the Restauradores to find it full of people waving Union Jacks and Stars and Stripes and jabbing the air with victorious fingers and V-shaped placards. She noticed blank flags being waved, too, and asked Luís what they meant.

'Ach!' he said in disgust, pulling away from the crowd. 'They're the communists. The hammer and sickle is banned by the Estado Novo so they wave these rags . . . I see that and I'm sick, I'm . . .'

He hadn't been able to continue and she couldn't understand his vehemence. So they'd left it, the thin end of the wedge already jammed in between them.

The first black day had come twenty months later when, after trying every siesta and every night to conceive another baby and after three consultations with different gynaecologists, Luís went

286

to see a doctor, a private one, not an army doctor, not for this. He took Julião with him for comfort and, she suspected, to show he'd already struck once.

He returned home, stunned and morose. The doctor had told him something he hadn't been prepared to believe and, on taking the first blast of Luís's outrage, let him look down the microscope himself. The doctor had said it could easily happen. A man, especially one in an active profession and a horseman, could go sterile.

Luís sat outside on the verandah in the January cold, staring at the slow, grey heave of the Atlantic. He was immovable and inconsolable. Anne, looking at the back of his bowed head, knew now that she'd never be able to tell him. After some hours she tried to coax him back in but he wouldn't respond. He even lashed her hand away from his shoulder. She sent Julião out to bring him round. He eventually picked the boy up, sat him on his knee, held him tight and when the two came back in an hour later she knew that something had been resolved. He formally apologized to Anne and looked down on his son's head in such a way that she knew, and it was almost with relief, that Julião would be the focus of Luís's life.

As the plane began its slow descent the adrenalin trickle started. They touched down at Heathrow just after midday. The taxi drove into London past office blocks, endless rows of houses, through traffic, and she knew she was in a foreign country. It was not her own. This was a country which had moved, was moving. She realized how stultifying Salazar's Estado Novo had become. In the first glimpses of London on a summer's afternoon driving through Earl's Court, seeing men with long hair, wearing red flared velvet trousers and vests, vests like the peasants wore except in bright colours and bleached with circles, she realized what Portugal was missing. This lot wouldn't have lasted ten minutes on the streets before being picked up by the PIDE.

The cab driver charged her two weeks' housekeeping to take her to her mother's house on Orlando Road in Clapham.

'It's on the meter, love. I doesn't make it up,' he said.

She paid and waited for him to go, prepared herself. The last time she'd seen her mother was Easter 1947, Luís had been on exercise and she'd flown back to London for a week. It had not gone well. London felt like a beaten city – grey, still rubble-strewn and ration-carded and peopled by dark-clothed shadows. Her mother had shown little interest in Julião and had made no alterations to her social or work arrangements, so that Anne had found herself alone with her son in the Clapham house for most of the week. She'd returned to Lisbon furious and since then she and her mother had phoned rarely, written letters which were strictly informative and exchanged presents neither of them wanted at Christmas and birthdays.

The only change in the street was a new block of flats where her piano teacher's house had been bombed out on the corner of Lydon Road. She walked up the path to her mother's house behind the privet hedge and had a momentary panic at the sight of the red-stained glass panels in the front door. She rang the door bell. Feet clattered down the stairs. A priest opened the door, saw the shock in her face.

'No, no,' he said, 'nothing to worry about. I was just dropping by. You must be the daughter. Audrey said you were arriving today. From Lisbon. Yes. Nice bit of weather we're having here so . . . yes . . . well, come in, come on in.'

He took her case. They stood in the hall, inched around each other for a moment. Familiar furniture appeared over the priest's shoulder like better company at a cocktail party.

'She's having a good day today,' he said, trying to recapture her attention.

'She still hasn't told me what's wrong with her,' said Anne. 'I tried to ask her last night on the telephone but she's being evasive.'

'Good days and bad days,' said the priest, who although bald, looked as if he was her age.

'Do *you* know, Father?'

'It would be better coming from her, I think.'

'She said it was serious.'

'It is and she knows it. She even knows how long . . .'

'How *long*?' she said, shaken by it, not prepared for that level of finality. 'You mean . . . ?'

'Yes. She's always playing it down, just says it's serious, but she knows it's only a matter of weeks. Weeks rather than months . . . so the doctors are saying.'

'Shouldn't she be . . . in hospital?'

'Refuses to stay. Won't have it. Can't stand the smell of the food. Said she'd rather be on her own at home . . . with you.'

'With me,' she said, out loud but to herself. 'Forgive me, Father, but you seem very cheerful, given . . .'

'Yes, well, I always am around Audrey. Most extraordinary woman, your mother.'

'I have to admit that I am quite surprised to see you here. I mean, she was never . . .'

'Oh yes, I know. Somewhat lapsed.'

'I mean, she's always been religious and quite strictly Catholic . . . that's how she brought me up. But as for . . . going to church, priests, confessions, Holy Communion, all that . . . no, Father . . . ? You didn't say . . .'

'Father Harpur. That's Harpur with a "u",' he said. 'Look, I'd best get going. I've put the tonic in the fridge.'

'Tonic?'

'She likes a gin and tonic at about six.'

'Is she in her room?' she asked, suddenly desperate for him to stay, help her through this . . . any awkwardness.

'No, no . . . she's out in the garden sunning herself.'

'In the *garden*?' she said, looking up the stairs.

'She just asked me to put something in your room . . . that's why I came from upstairs.'

'No, of course, but you said she was out in the garden in the sun.'

'Yes.'

'Have you heard my mother's confession?' she asked.

'Yes, I have,' he said, startled by the change of tack.

'Did she tell you when she last went to confession?'

'Thirty-seven years ago. It *did* take several days.'

'Well, that was probably the last time she sat out in the garden, too.'

'No, that would have been when she was in India.'

'Yes, I suppose it was.'

'You must go to her,' he said. 'I must get back to the church.'

They shook hands and he slipped out the door, black and silent as a cat burglar, a soul saver. She took her bags up to her room, which had been painted and new curtains hung. There were flowers on the dressing table. All her old books were on their shelves, even her battered, balding teddy lay on her bed like a valued but stinking hound. The smell of cigarette smoke drifted up from the garden and she saw herself twenty-four years younger sitting in front of the mirror, pretending to light a cigarette from a suitor's hand. She ducked to see herself in the glass, to inspect twenty-four years' worth of damage, but there was little on the surface. She could still grow her hair long if she wanted to and it was still thick and black with only the odd white strand, which she plucked out. Her forehead was smooth, although there was a little creasing around the eyes, but the skin of her face rested on the bones, there was no sag in her cheeks. Well preserved, they called it. Pickled. Pickled in her own genetic recipe.

On the lower floor she pushed open her mother's bedroom door. There was the strong scent of lilies masking another odour – not death, but the decay of live flesh. She shied away from it, went down to the hall, clicked across the black and white tiles to the kitchen and out into the garden. Her mother sat in the sun under a broad-brimmed straw hat with a tail of red ribbon. She had her neck back, her face up to the sun and the high trees which, in full leaf, screened the back of the houses behind. Smoke from a cigarette rippled out of her dangling hand. A tray sat on a stool and an empty chair next to it.

'Hello, Mother,' she said, nothing more momentous coming to mind.

Her mother's eyes sprang open in shock – shock and, she saw, joy.

'Andrea,' she said, as if she was crying the name out of a dream.

She kissed her mother. There was a moment's awkwardness as she crossed over to kiss the other cheek.

'Oh yes, of course, both cheeks in Portugal.'

Bony fingers fumbled across Anne's shoulders, thumbed her clavicle, seemed to be searching for something.

'Sit, sit, have some tea. It's a bit stewed but have some all the same. Did Father Harpur leave you a scone? He's a bugger for those scones.'

Her mother was thin. Her body had lost its compactness, the sturdiness. If there was any creaking now it wasn't from the bra or corsetry clasped to her but from old bones unoiled in their joints. She was wearing a flowery tea gown, and a loose light coat, cream and sky blue. Her pale face when kissed had lost its cool firmness. Now it was slack and soft, warm from the sun. Her features were still fine but faded and she'd lost that severity that had been so tiresome. For someone who was dying she looked good, or perhaps it was just what she was emanating.

'You met Father Harpur.'

'He let me in. I was surprised, I must say.'

'Really?'

'But he was very cheerful.'

'Yes, we do get on, James and I. We have such a giggle.'

'Giggle' wriggled like a worm in her mouth. Anne shifted in her seat.

'He told me he was your confessor.'

'He is, yes. And no, that wasn't much of a laugh, I have to say. He's a poet too, did he tell you?'

'We only met on the doorstep.'

'A good poet, as well. He wrote a very fine poem about his father. The death of his father.'

'I didn't think you liked poetry.'

'I didn't. I don't. I mean, I don't like that self-important stuff. People wandering lonely as clouds . . . you know. It's not me.'

There was a long pause while a wind worked its way through the trees and Anne had the feeling that she was being prepared for something. Softened up.

'Poetry's different these days,' said her mother. 'Like music, clothes, the sexual revolution. Everything's changing. You probably saw it on the way back from the airport. We even won the World Cup . . . was it last year, or the year before . . . anyway that was novel. How are Luís and Julião?'

Silence, while her mother smoked the cigarette to the end, her eyes closed, eyeballs fluttering against the thin lids.

'Tell me about Luís and my grandson,' she insisted gently.

'Luís and I had a bad falling out.'

'What about?'

'About the wars in Africa,' she said, immediately steeling up, not wanting to, but that was what politics did to her.

'Well, at least it wasn't about boiling his egg too hard.'

'He knows that these wars are not . . . if there is such a thing . . . good wars. They're not just.'

291

'He's an army officer, they're not normally given the choice, are they?'

'He should have kept Julião out of them, though . . . and now they're both in Guiné, or at least they will be in a few days' time.'

'It's what men do if they join the army. Combat is what they think they've always wanted from that life, until they get into it and come face to face with the horror.'

'Luís has even seen the horror. That first time back in '61 when we went to Angola . . . terrible . . . the things he told me he'd seen up in the north. But he's been hardened . . . inured to it. God knows, he might have even perpetrated some of the appalling atrocities they reported in Mozambique. No, there's no doubt that Luís knows. He knows absolutely what it's like. But the fact is, *he's* a full colonel, it's Julião who'll be in the front line. Julião's going to be the one who's leading the patrols out into the bush. The guerrillas . . . sorry, I have to stop, I don't really want to . . . I just can't think about it.'

Her mother reached out her hand and Anne thought she wanted more tea at first but found it clawing a way up her leg towards her own. She gave it over and her mother stroked it with a papery palm.

'There's nothing to be done. You'll just have to wait it out.'

'Anyway, that's why we had the falling out. I was supposed to go with them and I refused. Your call saved us from a formal separation.'

Some drops fell on the back of her hand and she thought it was raining and looked up to find the trees blurred as tears leaked down her cheeks. She was crying without knowing it, without understanding why. The start of some difficult unbuckling.

The sun dropped behind the trees. They went inside. Anne rattled ice cubes into glasses, poured the gin and tonics, sliced the lemon, thinking about the new openness of this undiscovered person she'd known all her life, working out the best way in.

'You mustn't spend any of your own money while you're here,' said her mother, shouting from the living room. 'I know what life's like in Portugal and I have plenty. It's all going to be yours in a few weeks so you might as well use it now.'

'Father Harpur said it'd be better if *you* told me what was wrong

292

with you,' said Anne, handing over the G&T, blurting it out, unable to keep up the light pretence.

Her mother took the drink, shrugged as if it was nothing much.

'Well, it started as a stomach ache, one that went on all the time, no respite. Nothing would cure it – camomile tea, milk of magnesia – nothing would even ease it. I went to the doctor. They prodded and probed, said there was nothing to worry about. Ulcer, perhaps. The pain got worse and the men in white coats got their machines out and had a look inside. There was nothing wrong with the stomach but there was a large growth in the womb,' she said, and sipped her drink, frowned.

Anne's own insides quivered at the news, at the thought of something terrible and life-threatening growing inside of her.

'Could I have a tad more gin in mine?' asked her mother. 'They always want to tell you how big it is – the tumour, I mean – as if it's going to be something that you're proud of, like those gardeners at country shows with spuds the size of their grandmother and tomatoes like boxers' faces. I've also noticed that the smaller tumours are always fruit. It's about the size of an orange, they say. I assume it's to give you the impression that it can be easily picked. Once it's bigger than a grapefruit they give up and thereafter it's bladders. They told me mine was the size of a rugby ball, which is a game I've never even followed.'

They roared at that, the glib release, the gin slipping into their veins.

'They took it out. I told them to send the damn thing to Twickenham. These chaps, though, they didn't laugh. Deadly serious. Said they'd taken everything out, kit bag, tubes, the lot – but they didn't think it had been enough. I told them I wasn't sure I had anything else to hand over and they said it was too late anyway. The secondaries were already established. A black day that was. Mind you, I never thought I was going to go on and on, not with the Aspinall track record. Death,' she said finally, 'it runs in the family.'

Anne cooked a piece of lamb, slow-cooked it with garlic and potatoes in white wine.

'I'm dying in here,' her mother shouted, still in the living room.

'I'm dying for another drink and from the wonderful smell of your cooking.'

'It's the way the Portuguese cook lamb,' said Anne, appearing at the door.

'Marvellous. We'll have some wine too, and none of that Hirondelle rubbish I give to Father Harpur. No. In the cellar there's a 1948 Chateau Battailley Grand Cru Classé which I think will suit the occasion of my daughter's return.'

'I didn't know you were interested in wine.'

'I'm not. Not enough to go out buying that sort of stuff. It's all Rawly's. You remember old peg-leg Rawlinson. He left it to me in his will.'

'You were still seeing him?'

'Good Lord, no.'

'But you were, weren't you? Back in '44.'

'Is something burning?'

'Nothing's burning, Mother,' said Anne. 'That was why I was packed off to Lisbon, wasn't it? You and Rawlinson.'

'I'm sure there's something . . .'

'There's no point in denying it, Mother, I saw the two of you in St James's Park after my interview with Rawlinson.'

'Did you now?' she said. 'I knew *something* had happened that day.'

'I followed you from your office in Charity House in Ryder Street.'

'Yes, well, I was working for Section V in those days. That's where Section V was. Rawlinson was in recruitment. I recruited you . . .'

'You *recruited* me?' said Anne.

'Yes, I recruited you, with Rawly's help, and made sure you didn't get sent anywhere dangerous. Thought you'd be safe in Lisbon.'

'Was that all?'

'Yes,' she said, going a little sheepish.

'But you wanted me out of the way as well, didn't you?'

'It wasn't the sort of thing a young girl should know about her mother,' she said, writhing in her chair. 'It was embarrassing.'

'But not now.'

'God, no. Nothing embarrasses me now. Not even dying embarrasses me.'

*　　*　　*

294

They sat down to eat. Her mother drank the wine and ate tiny scraps of the food. She apologized for not having an appetite. After dinner her mother was sleepy and Anne took her up to bed, helped her get undressed. She saw that frail white body, the small breasts gone to flaps of skin, her belly still swathed in bandages.

'We'll have to change the dressing tomorrow,' she said. 'If you don't mind.'

'I don't mind,' Anne said, pulling the nightie down over her mother's head.

Her mother washed, cleaned her teeth, got into bed and asked for a goodnight kiss. Anne felt a pang at the roles reversed. Her mother's eyes fluttered against sleep and the alcohol.

'I'm sorry I was such a useless mother,' she said, the words slurred and gargling in her throat.

Anne went to the door, turned out the light and found herself thinking about what she'd started on the plane – of her own inadequacy, how she'd loved Julião but always kept him at a distance.

'I'll explain everything,' her mother said, into the dark. 'I'll explain everything tomorrow.'

Chapter 28

17th August 1968, Orlando Road, Clapham, London.

Anne sat on her window ledge in the dark, the soft breeze blew through the cotton of her nightdress, rustled the trees at the bottom of the garden, drowned out the slow thunder of the city. A half-moon lit the lawn blue and there was the occasional faint few bars of music coming from a record player a few houses down. If she could have disembodied the sharp chunk of anxiety over Julião's safety she could have called herself happy. She was home and, after all the bitterness between her and Luís, now found herself near someone who had suddenly become reliable and all because of words, a few hours of words. A few hours to break the deadlock of forty-four years. Her mother not the person she'd ever known, behaving as if nothing was any different, as if she'd always been like this. Had the prospect of death done that? Given her a sense of freedom, of nothing to lose. She shivered. Old Rawly had been the tip of the iceberg, something that had broken the surface at the time. There was more. 'I'll explain everything.' That was the problem with becoming a different person, or returning to the original, everybody around you is changed as well. A little sickness crept into her stomach, a flutter in the gut. The nausea of truth taking off.

She was trying not to remember things but it was impossible, under these circumstances, not to look back. She tried to concentrate on the easy details – how she'd carried on working even after the war to the disgust of the Almeidas, Cardew leaving Shell at the end of '45 to go back to a different career in London and how that prompted her to start studying for her seventh-year exams to get a place to read maths at Lisbon University, none of her own qualifications being acceptable. But cutting into these bland facts were the other sharp, undeniable truths. Luís had drawn Julião to him, made him *his* son, not hers, and she hadn't resisted it and, at the time, she couldn't think why.

She'd busied herself with her maths and political observations. The harsh treatment meted out to the *ganhões*, the day labourers, employed at subsistence wages by the Almeidas' foremen was little different from what the city workers suffered in the factories and on construction sites. Under Salazar's fascist régime the conditions were terrible and any treacherous talk of union representation was rooted out by the *bufos* and the troublemakers handed over to the renamed, but equally brutal, PIDE. Her perception of these injustices hardened her and not just to the perpetrators. Luís became less of a husband, a more distant figure because he was away a lot, but also she thought of him as the father of her child – a job description whose irony never failed to make her uncomfortable.

She veered away from the start of that kind of thinking, lit a cigarette and paced the room, saw her first day at the university back in the autumn of 1950. The meeting with her tutor and mentor, João Ribeiro, a stick man built from pipe cleaners, a deathly pale individual who ate nothing, drank endless coffee in the form of small strong *bicas* and smoked packets and packets of Três Vintes. He was in constant pain from his teeth, of which only two were a yellowish white, the rest being brown, black or not there. From their first meeting, since he'd interviewed her for the place, he'd known that he had a brilliant student in front of him and they became close. When, a few months later, looking out of his window, they saw the arrest of several students and a professor by the PIDE, they exchanged a look and then risked some views on the matter. He felt safe because she was a foreigner but he was taking a risk, especially knowing that her husband was an army officer. After that groundbreaking moment their tutorials became maths and political symposiums and after some weeks João Ribeiro received permission to introduce her to some officials of the Portuguese Communist Party.

They were interested in her curriculum vitae although the written version didn't include her war service, but because there'd been Portuguese communist collaboration with the British Secret Intelligence Services at that time, they were aware of her role and were interested in her training. The communists had been decimated by a series of successful PIDE infiltrations and the subsequent arrests had included one of the main resistance leaders, Alvaro Cunhal. They wanted to make use of her SIS training to implement some safety measures within the cadres.

It became routine that after their tutorials João Ribeiro and Anne would throw themselves into Party work. She introduced a protection system whereby cell members would never know the identity of their controller, and all new members were given passwords, which were regularly changed. With João Ribeiro she developed new encryption codes for documents which, even when the PIDE raided a safe house in April 1951, proved to be uncrackable as there were no further arrests. Over the spring she introduced the whole idea of cover and initiated training programmes in role-play.

After the arrest of Alvaro Cunhal, the central committee had begun to suspect that they had a highly placed traitor in their ranks. Anne and João Ribeiro concocted a series of dummy operations in which each member of the central committee's discretion was tested with specific pieces of information leaked to them. Manuel Domingues, one of the most senior party members, failed the test. If Anne still thought she was engaged in intellectual games it changed that night. Domingues was interrogated and revealed to be a government spy and provocateur. *A Voz*, the Salazarist newspaper, reported the discovery of the body the next day, 4th May 1951, in the Belas pine forest north of Lisbon. He'd been shot, or rather executed, as she'd forced herself to accept.

In 1953 they launched the rural Communist Party newspaper, *O Camponês*, whose avowed aim was so close to Anne's heart – to campaign for a daily minimum wage of fifty escudos. The workers won their demands after a series of punishing strikes and brutal pitched battles between peasants and police, but not before a young and pregnant woman from Beja, Catarina Eufémia, was shot by a GNR lieutenant to become a martyr and symbol of the brutality of the régime. Her image emblazoned the front of *O Camponês* countrywide.

Anne stopped in her tracks across the room and looked up out of herself and realized that steely obsessiveness had returned. In falling back on those memories, she'd forgotten or rather been able to put aside, the moments of . . . what had she called it? Domestic pain. That made it sound like knife cuts and toe stubs, which is possibly what it had been, but they added up, maybe that was it, they added up.

In the morning her mother didn't tell her anything. She was sick and in pain. Anne changed the dressing on the livid, black-stitched scar across her mother's stomach. Her mother took pills and drifted, floated on a cloud of morphine through the slow, hot day. The next day was the same. Anne called the doctor. He inspected the wound, looked into the old woman's dull eyes, tried and failed to get any sense out of her. He left saying she'd have to go into hospital if she didn't come round. It must have penetrated her mother's unconscious state because it rallied some of her old stubbornness. She didn't take morphine the next day and slept through the morning.

The brilliant sunshine of the first days had been taken over by a growing oppression. The clear heat had become thunderous and the pressure leaned against the windows. Her mother ate a little lunch and read the newspaper. Anne took tea with her in the bedroom, sat facing the window with her feet up on the ledge. Her mother was sweating and held a damp flannel in her hand.

'It used to get like this in India before the monsoons came. The later the rains, the worse the heat. Everybody else went up to the north. Houseboats in Kashmir . . . that sort of thing. We . . . the missionaries, stayed. Terrible heat,' she finished savagely.

'It was the same in Angola.'

'What places for women like us to have been. They died in the streets in Bombay . . . just dropped to the floor like old carpets.'

'The smell,' said Anne.

'I don't think I could have lived with all that endless decay.'

'How do you mean?'

'If I'd stayed in India.'

'Would you have done?'

'No,' she said, after some time, 'no, I wouldn't . . . I couldn't have stayed.'

'Why not?' asked Anne, pushing now, sensing that they were coming to the nub of it.

Her mother stared at the lump of her feet at the end of the bed.

'You'd better bring me that box from the dressing table,' she said.

It was a reddish box and on the lid were carved two stylized figures, a man and a woman. Indian. Her mother opened it and tipped the contents of her jewellery on to the bedcover.

'This is beautiful,' she said and pushed her thumbs into the corners of the box below the hinges. The bottom of the box dropped like a jaw and two pieces of paper fell on to the sheet. 'You see, on the lid are the lovers and underneath are their secrets.'

The light outside had turned yellow. The sunlight strained against some dark centre like an old bruise. It screwed the pressure down in the room and the perspiration came up on their skins.

'You'd better sit down,' said her mother, and reached for her spectacles, which she held in front of her eyes without unfolding.

'Is this going to be a shock?' Anne asked.

'Yes, it will be. I'm going to show you who your father was.'

'You told me you didn't have any photographs of him.'

'I lied,' she said, and handed over one of the pieces of paper from the box.

On the back was written *Joaquim Reis Leitão 1923*. She turned it over. There was a photograph of a man in a light suit.

'Is there something wrong with this photograph?' asked Anne. 'Or the light? Perhaps it's just old.'

'No, that's what he looked like.'

'But . . . he seems to be very dark-skinned.'

'That's right. He's Indian.'

'You said he was Portuguese.'

'He was . . . partly. His father was a member of the Portuguese garrison, his mother was a Goan. Joaquim was a Catholic and a Portuguese national. His mother,' she said, and shook her head, 'his mother was stunning. You take after her, thank heaven. The father . . . well, he was a good man, so I understand, but beautiful? . . . Perhaps the Portuguese are different on their own turf.'

'My father was an *Indian*.'

'Half Indian.'

Anne took the photograph to the window but the light was so bad she knelt by the bedside lamp trying to discern the features.

'You look like the mother . . . lighter-skinned but . . .'

Anne squeezed the picture as if it was flesh and she was trying to extract something, not a splinter, but a tincture of life.

'So why couldn't you stay? Was it the cholera?'

300

'This was before the cholera.'

'What was before the cholera?'

Her mother dabbed her face and neck with the flannel.

'It's going to break soon,' she said. 'The weather.'

'They did all die in the cholera outbreak, didn't they?'

'Both my parents died in the cholera outbreak but that wasn't until 1924. This was in 1923.'

'When you got married? I was born in 1924 so . . .'

'We were never married. It didn't happen like that.'

The thunder rumbled way off in Tooting or Balham. The room was lit only by the bedside lamp which suddenly flickered and went off. The two women sat still in the ghastly light of the approaching storm.

'Was this your confession?'

'Yes. Father Harpur showed me his poem about his father afterwards. It was a great help for me. For the first time I managed to make sense of things . . . understand my stupid self.

'I fell in love with Joaquim. Madly in love. I was completely crazy for him. I was seventeen. I didn't know anything. I'd had this strict Catholic upbringing. The convent and then the mission. I knew nothing about boys . . . men. Joaquim was being trained by the Portuguese in medicine. My father got on well with the Portuguese. All Catholics together, I suppose. The Portuguese used to send the mission medicine and staff. One day they sent Joaquim. I was working as a nurse in the hospital at the time so I met him on his first day and everything I'd ever been taught, all my religious education, all my fear . . . it all went out of the window when I saw Joaquim.

'It was physical. He was the most beautiful human I'd ever seen. Dark brown eyes with great long lashes and skin like sanded wood. I just wanted to touch him and feel the texture of him on the palm of my hand. He had beautiful hands, too. Hands that you could watch doing anything and they'd lull you. I'm banging on, I know, but it was an incredible thing for me at the time. To have this feeling inside of me of, of . . . I never know how to say this because it was too many things at once – certainty, beauty, joy. You know what Father Harpur said? "Like faith, you mean?" And that would have been it . . . if sex was allowed to come into faith.'

'Sex,' said Anne, the word falling out of her mouth, prickly, like a horse chestnut, which grew to the size of a sea mine in the room.

'Yes. Sex,' said her mother bluntly. 'And before marriage, too. You'd have thought they'd only just invented that, the way they go on about it these days. Joaquim and I couldn't keep our hands off each other. We had the opportunity in the mission hospital at night. We even had a bed. We were young and reckless. I tried to keep count of the days . . . tried to be careful, but we were both incapable. I got pregnant.'

The thunder rolled nearer. The sound of the wooden tumbrel on a cobbled street was south of the Common now, the smell of rain already coming in through the windows. The pressure cracking. The electricity in the air fizzing.

'That was a terrible day. Joaquim was away, back in Goa. I'd been praying to come on. My father couldn't believe my sudden devotion. And one day it hit me. Two weeks after I should have had my period it came to me that this was it and I panicked. I lay in bed at night, my brain in a flat spin, trying to imagine myself standing in front of my father . . . you didn't know my father. It was inconceivable to have to tell him that I was pregnant and, not only that, I was pregnant by an Indian. I mean, they liked Joaquim very much. They loved the Indians but . . . mixed marriages. No. The Portuguese were different in that respect, they've always mixed with the locals in their colonies, but the British . . . a white British Catholic girl and a Goan. It wasn't possible. It was against the laws of nature. No different to homosexuality in those days. So, I panicked. I made up a story. I invented this very detailed account of how I'd been raped and become pregnant.'

'By whom?'

'A man. A fabricated man. One who didn't exist. It was easy to act it out. I mean, I was so damned upset anyway . . . almost mad at what I was having to go through.'

'And Joaquim?'

'He still wasn't there. The Portuguese had sent another medical student for a couple of weeks. I was on my own. I was in a desperate state and I knew something had to be done. So I told my father I'd been raped, broke down and wept in front of him, fell at his feet. Literally, I was a heap on the floor. I cried until I retched. My father called the police. The local police was headed by a fellow called Longmartin. He was one of those fearsome, muscular types, quite small, wire-brush moustache and with a neck in a permanent state of rage. He came round and took my statement, the statement of my completely flawless story. He also spoke to my father. I don't know what was discussed. I think perhaps they were asking my father whether he wanted it kept quiet in the district that his daughter had been raped. How open the investigation should be. I don't know. What I did know was that once those words of mine were uttered, they changed everything. I don't know where I got this from, my own mind, Father Harpur, a book . . . I don't know. The fact is that something started with a lie can only beget other lies, like a bad bloodline it will continue through to its terrible end.'

The wind thrashed through the trees, rattled the sash windows in their frames.

'What did Joaquim say when you told him?'

'There was nothing to be said. It was a *fait accompli*. He was racked with guilt that he'd brought this upon me . . . as if in some way I'd been unwilling in the whole affair. I've never seen anyone in such a torment of anguish. He was appalled that I'd had to take this stigma upon myself. The stigma of a defiled woman. He felt totally responsible. He wanted to go to my father. He wanted to take the blame.'

'Oh, my God . . . and did he?'

'You haven't heard the half of it yet.'

The first drops of rain hit the window. The smell of it on the hot tarmac filled the air. Thunder cracked overhead and lightning blitzed through the room. The net curtains billowed in the bay window and the roof took the full force of the colossal downpour.

'The way it happened,' her mother said, raising her voice over the roar of the rain, 'was that the police caught somebody. Yes, there's a crash course in colonial justice in this, too. They came to the house, Longmartin and two of his constables. They wanted me to identify someone. This was ten days after my supposed attack. I had myself under control by then, but when my father came to my room and told me I had to go with Longmartin, I went straight back into the terror. Of course my father said he'd go with me but Longmartin was a clever little bastard, that's why he'd brought the two constables along with him. There was no room in the car. He wanted me on my own. I rode in the back with him and he told me what was going to happen. There would be a line-up of six men, all Indians. They would be standing under the light behind some mosquito netting and I would be in the dark, so I'd be able to see them but they couldn't see me. I nodded through all this and then Longmartin started to say something else. He went from being the straightforward, almost brutally frank, police officer to somebody altogether quieter, more threatening, hopping backwards and forwards over the line of implication.

'He said that he was glad that they'd been able to clear this matter up. They were just beginning to have second thoughts about what had happened because they hadn't had the first glimmer of a clue. None of their informers had come back with anything except some rubbish about a Goan student at the mission. All the locals hate Goans, he said, because they're Catholics. Little hints but with an accumulative weight. By the time we reached the police station I was convinced he knew my game, so when he whispered in my ear as I went in front of the line up: "Third from the end." I didn't hesitate. I walked the line and went straight back to the third man from the end, whom I'd never seen before in my life, and pointed him out.

'Longmartin was very pleased. He took me straight home and handed me back to my father and said: "Very brave girl, your daughter, Mr Aspinall. Very courageous. Looked him in the eye and pointed him out. Very plucky, I must say." I hung by his side, a broken, spineless creature, while he snapped me up into pieces with his savage little ironies. I even thought I heard derision in his voice. I went to bed and, when I wasn't lying on my back staring sleepless into the mosquito net seeing that man's face behind it, I was writhing about as if . . . as I had been before they took this damned tumour out.'

'So Joaquim wasn't involved in the end.'

'Things were already going wrong in India. I know it was another quarter of a century before the handover but colonial rule was already in trouble even then. It had only been four years since that terrible business in Amritsar when General Dyer machine-gunned all those unarmed demonstrators. There was unrest everywhere. The man I'd pointed out was a leader of one of the local Hindu resistance militias. Longmartin had wanted him for years. When the Indians heard the charge against their man, they rioted and marched on the mission, but Longmartin was well prepared. The troops stepped in and broke it all up.

'Joaquim couldn't stand it. Everything had gone to dust. Our physical desire for each other had vanished. We could hardly bear to be in the same room as each other because we were so tormented by the developments. He saw it all as his fault. He was six years older than me and should have known better etcetera, etcetera. Now a man was going to hang in all probability because of him. He was outraged at the injustice. He said it would never have happened in Goa. He demanded to know my lie . . . how I'd said the rape had occurred. And he was fierce about it, Andrea, totally frightening. I told him everything and he handed himself in to Longmartin, admitted to raping the English girl, gave him my story verbatim.'

'And Longmartin accepted it?'

'I imagine Longmartin was furious. It was probably the one thing he hadn't anticipated. If you're ignoble yourself you can't foresee another's nobility. I know he would have resisted it strongly. I don't know what Joaquim said to persuade him but I think he must have scared him, given him a few ideas about how bad the rioting could get if the Hindus had categoric proof of their man's innocence. The end of it was that the Hindu leader was released and Joaquim was . . . Joaquim . . .'

Her mother was suddenly struggling against the unseen torment. She lay back, head thrown against the bedstead, her mouth wide, black and gaping, her shoulders convulsing with each chest-wrenching hack. She collapsed to her side. Anne sat next to her, put a hand to her shoulder, remembered that night when she was a child, her mother after the party sobbing to herself. Gradually the bird-like body underneath her calmed, the eyes opened and stared blankly into the room.

'Joaquim died in police custody,' she said. 'The official line was that he "committed suicide", hanged himself from the bars of his cell. Another version was that Longmartin was punishing him for ruining his little plan and he overdid it. As far as everybody was concerned, not just my parents and the people at the mission, but the whole town, Hindus and Muslims alike, justice had been done. Ten days later I was put on a ship to England. It was my peculiar fate that I, as the instigator of the whole rotten business, was to survive all of them. Thousands died in the cholera outbreak the following year including my parents, the Hindu resistance leader

305

and Longmartin. As a nurse in the hospital my chances would not have been good. As it was I became a living monument to my own moral cowardice. And Joaquim, the most honourable of men, died ... reviled by everyone ... even his father wouldn't collect the body and he was buried in an untouchables' grave on the outskirts of town.'

The rain moved off. The air blown into the room was cool and clear and brought with it the freshness of wet earth and mown grass. Her mother strained to sit up. Anne propped her up on the pillows. In her hand was the other piece of paper from the box.

'So that was my tale full of sound and fury. Shakespeare was right. It all comes to nought in the end. The slate is constantly wiped clean,' she said, and handed Anne a letter. 'This was the first, last and only letter he wrote to me ... from jail. One of the Hindu leader's men brought it to me. Read it. Read it out loud for me.'

Dear Audrey,
I feel clean for the first time in many days. My body is filthy, they don't let me wash, but inside I am scrubbed clean, the walls newly whitewashed and the sun bright against them so that I can hardly bear to look. I am happy in the same way that I was happy when I was a small boy.
    You must believe me when I tell you that what I did was for the best. What would have become of our love with that man's death between us? Better that we should hold it as something that was good and true although not to be. I know in these short lines that I might not be able to persuade you that none of what has happened is your fault. I am suffering the consequences of my own mistakes. You must sail away from here into the rest of your life with a clear mind and the knowledge that you have been my only true love.

    Joaquim

'It's not an excuse,' her mother said, 'but an explanation.'

Chapter 29

Autumn 1968, Orlando Road, Clapham, London.

The days shortened inch by inch towards the end of summer. The number of 'bad days' increased. If Audrey got out of bed it was only for a few hours in the afternoon. They spoke in the lucid moments before the pain took hold and the morphine smothered it.

Anne made a study in the room next to her mother's, put a desk in front of the window with one of her many photographs of Julião at one corner and read Number Theory books during the day and Jane Austen at night. When she wasn't reading she was thinking and smoking and watching the way the smoke was drawn up though the lampshade and into the dark.

One afternoon there were kids playing in the street, all gathered around one boy who was explaining the rules, and she saw herself years earlier looking out on to the lawn in Estoril at Julião and his friends. He'd only been eight years old and yet all the boys looked up to him, faces rapt with admiration, and she could only think of Julius and his last letter from the *Kessel* at Stalingrad. His men. It had started an ache in her chest. It was during the time they were launching *O Camponês* and she realized then that Julião was a passion she could have allowed herself, a cleaner, warmer passion than the politics she'd chosen, except it was a passion she didn't feel she deserved and it was one she feared, too. She could never rid herself of that sense of a payment due. She photographed Julião all the time, despite some dim memory telling her that primitive people thought that it was a theft of the soul. To her it had been a constant confirmation of his existence but now, fingering the frame on the corner of her desk, she wondered if it was her way of loving him at a distance.

*   *   *

She didn't sleep much in this period. Her mother would call out at all times of night and Anne would sit with her until she drifted off again. They covered old ground, her mother added detail to incomplete pictures.

The great aunt who, on Audrey's parents' death, had inherited and lived in the Clapham house with her niece and the illegitimate child, had died and left it all to Audrey when Anne was barely seven years old. Audrey had been working in Whitehall as a secretary for five years. The job had been arranged for her by her aunt and when she died it meant there was no one to look after the child, which was why Anne was sent to the nuns early.

'It was your Great Aunt, my Aunt G, G for Gladys, who started this régime of discipline. She was strict with both of us and I just carried it on. It wasn't me at all but it was a useful persona to hide behind.'

'What were you hiding from?'

'Your curiosity,' she said. 'My own guilt. I was quite different at work. I think I was seen as a bit of a good-time girl, always on for a drink, always ready for a party. I learned how to laugh. A loud laugh is very useful in England.'

'You must have had . . . offers.'

'Of course, but I didn't want anybody getting too close. Rawlinson was perfect. I have to say, there was something about his missing leg that attracted me. I couldn't fathom it at the time, especially as the only man I'd ever known had been physically perfect. It occurred to me only the other day that this was what I thought I deserved. I didn't want the full commitment so I didn't go after the whole man. I certainly wasn't his only girlfriend, either.'

'I followed him to Flood Street.'

'That was his wife. They didn't do much together. She never knew about the wine even. Terrible . . . the secrets, aren't they? We were bloody masters, Rawly and I. It's funny how they know, isn't it?'

'Who?'

'The Company. Once the war got going I was transferred into the Ministry of Economic Warfare. I was good with numbers . . . only numbers, mind, not *your* hieroglyphics. Secretaries in those days did most of the work and it was all top-secret stuff. They liked me. And when they moved Section V up from St Albans to Ryder

Street they sent me over there to keep an eye on the money.'

'What was Section V?'

'Counter Intelligence. And you know who was running it? Kim Philby. Yes, Philby was there from the beginning. I couldn't believe it when he fled to Moscow. 1963. It was a cold day. January some time.'

'You were talking about how they know.'

'Yes. How they know the ones who can keep a secret.'

'And?'

'They find the ones who've already got a secret to keep. I'd be useless now. Thrown it all away. Tell anybody anything, me. They'd call me Blabbermouth Aspinall and give me my cards.'

'And you were still working for the Company after you retired?'

'Oh yes, still in banking. You'll see them all at the funeral . . . except him.'

'You liked Philby?'

'Everybody did. Great charmer.'

Audrey suddenly directed her to the chest of drawers, left-hand side, under the bras and knickers, to a small leather box. Inside was a medal on a length of ribbon.

'That's my gong,' said Audrey. 'My OBE.'

'Why didn't you tell me?'

'My great triumph!' she said, punching the air weakly. 'Not much of one after forty years' service.'

'I'd liked to have known.'

'Now, yes. Now that we're talking,' she said. 'You know, it wasn't just because of Rawly that I sent you away. I *did* want you to be safe but . . . I wanted you out of my sight, too. You were a constant reminder of my weakness, my cowardice. You remember I couldn't stand the heat either. It brought back India. Terrible headaches.'

That night Anne sat even longer at her desk, the Jane Austen open but unread in front of her, just her own still reflection in the dark glass of the window pane and the trail of smoke rippling from the ashtray. After the afternoon's revelations she was thinking of her own secret life, which had continued after she graduated from Lisbon University with an offer from João Ribeiro to do a postgrad thesis on the new hot topic – Game Theory.

She'd snatched at the chance. Julião, under Luís's constant supervision, was becoming more embroiled in his young male world and drifting further from her already weakening orbit. Two years later she was stunned and a little sickened when he announced that he'd joined the boy's brigade, Mocidade, without asking her. To Anne, Mocidade was no better than the *Hitler Jugend* and it was only João Ribeiro who was able to mollify her, by saying it was a completely natural thing for a boy to want to do, to go off walking and camping in the hills with his friends.

It was then that the secret work had become even more important to her. She knew it was irrational but she saw Julião's actions as defiance, even, God help us, betrayal. The boy spent all his time with Luís, he was a brilliant sportsman and horseman, he was good at maths but not brilliant and he had a complete blindspot for physics. All that, and his pride in the Mocidade uniform, made her think that her son was all Almeida, that there wasn't a drop of Voss left in him.

It had come to her one day, as she was taking the train into Lisbon and looking at the faces in the carriage, that it was her secret life that made her different. She knew it brought her excitement but it was at that moment that she began to think it was bringing meaning, too. She lived for her document encryption sessions with João Ribeiro, the long meandering walks to the safe houses and secret printing presses of *O Camponês* and *Avante*, the role-playing sessions, the whole mechanics of the clandestine struggle.

For her husband she felt occasional affection, for her son – unconditional, if distant, love, for her mathematics – an objective, intellectual interest, and for her secret work – a deep need, an addiction stronger than the cigarettes she smoked end to end with João Ribeiro and the caffeine in the coffee they drank. It was what defined her.

She even recalled lying in bed one night next to Luís's snoring and feeling suddenly sufficient, enclosed, whole. She was thinking that guilt was being assuaged. Her secret work for social justice was an endless 'Hail Mary', penance for her self-confessed sins. It was part of the process of purification. And just as she arrived at this point she'd shaken the nonsense out of her head. She was a communist, an atheist – it had been muddled thinking.

She replenished her glass of brandy, found another packet of cigarettes and couldn't help immersing herself in the real glory years. In 1959 João Ribeiro and Anne planned what became, a year later, the brilliant and successful escape of their leader Alvaro Cunhal from the Peniche prison in the north of Portugal. They followed this with an even more outrageous scheme which would bring the attention of the world to the suffering of the Portuguese people. In January 1961 a group of Portuguese communists hijacked the cruise liner *Santa Maria* in the Caribbean. She referred to those two operations as the glory years but, looking back on it, they'd been short-lived. That was the high point of João Ribeiro's fame within the PCP. It was downhill after that. Members of the central committee became uncomfortable with his success and, when there followed a number of inexplicable arrests of communist cadres, suspicion seemed to fall automatically on João Ribeiro and his foreign assistant. João was sidelined into dull Party work but heard there was a plot to have Anne deported. He split away from her, told her to stay at home and destroy anything that could compromise her with PIDE.

Anne spent a month pacing the drawing room of the house in Estoril, smoking severely, waiting for the knock. Luís was away on exercise almost constantly. The knock never came. Her exit from the resistance stage arrived when Angola blew up in February 1961 and Luís and his regiment were sent out to quell the rebellion. Six months later, when the initial crisis was over and the fighting contained in the north of the country, she'd arrived by boat in Luanda with a sixteen-year-old Julião.

She sat back from the desk, turning the tumbler of brandy in her hands. She'd expected more from her memories. She'd expected some kind of emotional intensity to come with them but, as when she'd woken up from the nightmare back in Lisbon, it had come back to her as newsreel. She looked in on her mother who was fast asleep, the air rushing into her gaping mouth, and realized that she'd been more replenished in a matter of weeks than she had been by two decades of living.

Before the end of August the weather changed. A chill wind blew in from the north-east and summer was over. Audrey remained in bed all day, sailing on morphine. She muttered to herself, babbled lines of poetry while kids screamed outside and a football boomed against a car. A man, cross, roared at them and after a pause a small voice piped up:

'Can we have our ball back?'

'No, you bloody can't.'

Anne sat with her mother, holding her hand most of the day, squeezing it like a pulse, mulling over those endless days spent on the verandah in Angola while Luís fought the rebels and Julião played war in the garden. How it had all been leading to what she saw at the time as Julião's next betrayal, which was his dramatic announcement in 1963 on his eighteenth birthday that he'd been accepted by the Military Academy for Officer's Training. Why did she still think of it as betrayal? As if she'd spent years developing his political consciousness. A crack opened up in her mind and she'd just got her eye to it, her eye to a small chink of truth, when her mother suddenly said:

'You never told me about Karl Voss.'

It jolted her, whipped her head round to her mother, whose eyes were closed, her breath baffling and ricocheting in her throat.

'Mother?' she asked, but there was no reply.

Now there was regret at a chance missed. Her mother, working in Section V, must have seen the progress reports, must have read about her indiscretion with their double agent, the military attaché of the German Legation. In all their time together Anne hadn't spoken about Karl Voss and she'd had no intention of doing so. This was her mother's time, her mother's confessional. Earlier Audrey had urged her to go to Father Harpur several times. Anne even liked Father Harpur but she wasn't going to see him because she knew what he'd ask of her. He would compel her to tell Luís and Julião the truth and, whilst she could live with Luís's contempt, she would not be able to bear Julião's disdain. Now she thought that she should have told her mother, that it wouldn't have mattered. She wouldn't have made any demands. She would have listened and taken the secret to the grave with her.

She wrote a letter to a friend of João Ribeiro's, a mathematics professor at Cambridge called Louis Greig. His name and address had been given to her on her last afternoon in Lisbon while she'd put into action a half-measure, as she'd called it. She'd given João Ribeiro a wooden box from Angola containing the Voss family photograph and letters for safekeeping. She didn't want Luís to come across them if it ever came to him clearing her out of his life.

Louis Greig replied to her letter by return, urging her to visit. She responded, telling him about her mother but also jotting down some of her recent ideas and asking if there were any course possibilities, not in her doctoral thesis subject, Game Theory, which was a dead duck by now, but more in the line of pure maths. He wrote back saying that João Ribeiro had made contact and that there were definite possibilities for someone of her calibre. It was then that she began to see her half-measure as a full one and asked herself if she was ever going back to Portugal.

When she'd gone back to Lisbon in the past, from the various African wars, she'd gone back as the same person to find everything changed. Arriving back from Angola in 1964 she'd found the whole resistance movement stalled. Alvaro Cunhal had gone to the Soviet Union. João Ribeiro had spent two years in prison, his wife had died, he'd lost his job at the university and was now living in a single room in the Bairro Alto on very little money. The PCP had shunned him and he'd told her it was all over.

As it happened, she hadn't had much time to take it all in because the Mozambique rebellion started and Luís, with all his experience, was immediately posted to Lourenço Marques. It was in that tactically more brutal war that she and Luís began to fall apart. The Mozambique commander introduced techniques used by the British in Malaya and the Americans in Vietnam, giving the locals a stark choice – co-operate or face unrelenting suffering and death. News of the atrocities reached Anne in the army compound. She had pointless, violent rows with Luís. She threw things at him. She taunted him about the justice of the colonial wars, whether wars designed to maintain Salazar as an emperor were fit wars for his son. Luís spent more time in the mess. Anne drank cheap brandy and fulminated on the verandah.

She remembered the rage of that time as she sat with her first gin and tonic of the evening, with Louis Greig's reply on the desk in front of her, and knew she wasn't going back to that. She'd made the break. She'd had all that time to change, sitting on verandahs in Africa, but it had taken these few weeks with her mother, in the middle of a city striding into the future, to shrug off half a lifetime's inertia.

*   *   *

313

On 30th August she sat with her mother for the last time. Father Harpur had given her the Last Rites. She hadn't spoken a coherent word for twenty-four hours and it was clear the end was coming. At 2.00 a.m. Anne couldn't stay awake any longer. She stood to leave. Her mother's hand tightened and her eyes sprang open.

'They will come for you,' she said. 'But you must not go with them.'

Her eyes shut. Anne checked her pulse, shuddering at the ideas behind her mother's lurid visions. She was still there, breathing shallowly. Anne went to bed and overslept until midday. She woke up groggy, with her face crushed and creased. Her mother's room seemed more silent than usual and she knew there was nobody living beyond her door.

Her mother lay on her back, eyes closed, one arm out on the bedclothes. The slightly decaying lilies brought by Father Harpur from his church could not mask the odour of life's fluids curdling. Her face was quite cold. Anne looked at the body with a total absence of grief and realized the body meant nothing to her, that this was something that could be put in the ground.

She called the doctor and Father Harpur. She made herself coffee and smoked a cigarette in the kitchen. The doctor came and pronounced her dead and wrote out the death certificate. Father Harpur called a funeral director and stayed until tea, when the men came and removed the body. He left saying he would give a Mass for her mother the following morning. She went up to her mother's room after they'd gone. The bed was made. Audrey's slippers, swollen by the shape of her feet, lay beside the bed and it was that which reminded Anne of her loss.

The funeral was held on a cold, wind-whipped day. She'd followed her mother's instructions that a large party was to be held afterwards. The house was stocked with sherry, gin and whisky and she'd made a hundred sandwiches by dawn. She was still stunned by the extent of her mother's legacy, which included the Clapham house and a little over fifty thousand pounds in cash and investments. The solicitor said she never touched any of the capital left by her aunt. He also gave her a key to a safe-deposit box, number 718, held at the Arab Bank on the Edgware Road.

In the church she sat alone in her pew. Father Harpur gave a moving sermon about service to God, one's country and oneself. Afterwards, as the congregation converged on the grave site, Anne felt that unmistakable tug of the silver thread. As the men and women and a few older children moved through the old stones towards the dark oblong hole, she suddenly felt part of the race. This is what we humans do. We live and we die. The living salute the dead, however small the life, because we have all trodden the same hard track and know its difficulties. We will all go this way, into the ground or the air, president or pauper, and we will have all succeeded in one thing.

As they lowered the coffin it began to rain, as if on cue. Umbrellas exploded overhead, droplets formed on the varnished wood. Father Harpur said the blessing. Anne threw the first handful of soil and remembered something, but incorrectly, 'In your end was my beginning.'

Back at the house she began to see faces, rather than heavy coats and hats. They introduced themselves: Peggy White – assistant in Banking. Dennis Broadbent – Archives. Maude West – Library. Occasionally people just gave a name and she knew not to pursue it further. All the time one man kept finding his way into the corner of her eye. A fat, balding man. Someone waiting for his moment. Anne went into the kitchen for more sandwiches. He followed her, stood in the doorway, brushing the strands of hair across his bald pate with his hand.

'You don't know me, do you?'

'Should I?'

'You should . . . we were lovers once. Don't you remember? We spent a night together in Lisbon,' he said, smiling.

'I would have remembered that.'

'We did,' he said, '. . . on paper.'

'Jim Wallis,' she said.

They kissed on both cheeks.

'Fat and bald,' he said. 'I didn't age well. You look just the same.'

'Give or take a crow's foot.'

'You married,' he said, 'just after they moved me out.'

'Yes. Are you . . . yet?'

'I'm on my second now. Spent too much time in Berlin to keep my first. But I'm in London these days. Any children?'

'A boy. Julião.'

'Is he here?'

'No. He's a soldier . . . in Africa.'

'Ah yes, with his father.'

'You knew that much.'

'I was always interested, Anne,' he said. 'And not just on paper.'

'But now you're married . . . again.'

'Yes, two children from the last marriage. One of each.'

'And you knew my mother.'

'We all knew Audrey. Very important to be on the right side of Audrey, you know, when you're putting through your expenses and that. Bit of a stickler, she was. Never let it interfere, though. After the grilling there was always a drink down the pub. Yes, we were regulars at The French in Soho, she and I. Very sad. Going to miss her. We'll all miss her. Especially Dickie.'

'Dickie?'

'Surprised he didn't come back for a snort. Dickie Rose.'

'You mean Richard Rose?'

'*Lui-même.* You remember, took over from Sutherland when he blew up that time in Lisbon in '44. Dickie's heading for the high table now. Had a bit of a clearout after Kim left us in '63. Bad year that, with Profumo and all. Given him a clear street though. It'll be *Sir* Dickie before long and we'll all have to bow and scrape.'

'Richard Rose was a friend of my mother's?' she said, incredulous.

'Oh yes, Audrey had a knack of picking out the high-flyers. Big fan of Kim's, too. Bloody mortified when he pushed off. We all were. Smoke?'

He offered a B&H, lit it with a petrol lighter. They smoked and Wallis helped himself to three sandwiches stacked on top of each other.

'Shouldn't really,' he said. 'Bread's the killer for me. Got any plans, Anne, or is it Andrea?'

'It's still Anne.'

'Back to *Lisboa?*'

'No, I don't think so.'

'I see.'

'I did my bit in Angola and Mozambique. I'm not doing it in Guiné with both of them fighting.'

316

'Quite understand. Don't know what they're doing there in the first place. Mad war. Bad war. Can't afford it. Can't win it. Best chuck it all in, you ask me. I mean, what's it all worth? Peanuts. Peanuts and cocoa ... some door mats. Can't go throwing your money after that sort of thing. Pull out, Doc, that's what I say, pull out. The darkies'll be at each other's throats in minutes. Look at Biafra.'

'I thought I'd try and do some research at Cambridge.'

'Still doing your sums?'

'I've graduated in long division now, Jim.'

'Well *done*. Isn't it all about Game Theory these days? Strategy. How to keep the Russian balls in a vice. That sort of thing.'

'You should be a lecturer, Jim. Bring strategic thinking down to earth.'

'Tried it. Got pelted by the students at the LSE. Called me a fascist. They had a sit-in before my next lecture and that was it. Bloody long-haired ... they got somebody to come in and talk to them about disarmament instead. Don't know how the bloody layabouts learn anything.'

'You're sounding like a boiled colonel from Bagshot.'

He wheezed a laugh through his cigarette smoke.

'We're a dying breed,' he said, 'but we're needed. Have you seen a picture of Brezhnev? D'you think he's going to listen to someone wearing an Afghan, smoking pot and burning joss sticks? Actually I preferred Khrushchev. He said things, you know, blinked occasionally.'

'You only liked Khrushchev,' said a voice from the corridor, 'because you've got the same Philistine taste in art.'

'Ah, Dickie. Wondered where you'd got to. Just said to Anne here, unusual of you not to come back for a stiffener.'

Richard Rose had his greyish hair combed back with tonic. His eyes were still bright and his full lips twitched as if there was the prospect of a kiss. They shook hands. He brushed imaginary lint of his dark blue suit.

'What was it Khrushchev said about modern art, Jim, that you so wholeheartedly agreed with?'

'The lashings of a donkey's tail,' said Jim, in cod Yorkshire.

'Pure peasant. Potato farmer, no, shire horse. That was Mr K.'

'Drink, Mr Rose?' asked Anne, keen to get away from him.

'I'll fetch,' said Wallis. 'What'll it be?'

'Pinkers, I think, if you've got it.'

'The angostura's out there,' she said, annoyed with Wallis.

'My condolences, Anne,' said Rose, smoothly. 'Very fine woman, your mother. Tremendous. When she retired she left an unfillable gap.'

'I don't think she ever thought her services were that indispensable.'

'Perhaps not, but she gave style to her work, that's what's irreplaceable. Conscientious, severe even, but a great sport, too, terrific fun.'

They ran through the same question and answer exchange as she had with Wallis. That Rose was still unmarried was all the information he parted with.

'Who did you say you were talking to at Cambridge?' asked Rose.

'I didn't, but his name is Louis Greig.'

'What's his game?'

'I'm not sure any more. It used to be Game Theory back in the fifties and early sixties but I think he's moved over . . .'

'Ah yes, come to think of it his name has appeared here and there. Strategist. Think-tank bod.'

'Probably.'

'He was at RAND over in California for a while in the fifties,' said Rose, confirming it to himself. 'Research and Development, know what I mean?'

'That must have been after he finished his doctoral thesis at Princeton.'

'He's not a Yank, is he?'

'Eton and Cambridge.'

'Mmm,' said Rose, running aground on Anne's frosty shores.

Wallis turned up with the pink gin.

'To Lisbon station,' said Wallis, raising his glass.

'The good old days,' said Rose. 'My . . . we were all innocent then.'

'Here's another from the 1944 team,' said Wallis. 'This really is Lisbon station now.'

A man's hand thrust a pipe between the two men's shoulders and struggled through the gap between. He kissed her on both

318

cheeks before she had time to take him in. He held her shoulders at arm's length and looked her up and down like an uncle.

'I'm so sorry,' said Meredith Cardew, 'so terribly sorry, Anne. Shock for us all, wasn't it, Dickie, when she called us back in July. Brave woman. My God, I don't think I could have taken it as well as she did.'

He released her but kept an arm around her shoulder as if she were his protégée.

'Quite a little reunion,' said Rose. 'We're only missing Sutherland.'

'Poor chap,' said Cardew.

'Pinkers, Merry?' asked Wallis.

'I should say.'

'How's Dorothy?' Anne asked Cardew.

They were all gone by two in the afternoon. Wallis was the last to leave. He was supporting Peggy White, assistant Banking, who'd neglected the sandwiches and was paying heavily for the seven pink gins on an empty stomach. Anne cleaned up the house and sat at the kitchen table thinking about Wallis and Rose, how the two men, in their own way, had looked her over, sized her up for something. Rose couldn't be thinking of a job, not given their mutual dislike, but that was how it had felt. Wallis? Maybe Wallis was just looking for an affair. Bored with wife number two already. It seemed that family life was going to the dogs in England. No more sweating in the dark about getting pregnant. You just took the Pill and did what the hell you liked. Salazar would die rather than allow the Pill, Franco too. Her thoughts rushed down that trail until she arrived at her own family, split up, thousands of miles apart, the men fighting, and she found herself crying, alone in her big house, her mother's clothes already gone to the Oxfam shop, the worms already nosing against the smooth varnish of the coffin.

Chapter 30

Anne took the train up to Cambridge. She bought a newspaper at the station and for once reading the *Guardian* made her happy. On the first page of the foreign news section was an article about Dr Salazar, who'd been rushed to the Cruz Vermelha Hospital in Lisbon after suffering a collapse. A doctor announced later that an intercranial subdural haematoma had been found, and she smiled at how typically Portuguese that was, they could never have just said a blood clot on the brain. The article finished with a statement from a consultant brain surgeon who said that the Head of State would have to undergo an operation to remove the clot.

The sun broke through the clouds and streamed into the railway carriage. Anne lit a celebratory cigarette and mentally toasted the end of the fascist régime and its colonial wars in Africa.

Louis Greig had rooms in Trinity College overlooking the quad. He smoked cigars, a Swiss brand called Villiger. Anne smelt them from the bottom of the stairs and imagined a place in a state of controlled chaos, full of papers and books filed only in the occupant's mind. His rooms, though, were unexpectedly tidy. There was no loose paper. A section of the bookshelves was stacked with ring-bound notebooks, several hundred of them, and they were filed in bunches tied with different-coloured ribbons. Greig had not succumbed to the usual sartorial eccentricities of the maths don, such as socks and sandals with shiny grey trousers that ended above the ankle, a tweed jacket with elbow patches and a tie featuring a real bacon and egg motif. He was bald, but his remaining hair was cut close to his head, which was big and square. His body was solid, strong and fatless. From the way his shoulders and chest were packed into his suit jacket he appeared to be a regular at some sort of heavy physical exercise.

He was lounging back in his chair with a pair of black brogues up on the corner of the desk when she came in. By the time she'd closed the door, he'd leapt to his feet, skirted the desk and was behind her, a dark presence. She held out a hand. His felt hard and calloused like a farmer's. He kissed her knuckle. She smelt a faint cologne mingled with the cigar tobacco. He didn't let go of the hand but led her round and lowered her into a leather sofa. He sat opposite her on the front lip of an armchair. Close up she put him somewhere in his early fifties, but well taken care of.

'João Ribeiro did say you were exceptional, although he omitted to say in his letter that it was in a most evident way, too.'

'There were things he didn't tell me about you as well,' she said, batting his flattery off into the room. 'How you met, for instance.'

'Oh, João came here for a symposium on primes, I think. Then I went to Lisbon before I headed off to Princeton and gave a short series of lectures on Diophantine Equations.'

His eyes didn't leave her face. His hands, clasped together, fingers steepled, pointed at her. His head was sunk into his muscled shoulders and he'd dug his heels into the base of the armchair as if he was about to launch himself, dive into her. A metallic excitement uncoiled high in her stomach. She hadn't felt such brazen interest for more than twenty years. She had difficulty trapping questions long enough in her mind to ask them.

'Somebody I met the other day thought you'd been at RAND,' she said.

'I was. Two years. Bit of a hothouse that, all those brains steaming away under one roof . . . not totally dissimilar to working at Bletchley Park with Alan Turing during the war. That delayed my doctoral thesis, which was why I ended up in Princeton in the mid fifties. Then RAND . . . Santa Monica, you know, there's only two types of weather on the West Coast. Sun and fog. I missed my seasons. Nothing like an iron-hard frost and weak sunshine behind bare trees.'

'I missed the leafy summers and the smell of mown grass.'

'Who was it, who said I'd been at RAND?'

'Someone at my mother's funeral, I don't remember who.'

'I'm sorry. João didn't mention that.'

'I haven't told him yet.'

'He's been having a miserable time of it, João. Reading between the lines of his letter.'

'Maybe things will get better now. Did you read the news today?'

'About Salazar, yes. They say he won't be able to work again.'

'That might be good news for me, too,' she said, and sensed her reluctance, registered that first twitch of guilt.

'Oh you mean your husband and son fighting out in Guiné, yes, João said that you only *might* come . . . but here you are, so . . .'

They talked maths for what seemed like a short time because they got lost in the exchange. Greig was aggressive, starting most of his counter arguments with the words: 'That's trivial,' but Anne was an elusive opponent who, as soon as he'd nailed her down, tantalized him with another alluring possibility. By the end they'd hammered out a brief for a research paper. Greig said he would make inquiries about a place for her at one of the women's colleges.

She caught the train back to London and sat in a full carriage of American tourists who'd clearly journeyed down from Scotland and had thought that plaid made great jackets. Black Watch, yes, maybe, but Macleod? She couldn't believe them and suddenly felt like a staring hick. She went out into the corridor to smoke a cigarette and let her mind get crowded out by Louis Greig's physical presence, their intellectual connection and the smell of his cigars still on her coat. She put her face out of the window, her back to the wind so that her long black hair rushed past her face, blinkering her vision. The silver rails streamed out of the back of the train to Cambridge and she felt that tug again. She turned her face into the wind, the full blast of it too much to bear so that tears started in her eyes. Her hair flew behind in a thick lash and she was laughing at her life picking up speed, at the idea of events rushing towards her. Things, finally, happening.

The next day it rained and she sat in the dungeon dark of the Clapham house waiting for the telephone to ring, which it didn't. In the evening the rain stopped and sodden sunshine lapped into the room. She walked to her mother's grave and found that two expensive wreaths had been laid amongst the other bouquets – no names on them, only that of the florist's in Pimlico. She wandered amongst the other stones, her heels sticking in the turf, and took tea in a coffee house in Clapham Old Town. She ate cake and thought she might have imagined the attraction between them, overdecorated it in her mind. He was probably married. The lack of a wedding band meant little in England. She turned her own ring which wouldn't slip over her knuckle any more. Why would he be interested in her when there were all these sexually revolutionized twenty-two-year-olds on campus? She walked back home, skidding on the mash of autumn leaves and soggy litter.

The telephone was ringing as she opened the door and the five short steps to it made her breathless. Greig told her that he'd had the go-ahead from the head of the maths department, that he'd arranged a postgrad place at Girton, that application forms were being sent and accommodation was being looked into. He'd expect her to be up by the beginning of October.

She drank gin and tonic that night before supper and enjoyed one of Rawly's Pomerols with a pair of lamb chops. She went to bed drunk and woke up repentant.

London, still swinging in the sixties, rejuvenated her – the wild fashions, the incredible variety of music after Portugal's monotony, the sheer amount of stuff to buy. She bought winter clothes, went to Biba, wore jeans for the first time, smoked Gitanes, wondered why her mother had an entire collection of Herb Albert and his Tijuana Brass and ate her first hamburger at a place called a Wimpy Bar. It tasted like hell in a cotton wool bun. She did some practical things too, like getting the estate agents in to rent out the house on short company lets.

The application forms for the university arrived on the same day as a letter from João Ribeiro. The letter had been opened and read by the censors in Portugal, the tip of the flap stuck back down with glue. It was written in one of their codes and she had to dig out a copy of Fernando Pessoa's collected poems from the reference library to translate it.

Dear Anne,
You will have heard our good news by now but you will also,
no doubt, have seen from the state of this envelope that,
whilst the leader of the Estado Novo languishes brainless in
hospital, his security measures are still firmly in place. We hoped
for much but there has been no change. The government is
now in the hands of Marcelo Caetano, who is more

approachable than our old friend but, in getting the top job, will now find how much he owes to his pals in big business, the Church and the military. Nothing, I fear, will change. In fact, his first speech was directed at the ultra-right in which he said that the Portuguese, who have grown accustomed to being ruled by a genius, must now adapt to the government of common men. He's a donkey to Salazar's stallion and all we will get from him is a sterile old mule. I hope I am wrong. I hope the colonial wars end tomorrow and that the Portuguese can take their place among the civilized people of Europe.

I have lost three more teeth to the man in the street with the pliers. He told me that he is also a cobbler and I have given him my shoes to repair. He is taking care of me from head to foot.

I think of you and wish you all success.

João Ribeiro.

She smelt the letter, hoping to find some whiff of the sea, grilled horse mackerel or a freshly poured *bica* – smiling at herself as she fell for the Portuguese *saudades*, the longings – but all she caught was João's melancholy – despair tempered by humanity – which had penetrated the paper from the sweat of his hand.

Her pen hovered over the application forms, still undecided about one thing, still confused by the implications of João's letter. The telephone rang. She answered it in the chill hall and missed the man's name but heard that he was from the Portuguese consulate and would like to come and see her. She asked him what it was about but he declined to tell her. Only in person, Senhora Almeida. She agreed and hung up, only realizing then that he hadn't had to ask for her address.

He was there in less than an hour introducing himself from in front of his sticking-out ears as Senhor Martims. He was no more than five foot high and wore a black belted raincoat like a schoolboy's. They sat over coffee. He stroked his moustache downwards over his top lip obsessively, as if this was part of diplomacy, that he should never be seen speaking. They settled and his features became still and grave so that Anne immediately felt panic-struck and wanted to run from the room. He removed a letter from his pocket and held it on his knees which were pressed together. Anne saw her own name in Luís's handwriting. Senhor Martims looked down, gathered himself. His English came out quickly and barely made it through the gap between his teeth.

'It is my sad duty to have to inform you, Senhora Anne Almeida, that your son Captain Julião Almeida was killed in action four days ago in Guiné.'

There was a long silence. Senhor Martims' words did not penetrate her through the normal channels. She didn't hear them. They were hard words which hit Anne in the face, like torn-up cobblestones in a riot. They bruised their way in. They were not comprehensible as language. She understood them only as pain. Senhor Martims couldn't bear this silence in which he could only imagine the destructive power of his fast factual words. He started again and added more.

'Your son was leading a patrol in the forest and they were ambushed by guerrillas.'

Senhor Martims repeated it for her and she nodded at the words which headed off at different angles into the room.

'The guerrillas ambushed the patrol and your son, who was leading, was shot in the neck and chest. The fighting continued for an hour and his men were unable to come to his aid. By the time they had fought the guerrillas away your son had died from loss of blood. I am truly very sorry, Senhora Almeida.'

There was colour in these words, not just black and white information, and sound, too. They flung images into her head. The green forest, hooting and screeching. The first dull shots – cracks of poisonous sound. The red of blood on his neck and chest, darkening the green of his uniform. Julião lying in the long grass, the bullets zipping above him and the sky beyond the dark canopy, white, bleached to a harsh, glaring white, but growing dimmer as his life leaked into the pulsating ground, the heart beating under Africa.

'I am very sorry,' Senhor Martims was saying again, almost chanting. 'I have no way of softening this blow. This is the very worst thing to happen to a mother. I . . . I . . .'

Anne thought she should be crying, that she should be wailing her heart out, but these words had taken her to a much darker place. Crying was too small for this. You cried when you hit your finger with a hammer, not when the abyss has opened up inside you. She dug her elbows into her ribs to hold herself in. More words were coming her way from the small man but she was stopping herself from being split in two. The concentration for this was so hard and pure that the new battery of words came to her incomplete.

'. . . he felt responsible . . . fellow officers . . . nothing stupid . . . service revolver which I'm afraid he turned on himself . . . depressed . . . very proud . . . this terrible tragedy . . . two outstanding servants of their country. He left this letter addressed to you, Senhora Almeida.'

She didn't take the letter. She couldn't move her arms from her sides. Senhor Martims, at a loss, placed the letter on the arm of the chair.

'Do you have family here?' he asked, looking into her eyes as if she was shut in a box and he was peering through a slit.

'My mother died at the end of August,' she said. 'I have no family here.'

'You have no family?' said Senhor Martims, aghast. 'No friends?'

'Maybe . . . in Lisbon . . . still.'

'Friends of your mother?' he asked. 'You shouldn't be alone after such news.'

The only name that came to her was Jim Wallis and she said it. Senhor Martims found the number and spoke to Wallis in a murmur. Senhor Martims stayed with her, pacing the room, looking at the unopened letter on the arm of the chair, waiting for Wallis to arrive.

In her head she saw herself with her face out of the train window. These were the events that were rushing towards her, but blinded by the wind, they were just a blur, a sense of impending incident. Looking back she'd seen the silver rails but only through the incoherence of her own streaming hair. Now she was seeing a pattern, a terrible tragic pattern – her mother's story, her father's death, Julius Voss perishing at Stalingrad, his father's suicide, Karl's capture and execution, their son's death, the suicide of the surrogate father. 'Lies beget lies,' her mother had said, you have to tell another to keep the first one going. But tragedy is the same. It follows bloodlines. The one thing she'd never expected to be was tragic –

some jittery middle-aged woman, living alone in a large cold house, never going out because she could anticipate the next lightning strike. And here she was, a tragic figure. Pitied by Senhor Martims because she was a mother who'd lost everything and had no family. It made her angry and she tore open Luís's letter to see what he had to say for himself.

Dear Anne,
It is late and I've been drinking. The drink is not doing what it is supposed to do. I'm sweating and words, which were never my strength, float past me, but the pain, which should be dull by now, is still there, diamond hard, piercing, not one edge of it blunted.

The night and the noise of the insects are crowding me. My friends, fellow officers, have gone to bed. They see that I have taken it well. But I have not.

You and I left each other on bad terms because you thought that these wars were wrong. I saw it before – that first time in Angola – and I see it clearly now, but it is too late and I have lost everything – my son, and because you can never forgive me, you as well. The two of you were all that mattered to me and without you the future has no value.

I was never a man to do this sort of thing. I always savoured life. Perhaps if I wait I could persuade myself out of it and live the unendurable existence. But now, with the heat pressing against the walls, the vagueness of the world beyond the mosquito netting, the great distance between us and the colossal absence – I have no strength for it, no courage. Forgive me this, if not the other.

Your husband. Luís

She folded the letter up in its envelope and stuffed it down the side of the chair. Senhor Martims had stopped pacing and was now thinking about the English as a race. The words pity and admiration came to him. Why can't they explode? Why can't they squeeze out a tear? If she'd been Portuguese she'd have . . . she'd have fainted or fallen to her knees, wailing, but this . . . this bottled silence, this strapped-down stoicism. How do they do it? *Sang froid*, that was it, cold blood. The English were emotional reptiles. And as soon as he'd thought it he felt guilty. This was not the time for such thoughts. This woman ... the suffering ... it was unimaginable. Her mother as well.

But Senhor Martims was wrong. He didn't know it, but he was walking at the foot of a volcano. Plates had moved inside Anne, chasms had opened up and this boiling rage of molten rock was seething to the surface. Her hands, which were clasping her knees, trembled against her body's geology.

'Thank you, Senhor Martims, for coming to see me,' she said, her voice quaking. 'Thank you for your sympathy. I'll be all right now. You can go back to the consulate.'

'No, no, I insist on staying until Mr Wallis arrives.'

'I would like some moments to myself beforehand, that's all. If you would be so kind as to ...'

She engineered him out of the door. He went to his car and waited. Anne didn't go back into the sitting room but found the darkness of the dining room a comfort. She fell towards the table, retching with something too big to vomit out and barked her shins on a chair. The sharp physical pain was blinding and she stumbled over the chair, crashing with it to the floor. She lashed out at it with savage kicks, ripped the heel off her shoe.

'You fucking ... you fucking ... you little fucker,' she spat from between gritted teeth and, amazed at finding the available vocabulary, hauled herself to her feet.

She grabbed the back of the chair and dashed it against the wall. The back and rear legs split away from the seat and she brought this down with all her strength on another chair and broke off the two legs. She smashed the back into the wall and saw it splinter into matchwood. She took the front legs and seat and reduced that, too. She stood back, panting. The china quivered in the dresser. She threw open the doors, took out a plate and hurled it against the wall, another plate and another, the destructive satisfaction of it thrilling up her ribs. She swung each one harder and, as she got tired, she dredged up a screech of agony to launch the next plate with increasing venom. Just as her arm began to hang limp from her shoulder and her chest felt too full of organs, jostling for room, she found herself engulfed by a damp raincoat and Wallis whispering into her ear. More incomprehensible words.

She was taken up to a bedroom, her mother's room, and put into bed. A doctor was called, who came and sedated her. He left valium for later. She lay like a figurine in a cotton wool-filled box. The outside did not penetrate and inside was curiously muted, no thought or feeling could reach its pin-sharp conclusion.

She floated for what seemed like days and came into daylight with a strange woman in the room. She had to claw her way back into reality, a physical effort. The woman explained herself. Jim Wallis's wife. Anne tried to edge back towards what had happened but found herself removed from it. There was a padded bulwark between this new point and her past. She knew what had happened, the steel-fastened lock of muscles around her shoulder reminded her of that. She even saw the drift of shattered china up the wall but she could not recapture any of the intensity of the moment. She felt curiously bereft. The thought of her dead son and husband elicited sadness, which produced bleak, but quiet, weeping but there was no madness. She missed that madness. It had been right for the moment. Now she felt split, completely disconnected, not just from the incident but from the whole of her old life. The memories of it were as intact as they had been in the weeks while her mother lay dying, only now it wasn't even biography but more like history. It frightened her, this change of perception, until she realized that it was a modus vivendi, a truce after a mortifying exchange of artillery.

Wallis came by in the evening to relieve his wife. They talked on the landing outside the room. The day's report. Calm. Wallis sat on the bed, took Anne's hand. The front door slammed below.

'I'm back,' she said.

'It looks like it.'

'How long have I been . . . out?'

'Three days. Doctor's orders. He thought it best, in view of your mother as well.'

'Am I still on drugs?'

'Less than before, which is why you're back with us but probably a little fuzzy.'

'Yes, a little . . . fuzzy.'

She dressed as if she was watching herself do it and they ate something downstairs, the cutlery loud on the plates. Her surroundings, although sharp and recognizable, appeared unusual, as if oddly

329

lit. Wallis asked her what she was going to do with herself, but carefully as if she might be considering . . . what did they call it? Something stupid. The strangest thing was that the thought hadn't occurred to her – to kill herself. She assumed that she'd instinctively locked on to that stubbornness that her mother had possessed as well.

'I don't know,' she said. 'My life seemed to picking up some kind of momentum before this, I should try and recapture that, I suppose.'

'I could get you a job if you want.'

'Who with?'

'The Company, of course,' he said. 'They still haven't filled Audrey's position to Dickie's satisfaction. Every time someone new starts in the job Dickie just shakes his head and says, "Irreplaceable", and that's it.'

'Thanks, but Richard Rose and I, you know . . . I think I'm going to do this research project at Cambridge.'

'Any time you need help, Anne, we're here.'

Then something did come back to her and in focus. The reason why she'd hesitated to fill in her university application forms.

'There is something you could do for me now,' she said. 'You could get me my name back, my identity. I wouldn't mind being Andrea Aspinall again.'

Chapter 31

Her last act as Anne Ashworth was to go to Lisbon for the burial of Julião and Luís. Because of the African heat the bodies had already been cremated in Guiné but there was to be a Mass in the Basílica da Estrela and a burial service at the family mausoleum in Estremoz.

Anne stayed in the York House in Rua das Janelas Verdes in Lapa. The evening before the funeral she walked the familiar streets past the British Embassy on Rua de São Domingos, turned right into Rua de Buenos Aires, left into Rua dos Navegantes and down the railed slope of Rua de João de Deus. She hadn't been back in this neighbourhood for twenty-four years and, when she first saw the swaying jacarandas below the white dome of the basilica, she'd expected the memories to rush at her like excited children, but they held back, sidled off.

She stood in front of the old apartment building, its façade still the same with the green and blue tiles, black diamonds, the plaque, commemorating the death of the poet João de Deus, was still above the door.

She joined the Almeida family group on the steps in front of the basilica and, even though they'd never liked her, the foreigner, they took her in, accepted her in their mutual grief. They walked into the basilica together, Anne on Luís's mother's arm, and it confirmed to her what she knew about the Portuguese – they understood tragedy, it was their territory and they were united with anybody who was in it with them. They sat all night through the vigil – keeping watch over the urns.

Mass was held in the morning. Few people other than family came. The friends of Luís and Julião were all in Africa, fighting the wars. The Almeidas took the urns to Estremoz where they were laid in the family mausoleum, alongside other coffins, bunked on top of each other like soldiers in the barracks. The wrought-iron door was closed on the dead and their photographs placed in frames on the outside: Luís, as he'd always been in front of the camera, solemn, almost as if he was attending his own funeral, and Julião, still ready for life, his smile unbroken.

She stayed a night with the Almeidas and headed back to Lisbon on the train the next day. In the evening she went to see João Ribeiro, the last loose end to be tied before she flew out the next morning. João was living in a different room, but still in the heart of the Bairro Alto. He greeted her, kissing her hard on both cheeks and holding her tight to his thin body. She pulled away and he was weeping, pushing his handkerchief up under his specs until he realized it was easier to take them off.

'So, this is what has happened to me. This is what you do to an old man. How can you leave for such a short time and still make me so happy to see you? And sad. I am sorry for all your losses. More than anyone should have to bear in a lifetime, let alone a month. Life can be a brutal beast at times, Anne.'

'You should know, João,' she said, looking around the spartan room, his worn circumstances.

'This . . .' he said, sweeping his arm around, 'this is nothing to what you have had to endure.'

'You lost your wife, your job, the work that you loved.'

'My wife was always sick. It was a blessed release for her. The university? Under this régime it can't teach anybody anything. How can you learn with the newspapers printing their daily lies. And my work? I *have* work. This room is better than the last one, isn't it?'

'What work?'

'I teach arithmetic to children and their mothers how to read and write. I am a true communist, a better one now that I live among the people. They feed me, clothe me, look after me. But you . . . you must tell me what you are going to do after these terrible events.'

'There's only one thing I can do,' she said. 'I seem to have reached some sort of finality and yet I'm still here. I have to continue. I have to start again.'

She told him about Louis Greig and the research project and

they talked mathematics until a woman brought a tray of plates and grilled sardines and they sat down to dinner.

'It's not a bad life for an old man,' said João. 'My meals cooked, my washing done, my room cleaned and *fado* in the evenings. Perhaps this is how we should all live. I find it harmonious.'

The woman came back, cleared the table and left coffee and brandy.

'They know you are important to me,' said João, 'so they're making a fuss. They wanted to cook you something special but I told them sardines was what you liked, that you were one of us . . . as indeed is Louis Greig, for all his wealth.'

'One of us?'

'A mathematician and a communist.'

'I'm surprised. He told me he worked at RAND after Princeton.'

'But *after* McCarthy's witch hunts and anyway he's always been . . . safe.'

'His wealth, you mean.'

'His father owns a few thousand hectares of Scotland and is a Conservative MP, who I think was even in the shadow cabinet for a while. Louis went to Eton and never bothered with politics as an undergraduate. He kept himself clean and his eye on the larger game.'

'What about those lectures he gave here?' she asked. 'You, João Ribeiro, renowned communist, Head of Maths, must have invited him?'

'Me? No. That was the beauty of it. Dr Salazar invited him. Louis's father had business interests in Porto. Wine, I think. Connections were made, the invitation given. Louis was delighted. It looked like cast iron on his CV.'

'And you and he talked.'

'I was looking after him.'

'So he knew about you?'

'At his level the Communist Party is global.'

In the morning she sat outside Café Suiça in the Rossio square, taking a coffee and a last *pastel de nata* for what she thought would be a long time. Beggars nagged at her table – a man with no hands and his pocket held open with a stick, a woman with one side of her face burned, barefoot kids swatted away by waiters. She paid

333

for her coffee and went to a street of jewellers nearby and had her wedding band sawn off. The jeweller weighed it for her and paid her cash. She went back to the Rossio, distributed the money around the beggars, got into a taxi and left with a flight of pigeons for the airport.

The plane taxied to the end of the runway. As the engines built up power she waited for her favourite moment except that, as they were throttling up, she felt a rising surge of panic instead. She was terrified by the juddering of the plane's structure as it hurtled down the runway, had to close her eyes and fight the panic back down her throat as the wheels left the ground. The sense of nothing under her feet had never occurred to her before but now, as the plane powered into a steep climb, she felt powerless, rigid with fear at the approaching moment, when God might give up the pretence, let them drop from the sky and she would die in the company of strangers, unknown and unloved. They levelled out. A stewardess walked the aisle. The No Smoking light went out and Anne fought her way into her bag for her stalwart supporters.

Back in London Wallis came round for a drink on his own. He had a passport in the name of Andrea Aspinall, a national insurance number, everything she would need. They talked about Lisbon. He looked at the red dent left on her finger by the missing wedding band. Andrea steered the conversation round to his wife.

'She's a good girl,' he said. 'We get on, you know. She's self-sufficient, too. Doesn't need me around all the time. Don't have to worry about her at parties.'

'Is that important?'

'Don't like them clingy, Anne. Sorry, Andrea. Bit of space, if you know what I mean.'

'To play the field?'

'Well, yes, I suppose that's what I mean. Not that I have much luck these days.'

'Did you ever have any luck with that French songbird in Lisbon?'

'Everybody had luck with her except me,' he said, and rubbed his money fingers. 'Nothing's changed.'

'Maybe you wear your heart on your sleeve, Jim.'

334

'You think that's it?'

'We all want a bit of mystery, don't you think? You should be good at it. You *are* a spy, for God's sake.'

'Never much good at that malarkey, Andrea. Admin, that's me now. I was always talking too much. Not like you. Very spare with words, you are.'

'I wasn't then.'

'And now?'

'Had a bit of my stuffing knocked out, that's all.'

'Sorry. I didn't mean to be glib,' he said. 'It's a pity you're off to Cambridge.'

'You don't need me to give you mystery lessons.'

'No, no. Thought you'd come and work for us. Get you a job at the drop of a hat, you know that.'

'Even with Richard Rose in charge?'

'Dickie's not operating at a departmental level any more. He's practically government. Way back from the front line, he is.'

'Why's he going on about my mother's irreplaceability then?'

'Old school . . . they went back to the forties. He still took her out to tea once a week even after she retired.'

'Tea?'

'Their euphemism for a four-hour session in The Wheatsheaf. Christ, Audrey could put it away. Never saw her even stagger. Bloody marvellous sight. It was Dickie's way of keeping his finger in the pie. Audrey . . . Auders, as he called her. Follow Auders, he used to say. She knew everything. You always do if you're running the money.'

'I'm going to Cambridge, Jim.'

'Yes, yes, of course you are. All I'm saying is that if it doesn't work out . . . I'm, we're, the Company is here.'

Wallis tried to kiss her on the mouth as he left – five double G&Ts inside him and one down his shirt – she turned her face the fraction necessary so that he wouldn't feel bad. He stumbled down the path. She closed the door and watched him through one of the unstained diamonds of glass. He got into his car, started the motor and looked through the windscreen straight at her before pulling away. She didn't understand that look. It wasn't disappointment, vague humiliation or even anger. It was the look of a man who was working

335

on something and it was a long way from the bluff bonhomie that he churned out in her company.

She rented the house out to an American couple for a year. She went up to Cambridge on the train to find herself suppressing that same surge of panic she'd had on the plane coming back from Lisbon. Louis Greig had arranged a flat for her on the first floor of a semi-detached house in a leafy street not far from the station. She started work straight away but couldn't seem to remember the old social skills to make friends in her department. She became afraid of dead time. The English autumn was dark and squally. The rain scratched at her windows and she kept her head down because, if she stopped to look at her reflection in the glass, she might see dread in the empty room behind her.

Greig was away in Washington for the first two weeks which meant she had two Sundays when, in the early evening, *Songs of Praise* would come up from the television below her and Julião would appear in her head, lodge himself in her chest and she would pace the room until the pain went back into its crack, like a snake into a wall. At seven o'clock the pubs opened and she was always there with a half of lager, orbiting some sporty crowd of raucous and ebullient undergrads.

Greig came back in mid October and Andrea presented her first paper to him which he crushed as mercilessly as one of his cigar butts. He sent her out into the rain feeling empty, useless. She went back to her flat and lay on the bed, wondering whether her middle-aged brain was too hardened into its old patterns to be able to think originally any more. Greig came by in the late evening, hung his mac and umbrella behind the door and apologized for his brutality. Relief spread through her. He brought wine, something good from the Trinity cellars and a triangle of brie stolen from high table. She asked about Washington. He grumbled about the Yanks, how spoilt they were over there. He asked about Lisbon. Apologized for not inquiring earlier, he'd just had an ugly meeting with the dean about budgets. They talked about the Portuguese, the Almeidas, João Ribeiro.

'He's teaching arithmetic,' said Greig, amazed. 'The man could knock off Diophantine Equations before breakfast. What's he playing at?'

'Being a true communist, he says.'

'But he doesn't have to teach long division to street kids, for Christ's sake.'

'He's satisfying local demand. They don't need Diophantine Equations to sell their fish door to door.'

Greig's eyebrows seemed to float from his head with boredom.

'Isn't Salazar dead yet?' he asked.

'No, but still *hors de combat*.'

'That man's driving his country back to the Middle Ages,' he said. 'A thousand miles from his hospital bed there've been students rioting in the streets of Paris. The whole of European youth is on the move. We're in the middle of a cultural revolution while the Iberian Peninsula is in the hands of Edwardian stiffs, throwing money away on empire and grinding their people down into some pre-industrial slavery. They'll never recover. Sorry, Anne, I'm ranting . . . nothing like a good rail against our old fascist friends.'

'It's Andrea now . . . I wrote to you.'

'Yes, yes, of course it is. What's all that about?'

'I was a field agent for the Secret Intelligence Services in Lisbon during the war.'

'My God.'

'For some complicated reasons and a smattering of political embarrassment I had to get married under my cover name, which I was stuck with for twenty-four years until last month. Now I'm starting again. A clean slate for Andrea Aspinall.'

She was surprised to find Greig impressed. Bletchley Park hadn't perhaps had the kudos of action in the field. Cracking Enigma didn't have the dashing image. The keenness she'd seen in their first interview returned to his eyes, nailing her to the bed she was sitting on, did something strange to the muscles in her thighs.

'You're lucky we don't bother too much with proof of qualifications.'

'You're lucky I'm here at all,' she said, playing to him now, hands reaching shakily for some self-confidence. 'They wanted me for a job.'

'They?'

'The Company, as we call ourselves. The SIS. My mother worked for them, too. All her work cronies turned up at her funeral.

Some of them I knew from the forties in Lisbon. They were looking for staff.'

Greig leaned back in his chair. Andrea stretched herself out on the bed, propped her head up with a hand, sucked on her cigarette and tried to remember whether this was how seduction worked . . . if she ever knew.

'You're a dark horse,' he said.

'I'm dark,' she said, flatly.

He laughed, uneasily, suddenly finding blood converging on parts of his body – neck, groin – finding swallowing and crossing his legs suddenly a problem.

Her mother had been wrong. Sex *had* been revolutionized over the last twenty years or maybe Rawly had been much more of an interesting partner than Luís. After their first kiss she'd reached to stub out her cigarette and Greig had told her to carry on smoking. He put his hands up her skirt and she felt his hands shake as he found her suspenders and the bare skin above her stocking tops. He stripped down her knickers, roughly. He knelt before her, bent his head down between her thighs, cupped her buttocks with his rough hands and drew her to him.

He made love to her expertly. He was unembarrassed at making his demands and, continuing the tutor/pupil relationship, taught her things about men, like a tennis coach demonstrating grip. He asked her not to close her eyes in mock ecstasy but to keep them open, looking at him at all times, especially when she was kneeling in front of him. She ricocheted between embarrassment, lust and disgust. She was doing things within a matter of hours that Luís had probably never heard of and the discovery of this deep carnality in herself was disturbing, but oddly gratifying, too.

She fell asleep in the early morning and woke up alone, the morning so dark that she thought it was dawn when in fact it was close to eleven o'clock. She fingered her lips, which were sensitive, bruised. Her legs were as stiff as if she'd been out riding. In her gut she was both desolate and rampant. In her head she was ashamed and excited.

She had a bath and found herself rooting around for her best lingerie. She made herself up as she'd never done to go to the maths department and dressed in her new autumn clothes. He wasn't in the department. Her postgrad colleagues stared at her from beneath their crackling nylon shirts, their drip-dry, ever-creased Crimplene trousers. She moved on to Trinity and bumped into him coming out of the porter's lodge. He had his face turned back and he was holding his hand out.

'Come *on*, Martha,' he said. 'For heaven's sake.'

A woman, dazzlingly kempt, with styled blonde and lustrous hair, and a floor-length brown coat with a French silk scarf around her neck, took Greig's hand. Andrea stepped back, preparing to run. Greig turned, saw her.

'Anne,' he said.

'Andrea,' she replied.

'You're so awful with names,' said Martha, whose American accent grabbed the adjective and made of it innards on a butcher's floor.

Greig introduced his wife, asked Andrea to drop by his rooms at tea time. He pressed the automatic release on his umbrella, which burst open like a giant bat, and they headed out into the rain.

It had happened as quick as murder and the change was no less devastating. Andrea watched his broad back heading into town, Martha's narrow shoulders leaning into him. Desolation, bleak as the rain-slivered wind off the Fens, sliced into her.

She went home and thumped into the bed in her damp coat. The earlier emptiness had now been replaced by a full roll of barbed wire jealousy. Why anybody thought it was green, she couldn't fathom. Jealousy was a multi-edged blade and whichever way it turned it cut you.

By tea time she was exhausted and the walk back to Trinity in the rain was the trudge of a soldier making his way back to the front but, and she couldn't fail to notice this, she was going back. It was that inevitable. Choice was not in it.

Greig took the coat from her antagonistic shoulders, hung it up and showed her the leather sofa.

'I could see you were surprised by Martha,' he said softly. 'I thought João would have told you that much, but then it's not a natural way for his mind to think. Must have been a terrible shock. I'm sorry.'

She had nothing to say. All the savagely planned words suddenly seemed amateur, naïve.

'I hope you don't think that last night meant nothing,' he said. 'It wasn't just a one-off.'

Hope surged to absurd heights. What was she? Twenty again? Not one inch of emotional progress since girlhood.

'You're a beautiful woman. Extraordinarily gifted. Mysterious . . .'

'And your *wife*?' she asked, the word hacking through the air, serrated edge.

'Yes,' he said, simply – no excuses, no apologies, no denials.

She had questions stacked up inside her like punch cards for a computer programme but they were all binary banal and some of them, if asked, might have answers she didn't want to hear. What am I to you? A comfortable lay. A convenient screw. A charitable poke. That last one hurt because she knew how needy she was.

Greig sat next to her on the sofa, took her hand as if she was a patient. Where *did* he get those rough hands from? Nobody got hands like that from chalking equations on a board. His words leaked into her head like myrrh – exotic, nearly meaningless, except her insides quivered at them.

'The first time I met you I knew you were going to be important to me. I didn't intend to stay last night with you, but I just thought we'd suddenly connected and I couldn't resist that connection. The chance of knowing you, of getting closer to you. The way you smoked that cigarette, stretched across the bed . . . I was yours.'

As he spoke his hand came to rest on her knee. She knew, she saw what he was doing and did nothing about it, because she wanted this to happen. The coarse skin of his hand snagged on the nylon stocking as he pushed it up between her legs, over the stocking top, the soft skin on the inside of her thigh, until he brushed a hard finger over the outline of her sex beneath her best silk. The carnal jolt rushed up her spine, but something older, atavistic, recoiled. She stood and lashed her hand across his face. The slap fizzed on her palm. His face reddened. She slammed the door as she left.

Hours later she was back looking for him in the quad. No lights on in his room. She found his address from the porter's lodge and stood outside his house on the other side of the street, still wearing the same clothes, her make-up repaired. At 11.30 p.m. a light came on upstairs and Martha appeared in a bay window to close the curtains. Another light came on in the hall. The front door opened and Louis came out with a short-haired dachshund on a lead. She crossed the street, came at him between two parked cars and startled him as surely as if she'd had a knife.

'I'm sorry,' she said, partly for startling him, partly for the slap.

'I probably deserved it,' he replied, and continued on his way.

'You were taking advantage of me,' she said, catching up with him.

'I was,' he said. 'I admit it, but I couldn't help it.'

The dog trotted between them, doggedly disinterested in human drama.

'Do you have any idea what this is like for me?' she asked. 'I've been married for twenty-four years. You're only the second man I've known.'

The lie so smooth she even believed it herself. It stopped him in his tracks. The dog continued, yanked the lead tight, walked back huffily, looked at their feet.

'How am I supposed to know these things?' he asked. 'You don't tell me anything about yourself. And from my side, well, I sensed something. I was attracted to you. I did what any man would do. I went for you. It has nothing to do with my past, my marriage, your past or your previous marriage. It was just the moment.'

'And this afternoon?'

'I couldn't help myself. I find you irresistibly sexy.'

'Your wife,' she said, the word cutting her at the back of the throat, 'she looks . . . she seems very . . .'

'If I want strength, pragmatism, and efficiency, she's my girl. You have to understand, Andrea, Martha runs our lives, hers and mine, as a controlled experiment. My career, my work – what's that geared to? To achieving pinnacles of logic, zeniths of rationale. That's a mathematician's lot. Somewhere along the road I need passion, mystery, humour, for God's sake.'

They carried on walking. The dog leading, jaunty now that they were on the move again. They came on to an open expanse, a football pitch, and he let the dog off the lead.

'I thought you were walking into this with your eyes open,' he said.

'I was, but not with full information.'

The wind buffeted them. His mac flapped open. Her hair

341

streaked across her mouth and nose as if she were under the veil. He peeled her hair back, pushed his hand round the back of her neck and pulled her to his face. They kissed as they had done the night before. She pushed her hand into his jacket and up his shirted back. The dog reappeared, circled, snorted and tore off again.

The ground rules laid out, they started their affair. In that first term, the longest they ever spent together was after Sunday dinner when Martha, who was bored by the Senior Common Room, had an early night and Louis, instead of passing round the port, cycled to Andrea's flat and stayed there until 2.00 a.m. He also had a brass bed in his rooms in Trinity and they would occasionally take a tutorial in there. On spring afternoons they would go to his allotment, he was a gardener (those rough hands were from digging and planting), and she would read her paper to him while he worked and afterwards they'd lie down on the rough wooden floor of the shed amongst the forks and spades. Some evenings, if she became desperate, she would wait for him to walk the dog and join him on black, blustery nights. The dog would run off and they'd manage as best they could on a park bench, Louis looking around wildly as car headlights skirted the common.

The next term, when it was too cold to sustain anything in the frost-hardened air, they would slip into the back of his car, which he took to parking down the street from his house. They would trap the dog lead in the door and she'd end up with her face pressed against the quarterlight of a window, her breath fogging the glass, the dog outside looking up at her, questioning.

She couldn't believe what was happening, what she was doing. He would ask her to do things. Things like role-playing, which at first thought seemed absurd and, in practice, faintly disgusting but then she found herself doing them and as she did them more they would become less repellent, until they didn't seem revolting but were stimulating and then almost normal.

When he left her, as he did all summer to go to the States to idle on the beach with Martha and her family in Cape Cod, she stayed in Cambridge, researching to forget him. She lay awake at night, at first trying to work out what it was all about without ever be able to define her nebulous need for him and then realizing that she knew all along. With her mother, son and husband gone she felt unmoored, empty. Louis, her mentor and teacher, tethered her, filled her up. But the realization made no difference to her state and she saw that although this was what she expected of Louis, it never quite happened and yet it could . . . it could.

She had thought, at first, that Martha was the only barrier to her future happiness until it had occurred to her that Martha's presence was a part of the intensity. She and Louis were both hooked on the subterfuge – the secret meetings, the late-night assignations, the sense of the forbidden.

Memories of another age, another secret love leaked into her head to confuse the present.

During the next academic year Louis sensed a change in her, a change he did not like. She appeared confident. Louis responded by becoming slapdash about his other liaisons. Andrea would arrive just as another girl left, reapplying her lipstick. She found an earring in his room, a tiny pair of knickers, a used condom. Andrea never mentioned any of these finds. He had already become hostile and she didn't want to antagonize him further. That next summer he left for Cape Cod without saying goodbye.

She became prone to spontaneous bursts of crying which stopped as abruptly as they started. When the library shut for that summer she couldn't bear to go off on her own for a lonely holiday near families and lovers. Even when Jim Wallis invited her down to his cottage in the south of France, she couldn't face being with him and his not-so-new wife.

She stayed in Cambridge and counted the days to the beginning of term like a child with an advent calendar. As her loneliness crowded around her in her first-floor flat and the usual haunts of the undergrads fell silent, she sought out other pubs with life and noise, pubs whose regulars were labourers and builders, people who actually ordered pickled eggs from the jars behind the bar and ate them. She woke up in the mornings feeling as if she'd drunk every-thing including the wringings from the beer mats. She shuddered and squeezed the pillow to her face in a pathetic attempt to block out the creature she'd become.

Louis turned up late, three weeks into term. She was happy even when he trashed her summer's work, even when she could smell another woman on him.

As the Christmas break of 1970 approached she didn't know what to do with herself. She saw no way out. She was disgusted by her own weakness – announcing to herself every morning that this was the last time, that she was going to abandon the project, go back to London. Then she would methodically get dressed in her best clothes and go and visit the man who had made her into this.

Waking at four in the morning she would force herself to think of the good things from her life. She couldn't touch on Julião because her failure there was still too painful, but she went back to those last days with her mother and found things to sustain her. Her father's nobility. Her mother's honesty. Her own feelings of love for the woman she'd despised so much. She replayed conversations, thought about Rawly and his wine. His wife. And Audrey telling her that she only deserved the three-quarters man that Rawly was. Had the same happened to her? Was Louis all that she deserved, all that she wanted?

At the end of November she went to his rooms in Trinity, as usual, like the programmed toy she'd become. He barked at her from the door to go straight to the bedroom. He'd begun to enjoy command. She'd just undressed with Louis standing in the doorway, when they both heard Martha's voice at the bottom of the stairs. Martha never came to his rooms. It was an unspoken agreement. He shut Andrea in the bedroom. Martha came into his rooms without knocking. Her New England voice cracked like a whip. They were continuing a row they'd had the night before about going to New England for Christmas, rather than up to Louis's father in Scotland. Andrea, paralysed, sat naked on the bed and stared at the door. She thought she was praying for it not to open, but realized that this was just some superficial horror of social embarrassment, that in fact she *wanted* Martha to open the door. It would do something. It would move her situation one way or another.

Martha was breaking Louis down, dismantling him so effectively that Andrea thought that it wasn't a row about holidays at all. What was Martha doing here? Martha answered the question as if she'd heard it.

Martha opened the door.

She didn't open it gently. She was making a point. She flung it open. It swung round, smacked against the wall and slammed back shut in a fraction of a second – shutter speed. The image from both sides indelibly printed. Andrea naked on the bed. Martha transfixed.

The door was not reopened. It didn't have to be.

The silence was as crystalline as frost.

This time it wasn't Martha's voice that cracked like a whip. The slap must have stilled the quad. A door slammed. Louis burst into the room, tore off his trousers, wrestled her back on to the bed and pinning her wrists lunged into her and rammed her with directed, shuddering vehemence. It didn't take long and he collapsed on top of her. She shifted under his weight. He released her wrists, rolled off her and sat with his head in his hands for minutes.

'Fuck,' he said, after some time.

Andrea sat on the other side of the bed, back to him.

'I've always wondered how you and Martha stayed together,' she said, as if this might be some consolation.

'Because her father's a senator,' he said.

'Was that all?'

She rolled up a stocking and pulled it on, another.

'There's somebody I've been wanting you to meet for some time,' he said.

His words nauseated her. It was as if he'd been preparing her, bringing her to the right psychological pitch for some bad news. He went to the sink, washed himself, towelled between his legs. He pulled on his undershorts, trousers, flipped the braces over his shoulders, looking at her all the time, contemplating the new situation.

She reached for a cigarette and some tissues, wiped herself between her legs, lit the cigarette. She dressed without washing. She needed to soak for a week to get rid of this sordidness.

He made tea in his study. They sat at his desk. He stirred his tea a long time for a man who didn't take sugar.

'Who do you want me to meet?' she asked.

'Someone in London.'

'In London,' she said on automatic, now that the situation was changing she didn't want it to.

'We can't continue here.'

'You mean *I* can't.'

He went back to stirring his tea.

'This is an opportunity, a unique opportunity.'

'For you to get rid of me,' she said. 'I know bad news, Louis. I don't need it sweetened.'

'This is a job,' he said. 'And I know you'll be good at it.'

Chapter 32

1970, London.

They went to London on separate trains. Andrea had a nasty British Rail breakfast, cardboard toast and grey coffee. She smoked instead and wanted it to be pink gin time. Louis still hadn't told her who she was going to meet and he was no clearer on his cryptic remarks about the unique opportunity. This was what they had become. Not telling. Not talking. Circlers of each other. Unequal lovers. Bad maths. Mere satisfiers of each other's strange psychosexual needs.

Louis's intensity emanated from one source – his cock. What he admired in her was not what stirred him. He never talked about her beauty, her brain, her mystery as he had done before in those days which a madman might have called their courting. He was driven by the sex, but she had no idea what the connection was in Louis's head that was running his desire. As for herself, she didn't want to think about herself – a pair of scaley claws scratching about in the dust.

The train came into King's Cross Station. As it shunted to a halt and she reached for her bag she nearly grasped something about Louis, a nuance which wouldn't come back to her, but which had something to do with control.

She went to the RAC club in Pall Mall as instructed and asked for Louis Greig. The man at the desk gave her an envelope which contained a very long list of instructions. Go to Waterloo, take a train to Clapham Junction, then a bus to Streatham, another train to Tulse Hill, a bus back to Brixton and on and on. She set off on the interminable journey, annoyed with Louis for not telling her so that she could have worn flatter heels. She thought about the instructions as she made her way to Waterloo and found herself instinctively checking her tail. The instructions had the quality of spycraft about them. And on the bus from Tulse Hill to Brixton the man sitting next to her leaned over and said:

'Ours is the next stop.'

They got off on the Norwood Road and went into Brockwell Park. Her new companion took her to the bowling green in the middle, nodded her towards the clubhouse and disappeared. She was unaccountably excited as she tried the loose Bakelite handle of the clubhouse door. The interior was unlit and dark on what was now an overcast late November afternoon. In the weak light by the window, Louis sat with his back to the wall next to a thickset man in a dark, heavy overcoat and a grey-brimmed hat with a black band. She trod the wooden boards to where the men were sitting. The smell of creosote filled her nostrils. They were talking in low voices and she realized they weren't speaking English. They were talking in a language which she thought she should understand, it had the same sounds as Portuguese.

Louis and the man stood up and the light caught their faces. Andrea realized that this man must be a Russian. He took off his hat. His hair had the quality of wire wool.

'This is Alexei Gromov,' said Louis. 'He'll tell you where to go afterwards.'

He shook hands with the Russian and left, his retreating feet sounding like those of the first lord vacating the stage for the tragedians' big scene. Her heart was pounding in her chest, her system so shot through with adrenalin that breathing became a concentrated act and sweat formed on odd patches of her body.

Gromov's face had the stillness of someone accustomed to very cold weather, as if evolution had made the nerves retreat from the surface, to make life more bearable. His eyes seemed deep set in his head, not wary, but viewing with the advantage of cover. He showed her to a chair which he positioned so that her face was in the weak daylight and his head was backlit.

'We've been following your career with interest,' he said slowly in English.

'I'm not sure I've ever had one.'

'Politics is a belief. You might not practise it all the time, but it's always there.'

'You mean we communists never suffer from disillusionment?'

'Only if you've decided against the human race. Communism is of the people, for the people, by the people,' he said, opening his hands in front of him.

'And the state?'

'The state is merely structure,' he said, boxing his hands this time.

'Can't you be disillusioned by mere structure and still be for the people?'

Gromov found himself down an alleyway he didn't want to be in. He wasn't an ideologue, he'd never been strong on dialectic, and anyway it wasn't the purpose of the meeting. Greig had warned him of her cleverness, but seemed to have made a massive assumption about her commitment.

'We had heard that you were very committed to the cause,' he said.

'That depends on who you've been talking to.'

'One of our guests in the Soviet Union. A Portuguese guest.'

'I'm not sure that I know any.'

'Comrade Alvaro Cunhal.'

'I don't believe we ever met.'

'You planned his escape. A very bold and daring strategy.'

'I planned it, yes, but not alone,' she said, and for some reason it triggered off an old strain of anger. 'Do you know who planned that with me?'

'I think it was João Ribeiro, wasn't it?'

'Do you know what happened to him?'

Gromov shifted in his seat, the ride still uncomfortable, silently cursing Greig, who'd said she was psychologically prepared for the work.

'He left the party, didn't he?'

'They kicked him out, Mr Gromov. After nearly forty years of active, anti-fascist resistance, after some of the best operations ever planned against the *Estado Novo*, they kicked him out. Why *was* that?'

'The report said there'd been a security breach.'

'No. It was structure, Mr Gromov. Structure kicked him out.'

'I don't follow.'

'The central committee thought he was getting too big for his boots. They thought he was threatening their positions in the party.

349

So they planted their innuendo and rumour and João Ribeiro, one of the best, most loyal servants to the cause was removed from his office in the party. He ended up in prison and lost his job, Mr Gromov.'

'I'm not sure I understand.'

'Ask the central committee of the Portuguese Communist Party of 1961–2.'

'I can see you're angry.'

'He's a good and trusted friend. The PCP treated him badly.'

'I promise you a full investigation,' said Gromov, having no intention.

'Now tell me what you want,' she said, surprised at herself, angry and forceful now that she was out of Louis's orbit.

Gromov's hands were fists turned in on his knees. He'd lost the initiative in this meeting and he badly needed to get it back if this woman was to do what he wanted.

'We are entering a critical phase in our relationship with the West,' he said.

'And with the East, now that China's got the H-bomb.'

'It's not relevant to our relationship with the West.'

'Except that you're surrounded and you've made the West nervous after the Prague Spring.'

Maybe he should have asked Louis to stay and bring this wretched woman under control. She was impossible.

'In order for us to proceed into the next phase, the negotiating phase, we need to ensure that we have the very best quality information.'

'You want me to spy for you,' she said. 'You want me to give up my life, my research, my . . .'

'Love affair?' he asked. 'No, not necessarily. You'd only be in London.'

Love affair. That unbalanced her. How much detail had Louis given him? Those words. Love and Affair. They didn't really describe what was going on between Louis and her. But he'd said love affair and that meant that Louis must have said the same. She found herself suddenly on the downward spiral, clutching at the ludicrous to find hope.

'We want you to go and work for the British Secret Intelligence Service,' said Gromov, leaning in on her, seeing he'd hit home with something, but not sure what. 'If you are still sympathetic – no, I mean if you still believe in what *we* are trying to achieve, then we would like you to contact your old friend, Jim Wallis.'

'Jim's in Administration.'

'That is very good,' said Mr Gromov thickly, as if advertising cakes.

'Does that mean your aim is for specific or general intelligence?'

'You unnerved me earlier, Miss Aspinall.'

'I apologize if I was over-aggressive.'

'I thought you might have suffered an ideological shift,' said Gromov, thinking that's better, this is the tone.

'My argument was with the central committee of the PCP of 1961–2.'

'Some people when they come into some money, property . . . experience a change of view,' said Gromov, turning the knife now that it was in, punishing a little. 'From being in the street they are suddenly up high, looking down.'

'I've spent more than half my life in Portugal and its colonies under the dictatorship of Dr Salazar. You should have no fear of the bourgeoisie claiming me.'

'Yes. It is good, perhaps, that you have seen things from a different perspective.'

'I'm surprised Louis didn't put your mind at rest. If you didn't know already, he would have told you that I've lost a son and a husband to a fascist, capitalist, imperialist and authoritarian state.'

'It is refreshing to find someone both intellectually and emotionally motivated. I am sorry I doubted you. I don't know how I could have done, given your pedigree.'

The significance of that final word did not penetrate at first. She found herself thinking what exactly her pedigree was and got sidetracked by her earlier statement about Portuguese imperialism and the colonies. Gromov watched her mind at work from behind his glacial façade.

'Do you mind if I smoke?' she asked.

'Not at all.'

She scratched through the contents of her handbag, rooting around in her mind at the same time. She found a cigarette. Gromov provided the light. The word came back again with its full force – pedigree.

'Are you saying, Mr Gromov, that my mother used to work for you?'

'Yes, I am,' he said. 'She was an excellent servant of our cause. Her position within the Company's administration was vital.'

'I'm not sure . . . I'm not sure that . . .'

'She was never very clear to us about her motivation. You understand that some people who work for us are anxious to establish their reasons. It assuages their feelings of guilt. Your mother was not one of these. She was never a clandestine member of the Communist Party, for instance, like you were.'

'How was she recruited?'

'Kim Philby recruited her during the war.'

'Did he shed any light on her motivation?'

'Only that it was for very deep emotional reasons, which she was not prepared to divulge,' said Gromov. 'This is our preferred motivation. Those who do it just for the money . . . well . . . they are already demonstrating an untrustworthy capitalist tendency. We remunerated your mother for the considerable risks she undertook but she told me once that luxury made her feel very uncomfortable.'

'Was it you who laid those wreaths on her grave?'

'Yes. One was from me, the other from Comrade Kosygin. It was a small way of honouring her service.'

'She worked in banking.'

'A very interesting position.'

'I'm sure they've found someone satisfactory by now. It's been four years since she retired.'

'Just approach Jim Wallis . . . remind him.'

'You said there was something specific.'

'I don't think I answered that question,' said Gromov, on a roll now. 'But there is, yes. Something that your mother had been working on before she retired. As you know, the shared culture and language of the two Germanys makes our job of planting agents very easy and they are extremely difficult to uncover unless they are betrayed. We are in the process of entering into discussions with the West and, specifically, with the West German Chancellor, Willi Brandt. We have some very well-placed sources who are gathering excellent material to aid us with our negotiations. We have lost some of those agents, not important ones at the moment, but we don't want to lose any more. We are also losing the odd high-level defector to the West which is causing us a lot of . . . embarrassment. The problem is that since Philby left the Company our knowledge at an operational level has been very poor.'

'But not nonexistent. You do have people?'

'Your mother was one. Her retirement was a great blow. In spycraft, as in business, money is everything. It pays for things. You follow the money trail and you find out who it is paying.'

'That sounds simple.'

'Except that your mother traced every penny and concluded that the traitor on our side was either not receiving funds or receiving funds from a different source within the British Intelligence Service. We have since discovered that there is no separate source of funding for overseas operations.'

'So, you have a traitor who is not motivated by money.'

'It's even rarer than that, Miss Aspinall,' he said, which irrationally annoyed her for the second time. 'We have a traitor who is operating without expenses. Not many of our officers, KGB or Stasi, are prepared to fund treacherous operations out of their own pockets. These officers are privileged, but they are paid in Ostmarks and roubles, which don't go very far over the Wall.'

'So he gets his money from somewhere.'

'Possibly *she*. We are not even that far down the road.'

'By the sound of it you think whoever it is, is in Berlin.'

'Yes.'

'And you've looked at all your agents with access to West Berlin, checked their backgrounds and nothing's come up?'

'It's a long process.'

'But you've been doing it.'

Gromov shifted a foot, his first noticeable movement.

'It's in progress.'

'But easier and quicker through me?'

'You will be rewarded.'

'My reward will be to see João Ribeiro restored to his position on the central committee . . . if he wants it.'

'It will be done,' said Gromov.

'The other thing is, Mr Gromov, that this will be the only operation I will perform on your behalf. I have ideological faith but I do not have the same quarrel with my country that my mother did. I also suspect that this is the end of my research project at Cambridge. I imagine that I will have to tell Jim Wallis that it didn't work out. It will be a burned bridge. I'll need work. Admin within the Company may not be such a bad job, but I don't want to be a permanent *spy* there.'

Gromov nodded. He would work on her. She would come round to him in the end.

'The only clue we have on the identity of the traitor was something your mother overheard back in '66 from Jim Wallis. It was a codename she'd never heard of before and she could find no existing financial record for it. The name was: Snow Leopard.'

'Well, they're rare, aren't they, Mr Gromov?'

'Very rarely seen indeed,' he replied. 'I come from Krasnogorsk in Siberia, not far from the Mongolian border. At that point the Sayan mountains form the frontier, which is the natural habitat of the snow leopard. My father took me hunting when I was sixteen and while Wall Street was having its magnificent crash I shot the one and only snow leopard I have ever seen. My wife wears it today as a jacket when we go to the ballet.'

Andrea sat on a bench, high up in Brockwell Park, overlooking the Dulwich Road. The wind had got up and one side of her face was frozen, the eye tearful and her nose red. She hoped this discomfort would prompt some reasoned thought as to why she had just committed herself to spying for the Soviet Union. She had given Gromov good reasons. She wanted João Ribeiro to be rehabilitated. She had hinted that she was motivated in part by the death of her son and husband. Gromov had thrown up the pedigree business. It would appear that this was her family tradition. He'd also brought Louis Greig into the game. Her lover. Had she been considering that? Was it important not to disappoint Louis? His standing with Gromov would be enhanced. Would hers with Louis? Was that what she wanted? Were any of these the real reasons?

Then it struck her. The thought that had nearly penetrated at the end of the train journey. Control. Everyone, in this business and out, was looking for control. Louis had taken her as his lover because the secret of it gave him control over Martha. Andrea went along with it, with his demands, because she wanted to control Louis. As Louis sensed his control over Andrea waning, he drove her back into a vulnerable state. She allowed it, she wanted it, because she perversely interpreted this as regaining control over Louis by giving him what he wanted. She wanted to go back into the Company because, the spy's fantasy, it would give her ultimate control. Perhaps that was it after all.

This had become her nature. Gromov had talked about pedigree, and he was right. She was her mother's daughter. Her mother's revenge for Longmartin's injustice had been twenty-five years of treachery against her country. She wondered if she'd confessed that to Father Harpur.

Unable to stand the cold any longer she left the park. Gromov had told her that she was to meet Louis Greig at Durrant's Hotel in George Street in the West End which, it occurred to her, was not far from the Edgware Road. She checked her handbag to make sure she was still carrying the key to safe-deposit box 718 at the Arab Bank. She took a bus to Clapham Common and the tube into the West End. She came up into Oxford Street from the Marble Arch tube station and walked up the Edgware Road, wondering what instinct in her had prevented her from looking in the box before now.

Within half an hour she was sitting alone in a cubicle with the oblong stainless steel box, hands sweating, unaccountably nervous. Inside the box were sheafs of ten-pound notes. She didn't have to count them because there was a note in her mother's hand showing a total of £30,500.

Outside in the autumn wind she hailed a cab and, leaning against the passenger door, thought for a few moments and made her decision. She asked the driver to take her to King's Cross Station. She took the afternoon train back to Cambridge and spent the evening packing her things. She went to the pub, ordered a double gin and tonic and called Jim Wallis.

Chapter 33

15th January 1971, East Berlin.

The Snow Leopard stood three feet back from his living-room window and looked down from his fourth-floor apartment on to the empty packed snow and ice between the five concrete blocks which constituted his part of the not-so-new development on the Karl Marx Allee. He was smoking a Marlboro cigarette in a cupped hand and watching, and waiting, and thinking that life had become all about numbers – three feet, four floors, five blocks, all surrounded by nothingness, white, white zero snow. No cars. No people. No movement.

The two apartment blocks immediately opposite were completely unlit, not a square of light to be seen, not even the hint of someone stretching in a half-dark room, preparing for another all-night surveillance of nobody. The sky above was a muffled grey. The noise level was close to what city people knew as silence. The Snow Leopard's wife snored quietly in the bedroom, her door open, always open. He cocked his head as one of his two daughters squeaked in her sleep, but then his face went back to the window, his hand back up to his mouth, and there was the unmistakable taste of export America.

He went into the kitchen, dowsed the butt and threw it in the bin. He shrugged into his heaviest coat. It was minus twelve degrees outside, with more Russian snow due during the day. He put his hand to the radiator. Still working – glad they weren't on the tenth floor where the heating probably wasn't and State plumbers as rare as Omaha steak around here. He reviewed the situation one last time. Quiet. Two a.m. His time of night. His type of weather. He crammed a brimmed hat on to his head, picked up his uniform, which was protected by brown paper, and left the apartment, taking the stairs down to the garage.

He put his uniform in the boot and got into his black Citroën. He drove slowly over the ice-packed roads until he reached the cleared Karl Marx Allee, which had been the Stalin Allee, until Uncle Joe had been Khrushchevified, and then Brezhneved. He turned left, heading into the centre of town and the Wall. There was no traffic but he checked the rear view constantly. No tail. At Alexanderplatz he turned left on to Grunerstrasse, crossed the River Spree and parked up in Reinhold-Huhnstrasse. He took a brisk walk into an unmarked building, flicked a pass at two guards, who nodded without looking, and dropped down two flights of stairs into the basement. He went through a series of swept and swabbed tunnels until he reached a a door which he unlocked. This door, which he relocked, gave on to a small hallway and in four short steps he was walking southwards down Friedrichstrasse on the West side of the Wall.

He walked quickly and crossed the street at the Kochstrasse U-bahn. A hundred metres later he paid ten Deutschmarks to a swarthy, moustachioed man in a glass cubicle under a neon sign which read Frau Schenk Sex Kino. He entered through a large heavy leather flap and stood at the back, unable to see and unable to work out what was happening on the dark screen. Only the soundtrack told him that several people were approaching ultimate satisfaction with customary and prolonged ecstasy while the camera locked itself unerringly on their biological detail. Porn, he thought, the desecration of sex.

He reached the side wall of the cinema and walked slowly down to the front and another door, which let him into a passage lit by a single red bulb. A ginger-haired man, the same width as the passage, stood at the far end with his hands in front of his groin. Close to, the Snow Leopard could see that the man had the eye-lashes of a pig. He handed over another ten marks and opened his coat. The man patted him down, squeezed his pockets.

'Number three is free,' he said.

The Snow Leopard went into number three cubicle and closed the door. There was a binful of used tissues and some wishful graffiti on the walls. Beyond the tinted glass panel there was a girl kneeling on the floor with her face turned sideways, cheek to the ground, eyes closed, tongue roving her lips and her behind as high up in the air as it would go. She was fingering herself. He turned his back on the scene, checked his watch and tapped on the plywood wall. No answer. He tapped out his code again and this time received the correct reply. He took a roll of paper, a coded message, from the cuff of his coat and pushed it halfway through a hole drilled in the wall. It was removed from the other side. He waited. Nothing came back. A few minutes later the next-door cubicle was vacated.

He waited more minutes, his back to the glass panel, until there was a polite knock on the door. They always knocked, just in case. He followed another man down a passage, which curved to the right past other cubicles. The man opened a door to the left and waved the Snow Leopard through. The lighting returned to neon normal in this part of the building.

'Second on the left,' said the man, to the back of his head.

He went into the office. A man with a substantial belly stood up on the other side of a desk. They shook hands and the man offered coffee, which he accepted. The Snow Leopard laid a small white sachet on the sports page, which the man had been reading. The man set the coffee down, picked up the sachet, closed his newspaper and laid out a piece of dark blue velvet. He emptied the sachet on to it. He inspected the diamonds visually first, divided them up and then weighed them on a set of scales he had on top of the safe in the corner of the room.

'Three hundred thousand,' he said.

'Dollars?' asked the Snow Leopard, and the man laughed.

'Are you OK for cigarettes, Kurt?' he said, showing how seriously he took the attempt at negotiation.

'I've got plenty.'

'Did you bring any of those Cuban cigars with you this time?'

'What are we celebrating?'

'Nothing, Kurt, nothing.'

'That's why I didn't bring any.'

'Next time.'

'Only if it's dollars, not Deutschmarks.'

'You're getting to be a capitalist.'

'Who? Me?'

The man laughed again, asked him to turn his back. The Snow Leopard sipped his good, strong, real coffee down to the grounds and turned to find six blocks of money on the desk. He put them into the lining of his coat.

'Which way out?' he said. 'I don't want to go back through there like I did the last time.'

'Left, right, keep going until you get to a door and that'll put you into the Kochstrasse U-bahn.'

'Why couldn't I come in that way?'

'That way we don't get the twenty Deutschmarks entrance fee from you.'

'Capitalists,' said the Snow Leopard, shaking his head.

The man boomed another laugh.

The Snow Leopard got back into his Citroën on the East side of the Wall. He headed north through the old Jewish quarter of Prenzlauer Berg on the Schönhauser Allee. He took a right after the Jewish cemetery and, as the street narrowed, went up on to the pavement and parked under the arch of the *ersterhof* of a huge and decrepit *Mietskasern* in Wörtherstrasse. He waited with the engine running and then rolled into the first courtyard of the old nineteenth-century rental barracks, the terrible fortress-like forerunners to the kind of place he was now living in himself. He parked up and crossed the courtyard to the *hinterhof*, the back building, which never saw any sunlight. It was silent. The place was deserted, the living spaces totally uninhabitable, the damp, at this time of year, frozen on the walls. Chunks of plaster and concrete lay scattered across the stairs and landings. He knocked on the metal door of an apartment on the third floor. Feet approached from the other side. He took a full-face ski hat out of his pocket and pulled it over his head.

'*Meine Ruh' ist hin,*' said a voice.

'*Mein Herz ist schwer,*' he replied.

The door opened. He stepped into the heat.

'Do we have to have such depressing lines from Goethe?'

'I'll be changing to Brecht next week.'

'Another cheerful soul.'

'What can I do for you, Herr Kappa?'

The Snow Leopard took off his coat, laid it on the chair and removed an American passport in the name of Colonel Peter Taylor from the lining. Amongst its pages was a loose passport-size photograph.

'You know the deal. Take the old one off, put the new one on.'

The man, late thirties with bland, unnoticeable, dark features opened the passport, leafed through it with the familiarity of a border guard, which was what he had been fifteen years before. The nine years he'd spent in prison as a member of a five-man ring who'd been caught smuggling people to the West had not dulled his attention to detail, but rather sharpened it to a professional level.

'This is genuine,' said the man, looking up out of the corner of his head.

'It is.'

'I'll need forty-eight hours.'

'I want an entry stamp, too. I'll give you the date later.'

'Five hundred . . .'

'Same as the last time then.'

'Five hundred down and five hundred when I finish.'

'Since when did your rates double?'

'Like I told you, Herr Kappa, passports are the window into people's lives. I looked into this one and it seemed . . . cluttered to me.'

'Cluttered or sparse, it shouldn't affect your work.'

'That's the deal, Herr Kappa.'

The Snow Leopard took his uniform out of the boot and changed in the car. He went back to the Schönhauser Allee and headed north under the pillars of the S-bahn. He kept going and passed under the Pankow S-bahn, where he turned right and, as he pushed on, began to come out of the urban sprawl through Buchholz. Just before Schönerlinde he had to show his papers at a police post and was saluted and allowed through without even a glance into the back seat. He drove through the small village and headed north again through Schönwalde and into the pine forest beyond. A fine snow began to fall just as he turned off the road to Wandlitz and by the time he reached the guardhouse to the Wandlitz Forest Settlement, the idyllic lakeside village reserved for the ruling élite, he was swearing out loud. The snow was going to slow everything down.

The guard cracked his heels together and saluted.

'To see General Stiller,' said the Snow Leopard.

'Herr Major,' said the guard, and raised the barrier.

He drove through the settlement to the corner reserved for the Ministry of State Security, the Stasi, and parked up outside the villa belonging to General Lothar Stiller. The wind was blowing hard, buffeting against the buildings, needling the fine crystals of snow into the still sensitive side of his face. He'd think afterwards whether he'd heard anything, or if it had just been the thump of the wind on the edge of the villa.

He did hear something as he walked up the path to the front door, the snow swirling, feinting left and right, on the steps up to the porch. It was the door knocking against the latch. He pushed it open with a thick gloved finger and stepped into the dark carpeted hall.

Light came from a crack under a door to the left. It opened on to the remains of a party – three shot glasses for schnapps and vodka and larger glasses laced with the scum of beer foam. There was nobody in the room, but a tie lay on the back of one of the chairs. He skirted the furniture and headed for the general's bedroom.

He didn't see him at first. There was only a bedside lamp on and a bad sulphurous smell in the room. He turned on the main light. General Stiller was naked and kneeling in the corner of the room, hunched over an armchair on the back of which his light blue uniform was neatly laid out. There was a large, dark red stain over the pocket of the jacket which was working its way up to the medal ribbons on the chest. The white shirt next to it was flecked with blood. The bad smell was from the streak of diarrhoea down the general's hamstrings and spattered over his calves.

The Snow Leopard held a hand over his mouth and inspected the body. Stiller had been shot at point-blank range in the back of the neck. He knelt by his side. The exit wound was huge, an appalling mash of skin and bone and an ugly black hole where the nose should have been. The eyes seemed to be staring agog, as if amazed at seeing what had been a good-looking face sprayed over the back of the chair.

The Snow Leopard reached under the chair and came up with a ball of lacy underwear. He stood and took in the room. Four strides and he was in the bathroom. He pulled back the plastic curtain to the bath. She was lying face-down, peroxide blonde hair, black at the roots and now horribly reddened. She wore a black suspender belt and black stockings.

Back in the bedroom he flung back the covers. Something heavy hit the floor. The gun. A Walther PPK, no suppressor. He held it in his gloved hand, went back to the living room, opened the door opposite the curtained window of the front room. The girl's clothes were on the back of the chair. The bed had seen some action, all the covers hung off the end like a thick tongue and there was a large stain on the bottom sheet. He checked the rest of the house. Empty. The back door was open. The wind had eased up and the snow was now falling thickly. No tracks.

He picked up the phone and thought for a full minute of his options. He had to be careful. They always said that the phones in the Wandlitz Forest Settlement weren't tapped but anybody would be mad to believe that, given the ubiquity of the Stasi, and he should know.

Half of the money he had on him was due to a Russian, the KGB General Oleg Yakubovsky, and he would really have liked to call him and ask his opinion at this moment but that risked pointing a finger. There was no possibility of just driving away as he was logged in at the guardhouse. He knew he only had one option but it was worth fidgeting around his head just in case he miraculously came up with an alternative. But there was none. It had to be General Johannes Rieff, Head of Special Investigations.

Rieff's voice was thick with sleep.

'Who is it?' he asked.

'Major Kurt Schneider.'

'Do I know you?'

'From the Arbeitsgruppe Ausländer.'

'What time is it?'

'Five thirty, sir.'

'I'm not used to being disturbed for another two hours.'

'There's been an incident at the Wandlitz Forest Settlement. General Stiller has been shot and there's a dead girl in the bath who . . . is not his wife.'

'Frau Stiller hasn't been a girl for a long time, Herr Major.'

'The girl has been shot too . . . in the back of the neck.'

'What are *you* doing there?'

'I came to see General Stiller.'

'Yes, and that's quite normal at five in the morning, is it?'

'We frequently meet before office hours to discuss internal business.'

'I see,' he said, as if that was one of the world's most unlikely events. 'I'll be with you in an hour. Stay there, Major. Do not touch anything.'

Schneider put the phone down, sniffed the gun in his other hand. It smelled of oil, as if it had not been fired. He checked the magazine. Full. He tossed the gun back on to the bedclothes.

He inspected the ashtray in the middle of the table in the living room. Three cigar butts, one badly chewed, six cigarettes, three with brown filter, three with white, all six with lipstick, different colours. Two women. Three men. The women not drinking. He went to the kitchen. Two champagne saucers by the sink, both with lipstick, an empty plate with the faint smell of fish. One bottle of Veuve Clicquot in the bin. The girls came out for a talk, see how they were going to play it.

He opened the fridge. Three tins of Beluga caviar, Russian. Two bottles of Veuve Clicquot and one of Krug. One bottle of lemon vodka encrusted with ice in the freezer.

He went back into the spare bedroom where he found the girl's clothes, his brain just beginning to motor now. He swept a hand under the bed, lifted the covers. The handbag. He emptied it on to the stained bottom sheet. One passport. Russian, in the name of Olga Shumilov, her blonde hair perfect in the photo. He put everything back, threw the bag under the covers, suddenly remembered the original business and all the money in his coat.

He took the blocks of money out of the lining, stuffed them in the pockets and went to the car. He fitted the three packets under the front passenger seat and went back up the snow-covered path. Heavy flakes landed on his shoulders, he felt their delicate touch on his forehead.

He found a clean ashtray in the kitchen, began some serious smoking and light-headed thinking. The money, minus his twenty thousand Deutschmark tip and sixty thousand for Russian expenses, was to be split evenly between Stiller and Yakubovsky, who was waiting for him in the KGB compound in Karlshorst. The way the scam worked, as far as he'd been able to discover, was that Yakubovsky procured the diamonds, which arrived by diplomatic bag from Moscow. Stiller had set up a number of buyers, including whoever was the owner of the Frau Schenk Sex Kino chain. Not Frau Schenk, was all he knew. Schneider himself was just one of the sad old leg men who worked as an aide to Stiller and his Stasi friends, and who were occasionally on the end of a hard-currency bonus.

He was trying to work out why he thought this was a KGB job, even though the Russians had the tendency to shoot the other way round, through the face taking away the back of the head. He also couldn't quite square the girl being there. It was an inside job, of that he was sure, and *deep* inside, because admission to the Wandlitz Forest Settlement was very selective. Only the East German leader, Secretary General Walter Ulbricht, and his central committee members, plus top armed forces men and high-ups in the Stasi, or MfS as they saw themselves.

Stiller was not short of friends or enemies. There would be little sobbing over his grave. Certainly the handkerchief of the chief of the MfS, General Mielke, would not find its way up to his eyes at the funeral. General Mielke only tolerated Stiller because of the man's special relationship with Ulbricht, and his status as Ulbricht's head of personal security. Mielke and Stiller had the same interests, venality and power, which were competitive rather than comple-mentary. Even so, it was unlikely that Mielke would take him out of the game, and certainly not so ostentatiously, unless . . . back to the Russians. Perhaps the Russians had styled the execution and left one of their operatives as a decoy. This was pure paranoid thinking, of the type that could only possibly raise its head in East Berlin and it didn't come close to answering the fundamental question, which was: What had Stiller done wrong? He really had to speak to Yakubovsky about this, and preferably this morning.

Schneider's mind spiralled in and out from the incident without getting any closer to its meaning. All he knew, as a pair of headlights swept the front of the house, was that a death of this magnitude was going to see large forces manoeuvring for position and creating massive problems for him.

He let Rieff into the dark hall. The general, a heavy, dark man of about the same height as Schneider, stamped the snow off his boots. It was already ankle-deep out there. Rieff stared at the sole-patterned clods of snow on the mat and stripped off his brown gloves and peaked cap, preparing himself. He brought a strong smell of hair tonic with him.

'Do I know you, Major?' he asked, jutting his jaw, crushing his greying eyebrows together.

'I think you would have remembered,' said Schneider, clicking the hall light on.

'Ah, yes, your face,' he said, peering or wincing at him. 'How did that happen?'

'Laboratory accident, sir . . . in Tomsk.'

'I remember you now. Somebody told me about your face. Sorry . . . but you're not the only Schneider. Where's General Stiller?'

Schneider led the way, stepped back at the door. Rieff swore at the stink, slapped his thigh with his gloves.

'The girl?'

'Bathroom on your right, sir.'

'Probably shot her first,' he said, his voice echoing from the tiled room.

'General Stiller's gun is on the floor over there, sir. It hasn't been fired.'

'I thought I told you not to touch anything.'

'I came across it before I called you, sir.'

Rieff came back into the living room.

'Who's the girl?'

Schneider faltered.

'Don't treat me like an idiot, Major. I didn't really expect you to stand about with your thumb up your arse until I arrived.'

'Olga Shumilov.'

'Good,' said Rieff, slapping his hand with his gloves. 'And what were you and General Stiller up to?'

'I beg your pardon, sir?'

'Simple question. What were you up to? And don't give me any shit about work. The general's work habits were minimal.'

'That's all I can do, sir. That's all we discussed. They were minimal because he was an excellent delegator, sir.'

'Goodness me, Major,' said Rieff, sarcastically. 'Well, I'll let you think about that one and you can answer it in your own time.'

'I don't have to think about it, sir.'

'What would I find if I searched your car, Major?'

'A spare tyre and a jack, sir.'

'And this villa? What would we find in here? A piece of rolled-up Russian art? An icon? A nice little triptych? A handful of diamonds?'

Schneider was grateful for his burnt face, the mask of impenetrable plasticated skin which had no expression or feeling, other than it itched when he sweated. He kept his hands jammed in his pockets.

'Perhaps General Rieff has privileged knowledge about General Stiller's affairs . . .'

'I have *extensive* knowledge about his *privileged* affairs, Major,' said Rieff. 'What was in the fridge?'

'Material suitable for the refreshment and entertainment of Russian officers, sir.'

'Material?' snorted Rieff. 'He taught you well, Major.'

'He's my senior officer, sir. I'm stunned to see him in this state.'

'*I'm* surprised there weren't *two* girls in the bath . . . and a boy in the bed.'

This was true. There'd been some scenes. Schneider had heard and kept himself away from them.

'I hope I did the right thing in calling you, sir. It had occurred to me that this was sufficiently serious for General Mielke to be contacted.'

'I'm taking care of this, Major,' said Rieff severely. 'Where are you going now? I'll want to talk to you.'

'Back to the office, sir. I might be lucky to get there in time in this weather.'

'You don't fool me, Major,' said Rieff brutally. 'I've seen men who've met flame-throwers.'

Schneider, unsettled by the observation, didn't bother trying to correct him. He gave his salute and left.

His Citroën crawled through the heavy snow, back through the dark villages buried in silence. Snow-piled cars with two black fans scraped from their windscreens crumpled towards him, a swirl of moths in their headlights. He couldn't see out of the back window. Inside he felt muffled, suffocated. He opened the window a crack and breathed in icy air. This was a disaster, a complicated disaster. Rieff was going to brick his balls. Clack! He was no longer protected by the thick, rusting hulk of Stiller's corruption and that was the end of finance for his extra-curricular activities. A thousand marks for the American colonel's passport, that left nineteen thousand marks and then what? Unless. He could give Yakubovsky his half and keep Stiller's. Tempting, but insanely dangerous. His face didn't need the addition of a black, torn hole like Stiller's. He resealed the window, lit a capitalist cigarette.

The thump of the windscreen wipers lulled him. The warm, smoke-filled cocoon of the car was a comfort. He came into the centre of town. The snow-filled vacant lots, the crumbling buildings re-mortared white, the shells of deserted houses with their steps and window ledges stacked thick with pristine snow, all looked nearly presentable. How democratic snow was. Even the Wall, that raised scar across the face of the city, could look friendly in the snow. Icing on the cake. The death strip tucked up under a blanket. The watchtowers Christmassy.

He slewed the car into the Karl Marx Allee and joined the serious morning traffic of farting lines of two-stroke Trabants and Wartburgs, their black exhausts blasting and splattering the snow, already sludging up to pavement level. He eased through Fried-richshain into Lichtenberg and took a left before the Magdelen-strasse U-bahn into Ruschestrasse. He took one of the privileged parking spots outside the massive grey block of the Ministerium für Staatssicherheit. The only sign that this was the Stasi HQ was the number of Volkspolizei outside and the aerials and masts on the roof. The building itself was called the Oscar Ziethon Krankenhaus Polyklinik, which Schneider thought made it the largest mental institution in the world. Thirty-eight buildings, three thousand offices and more than thirty thousand people working in them. It was a town in a single block, a monument to paranoia.

He went through the steel doors, flashing salutes left and right, and went straight up to his office. He stripped off his coat and gloves, refused his secretary's grey coffee and called Yakubovsky on the internal phone. They agreed to meet on the HVA floor, the Hauptverwaltung Aufklärung, Main Administration Reconnais-sance or Foreign Espionage and Counter-espionage Service.

Yakubovsky's eyebrows came before him. Schneider wondered why a man prepared to shave his face clean every morning couldn't see the necessity of hacking back the brambles of his eyebrows. They saw each other and the Russian nodded and turned his grey back, which was wide enough to be tarmacked rather than clothed. Yakubovsky puffed on a thick white cigarette, from which he was constantly spitting flakes of black shag from his tongue. They began a slow walk. Yakubovsky's fat, slack as a brown bear's, shuddered under his uniform. Schneider delivered his news. Yakubovsky smoked, spat, turned his mouth down.

'The money?' he asked.

'It's in the car.'

'All of it?'

Tempted again, but no.

'Yes, sir.'

'Come to Karlshorst, five o'clock.'

'General Rieff is in charge of the investigation.'

'Don't worry about Rieff.'

Yakubovsky sped away suddenly, leaving Schneider jostled in the corridor.

At 4.15 p.m. it was dark. The snow had stopped. Schneider cleared his car windows front and back. He drove home first to see if Rieff was having him tailed. He parked up and stripped his DM19,500 from one of the packages. He drove a slow circuit of the blocks of flats before coming back on to the Karl Marx Allee and heading east down the Frankfurter Allee. He turned right into Fried-richsfelde, past the white expanse of the Tierpark, under the S-bahn bridge and then left into Köpenicker Allee. The KGB headquarters was in the old St Antonius Hospital building on Neuwiederstrasse. His ID card was taken into the guardhouse. A call was made.

He parked where he was told, pulled the packets of money out from under the seat. An orderly came out to meet him and took him up to the third floor, through an office he knew already and into a living room beyond, which he didn't. Yakubovsky sat upright in a straight-backed leather chair, next to a fire burning in the grate. He was smoking the last inch or so of a cigar. Schneider thought about the ashtray in Stiller's villa. It made him nervous but he told himself that anybody could smoke cigars.

The orderly appeared, carrying a tray on which there was a steel bucket of ice with a bottle of vodka stuck in it. Alongside was a plate of pickled herring and black bread, two shot glasses and a fresh pack of cigarettes with Cyrillic script over them. The orderly backed out, as if Yakubovsky was a man to keep an eye on.

The Russian crushed out his cigar. The end was soggy and

368

chewed up. Schneider twitched under his coat. He handed over the packets of money.

'Don't let me keep you from your guests,' said Schneider. 'I've already taken my twenty thousand marks. There's two hundred and eighty thousand left.'

'You're my guest,' he said. 'And you'd better take some more. There's not going to be anything for some time.'

He fished out a sheaf of notes from the lucky dip, which Schneider slipped into his pocket. Thick. Fifty thousand marks at least.

'Take off your coat. We need vodka.'

They tossed off three shots quickly, the vodka freezing cold, viscous and lemony. Schneider tried to loosen his neck off, his shirt collar chafing his scarred flesh. Yakubovsky threw pickled herring down his throat as if he was a performing elephant seal.

'Stiller is dead,' he said, which was no progress at all, but baldly stated the facts and filled the muffled silence in the room. The fire cracked off a spark up the chimney. More vodka. The good side of Schneider's face felt smacked. Black bread revolved in Yakubovsky's mouth like tights in a washing machine.

'Do you know who did it, sir?' asked Schneider, his voice sounding like someone else's in the room. 'And what was the Shumilov girl doing there? She was one of your agents, wasn't she?'

Yakubovsky tore open the pack of cigarettes like a savage and got one going.

'This is a delicate situation,' he said. 'A *political* situation.'

'Forgive me for being forward, sir, but you were there last night, weren't you?' said Schneider, the vodka steaming him open. 'Who else was there? That should throw . . .'

'I can understand your nervousness, Major. You probably feel exposed . . . out in the open,' said Yakubovsky from under his dark and threatening eyebrows. 'I *was* there, with General Mielke, if that satisfies your curiosity. We left at midnight. Stiller was shot about five hours later.'

'And the girls?'

'The girls arrived as we were leaving. They came with Horst Jäger.'

'The Olympic javelin thrower? What the hell was he doing there?'

'I understand he has quite a javelin in his trousers,' said Yakubovsky, eyebrows off the leash. 'And he doesn't mind throwing it about . . . or who's watching.'

'So who was the other girl?'

'Not one of ours, a girlfriend of Jäger's.'

'So when did Jäger and his girlfriend leave?'

'Four o'clock, according to the guardhouse.'

'Why was Olga Shumilov killed?'

'Because she happened to be there, I suspect.'

'And why *was* she there?'

'Probably to make sure that Stiller didn't go home,' said Yakubovsky. 'And under the circumstances, Major, I don't think you need to know the answers to any more of your questions. I've already told you that this is a *political*, not an intelligence, matter and that should indicate that any greater knowledge could bring its own pressures. Have some herring.'

They drank some more, finished the food. The Russian signalled the end of the evening by holding up Schneider's coat for him to get into. As he shrugged it up on to his shoulders Yakubovsky spoke quietly into his ear.

'We won't be seeing each other again on the same footing as before, you understand. Should anything happen to you, I will not be able to help. It would be inadvisable to use my name.'

The half-bottle of vodka prevented Schneider's fear from reaching the ends of his nerves which meant that the hair on the back of his neck stayed smooth as a seal's.

'Can I ask how strong General Rieff is in this matter, sir?'

'He is very well positioned. Look at his career before he became Head of Special Investigations.'

'And is he well-intentioned towards either of us?'

'No, Herr Major, he is not,' said Yakubovsky. 'He is of the ascetic school. A hair-shirt man.'

Outside an icy wind had got up and in the short walk to the car it effectively flayed his coat off him. He sat at the steering wheel, tearful, panting with the alcohol in his system. He stuck gloved thumbs into his eyes to stem the tears and force some concentration into his brain.

Yakubovsky was telling him that this was a KGB job and that the hidden agenda was political and, hard as it was to believe, bigger than himself. A Moscow directive, but aimed at what? And leaving Rieff so powerful.

Nothing came to him.

He started the car, drove back to the main gate and out on to Neuwiederstrasse. The sloppy suspension and his drunkenness threw him about the cockpit as if he was on a rollicking fair ride. He stopped on Köpenickerstrasse, pulled into the kerb near one of the still visible storm drains. He was gritting his teeth and hammering the steering wheel with rage and frustration. He took out the wad of Deutschmarks, felt their newness, sniffed their ink. New money. Real money. But too much of it if you were in the unexpected position he'd just found himself. He added his own tip to the bundle of notes, opened the door and threw the lot down the storm drain. Now he would even have a problem getting that passport back.

He drove home, parked up in the garage underneath the apartment block. He locked the car door, staggered to the stairs and walked into the sudden flare from a pair of headlights. Two men approached from the darkness behind, their shoes gritty against the cement.

'Major Kurt Schneider?'

'Yes,' he said, licking his lips.

'We'd like you to come with us for a . . . little word.'

Chapter 34

December 1970 to January 1971, London.

Andrea sat at her desk, the same desk that her mother had occupied for more than twenty years doing the same job. The work was not difficult and it meant that she met everybody who was doing any kind of operational work, and they all talked to her because they wanted to keep her sweet and lenient over their expenses sheets.

Andrea had had to endure a long interview with Dickie Rose, as he was now known, and a shy man called Roger Speke, who would only ask her questions through Dickie Rose and never directly. She had found out nothing about either of them, neither their work, nor their job titles. Meredith Cardew had seen her, too, but that was more of a chat about old times – Lisbon, sardines on the beach, and whether the restaurant Tavares was still running. It was only as she was leaving that she happened to mention how surprised she was to find him in the Company.

'Yes, well, got a taste for it during the war,' he said. 'Bored at Shell, so when I came over on a trip I arranged an interview. Stupid move, really. I'd have been much better off in the oil world but, you see, that was the other thing. Dorothy was fed up with the travelling, wanted to come back to the UK.'

'To London?'

'Good God, no, we bought a house in Gloucestershire. Happy as Larry out there. The girls have left the nest now, of course. All married. So now it's just grandchildren and the dogs.'

'And you've got the Company.'

'Heading for retirement now. Best days behind me. Berlin in the fifties, that was the time. We must have a drink, Anne . . . catch up on old times. Come over to the flat one of these cold evenings, keep an old man company.'

'I'm Andrea now, Meredith.'

'Of course. Sorry. Yes. And sorry about Luís and Julião. Jim told me the awful news. Terrible shock.'

The way he said it, as if it had happened last month and just as she was leaving, took her back a quarter of a century to the house in Carcavelos. Another terrible shock, as he put it. It set something off in her chest, a bird batting against her rib wall trying to get out.

She started in the early December. Wallis took her on a tour of the building. He reintroduced all the people who'd been at the funeral party. Peggy White, who'd assisted her mother in Banking. John Travis in Documentation. Maude West in the Library and Dennis Broadbent in Archives, who was the only one with anything to explain to her.

'I've got you down here as a Grade 5 Blue and Yellow. Grade 5 is medium security, Blue is for banking and Yellow is for Foreign, which means you're restricted to looking in files in that range and anything with a security rating of 5 and under. We all start on 5.'

'What's the highest?'

'Grade 10 Red. You can look at anything with that, including the Hot Room, but there aren't many Grade 10 Reds. Five in the whole building in fact and one of them is "C".'

'The Hot Room?'

He pointed to a door which had a card punch and a number pad by the jamb.

'All Top Secret and Operational.'

'What are the other colours I'm not allowed to look at?'

'Green is for Home/MI5, boring as hell. White is for Personnel, which you'll be cleared for in a few weeks' time.'

'Pink? Is there any Pink?'

'Yes, there is as a matter of fact.'

'What's Pink?'

'Sex.'

'Is that kept in the Hot Room too?'

'Under lock and key.'

'Who's got the key.'

'Roger Speke.'

'It's always the quiet ones, Mr Broadbent.'

'Just like your mother,' said Broadbent, laughing. 'Uncanny.'

*　　*　　*

373

Peggy White took her through the Banking procedures, sipping her way through glasses of water, as her small lips pursed themselves over International Money Transfers, Expense Sheets, Contingency Funds, Emergency Funds, Quarterly Finance Presentations, Cash Flow, Budgeting and all the other bean counting jargon.

'It's been pretty quiet recently. The last big flap was '68, after the Prague Spring. Agents flying this way and that. The money going all over. Your mother was retired by then. Yes, the Prague Spring did for her replacement. Terrible hash she made of it. Anyway, we really thought that was going to be it, you know. The Reds were going to pull back the Iron Curtain, charge through, and keep going until they hit Holyhead. Still, it's all died down now. I do love it when the days hurtle by like that. To be honest, they're dragging at the mo'. But . . . with the Russkies, anything can happen.'

Andrea settled into the work and made friends with everybody, especially Broadbent. He would leave her alone in Archives so that she could wander the files which she hadn't been cleared for and she could also watch who had access to the Hot Room. Only Rose, Speke and Wallis ever used it. Broadbent revealed that there was a card with magnetic tape and a set of four numbers was issued every week by Roger Speke.

By mid December she'd been through most of the main body of the archives and found nothing of any interest and no reference to the Snow Leopard anywhere. Ten days before Christmas the Americans finally moved out of her house in Clapham and Andrea left Wallis's attic room and set up at home. She met Gromov again at the bowling green in Brockwell Park. He told her what she already knew, that she was going to have to gain access to the Hot Room and look at the operational files to find any reference to the Snow Leopard. If she could get him a card he would arrange for a duplicate to be made overnight. Once she had that, all she had to do was get the weekly number code. Easy. Easy for Gromov in his big coat with his chilled face sucking his one capitalist weakness, sherbet lemons.

She went back to watching the Hot Room users and where they kept their cards. Wallis and Rose were less frequent users than Speke and they kept their cards in their wallets. Speke, who went twice a morning, kept his in the breast pocket of his jacket. She watched Speke for a week and noticed that he only did Hot Room work in the mornings. Grade 10 Red files were not allowed to be removed from the Hot Room. The men worked in there and could only take notes. No photocopying.

She noticed that Speke was a very correct man, fastidious in his manners and dress, the sort who always had a comment about the single vent versus the double vent, and he never worked with his jacket on. He would wear it between rooms but would always remove it before sitting down. He wore a cardigan underneath the jacket and the jacket was always hung on a hanger on the back of his door. The only problem was that she never had access to Speke. He didn't speak to her, or anyone for that matter, apart from the other section heads. He left at five thirty every afternoon and never stopped for a drink. She wasn't surprised that he hadn't been at the funeral – not her mother's type.

She was getting desperate and thinking about how she was going to find out who the fifth card holder was when an expense sheet appeared on her desk with a request for more funds. She checked back in her files and found that the agent, codenamed Cleopatra, should still have had £4,500. Cleopatra's base was given as Tel Aviv. The Middle East was Speke's section.

She waited until two minutes before lunch and knocked on Speke's door. He was standing by the window, looking out on to Trafalgar Square, hands in pockets, stretching the cardigan out in front of him. He was startled to see her and made for his desk as if he had a gun in it. Andrea was sweating under her woollen suit, her blouse sticking to the small of her back. She handed him the expense sheet and talked him through it. He scratched the end of his nose and blinked behind his bifocals. He reached for his phone. She told him she'd be back in the morning. He stood as she backed away. He headed for the window again. Andrea opened the door. Speke stooped to fuss over a plant on the mantelpiece. She put two fingers in the breast pocket and lifted the card, closed the door.

Back at her desk, Peggy White asked her if there was anything wrong.

'Institutional central heating, Mrs White. I can't take it.'

'Your mother was just the same,' she said.

Andrea went out for lunch and queued for a passport photo in Charing Cross station. A man stood behind her. She went into the

375

booth and slipped Speke's card behind the sample photos board. She stood and waited for her photos to be developed. The man behind her came out after his session but didn't wait. Her photos came out. A few minutes later the man's came out black.

The following morning there were two cards in the letter box at home, original and copy. She got to work early, in case Speke went straight to the Hot Room. He arrived. She gave him a few minutes and went to see him. He still had his jacket on. She blinked the intensity out of her eyes, slowed herself down. He was at his window again, looking out on the brittle, frosty morning. Speke, poor, portly Speke, who liked ten minutes to recover from his tube journey in the morning, stiffened.

'I'll come back,' she said.

'No, no, no, what is it?'

'Cleopatra's expense sheet.'

'We must change that codename, you know.'

'I agree. It's absurd to think such mundane things of Cleopatra.'

'Quite. One day we'll find at the bottom: one asp – £3 9s 6d,' he said, and laughed at his own joke. Poor Speke, he'll never be able to go decimal.

'Let's hope not, Mr Speke,' she said. 'Shall I take your jacket?'

'Oh . . . thaggadee,' he said, five options colliding in his brain.

She lifted the jacket off his shoulders, replaced the card, hung it up.

'You're right,' he said, 'Cleopatra should not be requesting more funds. I shall send him a message forthwith. What do you think it should say . . . Miss Aspinall?'

'I wish you all joy of the worm?' said Andrea, knowing that Speke would appreciate Shakespeare.

Speke's laugh came out higher pitched than a hyena's in the bush at night.

'That might be a little too sinister,' he said, 'but excellent nonetheless. Put the wind up in Tel Aviv. Nothing wrong with that.'

Andrea came away exhausted. These things seemed so easy in films but they tore her nerves to shreds, like stealing sixpences from her mother's purse, except it was ten years in Holloway for this kind of domestic pilfering. And she still had to get the weekly access code. And she still had to get into the Hot Room with enough time to achieve something. She knew what she was up against in there. Hundreds of files, and that was just the Berlin/Soviet section.

Cardew asked her over for drinks and supper in his flat, a one-bedroomed affair in a mansion block in Queen's Square, Bloomsbury. They drank gin and tonics while Cardew made a Bolognese sauce in his galley kitchen, *Don Giovanni* on the record player.

'Spag Bol's my staple,' he said, looking a bit sad from behind, grey trousers hanging off his backside. 'I think I'm going to try something else but I always gravitate towards the minced meat and the tins of tomatoes. Pathetic, really. We ate so well in Lisbon.'

'I miss the fish,' she said. 'I even miss the salt cod and I never thought I was going to miss that.'

'Fish only comes in a finger these days,' he said. 'You know, I liked the salt cod with the cured ham on top. Ever try that? One of our girls came from up north and that was how they did it up there.'

'Doesn't Dorothy ever come down and cook you something up . . . or go to the theatre?'

'Dorothy wouldn't be seen dead in London. Hates the damned place. Filthy dirty. Full of Flash Harrys. I'm all right, Jack, and eff you, is how she sees it. Pity, really. Lonely old life I lead down here. G&T, Spag Bol and opera in the evening.'

They ate the pasta and salad, started on the second bottle of red. Cardew's conversation drifted towards work.

'Yes, the fifties were terrific once we got rid of bugger boys Burgess and Maclean. Thought we were right on top of the game, only to find it was a complete bloody farce, with George Blake spoon-feeding the KGB the whole Berlin works and Kim in London doing the dirty here. Made fools of us all. Khrushchev said to Kennedy once that we should give each other a list of all our spies and we'd probably find they read the same. Too bloody right. Another drop, dear?'

He refilled the glasses. Sweat glistened on his top lip. He was on his way.

'It's much more secure now,' said Andrea. 'They seem to have cut admin away from operations. We're all boxed off. Nobody knows what anybody else is doing.'

'As if that was the bloody problem. They've got completely the wrong end of the stick, as per u. Nothing was leaking out of admin. It was ops, that was the holey bucket. Now we sit trussed and blindfolded in our offices, not daring to do a damned thing. And they put us all through the wringer back in the sixties, I can tell you. I held on to my Grade 10 Red status . . . a lot of the others didn't. Plenty of early retirements, one or two arrests. Gutted the Company. Barely ticking over now.'

'I don't see much of you in Archives,' she said. 'Flashing your Grade 10 Red status.'

'Not the way I do things, Andrea. Not my style. Never been a bookworm. Not like Speke. He loves those files. That's his nest. He's the one who devised the system. Gave us all our little bloody cards. Comes round every Monday morning and tells us the weekly code numbers. I can never remember the damn things. Once he told us the numbers and forgot to reprogramme the lock, decided there'd been a security breach and they set the dogs on us again. Yes, he was a bit sheepish after that, old Speke. Bloody right, too.'

They finished the wine. Cardew put on the *Magic Flute*, poured himself a whisky and a brandy for Andrea. He stood in front of the gas fire and conducted an imaginary orchestra. The whisky bottle found its way to the rim of his glass once every half an hour and after the third he hunched himself over and made a ghastly face and said:

'The Bells, The Bells,' as he poured himself another, trying to divert attention from the fact that he was hitting it hard. It was Teacher's, too.

Andrea sipped through her brandy and said she had to leave. At the door Cardew held her coat to his chest in a neck lock, very drunk now, eyes fluttering.

'Don't suppose you'd care to make an old man happy?' he asked, and before she could disappoint him, 'no, no, no, bloody ridiculous thing to say. Four sheets to the . . . no, ten sheets to the wind. Don't know what I'm saying. Take no notice. Always thought a lot of you, Anne. Yes . . . liked you very much. Very, very much. Very . . .'

'Can I have my coat please, Meredith?'

'Sorry, sorry, sorry. Course you can. Strangling the poor fellow.'

He helped her into it and at the door planted a ludicrously chaste but very wet kiss on her cheek.

'Wonderful,' he said, and fell back against the wall.

The next Monday morning, the second week in January, she was in Cardew's office when Speke came to give the numbers. She witnessed the absurd sight of a grown man whispering in another's ear behind a cupped hand. As soon as Speke left the room Cardew wrote down the numbers on a pad.

'Don't know why I bother,' he said. 'But you know the one time I did need to go to the Hot Room and I went to ask Speke to repeat the week's numbers, the bugger wouldn't tell me. Worse than school here, Andrea. If anywhere could be worse than Charterhouse.'

As she stood at the end of the meeting she read the numbers off upside down. She had one week's access. Now she had to get past Broadbent.

Broadbent worked from nine to five thirty with an hour off for lunch. Usually he cleared the archive room and locked up while he went for his sandwich and pint in the Coach and Horses in Soho. Andrea persuaded him to let her stay. He could lock her in there while he went out.

'Just for a few days while I get on top of this,' she said. 'It's getting all the background that's so important, Mr B. Peggy White can only tell me so much.'

'I'm surprised Mrs White can tell you anything,' said Broadbent, swigging his hand. 'That's not water she's knocking back, you know.'

He locked her in the archive room. She sat reading her files for five minutes and went to the Hot Room. She slipped in the card, punched in the numbers and the lock clicked back. She took off her shoes and put them on the table. She'd been washing herself in non-perfumed soap since this campaign began and she hadn't washed her hair over the weekend to make sure she was odourless. She went straight to the Berlin/Soviet section and went through all the active personnel files, each one fronted with the agent's codename. There was no Snow Leopard, but there was a file headed Cleopatra, which she opened only because of the business with Speke and the curiosity of finding a Middle East agent in the Berlin section.

379

According to the file Cleopatra was not working out of Tel Aviv but was in the Political Section of the Secret Intelligence Service in Berlin recruiting KGB officers for intelligence purposes. She memorized the recruited names, all Russian except one German. The back of the file opened in a gatefold and showed the monies paid to the men and the totals. None of the amounts were insignificant. She looked at the dates. She went back to the front of the file. Cleopatra had been installed on 1st August 1970. She replaced the file, looked around the room, found the London section. There was no admin section and all files were headed with codenames. There was a click, the same click as when she'd opened the Hot Room door herself, but not from her end of the room. The noise went through her like a slaughterer's bolt.

She snatched her shoes from the table. The noise had come from beyond the stacks to the right. Another click as the door shut. Footsteps on the lino floor. She moved alongside one of the Dexian stacks with their woodchip shelves. Speke walked down the aisle on the far side, a cardboard folder under his arm. There was another door. It should have been obvious. How were the section heads expected to access files after hours? She backed behind the stack, viewed him from between the files, looked at her watch. She had twenty minutes before Broadbent was due back. The sweat seemed to pounce out of her.

Speke threw his folder down and went to a caged section beyond the Soviet/Berlin area. He took out a bunch of keys connected to his trousers by a chain and unlocked a padlock at the front, opened the barred doors. He let his fingers play along the shelves and pulled out a file. He went back to the table in the middle and put it down. He removed his jacket, hung it on the back of the door, sat down and opened the file. He went through the papers until he got to a buff envelope, put his hand in and drew out a set of colour photographs. A small groan emanated from deep in his throat and he looked around suddenly and directly at her so that everything in her retreated to her spinal column. Speke laid the photographs on the table and leaned forward over them. In the foreground was a naked woman on all fours with a man in front and a man behind. Broadbent hadn't been joking. This was Speke's personal erotica section. The needle of the second hand on the wall clock behind Speke flickered as it devoured each chunk of time. Speke sat back and then jolted forward as he picked up some other unseen detail.

By five to two Andrea's physiognomy had changed. The desire to scream that had been confined to her throat had now spread over her entire body. She couldn't swallow, she couldn't blink, her brain had seized, its cogs crunched together like a traumatized gearbox. The second hand flickered two hundred and thirty more times until she was sinking her teeth into pure air.

Speke suddenly looked at his watch, started, packed up the photographs, slung the file back together and threw it into the caged section. He relocked it and headed for his door so quickly that Andrea barely had time to shift around the end of the stack.

She heard the lock go, the door shut. She counted to fifteen, forced the seconds out of her. Then slammed her card into the door and tapped out the numbers. No click. The lock didn't shoot back. She tapped the numbers again. Nothing. She knew the numbers were right. She never made a mistake with numbers and not with this number. This number was a famous number. This number was 1729. No mathematician could forget that number. It was the smallest number expressible as the sum of two cubes in two different ways. Her brain was crashing down a cresta run of pure panic, white, white, white.

She took two deep breaths. Slowed everything down. Tried the numbers backwards, thinking Holloway, Holloway. The lock clicked back. Broadbent's keys were rattling in the outer door. She sprinted to the desk, threw her shoes down and hit her chair so hard with her behind that she had to save herself from crashing to the floor.

'Still here, then?' said Broadbent.

She rattled a pencil between her teeth. Started as she noticed him.

'What?'

'Still here?'

'To be honest with you, Mr B., I wasn't.'

'Oh, really?'

'I went to Lisbon for lunch. Grilled lobster and white wine on the terrace.'

'All right for some,' he said, monotonous, morose.

Her stomach disentangled itself from her heart and lungs and headed south.

She met Gromov at night in a safe house just off Lordship Lane in Peckham or East Dulwich. A balding, grey-haired man let her into the semi-detached house halfway down Pellatt Road, behind a hedged front garden of various gnomes at work. She followed his large rubber-soled slippers into the living room where Gromov was sitting by a tiled fireplace, with a clock on the mantelpiece and a figurine of a woman in a bonnet with a trug of flowers. The Russian looked awkward with his still, grey face next to a print of two sweet little girls entitled 'Nature'.

'I don't think I've ever been to this part of London before,' she said. 'Brockwell Park, now Lordship Lane. I thought it was all supposed to happen on Hampstead Heath.'

'Not at this time of year, and in the summer it's full of civil servants with their boys in the bushes.'

'I had no idea.'

'Some of them are our boys,' he said, and didn't laugh.

'You're everywhere, Mr Gromov.'

'Nearly.'

She told him that there was no record of the Snow Leopard in the active personnel files and Gromov nodded as if this was common knowledge. She said she hadn't had time to look through the operations files because of Speke and she made it clear that she wasn't going to try again, given the dangers.

Gromov blinked, accepted it, not upset at all. His reconciled silence needled her. She told him about the Cleopatra file and got his attention. He was pleased to see that she was operating off brief. She told him of the oddity of the file, Cardew's insights into the Company, the atmosphere of distrust, the rift between ops and admin. She gave him details of what was in the file. Gromov still did not register surprise.

'There were six names on the list,' she said.

'Six?' he said. 'Are you sure there were six?'

'I was a postgrad mathematician until six weeks ago, Mr Gromov. I can count.'

'Give me the names.'

'Andrei Yuriev, Ivan Korenevskaya, Oleg Yakubovsky, Alexei

Volkova, Anatoly Osmolovsky and one German, Lothar Stiller.'

'This will have to be checked,' he said brutally.

'Checked?'

'You have done very well.'

'How do you *check* this, Mr Gromov?'

'I send somebody else in ... somebody with Grade 10 Red status.'

Hard silence from Andrea.

'You have proved yourself,' said Gromov. 'That was what was important about this exercise.'

She was furious.

'Do nothing until you hear from me again,' he said and went to his coat.

He handed her an envelope.

'What's this?'

'Five hundred pounds.'

'I don't want your money.'

'Your mother wasn't so proud,' he said, and she remembered safe-deposit box number 718 sliding back into its wall.

At the weekend Louis Greig appeared outside the house. He rang on the door bell and she didn't answer it. He stayed there, pacing up and down the pavement outside, checking the front-room window and peering through the stained-glass panels of the front door. He went away and came back after lunch and she knew she was going to have to see him or be besieged in her own home.

She wanted to confine him to the doorstep but he stepped straight past her into the hall. He looked hunted. His customary neatness had gone. His hair stood up so that he appeared frayed. His eyes were dark with sleeplessness.

'I've been trying to find you,' he said.

'I was staying with a friend until ...'

'Yes, the Americans, your tenants, told me.'

'I've only just moved back in,' she said, keeping it banal.

'Martha and I were in the States.'

'So you went in the end.'

'She went and I followed on later,' he said. 'I was going crazy in Cambridge.'

There was a very long silence in which the stink of his desperation became unbearable. She couldn't think of anything to alleviate it.

'I'm sorry,' he said, his lips thinning to white lines as he pressed them together, trying to keep the extent of his wretchedness to himself. It made her feel cruel. 'I just . . . I can't . . . I'm completely desperate, Andrea.'

'There's nowhere for this to go, Louis. It's finished.'

'Couldn't we . . . ?'

'What?'

'Talk?'

'We have. You're forgiven. Now go.'

'It's just that I can't . . . I have to be with you. I can't stop thinking about you.'

'How do you think about me, Louis?' she asked, turning vicious. 'On the park bench, in the back seat of the car, on your brass bed . . . in the potting shed?'

He grew more agitated.

'Martha's left me,' he said. 'We . . . we could be together . . . properly.'

'No.'

He brushed back his flyaway hair, again and again, touched his anxious face.

'Couldn't we . . . ?'

'No.'

He closed his eyes, bringing himself to the marks. The real reason he was here.

'Just one more time,' he said. 'Please, Andrea. Just one last time.'

She was revolted by him and opened the door.

'Just touch me how you used to touch me,' he said. 'Don't you remember . . . out on the common . . . the way you, the way I taught you to.'

'Get out, Louis.'

He swallowed.

'Just one touch and I'll go.'

She got behind him and shoved him out. There was surprisingly little resistance. He'd gone kittenish. She slammed the door on him. He put his face up to the glass panels.

'Don't you remember how it was, Andrea? Don't you remember?'

*   *   *

384

At work on Monday morning the atmosphere had changed. There was palpable tension like she'd only ever felt at school when something had gone drastically wrong. Peggy White was already halfway down her first glass of watery gin and it wasn't even five past nine.

'They want to see you,' she said.

'They?'

'All the section heads. They're in Speke's office.'

Andrea was panting. Her heart beat in tight spurts and tapped like a knuckle against a high rib. She'd left the card with Gromov. She'd been careful all the way. It had taken her for ever to get to Pellatt Road making sure she wasn't tailed. She covered her nose and mouth with her praying hands, closed her eyes, said a few words to a God she'd forgotten and knocked on Speke's door. Cardew opened it. Speke was at his window in his cardigan. Wallis leaned against a wall in the corner. She was asked to take a seat in a chair in the middle of the room. Speke moved back to his desk. Cardew loomed to her left.

'This is intimidating,' she said. 'I hope I haven't been too hard on your agents' expenses.'

'It's not meant to be,' said Speke. 'It's just serious, that's all.'

'I haven't even been here long enough to make a quarterly statement,' she said. 'I don't see how I . . .'

'This is something different, Andrea,' said Wallis, sitting on the bars of the radiator in front of the window.

Her fingernails were blue with cold.

'Wallis has been running a double agent in East Berlin for the last six years,' said Speke. 'None of us here knows anything about him, no name, nothing. All we know from the quality of his intelligence is that he has contacts in both the KGB and the Stasi. Apart from his intelligence, which has always been perfect, he has facilitated a number of defections. He has managed to retain complete anonymity by being self-financed and not demanding any payment. We have no idea how he finances himself but he has always been able to meet the not inconsiderable expenses that his work demands. However . . . now there is a problem.'

'Well, there's plenty of money in both Emergency and Contingency,' she said.

'Thank you,' said Speke.

'This isn't a banking matter,' said Wallis.

'The agent was in the process of arranging a defection of a man whose specialized knowledge would give us a more complete understanding of ICBM deployment in the Soviet Union. Now a number of things have happened which have made the agent's life awkward. We need to give him temporary support until he can get this defector out. After that he can disappear back into his cover and rebuild his system.'

'Support? What sort of . . . ?'

'Operational support.'

She looked at the faces of the men around her. They looked back.

'I'm admin,' she said, quoting Jim Wallis back to them.

'At the moment,' said Speke.

'I was trained as an agent back in 1944. My active service was less than one week and, as Jim knows, that wasn't entirely successful.'

'But it wasn't your fault, Andrea,' said Wallis. 'The whole operation was a cock-up from the start.'

'But surely you can find someone with a bit more experience than me. I mean, Cold War espionage is . . .'

'Not so different,' said Cardew, 'the Americans still don't tell us what they're doing and the West German BND have their own agenda. A week's training in Lisbon back in 1944 will stand you in very good stead.'

'The point is,' said Wallis, 'our man doesn't want anybody with experience. He doesn't want anyone with a track record in post-war espionage. He wants someone, as he puts it, with a clean bill of health.'

'Then there must be someone in training. I mean, it's ridiculous to send a bean counter on operations.'

The men looked at each other as if this might well be the case.

'It's the fact that you've just started here from a ready-made background that's decided us,' said Cardew. 'There's nobody in training at the moment who we could get into East Germany as easily as you.'

'East Germany?'

'You have a very particular background,' said Speke. 'We've spoken to the head of the maths department in Cambridge and it seems that there would be some point in you paying a visit to a Professor Günther Spiegel, who is a senior lecturer at Humboldt

University in East Berlin. An invitation is in the process of being arranged for you.'

'In the process sounds as if . . .'

'There's a certain amount of urgency,' said Speke.

'It sounds as if you're not giving me any choice in the matter.'

'You *could* refuse,' said Speke.

'And we would lose a very valuable defector,' said Wallis. 'And possibly an agent, too.'

Silence while they let the weight of that press on her conscience.

'This Gunther Spiegel,' she said, after a lengthy pause, 'is he one of us?'

The men leaned back, the pressure subsided.

'No, no, he's a maths professor. He's your ticket in and out, that's all.'

'And what am I expected to do?'

'Do as you're asked. Think on your feet,' said Speke.

'Who is the defector and am I supposed to be involved in helping with that?'

'You will be told who the defector is in due course, and yes, you will be expected to assist.'

'And who do I do this for?'

'Contact will be made.'

'How will I know the contact?'

Speke nodded at Cardew and the two men left the room. Wallis tore a piece of paper off a pad and put it on his knee.

'He will ask you this question,' he said, writing.

He handed her the paper. It said: 'Where do the three white leopards sit?'

'And what would be your reply?'

She wrote: 'Under the juniper tree,' and handed it back.

'I knew we could rely on you,' he said, and lit the paper, threw it in the metal bin.

'Does he have a codename?'

Wallis leaned over, put his lips to her ear and whispered: 'The Snow Leopard.'

Chapter 35

15th January 1971, East Berlin.

The first hint that the Snow Leopard had that this might not be a civilized little chat was when one of the men asked for his car keys. Schneider was put in the back of their car with the other man and they drove in convoy out of the estate and on to the Karl Marx Allee. The second hint came when they didn't go to the Stasi HQ but headed north of Lichtenberg, to the Hohenschönhausen Interrogation Centre where the meat wagons used to arrive bringing food for the massive Nazi kitchens during the war but now emptied out live, suspicious flesh for questioning in the dark cellars known as the U-boat.

His name was logged at the front desk and the contents of his pockets and wrist watch were put into a buff envelope, which one of the men took, along with Schneider's coat, to a room down the corridor. There they asked him to strip down to his underpants and take off his shoes. The clothes and shoes were added to the coat and taken away. The remaining man told him to put his hands up the wall and spread his legs. A man in a white coat appeared and searched him thoroughly – hair, ears, armpits, genitals and the final indignity of the greased, gloved finger in the rectum. He was taken back out into the corridor and downstairs to the cellars. Behind a soundproofed door he entered a sodium-lit cavern of freezing cold and hellish noise. Loudspeakers relayed endless torture sessions of men screaming and screaming, until it seemed impossible that their larynxes could take any more. They put him in a cell with no furniture whose concrete floor was scattered with shards of ice. They locked the door and left him in total darkness. A few minutes later a light of surgical brightness came on and after half an hour he did what he'd heard other inmates of the Hohenschönhausen used to do. He knelt on the floor, made fists of his hands in front of him and rested his head on top of them. He disappeared into his thoughts. He was well aware of Stasi methods. They were not beaters and bludgeoners. They played the long game, the slow, psychologically destructive game. After a while he moved beyond these thoughts into a region where nothing happened, where the physical being was suspended, senseless, like a bat in daytime.

He heard the key in the door and stood to attention, face screwed up in agony under the light. They took him back up to the room where he'd been searched. He asked for a cigarette. They ignored him, sat him on a chair and left him with the door open. He waited for the psychological point to be made and after a few minutes his wife and two daughters filed past in the corridor.

'Kurt?' said his wife, confused.

'*Vatti*,' said the girls.

They were moved on. He was taken back down to the cell with the knowledge that his wife and daughters were being questioned and the apartment searched. Still calm. They knew nothing and he'd always made sure there was nothing in the apartment. No spy paraphernalia, no illegal currency, no documents. Thank God he'd dropped off the American passport on the way up to Wandlitz.

It was probably past midnight when they came for him again. They took him into an interrogation room. Two chairs, no table, a panel of mirrored glass on one wall and maybe an audience beyond. They stood him in the middle of the room and started the questions, endless questions, repeated endlessly, which, whatever tangent they appeared to come in on, always ended up probing the same nexus. His relationship with Stiller, Stiller's activities in West Berlin, Stiller's interest in the Arbeitsgruppe Ausländer.

It was a softening up process and Schneider allowed himself to be softened. He let his head loll and jerk up as if out of sleep. He paid out confusing lines, let them pick up on them and truss him up with them later. He constantly asked for things – cigarettes, coffee, water, the toilet. They circled him, drove the questions into him from all angles, worked his brain over like a piece of dough. His knees buckled after six hours standing and they forced him to stand in 'the statue' – leaning against the wall, arms outstretched, weight supported by the fingertips. The pain was quite quickly excruciating. Answering the questions became almost impossible, just barely audible words between grunts of agony.

After three hours alternating between standing to attention and 'the statue' he didn't have to pretend so hard. One of the interrogators disappeared for some minutes and then brought back his shirt and trousers. They told him to dress and then marched him down corridors and up stairs until they reached an unmarked door, which they shouldered through. He was left in an office with a desk and two chairs. He sat in one of the chairs and instantly fell asleep.

He came to with his face being lightly batted by a pair of thick brown gloves. He focused on General Rieff, sitting on the edge of the desk, performing this task of light dusting.

'There's some coffee for you on the side, Major,' he said.

Rieff was going to have to do a lot better than this to break him down.

The general threw him a packet of Marlboros and held out a light.

'There's a bread roll there, too, some butter, cheese.'

'You're killing me with kindness, General. What do I have to do?'

'If you want to, you could start by telling me why you killed General Stiller and Olga Shumilov.'

Schneider sat back, crossed his legs, drew on his cigarette.

'Even you know that's not true, General Rieff.'

'Do I? We've had an autopsy done. You might care to read the report. Time of death should interest you.'

Schneider took the paper, ran his eyes down it.

'Between five and six in the morning,' he said. 'That's very convenient.'

Schneider helped himself to coffee, broke the roll, buttered it, added a slice of cheese. He chewed his way through it, taking his time, showing that Rieff's scare tactics weren't working.

'Where's the gun, General Rieff? There's no gun.'

'On the contrary, we've found General Stiller's Walther PPK on the floor with two bullets missing from the magazine. You might like to read the ballistics report.'

'It might make predictable reading.'

'The good thing about a life sentence in a labour camp, Major,

390

is that it's never as long as the original life would have been. Yours would probably be all over in a matter of fifteen years.'

'Rather than breaking down the bag man, General Rieff, I should have thought your time would be better spent pursuing General Stiller's real murderers. You must know by now who was in that villa . . .'

'Don't be ridiculous, Major,' roared Rieff. 'If you're going to persist with that kind of attitude I'll send you back downstairs, and for a little more than ten hours this time. A week should see you right. You'll have a brain like calf's-foot jelly by the end of that.'

Schneider drank the coffee down, cleared his mouth of bread and cheese, poured himself another. He picked up his still smoking cigarette and returned to his seat.

'I can't think what there is for me to tell you that you don't know already. I imagine you were on the receiving end of some of General Stiller's generosity, yourself. You know that he was operating beyond the limits of a general's pay. You know that he was venal and depraved. I can supply the unsavoury detail, some of it titillating in its salaciousness, but I'm not sure how that will advance your cause.'

This seemed to strike Rieff as true, because he suddenly had the look of the bull surveying the shattered china shop, wondering what he was doing with all this porcelain crunching underfoot.

'What were you doing for General Stiller in West Berlin?'

'I was running errands for him,' said Schneider. 'That's what I was, General Rieff, and you know it, an errand boy. I'm not proud of it but I was given no choice in the matter.'

'What were these errands?'

'From the questions you asked me in the villa you know this already. Diamonds. Art. Icons. Selling them to the West.'

'So who was running the Russian end of this operation?'

'That I can't tell you.'

'You don't know?'

'If I did, General Rieff, and you acted on it, how long do you think I would last?'

'Was it General Yakubovsky?'

'I can't answer that,' said Schneider. 'But that should be enough for you, shouldn't it?'

Rieff nodded, walked once around the table.

'Did you ever make contact with foreign agents?'

'I work for the Arbeitsgruppe Ausländer. It's my job to deal with foreigners, following them, checking their contacts . . .'

'I mean, on behalf of General Stiller.'

'This was only ever about hard currency, General Rieff,' said Schneider. 'It was never treachery.'

'Ninety per cent of spies betray their countries for money.'

'I'm sure it's not as simple as that,' said Schneider.

'Have you ever heard of a foreign agent codenamed Cleopatra?'

'No. Which agency is she with?'

'The British Secret Intelligence Service.'

'In West Berlin?'

'Yes.'

'How is she relevant?' asked Schneider.

Rieff didn't answer. He walked around his desk and slumped in his chair, thinking. Here was a man caged by his own paranoia, determined to know everything about everybody, and when he didn't know something it ate into him. He didn't know who Cleopatra was, or how she was relevant.

'You think that Stiller was contacting an agent called Cleopatra and selling intelligence to the West?' asked Schneider.

'Yes, I do, and I think you were making that contact. You were his creature, Major Schneider.'

'I have never contacted any agency on his behalf. I did what I was told to do – picking up for him. And *you* know that once you've been asked to do something like that you can refuse, but your future will look bleak. I did what Stiller asked and if I hadn't I wouldn't be here, but there would be someone else in my place, you can be sure of that.'

'Until I've cleared up this business you're not going to do anything for anybody,' said Rieff.

'I'd like to remind you, General, that I *did* call you when I found Stiller's body and you should know from the guardhouse that I did that within ten minutes of arriving at the Wandlitz Forest Settlement. The incident was also sufficiently serious for General Mielke to be informed, but I left that for you to do.'

Schneider thought it a point worth reiterating.

'That's why I'm going to release you, Major. I'm not going to let you travel to the West any more and I'm keeping your car for the moment, but you're free to go.'

'Free? You think I can do my job properly under these circumstances? If you're going to send me out under twenty-four-hour surveillance I might as well stay in here.'

'If that's what you want . . . I'll get the guards to take you back down,' said Rieff. 'If not, the rest of your clothes are behind you.'

No, he didn't want to go back downstairs. Fresh air. *Berliner Luft.* That was what he needed. He dressed in his unstitched clothes, the shoes parted from their uppers, his coat with the lining stuffed in the pocket, the buff envelope in the other. He stood in the middle of the room, putting his watch back on, thinking up a negotiating stance.

'A car will take you back to your apartment,' said Rieff.

'If I can get you information on Cleopatra, will you give me freedom of movement?' asked Schneider. 'I can find out. I have the contacts who can find out, but I'm not going to compromise my network doing it.'

'I won't let you out of East Berlin, if that's what you're after.'

'I just don't want people on my back.'

'I'll give you forty-eight hours without surveillance, then you report back to me.'

The car dropped him off outside his apartment block. It was six in the evening. He flapped up to his apartment in his ruined shoes, found his keys in the bottom of the buff envelope. His wife was sitting with the girls, playing cards in the living room. He kicked off his shoes, took the rush of his two daughters into his arms, clasped the tiny ribcages under their woollen cardigans, kissed the tight smooth cheeks of the ones who loved his own ruined face without question. He put them down. Elena, his Russian wife, sent them to their room. They sat at the table with coffee and brandy and smoked at each other, while he talked her through the surface of his problem with Rieff. He asked her if they'd been treated badly and they hadn't, just made to wait around before being taken back to the apartment. He asked if the apartment had been searched. She handed him a Polaroid of one section of the living room. Polaroids which would enable them to put the apartment back as they'd found it.

'They must have dropped this,' she said.

'I suppose they could have wrecked the place if they'd wanted to.'

Elena, who seemed to have some natural understanding of these kind of events, went into the kitchen and made supper. She was always calm, not through any innate serenity, but more out of an acceptance of the workings of the State. Schneider, cleaned up and dressed, sat at his desk and wrote out a coded note. They ate supper as a family and the girls went to bed. At 10.00 p.m. he went out. Elena didn't ask for any explanations. She never asked him questions. She was watching women's volleyball on the television.

Schneider walked up to the Karl Marx Allee, past the Sportshalle where the volleyball his wife was watching was being played. He went into the Strausberger Platz U-bahn station and back out again. He turned right down Lichtenberger Strasse heading for the Volkspark Friedrichshain. Rieff had been as good as his word. He was clean. He hovered in Leninplatz around the new statue of the great man, taking a last look around him to be sure. The nineteen metre statue, backed by red granite blocks, looked ahead, smiling benevolently on the grim city. He cut across the square into the dark, snow-covered park, made his dead-letter drop and walked back home.

Elena was already asleep. She slept with the bedroom door open, even now, in case the girls needed her. He watched her calm face as she slept, a woman at peace, an unquestioning person. He wondered if there was a part of herself that he didn't know about, that she was living her life for, because he only ever saw her engaged if she was with him or the children. She could watch television until the screen went blank. It didn't matter what. Secretary General Ulbricht boring a trade delegation, the four-man bobsleigh team, Brezhnev overseeing the weaponry of the Soviet Union in Red Square, *skilaufen*. She was never bored, but also never took any greater interest than what appeared on the screen. She didn't read newspapers or books. She used television to fill in time between engaging with those that mattered to her.

Schneider cared for her. He'd tried to push himself beyond just caring but it required taking her with him, and she was an unwilling traveller. In fact, she didn't like physical travel either. She'd hated leaving Moscow to come to this halved, tormented city. She was envious of his trips back there, even if they were for shudderingly dull conferences and hair-raising debriefs with KGB seniors. He brought back caviar, which he thought she might consider killing for, yes, that was a passion – fish eggs, roe. He should have taken some from Stiller's fridge but that would have given Rieff another stick to beat him with. He suddenly felt exhausted, almost too tired to undress. He wanted to just lie down, scratch a cover over himself, some leaves perhaps, hibernate, dissolve for a season and wake up in spring.

It was late. Schneider's body craved more sleep. The covers weighed a hundred kilos. Leaving the warm sheets was like struggling out of the arms of a woman, but not Elena. She wasn't the type. She was already up, giving the girls their breakfast. They never made love in the mornings. He couldn't bear her looking over his shoulder to make sure the girls weren't at the door. She couldn't bear . . . all that mess, as she put it.

In his office twenty-four hours of paper had built up on his desk. Twenty-four hours of endless reports on what this foreigner had drunk in which bar, who that diplomat had lunched with at what restaurant, what that businessman had said to which girl and what they had done together . . . sometimes with photographs. Nothing surprised him, except that any work was done by these people at all. They were either drinking, eating or fucking. He leafed through, reading the summaries only, his eyelids heavy. At 11.00 a.m. he was summoned to a meeting in the HVA Dept XX, which handled dissidents and was overseen by the KGB General Yakubovsky. He put a call through to the general, hoping for a corridor chat, but he wasn't in.

The meeting was opposite a colonel, who informed him that another deal had been concluded. The sale of two East German politicals had been agreed and there was to be a handover on the Gleinicke Bridge on Sunday at midnight. Schneider would be the driver. This surprised him. It meant that his under-investigation status was not yet common knowledge. Rieff had put him back into the sea.

After work he passed by the Volkspark Friedrichshain and picked up from his dead-letter drop. The note was short. A British intelligence agent posing as a British Steel delegate, codenamed Rudolph, would meet him in the usual place, a deserted *Mietskasern* in Knaacke-strasse in the Prenzlauer Berg district at 10.00 p.m.

Schneider performed his family duties and went out into the cold night to catch a bus to the Alexanderplatz and then a U-bahn to Dimitroffstrasse. From there it was a short walk to the *Mietska-sern*. He passed under the arches and crossed the courtyards of the massive boarded-up complex and went up the staircase of the *Dreiterhof* to the fourth floor. He went to a room above the arch and waited. He was half an hour early. He was always early.

He took the full-face ski hat out of his pocket and fitted it on to his head. He didn't pull it down because the wool itched against his scarred flesh. Twenty-five minutes of refrigerated silence passed and he saw the British SIS agent arrive. He rolled down the ski mask. The footsteps came up to the top floor and approached. He stopped them with his introduction and received the right password back. He clicked on a torch for the SIS man, who had always been annoyed by his codename and especially at this time of year. They went to a table, stood over it and Schneider produced cigarettes which they lit up. Rudolph looked very young for this kind of business, not even thirty. He had the feeling of an undergraduate about him – dissolute, uncaring, loose – a very bad combination for a spy, thought Schneider.

'What's the problem?' asked Rudolph, staring fixedly at the ski mask.

'Apart from the ones outlined in my note, you mean?'

'You asked about Cleopatra. How's that relevant?'

'That's what I want to know,' said Schneider. 'I've got somebody standing on my neck. I said I'd find out about Cleopatra for him.'

'What's the background?'

'My funding comes from extra-curricular work I do for General Stiller . . .'

'Ulbricht's head of personal security . . . the one who got shot yesterday with a girl.'

'Olga Shumilov . . . KGB. I didn't know what to make of it. Still don't. I had to call General Rieff.'

'Who's he?'

'Well, the last time I bumped into him was years ago and he was running the HVA Dept X, which is Disinformation and Active

Measures. I don't know where he went from there,' said Schneider, 'but now he's operating under the umbrella of the Ninth Main Directorate, which is the Stasi's investigative arm.'

'That sounds a very Kafkaesque department.'

'General Rieff is putting me through the wringer. So far only my fingers have gone through. A little bit of pain to see if there is anything more to come out. I don't want him to feed me all the way through . . .'

Rudolph sniggered.

'Sorry . . .' he said. 'Just an image . . . that's all.'

'You should try it. A quick twelve hours in the U-boat in Hohen-schönhausen would further your education.'

'Carry on . . . sorry.'

'He mentioned Cleopatra, asked me who she was. In return for staying off my back, I said I'd get him some information.'

'Well, now . . . Cleopatra,' said Rudolph, preparing himself, 'you might find this surreal.'

'It's all surreal,' said Schneider.

'This, even more so. Cleopatra is an American idea. She recruits senior KGB officers. She pays them for intelligence. That intelligence is then circulated around the SIS, CIA and the BND. Between the British, American and German intelligence agencies we try and work out from the disinformation the KGB seniors supply and the real information we're getting from our reliable agents . . . a picture.'

'My God.'

'It's what it's come to. Nobody knows what's real any more, so we examine and qualify untruth to get closer to the truth.'

'I don't know whether I can get Rieff to believe that. He's old school, you know.'

'They're all old school on this side of the curtain. That's why everything stays the same. You've got flat-earthers in charge.'

'Thanks for that, Rudolph,' said Schneider. 'What did Stiller have to do with Cleopatra?'

'His name was put forward for recruitment by General Yakubovsky. Stiller was the only German on the list.'

'And the only one to get shot,' said Schneider, and they lapsed into silence.

'Do you want London's theory?' asked Rudolph.

'Might as well, seeing as we're here.'

'Yakubovsky wanted to get rid of Stiller.'

'Doesn't make sense. Yakubovsky's making money out of Stiller's contacts in the West.'

'What if he's been told by Moscow that Stiller's got to go? All his commercial concerns go out the window. Oleg's job is on the line.'

'Why would Moscow want to get rid of Stiller?'

'You said he was Secretary General Walter Ulbricht's personal security man.'

'*You* said that.'

'Wouldn't that suggest they're trying to weaken Ulbricht?' he said. 'They take Stiller out of the game. He's corrupt and deserves to go. If Ulbricht cries foul, Moscow shows him he was on the take, not just for money but intelligence as well. Ulbricht has to swallow his bitter little pill.'

'What's wrong with Ulbricht?'

'Brezhnev thinks he's too full of himself. So full that he thinks he doesn't have to pay attention to Moscow any more. He's getting to be a loose cannon ... and then there's all that stuff with Willi Brandt.'

'What stuff?'

'Ulbricht hates him. You remember Erfurt, March last year. Willi got a big reception. Crowds cheering him outside his hotel window. Biggest crowds ever in East Germany for a pol. And if you don't know Ulbricht, we do. A CIA man said to me the other day: "That guy Walt's got a personality cult following ... of one."'

'We all want to be loved ... even communists.'

'Well, it's made Ulbricht a difficult customer to handle. Brezhnev doesn't want the West riled up, what with the Chinese and their H-bomb in the east. And if he wants to keep the whole communist edifice in place he has to make it look as if he's moving, when in fact he's still on the same old treadmill. Hence détente. Given Ulbricht's antipathy to Brandt, Moscow doesn't think his contribution to any negotiations is going to be positive. *Ergo* they want to give Walter his cards and find someone who will toe the line and be less of a maverick.'

'That makes sense, Rudolph,' said Schneider, surprised that the boy had it in him.

'Well, there's as much truth potential in it as anything else, I suppose.'

'Another thing . . .' said Schneider. 'The money. I need money.'

'Don't we all,' said Rudolph, still dazzled by the brilliance of his analysis.

'To get Varlamov out, Rudolph.'

'Oh, yes, sorry, I'd forgotten about him.'

'I'll need help too. The kind of help that's not going to compromise me.'

'OK. First of all, the money. London have assured me that they're going to deliver your money with a one hundred per cent guarantee of anonymity. They also said you can spill it about Cleopatra. She's a closed operation. I think that should keep you snug with General Rieff, by the sound of it.'

'Or it might just increase his already very suspicious mind,' said Schneider. 'He accused me of being a double today.'

'The way the money is going to come to you, I have been assured, will make you cast iron with Rieff, with Mielke, with Yakubovsky, and with Lord Leonid Brezhnev himself, too.'

Chapter 36

16th January 1971, safe house, Pellatt Road, London.

Gromov sat in the armchair in the front room of the safe house in Pellatt Road. He'd slipped his shoes off and was warming his toes on the tiled hearth. Andrea sat opposite, not wanting to smell whatever vapour was coming off Gromov's feet. She had just reported the conversation with the section heads and Gromov was digesting it, along with two biscuits which had showered crumbs down his front. She lit a cigarette and tossed the match into the fire over Gromov's wriggling toes.

'A very interesting development, don't you think?' said Gromov, flat as beer from the drip tray.

'It seems to be progress.'

'Is this a money-related problem that the Snow Leopard has?'

'Wallis said, "It's not a banking matter."'

'Not a banking matter, yes. So what is his problem?'

'Something to do with the defector?'

'The defector. An expert in ICBM deployment in the Soviet Union,' said Gromov. 'There is a Russian physicist due at Humboldt University to give two lectures, attend a dinner, receive a prize, and spend the night before returning to Moscow. His name is Grigory Varlamov.'

'Is he a known defection risk?'

'If he was we wouldn't be sending him to Humboldt University,' said Gromov. 'When do you leave for Berlin?'

'Tomorrow morning.'

'Varlamov arrives the following day ... in the afternoon and stays for twenty-four hours,' he said, and then, thinking out loud: 'If Varlamov's satisfactory defection is the goal of the SIS's operation then what could be giving the Snow Leopard his problem? If it's not money, it must be that his situation has changed

400

and, for whatever reason, he's finding it difficult to manoeuvre.'

Gromov came up with a crumpled white paper bag of the sort given in sweet shops. He offered it to Andrea and she turned her head. He fished out a miniature rugby ball of yellow sherbet lemon and threw it in his mouth. He rattled the sweet around on his teeth.

'You gave me Cleopatra's list,' he said. 'There was a name on it that shouldn't have been there. When I sent that list back to Moscow I was told that General Lothar Stiller who was Secretary General Walter Ulbricht's personal security chief did not have permission to enter that operation.'

'Was?'

'Stiller couldn't come up with any explanation that could save him,' said Gromov, and Andrea whitened. 'No, no, no . . . nothing to do with your intelligence. I've since learned that he was already under a death sentence. It was the KGB who put his name forward to Cleopatra. His appearance on the list in London was just some paperwork to legitimize his termination.'

'To whom?'

'The East Germans, of course. If we show them categoric proof that their man is a traitor – on file as a traitor in London – there can be no argument.'

'Why did Moscow want to get rid of Stiller?'

'He was a disgrace to communism and because of his corruption or his generosity, whichever way you choose to look at it, he had a comprehensive and far-reaching power base within the Stasi. And that is all I'm prepared to say at the moment. There's a political angle to this development that cannot be discussed. My point is that the Snow Leopard's problems started after Stiller's death.'

'So now you are investigating Stiller's contacts?'

'I said they were comprehensive and far-reaching. We have begun an investigative process but there are hundreds of people involved and given that Varlamov will be arriving in East Berlin within the next thirty-six hours, and presenting the SIS with twenty-four hours to get him out, we have very little time. Breaking men down *takes* time. Your action will be faster, more direct.'

'Do you really expect me to believe that?' said Rieff.

'I told my contact you wouldn't,' said Schneider, who'd just finished telling Rieff the bare bones of Operation Cleopatra, no theory, no mention of Stiller, just that the Americans had set it up to buy Soviet intelligence with the certain knowledge that they were receiving KGB disinformation from which the Allied Intelligence services hoped to be able to draw conclusions as to the real picture.

'It's absurd.'

'It's the point at which we have arrived in the ... er ... *impasse*,' said Schneider, which seemed to strike home with Rieff, because he gave a little jump in his seat.

'You know, it would be typical of the KGB,' he said.

'What?' asked Schneider, dismally stirring the rough Cuban sugar into his weak black coffee.

'That the KGB should mount an operation without telling us *and* without showing us any of their results.'

'What's there to show?' asked Schneider. 'That we've reduced the enemy to such absurdities? I suppose it might improve morale.'

'You think morale is low?'

'I mean give an extra fillip to our already high morale.'

'You don't fool me with that plastic face of yours, Schneider. The result of your so-called laboratory accident,' he said scornfully.

Schneider didn't like this about Rieff. The way the man hugged you to him, conspiratorially, and then thumped you in the gut just as you thought you were friends. He said nothing.

'In your work for the AGA you meet a lot of foreigners,' said Rieff. 'You must have quite an extensive network on both sides of the Wall.'

'I've been working at it for seven years.'

'In those seven years have you ever come across an agent code-named the Snow Leopard?'

'No, I haven't. Why do you ask?'

'Because I want to find him.'

'What's his game?'

'He's a double, who's successfully blown several of our under-covers in the West as well as having arranged at least three high-profile defections.'

'Has he been operating long?'

'In the region of six or seven years.'

'I'll put the name around my network, see if I come up with anything.'

'I doubt anyone will.'

'Why not? It's very difficult to operate completely anonymously. You shouldn't be so pessimistic, General.'

'I only doubt it, Major, because I think *you* are the Snow Leopard.'

Andrea took an Interflug flight into the Schönefeld Airport in East Germany. The East Germans had only been prepared to accept her as a visiting mathematician to Humboldt University if she came as a guest of the DDR, although it didn't mean they paid for her flight or hotel, which were expenses she would have to cover in hard currency.

She went through a lengthy document check, during which her two letters of invitation, one from the chancellor of the university and the other from the head of the maths department, Günther Spiegel, were verified by telephone. Her luggage was dismantled and left for her to put back together again, but there was no personal search. She made a currency declaration and bought the standard twenty-five Ostmarks from the State bank. A driver sent by the university was waiting for her, with her name misspelt on a card. He took her straight into the centre of town, into the flattest city she'd ever been in, and dropped her at the Hotel Neuwa on Invalidenstrasse. He didn't speak a word, not of his own volition and not to answer any of her questions.

She ate lunch on her own in the hotel. A terrible piece of gristly pork with a mush of red cabbage and waterlogged potatoes. The driver returned and took her in his usual surly silence to the university. He led her up the stairs to the first floor, pointed to a door and left. A woman answered her knock and, in asking her to come in, offered her the first words of welcome since she'd been in the country. She had an initial meeting with Günther Spiegel, who at the end of it asked her to attend one of his lectures later in the afternoon with a group of his postgrad students.

She found her own way to the student canteen, where she sat alone with a cheap coffee, but even nastier than on British Rail. People looked at her but nobody dared to approach. After her lecture with Spiegel he invited her back to his apartment for dinner.

'I would have asked you earlier,' he said, 'but it had to be cleared first.'

Back in the hotel she found that her room had been searched, her clothes unpacked and repacked with near precision. She ran water into the bath, stripped naked and peeled off a dressing from the small of her back and unpinned a sanitary towel from the gusset of her knickers. She opened them and removed twenty thousand Deutschmarks in soft used notes which she wrapped in tissue.

The bath water was lukewarm and brown, and whatever was suspended in it making it brown clung to the soap, producing a frothy scum on top of the water like effluent. She dressed, putting the money in the small of her back just below the elastic of the waistband, always in the bathroom. She lay on the bed and read a book, turning the pages without taking in a word. Reception called at 7.30 p.m. to tell her the driver was waiting for her downstairs. He took her on a short drive to a modern development called Ernst-Thälmann Park.

Günther Spiegel's apartment was on the eighth floor of a high-rise block overlooking the statue of Ernst Thälmann himself, all thirteen metres of black Ukrainian marble. Spiegel stood with her at the window, shaking his head, drinking wine as they looked out over the flat expanse of the city, still covered with a crust of ice-hardened snow.

'We moved here from a beautiful nineteenth-century tenement in Belforterstrasse because the old place was falling to pieces, the plumbing didn't work and the electrics were life-threatening, all of which the State refused to repair. They insisted we move here. It was brand new. And now it's as bad as the hundred-year-old places. You have been fortunate to find the lift working, although the eight-floor climb means that for the first hour you are warm when the central heating breaks down and, of course, State plumbers hibernate in winter . . . it's well known.'

The meal was marginally better than the one in the hotel and both Herr and Frau Spiegel apologized separately for the poor quality of the meat.

'The State moved into pig production in a big way recently,' said Spiegel, 'so now we get no vegetables and all our terrible meat is sold to the West for pet food.'

'Your poor dogs,' said Frau Spiegel.

After the meal Spiegel beckoned her into the bathroom and

asked her if she had any spare hard currency. He must have done this before, and with visitors more important than she, because he showed no signs of embarrassment or humiliation.

He told her they would have to find a taxi near the S-bahn station because the usual driver was off for the night. They went down together and found one cruising the estate. Spiegel spoke to the driver while Andrea got into the back.

The cab driver didn't go back the way she had come, but headed off down Greifswalderstrasse and kept going until a park appeared on the left.

'Volkspark Friedrichshain,' he said.

They headed along the south side of the park and passed a statue.

'Statue of Lenin,' said the driver, in bad English. 'New. Nikolai Tomski.'

'I'd prefer to go straight back to my hotel,' she said.

'No problem.'

He turned back into the centre and headed into the Prenzlauer Berg district.

'Volksbühne . . . theatre,' he said, their eyes meeting in the rear-view mirror.

'Hotel Neuwa, Invalidenstrasse,' she replied. 'Please.'

'Patien',' he said.

At the Senefelderplatz U-bahn he bore right up Kollwitzstrasse, past the Jewish cemetery and right on to Belforterstrasse, where Spiegel had said he used to live. The driver turned left again, checking his mirrors all the time.

'Water tower,' he said. 'Nazis use to murder people in cellar.'

Andrea didn't say anything this time.

'Good. You relax now,' said the driver.

He crossed the Kollwitzplatz, keeping on the Knaackestrasse, and swung hard left into a *Mietskasern*, driving swiftly under the entrance arch, through a courtyard and another arch, until he parked up in the total darkness of the second courtyard. He opened her door, took her by the arm and led her to the staircase.

'Top floor. Right side,' he said. 'Hand on the wall. Very dark. I wait for you.'

She shivered, not cold, involuntary, as if fingertips had brushed her ribs.

* * *

405

The Snow Leopard saw the car arrive and put on the ski hat. He had arranged two piles of cement blocks on either side of the table as stools to sit on. He had a torch in his pocket. He heard the uncertain steps coming closer, feet searching across each landing to the next flight. He yawned until tears came into his eyes. He was surprised to find so much adrenalin in his system. He pulled the mask down over his face.

The feet reached the top floor and moved down the corridor. He turned on the torch, pointed it at her feet, stroked the stockinged ankles with the light. She stopped, he asked her where the three white leopards sit and she replied. He led the feet into the room and laid the torch on the table. The fog from their breath met at the edge of the low light. He took out a packet of Marlboros and a lighter. She slid one out. He lit her face with the yellow oily flame from his petrol lighter. His hand shook. She steadied it. He lit his own cigarette and there followed a long silence of the sort that rarely happens at the beginning of a meeting.

'They said you would wear a mask,' she said, to break the deadlock.

'Do you mind if I look at your face? Shine the torch in your face?' he asked.

'If that would help . . . we'll have to know each other properly eventually . . . I expect.'

He shone the torch at her from several angles. She looked straight ahead without closing or screwing up her eyes. The defined circle of light in his hand trembled.

'Do you mind if I turn it off for a moment?' he asked. 'I need to hear your voice without distraction.'

'That's fine.'

He turned off the torch. They sat in darkness, only the two coals of their cigarettes provided any light. His heart was like thunder, no distinct beats, just a tremendous roll of noise in his chest.

'Do you know me?' he asked.

'How could I?' she said. 'I don't know what you look like.'

'What does anyone know from just looking?'

Silence.

'You're the expert,' she said. 'You're the spy.'

'Everybody's a spy,' he said. 'We all have our secrets.'

'But . . . but you're the professional.'

406

'Unpaid. Remember. That's why you're here.'

'Ah, yes, the business,' she said, relieved. 'I have your money. Twenty thousand Deutschmarks.'

'You'd know me by my voice now, wouldn't you?' he asked. 'You listen carefully.'

'I don't know how you've arrived at that conclusion.'

'They say a child will always recognize its mother's voice.'

'But I'm not your child,' she said, something shaking inside her or rather outside, as if there was an earth tremor, something completely strange. 'Can we have the light on now, please?'

'Would the same apply to a lover?' he asked, ignoring her. 'Between lovers?'

'It's not the same, is it? It's not a blood tie.'

'Have you ever been in love?'

'I haven't risked coming here to discuss that with a total stranger.'

'Of course. Not to talk about those kind of secrets . . . but other ones . . . duller ones.'

Silence again.

He pulled off his mask, flattened it on the table.

'Would *you* answer the same question from someone you didn't know?' she asked.

'I might.'

'Have you ever been in love?'

'Only once.'

'Who with?' she asked, her heart undecided about its next beat.

'You . . . crazy.'

She coughed against the sudden knot in her throat. Her cigarette wavered in the dark.

'Now do you know me?' he asked.

No answer.

'Do you?'

'Yes,' she said, and after another long silence, 'I'm not sure I know myself.'

'We've changed . . .' he said, almost blasé, distant, 'that's normal. Isn't that completely normal? I'm not as I used to be either.'

He recognized his own coldness and reached over, found her hand.

'Let me see your face,' she said.

'I've only half a face you'll remember.'

'Just show me.'

'The good news or bad news?'

'Where I come from, we always ask for the bad news first.'

He turned his head to the right, switched on the torch and held it at table height so that he looked ghostly, ghastly, horrific.

'That's the worst news,' he said.

He turned his head to show the other profile, and there was Karl Voss, almost as she'd first known him. She put her fingertips to his face, touched the bones which were still prominent, still vulnerable under the tight skin.

'That's the slightly better news,' he said. 'A Russian flame-thrower grilled the other side.'

'They told me you'd been shot in the Plötzensee Prison.'

'A lot of us were,' he said. 'I was in a line up but they were firing blanks that day. Scaring us to death.'

'Rose said you were involved in the July Plot.'

'I was. I was their man in Lisbon.'

'How did you survive that?'

'I happened to be interrogated by a man called SS Colonel Bruno Weiss who, although he was a very nasty piece of work – I think they hanged him in '46 – was someone I knew from my days in the *Wolfsschanze*. I had a particular connection with him there.'

He stopped, because she was looking at him, transfixed, tears rolling silently down her face.

'It *is* me,' he said. 'I *am* here.'

'Can *you* believe it?'

'No. I'm trying not to think about it.'

'I'd forgotten you.'

'Had you? That wouldn't surprise me. I imagine you were told something, a few lines, I don't know, maybe only several words. Voss has been shot. They were wrong, that's all.'

'This is what Rose told me, he said: "We've had news of Voss, by the way. Not good. Our sources tell us that he was shot at dawn in Plötzensee Prison last Friday with seven others." That's what he said. Those were his words.'

'I never liked Rose but he did happen to tell you the truth. Perfect intelligence. It was a Friday. Yes. And there were eight of us. We were shot too ... but only shot at.'

'That lie has . . .'

'It wasn't a lie . . . only an untruth. I doubt he knew and if he did, he probably thought it would make life easier for you. You were young. You could recover.'

'No,' she said, quickly. 'It made it hard, incredibly hard. If I'd known you were somewhere, even if I couldn't see you, there would still be possibilities. That word "never" would not have got stuck in my vocabulary.'

'You're angry.'

'Because I thought this could never happen, I've never considered it. If I had, anger is not what I would have expected. I'd have thought that we'd flood back into each other's arms, like they do in films, but it's twenty-seven years, isn't it, Karl? It's the nature of frost that after time it becomes permafrost. It doesn't thaw out in ten minutes, and definitely not in this climate.'

'It *is* cold,' he said. 'And you're right. I never had to live with the loss. That would have been hard.'

Silence again.

'It's warmer when it snows,' he said, and she knew he was thinking.

'Then let's talk,' she said. 'Tell me about that particular connection to Bruno Weiss.'

Silence while he finished the cigarette, rubbed his thighs up and down, went back to that black trunk with the white stencilled address in the furthest recess of his memory.

'I planted a bomb for him, which killed a great man,' he said. 'Fritz Todt. A *great* man and *I* killed him. I didn't know that I was killing him, but I did and afterwards I entered the world of SS Colonel Bruno Weiss and, what's more, I accepted it. I didn't just keep my mouth shut. I went a step further and planted a lie for him. He sort of returned the favour some time later by trying to help me get Julius out of the *Kessel* at Stalingrad but . . . it was too late.'

'But he got you off the hook after the July Plot.'

'Off the hook, yes,' he said, thinking about the irony of that. 'He chose to believe me, that was all. There were others, who I knew were innocent, whom he chose not to believe and he tortured them and executed them. But me . . . he didn't exactly let me go. I ended up reduced to the ranks on the East Front. But even there, you know, this appalling luck pursued me and within a few months the shortage of officers was such that I was back in a captain's uniform. Some of my men said I was "blessed", as if that could possibly be the right word for being allowed to continue in that hell.'

'That depends on what you believe.'

'Yes,' he said, almost aggressive. 'What do I believe in?'

'Perhaps, like me, you'd begun to think there's nothing beyond the door into the dark.'

'That's true. I certainly didn't want to see behind that door. Not then. I can't think why. There was every reason. Being embraced by the dark should have been a relief.'

'And the Russian flame-thrower?'

'I'd like to tell you that was purification by fire, but I think it was just simple luck again. We were retreating, every day we were retreating in front of that Russian onslaught. We were on the outskirts of Berlin. I was pushing a car out of a mudhole so that my men could get a piece of artillery through and, as I grunted against the back window, I came face to face with General Weidling, who was an old friend of my father's. He recognized me but couldn't place me. We had one of those absurd chats, where a world war seems to stop for a few minutes, and he tried to think where he'd seen me before but I'd already changed my name by then. It had been easy enough in the confusion, amongst all that death and destruction, to pick up some ID tags. My men knew my history, they even came to me with Captain Kurt Schneider's documents one day, found them on a body in a shell crater. They knew it would be hard for me if later the Russians traced me back to the Abwehr. Military intelligence. Spying. It never looks good. So I told Weidling I was Kurt Schneider but, as with Bruno Weiss, Weidling and I had made some strange connection and he asked me how well I knew Berlin. I'd lived there all my life before going to Heidelberg so I knew it very well. He ordered me to take him to the Führer's bunker, which I did, and when I got him back in one piece he made me a member of his staff. My men couldn't believe it.

'It helped being on Weidling's staff but I wasn't out of the war. Occasionally the fighting caught up with our constantly mobile HQ – it was all street to street, house to house with the Russians.

410

Terrible fighting. Terrible loss of life. And one day some of the original Kurt Schneider's luck caught up with me and I got my leg stuck under some rubble after a tank blasted a hole in a house wall. A Russian cleaned out the room with a flame-thrower. I was left for dead and picked up only after the fighting had more or less stopped.

'When the Russians found out I'd been on Weidling's staff I was given some medical treatment and eventually flown to Moscow on a planeload of loot. They did some rough repair work on my face and I was taken to a prison camp north of the city called Krasnogorsk 24/III. Weidling was being interrogated in Moscow and one day the NKVD came to see me when they heard that I'd been in the Führer's bunker with him near the end. I told them everything I'd seen, which wasn't much, waiting at the bottom of the stairs while Weidling delivered the latest atrocious news . . . but I embellished. Then I mentioned I'd studied physics at Heidelberg University and I slipped in Otto Hahn's name, and that was it – anything to get out of that camp.

'They interviewed me, sent me to some technical centre in Moscow and then out to Tomsk, where I was a lab assistant in a research laboratory for twelve years, until 1960. I married and, maybe because of my father-in-law's contacts, I was offered a place at the M-P school, which was the Soviet Intelligence Academy in Moscow. I leapt at it, because they said it would get me back to Germany. They gave me a Berlin posting in '64, so here I am – Major Kurt Schneider, Ministry for State Security, Arbeitsgruppe Ausländer – I monitor foreign visitors to East Berlin. *Wilkommen nach Ost Berlin.*'

'You're married.'

'With two daughters. And you?'

'I was married. I got married straight after I was told that you'd been shot. I had to. I thought I had to at the time.'

'Yes, of course. Any children?'

She stared into the table. The wood was stained with rings from mugs and glasses, creating a series of Venn diagrams. Connections. Overlaps. Differences. She opened her bag and took out a photograph of Julião. She slid it across the rough surface. He tilted it towards himself. Frowned.

'My God,' he said.

411

'I called him Julião.'

'But that's extraordinary,' he said, flicking the corner of the photograph, until finally he took the torch to it and inspected the face minutely.

She fought it back down several times – the instinct to lie, to dissemble, still strong, even in front of the one person who she could and should tell.

'The Portuguese and their *fado*,' she said. 'Do you remember that?'

'We heard some that night we went walking in the Bairro Alto.'

'It seems we're destined to live our lives in minutes and hours, instead of years and decades. My life's been two weeks long, where everything that has happened to me is as a result of that short fortnight and its endless repercussions.'

He flicked the torch up at her, to see if her face said more than her words.

'Why do you think he looks like Julius?' she said.

He stood up, paced the room, snatched at the cigarettes and lit two up, gave one to her in passing.

'I can't think,' he said. 'I can't think. Don't talk. I can't hear. I can't speak.'

Her hands trembled the cigarette to her lips. Her lips trembled the cigarette back into her fingers. She laid it on the edge of the table, interrupted his pacing, grabbed the lapels of his coat.

'Where is he?' he asked. 'Just tell me where he is, so that I can imagine him there.'

She was suddenly aware of how cold it was in the room. Standing close to, they were immersed in each other's breath. The air was freezing in her mouth and nostrils, chill in her lungs, ice around her temples.

'He's dead, Karl. He was shot and killed out on patrol in Guiné in Africa in 1968. He was a soldier . . . like Julius.'

For a moment he looked as if he'd breathed in pure frost, it stiffened him, froze his guts and weighed him down. He slumped on to the cement blocks, his head hanging from his shoulders, as if suddenly broken. He took her limp hand and put it to his good cheek, shook his head against it, not so cold now.

'No wonder you don't know yourself,' he said.

'And you?'

'Living my son's life in fifteen seconds . . . it's not the same. Losing a child after a lifetime, that's an unbearable thing.'

'Like your parents did,' she said, automatically because she'd thought that years ago, too.

'Yes,' he said, and stared into the concrete floor.

His head came up slowly. His eyes fixed on a thick crack in the plaster of the wall. He followed it up to the ceiling, where it parted into two thinner cracks, which eventually merged into nothingness.

'Tell me,' she said.

'I'm thinking.'

'You haven't stopped thinking since you shone that torch in my face.'

'Now I'm thinking what I was trying not to think earlier.'

'And failed.'

'Yes, I failed . . . I've been wondering why Jim Wallis would send *you* to contact me.'

'Did Jim recruit you?' she asked, a feint, a diversion.

'*I* recruited *him*,' said Schneider. 'He came over to East Berlin on a trade delegation, soon after I got here. He was fat and bald, but I could still see that schoolboy's face of his staring out. He was travelling under some name or other, but I knew it was him. I had him picked up, grilled him, had him with his claws stuck in the ceiling. Then I personally drove him back to the delegation and told him who I was. I proved it to him as well . . . using your names. Anne Ashworth, Andrea Aspinall. I'd already decided that the only way I could make myself feel better about what I'd become – this Stasi officer who spies on foreigners – was to work against the system from the inside, use my position to get defectors out and point the finger at East German undercovers in the West. I said I'd work for him on condition that he was the only person to know about me and that there would never be any link between me and British Intelligence. Complete anonymity. No money to be allocated to me so that I could never be traced. But he's clever, Jim, because he remembered that there *was* a link. The original link. You.

'And our arrangement was all working perfectly . . . until I came under investigation after the KGB shot General Stiller, which I can only think was a political assassination with top-level authority from Moscow, because since then I've been under some very heavy

413

internal pressure. I needed help, Russian help but, as you can imagine, my KGB friends deserted me so . . . Jim comes up with a plan to give me support without compromising my conditions of service. Or to use the words of the contact agent, in a way that would leave me "cast iron with Lord Leonid Brezhnev". And what does Jim do? He sends *you* to contact me. Which means . . .' he said, looking not at her but into her, organ-deep.

'What?' she said, shuddering under that look.

'You're working for them, aren't you? The Russians. And Jim knows it, too. You're a double,' he said. 'It's clever, isn't it? And very sick, too. This *is* a cold war, they're right on that. The level of absurdity is such that nothing can be believed, or is believed any more, except the old reliables. Wallis would never let me fall through the net because I am one of the few agents he's got on this side of the Wall who delivers consistently good intelligence. He will do anything to protect me. He will use my only love, because he knows that she is the one person in this world who would never give me up.'

Silence.

'Or is he wrong?' he asked, raising a corner of his forehead where there should have been an eyebrow. 'Did they scrub your brain, Andrea?'

'He's right,' she said quietly.

'My luck holds,' he said. 'But yours doesn't.'

'Why not?'

'Jim's decided to sacrifice *you* for me.'

'How?'

'You've been sent by the Russians to find me. The Snow Leopard. And now?' he asked. 'Now you're *not* going to find the Snow Leopard because you won't give me up to the Russians. So, as a double agent, what the hell are you going to do?'

'I'll say I never saw you.'

'They won't believe you. What have you been doing this last hour? They'll check with the hotel. Everybody's watching everybody else. This is wartime Lisbon cubed.'

'I didn't see your face.'

'But what can you say you were actually doing for an hour?'

'We were planning the Varlamov defection together.'

'And that's it? You never see me again? The Russians won't

accept that. There will have to be another meeting and they'll want to know about it. If you don't find the Snow Leopard . . . you might not be going back to London.'

'Do your thinking, Karl.'

'That's all I can do.'

'I'll do anything, you know that.'

'Anything?'

'Except give you up.'

'Maybe you won't have to give up *the* Snow Leopard, just *a* Snow Leopard,' he said, and then to himself, 'Whatever . . . Jim's going to have to do without Varlamov.'

Chapter 37

17th January 1971, East Berlin.

She lay on the bed, not sleeping, always uncomfortable, always some part of her uncovered and cold because the cover was too small and she got cramped with her knees up to her chest. She writhed and rucked up the bottom sheet, which was too short as well. What's the matter with this country, that they torture their guests with linen?

They had kissed, and she still felt the halfness of that kiss on her lips. The one half as she remembered it, the other smooth and hard like a beak, but not of a bird, more like a squid. Strange that it hadn't repelled her when the idea of it was so unpleasant. His new imprint.

He'd asked her why she was working for the Russians and the lies queued up with amazing alacrity, ready to file out: In Portugal I grew to hate fascism. I became a communist out of resistance to fascism. I loathed the authoritarian imperialism of the *Estado Novo*. I lost a son and a husband in the maintenance of empire. It was all very impressive, but she used none of it. It was all unacceptable, more than a disgrace, to attempt to speak those words to his lashless, browless eye. Even the loyalty to João Ribeiro, which she'd used to beat Gromov, looked tarnished in the glow of that torch between their half-dark faces, their visible breath joining in the cold air. She'd started on that new line of thinking, her need for control, everyone's need for control, but even without being able to see him clearly, she knew he wasn't having any of it.

'When I was in Lisbon, Richard Rose was always throwing lines of literature at me,' he said. 'He gave me a line once from a poet, who he told me afterwards was called Coleridge. I'd never heard of him. The line was "the secret ministry of frost". How silently and stealthily frost transforms the world. We don't know it's happening until we wake up on a white, still morning with everything frozen in its moment. Perhaps this was supposed to be a vision of beauty, I don't know. But one morning, before I'd made contact with Jim, when I was sitting in a car, out on surveillance, I saw the secret ministry of frost. It had been raining and then the temperature started to drop. It happened in front of me, no secrecy. The water hardened on the windows around me into clear slivers of ice at first, and then, as it grew colder, they crystallized, blurred and whitened until I couldn't see out and nobody could see in. And it hit me, threw me into a blind panic, that this was what had become of me. I had disappeared under the secret ministry of frost, I was impenetrable, I was blank . . . except that it wasn't frost. It was hate. I hated myself, what I'd become.'

She lay now, cold in her bed, thinking about her mother, because it was easier to think about her than to get personal. She remembered her mother's remoteness, her white moon face, peering up the stairwell out of the dark hall, that hardness of her cheek, the coldness of her hands, the unreachable mother trapped behind her frosted windows. She'd come to see her hate of Longmartin clear enough, but had she ever taken it that one step further, as Voss had done? Father Harpur might know. She might have confessed to him that she was betraying her country and found salvation that way.

Andrea propped her head up, lit a cigarette, placed an ashtray on her chest. She already felt different, still too trussed up by fear, perhaps, to see it clearly but she was beginning to understand the simple beauty of the 'whitewashed walls' in her father's last letter to her mother. The cleanliness. She'd been lucky, or was it a different destiny for her, to find the one person to whom she could possibly admit her appalling weakness? In the drear light behind the curtain she saw how she'd been formed by that weakness. How she'd used her strengths to hide it. How that weakness had become her secret. That was an equation. Secrets equal weaknesses. She sucked on the cigarette and savoured the irony that it was her secrets, those weaknesses, that had made her unknowable. They gave her mystery and they made her attractive, too. Some men, like Louis Greig, knew it and used it to satisfy their own depraved needs. The others were hopelessly misinformed.

There was a knock on the door. She stubbed out the cigarette.

417

Another knock, more urgent. He'd told her the Russians would come for her and that it would be in the night. She opened the door. A man stepped past her, another stayed in the corridor. The man stood at the window, told her he'd come to take her to General Yakubovsky and that she should get dressed.

The Snow Leopard had watched her leave. She hadn't let him keep the photograph, more cautious this time around, and right, too. He kept his eye to the crack in the boarded window and counted her steps across the courtyard to where the taxi driver was waiting. That kiss. He touched the ruined half of his mouth. Had that kiss disgusted her? Something shuddered in his torso, a wrack of old pain. Seeing her, opening that black trunk, bringing back all those dark memories. His mother's death, perhaps, in the firestorm of Dresden. Was that it? He braced himself against the window, eye still to the crack, as the taxi pulled out of the *Mietskasern*. Another shudder. Pain streaked across his chest. He coughed as if he was hiding and was desperate not to be heard. He dropped to his knees and sobbed into the back of his gloves, over the years of not knowing, over the years that he would never know, and that possibly he might never have known. Julius, his father and mother all staring into the camera, behind his son's unbreakable smile.

He pulled himself together. He collected up the cigarette stubs, stamped the ash into oblivion. He took a different route out of the *Mietskasern* and crossed Wörtherstrasse into another. He went to the *hinterhof* and up to the third floor, trying to remember his Brecht, pulling the mask over his face and knocking on the door.

'*Und der Haifisch, der hat Zähne,*' said the voice.

'*Und die trägt er im Gesicht,*' he replied.

This time the man offered him a drink, which meant that this was not going to be a smooth operation. *Molle mit korn.* Beer with schnapps. Not the time of day for it, but it seemed right. They knocked back the schnapps and sipped the beer.

'Is it ready?' asked the Snow Leopard.

'Except for the entry date.'

'I don't need an entry date any more.'

'It's not going to make it any cheaper, Herr Kappa.'

'It should.'

'I know who this is,' said the man. 'I've been reading the news-papers.'

'I'm amazed someone like you bothers with those rags.'

'He's Grigory Varlamov. The physicist. He's going to give a couple of lectures. They're going to present him with a medal at some dinner and then what? Hup, hup over the Wall. You've got to be crazy, Herr Kappa.'

'I'm not asking you to go with him. Just to do your job.'

'This is very, very cluttered, Herr Kappa.'

'Did I ask you to sign your work? Nobody's going to look at this and come knocking.'

'If you take Varlamov over the Wall the heat's going to come down hard on all of us. Nobody will move a muscle for months.'

'Just tell me.'

'I'm doing myself out of a job.'

'You're nearly there.'

'I've got people I have to run. People who've collected their wolf's ticket years ago . . . they rely on me.'

'Keep going.'

'Five thousand.'

'And finally we have it. The price of freedom.'

'Five thousand.'

'I heard you the first time,' he said, steeling up. 'Let's see the work.'

The man left the room and returned to find the Snow Leopard counting out the money. The man was relieved.

'It's the best bit of work I've done for a long time,' he said.

Schneider looked at the passport, held it up to the light, sipped his beer, suddenly weighed down by sadness. He put the beer down, handed over the money, slipped the passport into his pocket.

'Who've you spoken to about this?' he asked.

'I never speak to anyone.'

'You'd better count that money.'

The man thumbed through the notes. Schneider hit him hard in the throat. The man went down and Schneider knelt on his chest and jammed his gloved fingers into the man's windpipe and held him, looking up at the door so that he didn't have to see the man's face. The fist in the throat had taken everything out of the man. He died with barely a struggle. Schneider picked up the money, cleaned out his two glasses and stood over the body. He was angry at what the man had forced him into but he felt ruthless, too. He wasn't going to leave a man like that out there, with Andrea taking her risks.

'Stupid,' he said, and left.

Andrea sat in the back of the car, the two men in front speaking in Russian, animated, talking about football, she gathered from the head movements. She smoked her duty-free cigarettes and thought about his body. The body she had just held, had put her hands into his coat and grasped, was thin and hard as a rail. She knew from looking at his throat, the veins standing out of his neck, that he had not put on any weight and when she put her hands on him he seemed even thinner than she remembered. His big bones protruded, large hard knuckles around his shoulders, elbows, wrists. He'd told her that his two years in Krasnogorsk on bread and vegetable soup, with the odd piece of fish, had left him like this. He couldn't flesh out however much he ate. It was as if there was something else inside him eating the food, a worm, or something bigger, a snake. Thin or not, she still wanted him. She still had the taste of his salt in her mouth, even after all these years.

The car turned off the main street and into another. A white expanse, which disappeared into greyer lines to black, flashed past in frames. The word 'gulag' formed in her brain, stuck in her throat, which was not a good sign.

She'd asked him about his wife. Elena. A Russian. He'd said he'd married her out of loneliness. He didn't know her, but he thought that was because there was little to know. His girls. He loved his girls. His wife made him feel lonely still, but his girls filled him up.

This was how they'd been together a quarter of a century on. A generation between meetings, and yet no time at all.

They pulled up at the barrier to the St Antonius Hospital, the car's exhaust crowding the foot of the guardhouse. Minutes later they were stomping up stairs and down corridors, through an office, into a living room where General Oleg Yakubovsky, the fat man with the eyebrows Schneider had told her about, was standing in front of the fire, warming his buttocks. She introduced herself. He offered coffee, or something stronger. She took both. He seemed pleased.

'You have made contact with the Snow Leopard,' said Yakubovsky. 'We watched you get into the taxi in Ernst Thälmann Park but decided to let you have your first meeting alone.'

'I'm not sure where we went. The driver took me on a tour. A park, a statue of Lenin.'

He asked her to describe where they'd met and what the Snow Leopard looked like.

'I didn't see his face because he was wearing a ski mask. He was taller than me by some inches. He wore gloves and a grey coat. He was broad, thickset but not fat. The only skin I saw was at his neck between the mask and the collar of his shirt. There was some dark hair and his skin colour was dark, too. The shape of his head was wide, square. It looked like a heavy head.'

'What did you discuss?'

'I gave him twenty thousand marks and an American passport in the name of Colonel Peter Taylor. He spent some time inspecting the passport, but he never removed his gloves.'

'What colour were the gloves?'

'Brown.'

'What does he intend to use this passport for?'

'To get Grigory Varlamov into the West.'

Yakubovsky didn't react.

'You were with him a long time,' he said.

'I wouldn't know.'

'Your taxi didn't come back to the hotel for over an hour.'

'I was building his trust. He was very nervous. I told him about myself. I wanted him to talk about himself, but he was cautious. I told him I was attending lectures at Humboldt University where Varlamov is due to perform. I wanted him to make use of me, but he was a very difficult man, General. He said he needed twenty-four hours to change the passport photo and then he would need to get the passport to Varlamov. I offered again and this time he accepted. We've agreed to meet again and finalize how I should approach Varlamov.'

Yakubovsky wrote out two numbers on a card, which she should ring when the Snow Leopard made contact again. He told her she would be followed from now on and she protested, saying that it was too dangerous, that she didn't want to lose him when they were so close. Yakubovsky agreed, reluctantly. She finished her brandy. He held her coat.

'The Snow Leopard also said that this would be his last job for some time. That his position was changing in line with some unspecified political shift here in the DDR. He said he would be going back into cover.'

Yakubovsky walked her to the door.

'This place where we met,' she said. 'It was massive. Hundreds and hundreds of rooms, on four floors, building after building.'

'Yes. The *Mietskasernen* were built as accommodation for working men and their families in the time of Frederick the Great. They're no better than slums.'

'If the Snow Leopard had any chance to run I doubt you'd find him in that place, even with a whole battalion of men. There must be lots of ways in and out. There's probably access to the sewers. It's his place of choice.'

'What is your point?'

'Mr Gromov, back in London, told me that the only Snow Leopard he ever saw was back in 1929 in the Sayan Mountains. He shot it and his wife wears the pelt as a jacket. I think we should be applying the same ruthlessness to *this* Snow Leopard.'

'We will have KGB marksmen at hand.'

'I've told you that he is very cautious. He's a professional, a nervous professional. To cover a building like that you would need ten or fifteen marksmen. They would create a presence which the Snow Leopard would pick up. It's possible, too, that he will give me very little notice. How are you going to position your men in an unknown building in, say, half an hour? No, General, no marksmen. There is only one way to be certain of catching this Snow Leopard. The person closest to him will have to shoot him. It's not something I want to do, or ever thought I would have to do, but I think it's the only way. I want you to supply me with a gun.'

Yakubovsky, the soldier now, looked into her to see if she had the mettle for this. He went back to his desk and took out a handgun from the top drawer. He checked that it was fully loaded, showed her how to operate it. He asked her if she'd ever fired a gun before.

'I was given small arms training during the war, General. Mr Gromov must have told you that I haven't always been a mathematician.'

She was taken back down to the car, her legs were weak, her stomach sick, the alcohol and coffee toxic in her blood. On the trip

422

back to Invalidenstrasse she sat in the middle of the back seat, supporting herself with her hands on either side, exhausted by the performance.

The Snow Leopard stood over his sleeping wife at the end of the bed. She was lying on her back, her mouth slightly open, the air rushing in and out with her every breath. He tried to think of any memorable sexual moment they'd had together. He couldn't. A colleague had told him once that he'd known when he and his wife had conceived their first child. It had been special in some way. There'd been some extra surge that night. Schneider had been sceptical, had tried not to allow his imagination to tangle with the biology. Both his own conceptions had passed without any notice-able change in the electric current. And yet all he had to do was think of that room in Estrela, that bed, the sofa, the thick lash of her black hair, her brown coin-sized nipples, and he'd feel the blood uncoiling him. Yes, that had been memorable and they'd conceived too, although he still hadn't had any sense of that. Such is the persuasive power of self, he thought. We'll believe anything we want to.

He got into bed next to Elena. It was like an act of infidelity. He turned his back on her. She rolled and her hand rested on the fan of muscle below his shoulder and he found himself thinking of the job he had to do later that week, driving the two dissidents across the Gleinicke Bridge, and he thought about keeping on driving, and driving, and driving.

.

Chapter 38

18th January 1971, East Berlin.

Schneider arrived in the office early. He hadn't wanted to be around family that morning. He put a call through to an old friend in HVA Dept X and asked him where Rieff had gone to after he'd left Disinformation and Active Measures. He told him that he'd done three years on National Security running the Wall and the Curtain under the direct orders of Secretary Erich Honecker.

He went through his in-tray until he came to the report he'd been looking for. Her face looked up at him. A bad photograph but it still quickened his blood. He leafed through the surveillance report. Everything normal. They'd even lied about her taxi ride from Ernst Thälmann Park back to the hotel, saying she'd gone back directly.

At 9.00 a.m. he put a call through to Yakubovsky, who growled, but agreed to a corridor meeting outside HVA Dept XX. Schneider prepared himself for the meeting by running up the stairs so that he would arrive out of breath, panicked. He overdid it. Yakubovsky took one look at him from the end of the corridor and nearly bolted back into his office. Schneider calmed, drew alongside.

'I told you I couldn't help you,' said the Russian, annoyed.

'It's Rieff.'

'I also told you that Rieff was not our friend. It is up to you to deal with him in your own way.'

'But he's like a wild dog after me. He knows everything about Stiller, what he was doing in the West . . . he's even mentioned your name.'

'And what did you say?'

'I denied your involvement,' said Schneider. 'But that's not the problem. If it was just that sort of thing I could handle it . . . we could come to an arrangement. But this is not enough for him. He wants my blood. He's accused me of being a double agent called the Snow Leopard. I've been through all the files at the AGA and I can't find any reference to a Snow Leopard. You have to help me on this. Corruption is one thing. Prison, or maybe a labour camp ... But treason ... treason's the guillotine.'

Yakubovsky stopped at the first mention of the Snow Leopard and let his eyebrows give Schneider their full attention.

'What did Rieff say about the Snow Leopard?'

'He's furious with the KGB, too.'

'But what did he say, Major?'

'He says the KGB never share their information. They conduct their operations without ...'

'Major Schneider,' said Yakubovsky, gripping his shoulder, 'just tell me what Rieff said about the Snow Leopard.'

'He said ... he asked me about the Snow Leopard and, when I said I'd never heard of him, he replied that he didn't think I would have, because ... and these were his words: "I think *you* are the Snow Leopard."'

'Calm down, Major,' said Yakubovsky. 'You have nothing to be afraid of. You are not the Snow Leopard. The Snow Leopard is a KGB operation which will culminate in the next twenty-four hours. You are not to speak to anyone about this and especially not to Rieff. Afterwards, I will personally speak to Rieff.'

They parted, the Russian hitting him on the shoulder with his padded palm. Schneider went straight down to the toilets on the AGA floor, leaned his hot face against the cool cubicle wall and lit a cigarette, which did not calm him down.

Back in his office he put a call through to one of his patrol cars and ordered them to bring in a British national called Andrea Aspinall, a visiting maths postgraduate staying at the Hotel Neuwa and attending lectures with Günther Spiegel at Humboldt University. At lunchtime he was informed that the woman had been picked up and was waiting in Interrogation Room 4.

He shook himself down and felt for the passport and money in his pocket. He checked there was a full tape running for Interrogation Room 4 and went in. Andrea was sitting with her back to him, smoking.

'I am Major Schneider,' he said. 'Have you been offered coffee?'

'No,' she said, annoyed.

'I'm sorry. This isn't supposed to be anything threatening. It's just a routine matter, you understand. Our enemies have forced us to erect this anti-fascist protection barrier . . .'

'Is that what you call the Wall?'

'That's what it is, Miss Aspinall.'

'My God . . . when they sent your brain away, Major Schneider, it came back whiter than white.'

'I can, if I wish . . . if you want to be rude to me, make this go very badly for you.'

Silence.

'Sorry . . . you were saying . . . I think you were about to give me a lecture on enemies of state.'

'Yes . . . we have built this wall to protect our citizens, but our enemies continue to make frequent attempts to penetrate it. They send people to spy on us. People such as visiting mathematics postgraduates from Cambridge. It is my job at the Arbeitsgruppe Ausländer to weed out the false and leave the true. I have two conflicting reports here, which is why I've had to bring you here for questioning.'

'I'm not in East Berlin for very long, Major. This interruption cuts into my very short stay. I would be grateful if you could move it along.'

'Of course. You arrived yesterday, took lunch in your hotel, the Neuwa, went to see Dr Spiegel, had a coffee in the canteen, attended a lecture, went back to your hotel and then went out to dinner with Dr Spiegel in his apartment in Ernst Thälmann Park.'

'My God,' she said. 'I'd like to be able to say I find your surveillance comforting, Major, but I don't.'

'This is where we have the conflict. My report says you took a taxi back to the Neuwa Hotel.'

'Which I did.'

'The taxi picked you up at 21.55.'

'Probably.'

'The Neuwa Hotel reception reported that you came in at 23.10. That's an hour and a quarter to go from Ernst Thälmann Park to Invalidenstrasse, which would leave approximately one hour unaccounted for.'

Silence. Over a minute of it.

'I can't believe this country.'

426

'Believe it?'

'Is that all you do all day ... watch each other? Wait for each other to fall over so that you can report it? Ask the taxi driver. He took me on a tour of East Berlin. The Volkspark Friedrichshain, the statue of Lenin, the Volksbühne theatre, the ... the famous water tower where the Nazis murdered communists back in the thirties. It was all very instructive and time-consuming.'

'That still doesn't account for the hour, Miss Aspinall.'

'You said there was a conflict, Major. When did the surveillance people say I got back to the hotel?'

'At 22.15.'

'So who do you believe?'

'On this occasion the Hotel Neuwa reception,' said Schneider. 'And you're not going back to the university until that discrepancy's been explained to my satisfaction.'

'Before I left England they told me that the Stasi was no different to the Gestapo and, you know what ... they were wrong. You're worse.'

'I have all day, Miss Aspinall. The rest of the week. A month. We are blessed with time on this side of the Curtain.'

They sat in silence for ten minutes, smiling, looking at each other.

'This is ridiculous,' she said.

Schneider stood and walked around the room. He came back to her, brought his face down to her level and put the passport and money into her open handbag.

'Just tell me what happened in that hour, and as long as you weren't spying or taking photographs of sensitive buildings, making contact with people without authorization ... then you can go back to your hotel. If you don't, I will have you taken down to a holding cell and ...'

'I want to speak to General Oleg Yakubovsky,' she said, severe now.

Silence while Schneider blinked that information into his brain. Andrea slowly turned her head towards him. Their faces were only inches apart, their lips.

'Did you hear me, Major?'

'I did, yes,' he said. 'I'm just wondering why ... I mean, *how* you know General Yakubovsky.'

'I am operating under his authority . . . and that of Mr Gromov in London.'

Schneider stood, went back to his seat, his heart hammering away, even though he knew what was coming.

'What is this operation?'

'It is called Operation Snow Leopard and that is all I am saying, until General Yakubovsky is informed.'

Schneider stood, kicking his chair back as he did so. He offered his hand.

'Please accept my apologies,' he said. 'We were not informed of your presence here. I hope I haven't inconvenienced you unduly.'

'You have, Major,' she said. 'And I'm wondering why you don't call General Yakubovsky.'

'It's not necessary, Miss Aspinall. And . . . I would be very grateful if you could possibly not mention this to the general should you speak to him.'

She stood, picked up her handbag, refused his offered hand.

'I'll think about it.'

'Would you allow me to drive you back to the university or your hotel?'

'You're quite pathetic, Major, aren't you?' she said, and they left the room.

Schneider called up a car and, while they were waiting, retrieved the tape of the conversation. He drove her back to the university and returned to his office. He called General Rieff. The general was out and not due back until four o'clock.

General Rieff's secretary kept him waiting with his tape and file for thirty minutes before she put the call through. Rieff added on another fifteen minutes before asking him to be sent in. Schneider laid Andrea's file on the desk and asked permission to play the tape. He spooled it up and sat back to watch while General Rieff alternately rapped and slapped the arm of his chair, listening to the tape, half bored by what appeared to be the usual grind, until he heard her mention General Yakubovsky. Then he was still and listened intently through to the end.

'Why didn't you call General Yakubovsky?'

'I'd already spoken to him.'

'Why?'

'I'd asked him to help me. I told him that you'd accused me of being the Snow Leopard. I was desperate for him to intercede on my behalf. All he did was ask me how you knew about the Snow Leopard. And, of course, I didn't know. Then he put his hand on my shoulder and told me not to worry, that I wasn't the Snow Leopard, that the Snow Leopard was a KGB operation which would be concluded within the next twenty-four hours. He told me not to speak to anyone, and especially not to you.'

'Did he?'

'I've checked on Miss Aspinall and she's flying back to London tomorrow at 11.00 a.m.,' said Schneider. 'I also personally drove her back to the university in order to ingratiate myself, so that she would not report the incident to General Yakubovsky. She has agreed that it would be between us.'

'The Snow Leopard is *not* a KGB operation,' said Rieff. 'It is the codename of a double agent and we have as much right to him as the KGB. *More* right to him, because he is here, now, in this building giving away the names of our agents in the West, helping defectors . . .'

'I'll tap her phone and maintain surveillance on the Hotel Neuwa.'

'*You* and only you, Major, will listen to the phone tap, and all surveillance will report back to you if she moves. Nobody else in this building is to know about it,' he said, picking up the file. 'Is this hers? Have you done a background check on her?'

'I have, sir. There's nothing out of the ordinary. She has spent the last two years doing pure maths research in Cambridge and before that she was a maths postgraduate at Lisbon University. I also checked on Mr Gromov, who she mentions on the tape. He has diplomatic status in the Soviet embassy in London, but he also holds the rank of colonel in the KGB.'

At 7.30 p.m. Andrea got back to the Hotel Neuwa from Humboldt University. She sat on the bed with her head in her hands and looked at the telephone. Her gums itched and she had a fit of gaping yawns. She picked up the phone and dialled Yakubovsky's number.

'The Snow Leopard's made contact again,' she said.

'Where?'

'A note was given to me in the university canteen.'

'Has he asked for a meeting?'

'Of course, he has to, he needs my help.'

'Where is the meeting?'

'You remember what I said to you ... I don't want anybody there. We have to think of him as the kind of animal that he is.'

'Of course, but I will have to make my report.'

'The meeting will be above the arch on the third floor of the *dreiterhof* in the *Mietskasern* at number 11 Knaackestrasse in Prenzlauer Berg, at 22.00.'

At 7.38 p.m. Schneider relayed the phone tap to General Rieff.

'What do you think this means?' asked the general. 'When she says, "I don't want anybody there."'

'My understanding of that, sir, is that she is going to deal with the Snow Leopard herself.'

'No.'

'No?'

'I will not permit this to happen. The Snow Leopard must be interrogated. We have to find out the extent to which he has compromised our agents and who he is planning to help defect. If she kills him we will lose all this valuable information. We will lose the opportunity to become the Snow Leopard ourselves ... the possibilities for disinformation are enormous. I will not allow it.'

'Do you know this place where she's going to meet him?'

'Vaguely.'

'So you know why she's proposing to deal with the Snow Leopard herself?' said Schneider. 'It's the only way she can be certain.'

'You will leave me now and I shall think about this and decide on a course of action.'

'To control one of those *Mietskasernen* I would suggest you need a hundred men, and if you turn up with a hundred men I am sure you will not see the Snow Leopard.'

'Thank you for your advice, Major ... you have been indispensable.'

'May I add one other thing, General Rieff? That if you interfere I would suggest that it could lead to a lot of bad feeling between ourselves and the KGB.'

'Herr Major?'

'Yes, sir.'

'I shit on the KGB.'

At 9.00 p.m. Andrea checked the gun. It was still fully loaded, as it had been the last fifty times she'd looked at it. She left the hotel and walked straight into a waiting taxi and asked him to go to the Jewish cemetery near Kollwitzplatz. She stood in a dark corner and watched. Nobody was following. Yakubovsky appeared to have kept his word and Schneider had made sure that nobody was tailing her from the hotel. She went back up Husemannstrasse, turned left into Sredzkistrasse.

Her breath clouded the air and dispersed into the still, freezing night. Her heels on the silver cobbles were the only sound in the street. As she hit Knaackestrasse she bore left and walked straight into the entrance of the *Mietskasern*. She leaned against the wall and dragged the icy air up her nostrils, tried to clear her mind, prayed for it to be twenty-four hours later and everything done.

He'd told her not to think about it. He'd told her to keep acting, never stop, never pause for a fraction of a moment's thought. When she'd told him that she couldn't, he'd reminded her of the ruthlessness with which everybody else was acting.

'You just have to find your own values,' he'd said, 'the ones you're prepared to protect with the same ruthlessness.'

An image came to her from God knows where in her memory. One she'd never seen. Judy Laverne in the flaming cage of her car crashing down into the ravine. Lazard had been ruthless. Yes. Beecham Lazard. The sight of that bullet tearing out his throat, the crashing noise of the gun, the blood. That was the only time she'd ever seen anyone killed close up, as close as she was going to be to this man. This man, who she didn't know. The one who was going to save them. He'd told her how she would know the man, how she would know that he was there and the right man. He'd also told her the terrible thing she had to do, how to make it certain, how to make it look right. It was going to demand more of her than any other act in her life. Yes. Act, he'd said. Always act. It will not be you, he had said, but it was her.

She set off across the courtyard between the *ersterhof* and the *zweiterhof*, through the arch and into the next courtyard. She angled her walk towards the left-hand corner. She took out a torch she'd bought and walked up the stairs to the third floor, slowed down. She turned off the torch. Waited. She smelt the frozen air cut with the mustiness of degrading plaster, the mould of rotting timber. Her hand closed around the gun in her right-hand pocket. She walked steadily down the corridor until she arrived above the arch. She looked at her watch. A minute past ten. She shone her torch into the room, at the two piles of cement blocks on either side of the table. She sat on one of the piles, put her hand under the table and found the woollen ski mask, tucked it into the same pocket as the passport and money. She waited, desperate for a smoke but wanting to keep the air clear. Six minutes past ten. She turned off the torch and slipped out of her shoes.

She reached for the door, turned left down the corridor, one hand to the wall, the other holding the gun at waist height. She reached the first doorway, put her face into the blackness of the room, breathed in. She moved on to the next doorway. Nothing. Even before she reached the third doorway she could smell the unmistakable perfume of hair tonic. She stood in the doorway and clicked on her torch. Rieff was in the corner, gun hanging from his hand at his side, eyes wide in the torchlight. She fired quickly, three times. Three thuds into the heavy coat. His gun fell to the floor. She rushed at him as he began to fall forward and drove her shoulder into him so his knees buckled and he fell sideways against the wall. She tore the mask out of her pocket and stretched it over his head, not thinking, only acting, and to make it certain, to make it look right, fired a fourth shot through the ski mask into his face. His heavy head cracked back, destabilizing him, and he slid forward off the wall and ended face-down on the floor. She picked up his gun and stuffed it in his pocket. She took the passport and money out and put it into his other pocket. She ran out of the room, back down the corridor and into the room above the arch. She stepped into her shoes, sat on the cement blocks and put her head on the table and vomited between her feet.

Footsteps ran across the courtyard, sprinted up the stairs. Other, slower footsteps followed. Torch beams ricocheted down the corridor. Two armed men in combat gear appeared at the door. One stayed, the other moved on. The slower footsteps took forever to get up the stairs. They lumbered down the corridor. There was an exchange of Russian. Yakubovsky looked in on her and continued to where the other soldier was standing.

An order was given. The soldier reacted. There was a stunned silence. Another order was barked out. Yakubovsky moved back up the corridor, appeared in the doorway, passport in hand. He muttered something else and the soldiers staggered past with the body between them. He unhooked Andrea's fingers from the gun and put it in his pocket with the passport. He picked up the torch, offered Andrea his arm and they left the building.

'It's always distressing,' he said, 'to find that one of one's most valued colleagues is, in fact, a charlatan.'

In the morning, as a measure of respect due to a valued servant of the Soviet Union, General Yakubovsky ordered Major Kurt Schneider of the AGA to take Andrea to the airport. He picked her up at the hotel and they headed south out of the city, not talking for the first few minutes of the journey. Andrea sat in the back staring out at the greyscale of the framed cityscape.

'You're blaming yourself now, aren't you, for what I had to do?' she said to the back of his head.

'I keep thinking that there must have been another way.'

'I'm the strategist, remember, and there was no other way. The only uncertainty was that he would be there at all. When he was, I did as you said. It was ironic, that's all.'

'Ironic?'

'My piano teacher was killed by a direct hit on his house back in the Blitz in 1940. I was sixteen and I said to myself then that I would kill a German. When the time came for me to even the score . . . I couldn't find any of that old hate, only fear and certainty. I did it and there was no satisfaction.'

'Certainty?'

'From that ruthlessness you talked about.'

'You shouldn't have been put in that position in the first place.'

'Now you're going to blame Jim Wallis.'

'I am.'

'The way I see it is that I put myself in that position. I agreed to work for Gromov back in London. I took the step of going back to the Company. Jim Wallis just did his job,' she said. 'It surprised me to find he had that kind of toughness in him. I thought he was soft . . . good-natured.'

He took a buff envelope out of his pocket, handed it to her between the seats.

'Your security,' he said.

'What is it?'

'Don't open it. Don't look at it. Just give it to Jim, and tell him the negative is in safe-keeping in East Berlin.'

'And what is it?'

'It's another one of those sad, seedy sideshows to our great intelligence industry,' said Schneider. 'It's a photograph of Jim Wallis being buggered in a public lavatory in Fulham.'

'Jim?' she said, astonished. 'Jim's on his second marriage.'

'Maybe that's why the first didn't work out,' he said. 'The glue that holds us together is, not infrequently, our shame.'

'Even with this I'm going to get a hard time for sacrificing the Varlamov defection.'

'Varlamov,' said Schneider to himself. 'Varlamov didn't smell right from the beginning.'

'Is this retrospective genius?'

'Probably. When I was told to set the defection up, they were very firm on one point . . . that I should never make contact with the subject until they gave the go-ahead. I'm still waiting. Varlamov was going to be leaving today.'

'Yakubovsky said they're going to take him back to Russia in chains.'

'I don't think Varlamov wanted to defect. Jim Wallis used him to keep the KGB distracted. They thought that he was the goal of the operation whereas . . . well . . . everything's worked. My cover is still intact, as is yours with the Russians, and Varlamov, a great servant of the State, has been discredited.'

They passed under the S-bahn between Schöneweide and Oberspree and the traffic eased up on the Adler-gestell. He put his hand back between the seats and she held it, stroked the knuckles with her thumb.

'Why did you tell me about that dissident exchange you're doing on Sunday night?' she asked.

He threaded his fingers through hers.

'I thought about going with them,' he said, and she squeezed his hand, suddenly anxious. 'I thought about driving them to the

434

middle of the bridge for the exchange and then just keeping on driving. It . . . it would be possible . . . in my head.'

'So you're not going to do it.'

Their eyes connected in the rear view.

'Elena and the girls,' he said. 'They'd let them drop through the floor.'

She turned her head, let her eyes fall on the road markings flashing past the car, the dirty snow, the bare trees.

At Grünau he took his hand back and they peeled off the Adlergestell, turned back underneath it and headed south-west on the autobahn to Schönefeld. They went through a document check at the police post to leave Greater Berlin and from there it was a few minutes to the airport.

'So this is it, for us?' she said. 'One day we might be on the same side.'

'Our ration for the next quarter of a century,' he said, putting his hand back to her again. 'And we *are* on the same side . . . *our* side . . . where nobody else matters.'

'Twenty-five years. That'll be 1996,' she said. 'I'll be seventy-two. They should have let me out of prison by then.'

'They won't send you to prison, and there's always *détente*,' he said. 'We have to have faith in *détente*. London thinks that Ulbricht's finished. Yakubovsky said that Rieff was well placed. Rieff used to work with Erich Honecker. I think Honecker will be Moscow's new man.'

'And what's he like?'

'A dry man but not arrogant like Ulbricht, not full of his own importance or hate for Willi Brandt . . . a better chance for *détente* . . . possibly.'

'Or a better chance for the Russians to retain control,' she said. 'Dry doesn't sound very flexible to me.'

'Maybe it's better . . . maybe he's breakable . . . crumbly.'

'In the end, Brezhnev dictates,' she said, and was suddenly depressed. 'You know why they use the word "*détente*"? I think it's because it doesn't sound as easy as "relaxation".'

He swung into the airport and parked up close to departures.

'We can add another two hours or so to our total,' he said. 'I worked it out once when I was in Krasnogorsk. We still haven't managed a whole day together . . . yet.'

435

He squeezed her hand. The moment suddenly on them.

'I know it hasn't been a day,' he said, 'but I know you. I said it once to myself out loud in the apartment in Lisbon. I am not alone. It sounded stupid, like all these things do, but it's what has mattered to me all this time, that at least there's been somebody.'

'When I flew back from Lisbon after putting Luís and Julião in the family mausoleum, I was panic-struck. I thought I'd become afraid of flying. But then I realized that it was the fear of suddenly finding myself alone. It was a sudden terror of crashing and dying in the company of strangers . . . unknown and unloved.'

'We're all strangers,' he said. 'Even more so in this business.'

'That's the point, Karl . . .'

'Or is it Kurt?' he said, his one operational eyebrow arched, and they both laughed.

She reached for the car door and he asked her for one last look at the photograph of Julião. He nodded it into his head.

He took her case, walked across the dry, frozen tarmac, cleared snow piled at the edges in solid ridges. He gave the case to a porter. They stood at the entrance, their breath joining in the icy air. He shook her hand and wished her a safe flight, stepped back and saluted her. He walked off without a backward glance, got into his car and drove away into his colourless world.

Wallis met her at the airport, took her by the arm as if he was going to march her straight into a waiting police car. They got into the back of a cab.

'Clapham,' he said, and sat back, pleased with himself.

'There's a police station at the top of the Latchmere Road,' she said.

'Come on, Andrea. No need for that. You did a great job.'

'By accident, rather than design.'

'Oh no, no, no, *I* think it was by design.'

'And now?'

'This isn't Russia, you know. We're not the KGB. No salt mines here, old girl. We take care of you. You go back to Admin, work hard, get your gong, take your pension.'

She checked him for sincerity. He returned her look. Karl had been right, he was still young behind that fat face, willing and eager to please. He made it all sound cosy.

436

'And, of course,' he said, 'in return, we hope you'll be amenable to maintaining a relationship with Mr Gromov.'

'And if I'm not?'

'Do not pass Go. Do not collect two hundred pounds. Go To Jail.'

'I told Gromov I'd only do one job for him.'

'Really? Why was that?'

'I wanted that pension you're talking about. I didn't want to live my life in a constant sweat. And, besides, the hate's gone. There's nothing left in me to keep me going.'

'Hate?' asked Wallis. 'Not sure what you're on about there, old girl.'

'How Louis Greig got me to work for Gromov in the first place.'

'But "hate"? Who do you hate? Louis Greig?'

'Louis turned pathetic,' she said, and after a laden pause: 'Perhaps I hate the same person you hate.'

'*I* don't hate anybody,' said Wallis, shifting to the corner of the taxi, turning to her. 'Hate ... you know, Andrea, it's not a very British thing that, is it? We don't have those sort of ... feelings.'

'I know, Jim, you don't even hate your traitors, do you? Or maybe you would if they were really close, right deep inside ... I mean, in the Hot Room ... that far inside.'

'We've cleaned our house, old girl. Bad show in the sixties, but we're spic-and-span now,' said Wallis, defensive, taking this as a strangely personal attack.

'Are you?' she asked, deflected for the moment. 'You know, when I told Gromov the contents of the Cleopatra file ... the names.'

'Yes, Cleopatra,' said Wallis, taking it away from her, relieved, back to being high on the hog, 'that was all a blind, just to test the ... er ... lines of communication between London, Moscow and Berlin. Moscow wanted to weaken Ulbricht, clear out his cronies, including Stiller. So Yakubovsky put Stiller on the list. You found out, told Gromov. Gromov presents the case to Moscow. Moscow ask Mielke what the hell is going on. Yakubovsky gets the order to execute. Andrea Aspinall passes her initiation test with Gromov.'

'I see ... so you planted the Cleopatra file on my desk and then *let* me get into the Hot Room?'

'You pilfered Speke's card.'

437

'How did you know I was working for Gromov?'

'Because we've been watching Louis Greig for the last five years.'

She nodded, remembering Rose's interest at the funeral party.

'You still haven't let me tell you what Gromov said.'

'After you gave him Stiller's name?'

'He said that the information would have to be checked. I was annoyed after the sweat I'd been through and asked him what he meant. He said: "Checked by somebody with Grade 10 Red status."'

'Pure mischief,' said Wallis.

'Is it? Why?'

Wallis tapped his lips with his forefinger, something not quite right. Day spoilt. Bloody shame.

'You're not going to turn me on Gromov,' said Andrea. 'There'd be no point until you've cleaned out your own house.'

'They'll stick you away, Andrea.'

'No, they won't,' she said. 'Because you'll give me your full support, Jim.'

'Only so far.'

'No . . . all the way,' she said and handed him the envelope. 'To the hilt.'

'What's this?'

'A gift from the Snow Leopard. He said that the negative was in East Berlin for safe-keeping. He also said you might not want to look in there. He told me not to and I didn't.'

'Not following you again, old girl,' he said. 'Bloody mysterious, aren't you? Always have been.'

'We're back to talking about that person, the one we hate, the one who's with us all the time, the one we can never get away from, the only one we can possibly know if we ever allow it.'

Jim Wallis shook his head. Cuckoo.

'Did they put something in your water over there, old girl? Flipped your marbles? Bleached your brain?'

He pushed his finger under the flap and drew it along. He eased out the photograph as if he was hoping it was a lucky card and even his thirty years of professional dissembling couldn't stop him from blanching.

On 3rd May 1971 Walter Ulbricht was delayed from attending the 16th Plenary Session of the Central Committee by two new bodyguards, appointed by the Stasi chief General Mielke. They took him for a long and exasperating walk along the River Spree. By the time he arrived at the session, Erich Honecker had been elected Secretary-General of the Central Committee and Chairman of the National Defense Council.

Book Three
The Walking Shadows

Chapter 39

September 1989, Andrea's cottage, Langfield, Oxfordshire.

'It was the only structural change I made, knocking down that wall,' said Andrea. 'I didn't want to spend my time endlessly walking from kitchen to dining room.'

'Talking of knocking walls down . . .' said Cardew.

'You promised not to mention him,' said Dorothy.

'Who?'

'You know damn well – Gorby.'

'My only conversational embargo is on property prices,' said Andrea.

'Hear, hear,' said Rose.

Only four of Andrea's guests for her first dinner party had not been honoured by the queen. Her next-door neighbours, Rubio and Venetia Raitio, were sculptors. He was Finnish. Sir Richard Rose had bought his Thai dancer boyfriend along, who was called Boo and occasionally called himself Lady Boo if Dickie became too pompous. Sir Meredith and Lady Dorothy Cardew and Jim Wallis MBE with his fourth wife, a Frenchwoman called Thérèse, made up the party.

'Where did you get this table?' asked Dorothy Cardew, determined to have her say. 'It's a Queen Anne refectory, isn't it?'

'A copy, Dorothy. A copy.'

'He says all the right things – *Gorby*,' said Cardew, scathing. 'All this *glasnost* and *perestroika* . . .'

Dorothy rolled her eyes.

'I always thought that was a horse-drawn sleigh,' said Venetia, trying to keep it light.

'That's a *troika*,' said Rose. '*Perestroika* is reconstruction.'

'How dull,' said Boo, who'd learned most of his vocabulary from Rose.

'I rather like the sound of sleigh bells,' said Dorothy, trying to pinch the conversation back.

'And *glasnost* is openness,' added Rose, explaining to the morons.

'I don't think you're right,' said Venetia, deciding to puncture Rose. 'I'm sure it's a Moscow directive that everybody should get out their open-top sleighs, put on their best fur mufflers and jingle about in the snow.'

Rose threw up his hands. Boo slapped him on the leg.

'Amounts to the same thing,' said Wallis. 'If you ask me, Gorby's a tricky customer. Whatever anybody says, he's still a red. We only like him because he's got a cracking wife.'

'It's *impossible* to hate someone with such a *tache de vin* on 'is 'ead,' said Thérèse. '*Il est très, très sympa.*'

'What's she on about?' asked Cardew.

'She likes Gorby's birthmark, dear,' said Dorothy. 'That archipelago on his head . . . it is rather endearing.'

'He'll come down with the iron fist eventually,' said Cardew. 'You'll see. The *politburo* will rough him over and he'll be breaking heads by Christmas.'

'I think he'll do it,' said Andrea.

'What?' said Cardew, spoiling for a fight.

'You said it yourself – "talking of knocking down walls". I think he'll open it all up. Get shot of all the satellite states. He can't afford them any more. He'll tell them to get on with it on their own.'

'Not in my lifetime, he won't,' said Cardew. 'Mind you, that might not be so long.'

'But you're so *young*,' insisted Thérèse, flashing her jewelled fingers. 'And so 'andsome.'

'He's depressed about being eighty in November,' said Dorothy.

'No need to go telling everybody,' said her husband.

Andrea bought a television and a dog at the beginning of October. They were both things she'd thought she'd never buy, but she liked the feeling of someone else in the house. The dog, a long-haired dachshund, seemed superior enough to be called Ashley.

A week later the television rewarded her. Gorbachev went to

Berlin and told that dry old stick Honecker, 'When we delay, life punishes us.' Andrea punched the air. Ashley was more circumspect.

She sat on the floor of the still empty living room and read the newspapers, watched and listened to every minute of news on the TV and radio. She felt that excitement again, the tug of the silver thread.

The beginning of November was even better, the boldness of the East Germans was building. She started living in her own world now, just as she'd seen other oldies, who'd committed themselves to a golf tournament, a tennis championship, or worst of all World Snooker. She didn't dare go out in case she missed something. She lived on coffee and cigarettes. Ashley went next door and was fed by Venetia.

On 9th November she'd just poured her first gin and tonic of the evening when she heard the bizarre announcement that free travel would be permitted for East Germans with immediate effect. Andrea didn't know what this meant. It was too banal. It sounded as if they'd just given up their strongest card – the Wall. Was this how such a régime ended . . . with a blunder?

Five hours later she was kneeling in the middle of the living room, a full ashtray and a bottle of champagne on her right and the phone on her left. The scenes on the television were beyond belief. People were standing on the Wall, Wessies were dancing with Ossies in the street, they were all drenched in beer and *sekt*, a lot of them were in their nightgowns and slippers, some were holding babies aloft and a drift of super-strength Kleenex was building up behind Andrea. Ashley lay with his chin on the ground, swivelling his eyes, wanting it all to be over so that they could go back to regular meals and walks.

Jim Wallis had been the first to call.

'Have you seen it?' he roared.

'Have I seen it? I've been living it, Jim. This is better than twenty-fifth April '74.'

'Twenty-fifth April?'

'The Portuguese Revolution. The end of European fascism, Jim.'

'Completely forgot about that, old girl. End of fascism, of course.'

'But this is the end, the real end of all that . . . all that stuff.'

'Thought you were going to say the "H" word for a minute.'

She woke up at 4.00 a.m. lying on the floor, the television screen blank, the champagne bottle on its side, the ashtray overflowing and her mouth like the inside of an animal-feed sack. Was this any way for a pensioner to behave? She dragged herself up to bed. She slept and woke up feeling dead and empty, as if the whole point of her existence had been removed at a stroke. She drifted from room to room, most of them still empty of furniture because she'd sold every stick from the Clapham house. She decided that this was the day to give up smoking. When depressed, deepen the depression by doing something that's good for you.

She wanted the phone to ring. She wanted *him* to call, but how would he know where she was? Jim Wallis had dropped operational contact with him years ago. They'd lost track because it was too dangerous to keep track. She thought about flying to Berlin and trying to root him out. Then she started worrying because he was Stasi and there were bound to be reprisals, lynch parties. He'd have to keep his head down and it would do no good to have her poking about in the cadaver of the system, trying to find him.

She put it from her mind. She went to work on the house. She refurbished the attic for no other reason than it seemed right to start at the top, to reorder the head first. She redecorated the bedrooms, put beds in them even though she rarely had visitors who stayed. She made a study downstairs, bought a new computer which sat on her desk and had the same power as the one she'd used at Cambridge years ago which had occupied a whole room. She decided to involve herself more in village life and began to frequent the village shop, buying little and staying long because she liked the divorcée, Kathleen Thomas, who was running it with the proviso that she was always going to shut the next day because of the competition from Waitrose in Witney.

Only five people used the village shop until that Christmas, when a sixth joined this very expensive club. Morgan Trent was forty-five, he was a major who'd just left the army and was renting whilst trying to find somewhere to buy. He wanted to set up a garden centre. Andrea didn't like him. He fitted her mother's description of Longmartin, which seemed as good a reason as any for some natural animosity. Also, Kathleen Thomas fancied him, which meant Andrea had to listen to their endless badinage while Morgan bought things that he didn't need three or four times a day.

Maybe it was because of Trent's business plans that she decided to start work on the garden in the spring. She didn't want to have to buy anything from him when his garden centre opened, although those plans didn't seem to be maturing with the speed that he implied. That summer she hired a skinny little kid from the council houses at the end of the village to come and mow her lawns. He was sixteen and called Gary Brock. She thought he was all right but Kathleen told her he was a glue sniffer and a threat to society. Morgan Trent agreed with her, but he was bedding her by now so he was bound to.

In the late summer Andrea came back from a treacherous shopping trip to Waitrose and found the lawn mower had gone. She mentioned it to Kathleen, who said that she'd seen Gary Brock walking it out of the village earlier that afternoon. Andrea announced she was going down to the council houses to speak to him.

'Watch those dogs,' said Kathleen.

'What dogs?'

'His father breeds pit bull terriers.'

'Sells them to drug dealers in Brixton,' shouted Morgan, from the living room.

'Shut up, Morgan,' said Kathleen.

'He bloody does.'

'Anyway, you've got the idea,' said Kathleen. 'Mr Brock senior isn't what you'd call genteel.'

'Not the type you fought the war for, Andrea,' shouted Morgan.

'How do you know I did anything in the war, Morgan?'

'Everybody did in your generation.'

On Marvin Brock's gate was a hand-painted plywood sign that said 'BE WEAR THE DOGS'. She rang the door bell, which set off savage barking from all over the house. She took two steps back as if that would give her a half-chance of escape. Through the frosted glass she could make out a large person struggling down the corridor.

'Come on now, matey,' said the voice.

Marvin Brock opened the door. Daytime TV blared from a room behind him. His head was shaved and he wore jeans and a Swindon Town football shirt; wrapped around his wrist was a thick leather lead, which was attached to a dog of such alarming power and potential ferocity that it didn't have a collar but a full leather harness. Andrea flinched at its name written in metal studs on the thick strap across its chest. Can you call a dog that nowadays? Isn't there a law? The dog was straining against the lead, pushing a twitching black nose in her direction.

'Come on, Clint,' said Marvin, 'back down, back down, there's a good lad.'

'Oh, Clint,' said Andrea, relieved.

'Yairs, after the actor. Greatest living actor. Clint Eastwood.'

'You're Gary's father, aren't you?'

'Yairs,' he said slowly, used to this opening question.

'I'm Andrea Aspinall. Your son Gary mows my lawn. He appears to have walked off with my mower.'

'Walked off?' said Marvin. 'Well, he's prob'ly gone to mow someone else's lawn.'

'I didn't give him permission.'

'I see.'

'Can you get him to bring it back please, Mr Brock.'

'No probs, Andy. No probs. Sorry about the mix-up.'

A week later there was still no mower and Andrea reported its theft to the police. Gary had stolen the mower and sold it, but it was just one in a long line of minor offences ending with a drugs charge. Andrea was called as a witness. She spent a full three minutes in front of the magistrates. Gary Brock was sent down for eighteen months.

In late May of 1991 she was mowing her own lawn and wondering why she'd ever bothered to pay Gary Brock to do it. It was so satisfying, even mathematical, especially that last square in the middle of all the other concentric squares.

As she put the lawn mower away she was aware of a presence leaning against her car in the garage.

'You remember me, Mrs A, don't you?' said a voice, with threat and lots of Oxfordshire threaded into it.

448

He was thickset, wearing tight jeans and mahogany Doc Martens. His T-shirt was stretched over slabs and ridges of muscle and clasped his biceps, which had a thick worm of a vein over them.

'Gary Brock, Mrs A.'

'You've been let out early, Gary.'

'Been on my best behaviour, 'aven' I, Mrs A?'

'You've been weight training too, haven't you, Gary?'

'Yair, I 'ave. You know why, Mrs A?'

'I expect being locked up's a bit boring, isn't it?'

'Not to start with, it isn't, no.'

'Why's that?'

'Because everyone wants to fuck a new arse, Mrs A.'

Silence.

'What are you doing here, Gary?'

'Just telling you what it's like inside, Mrs A.'

'You didn't got to jail because you stole my lawn mower, Gary.'

'You were quick to get up in that box against me though, weren' ya?'

She made for the door. Gary blocked her way. She was scared now. Rubio and Venetia were away and Gary would know that. The garage was hidden from the road at the back of the house. This was what happened, she thought, you survive the worst possible scenarios without a scratch only to be assaulted by a teenage lout in your garage at home on a summer's afternoon.

'What do you want, Gary?' she asked, angry now.

Gary's head suddenly twitched. Footsteps on the gravel drive. He stepped back to look. A tall male figure stood in the garage door, silhouetted against the bright light outside.

'Well ... what *do* you want?' the man asked Gary in accented English.

She knew that voice. Gary lumbered over. Andrea moved into the light, made a negative sign with her hand.

'What *are* you doing here?' Voss asked, in a voice that had known men a lot worse than Gary. Voss put the terrible side of his face up to him. Gary pulled back from the power of such damage. A man, even in his seventies, who looked like that, who could walk around like that, had his own strength.

'I came to say hello to Mrs A, that's all,' he said, edging around Voss. 'Been away, I 'ave.'

Gary moved off, trying to look light and unselfconscious. Voss put an arm around her shoulders, gripped her tight.

'You have a talent, Karl Voss . . .' she said.

'I have my uses.'

Chapter 40

May 1989, Andrea's cottage, Langfield, Oxfordshire.

As soon as she sat him down in the kitchen and made him coffee she knew that he was different. They didn't just walk into each other's lives and take up residence as they had done before. Her instinctive understanding of him had disappeared. He'd made himself unreachable.

He told her he hadn't contacted her before because Elena had been ill. She'd died only last month. He'd just left his youngest daughter in Moscow after she'd got married to a research chemist two weeks ago. His eldest was in Kiev, married to a naval officer and pregnant with her second child. That was all he had to say about his two little girls. He mentioned, too, that he'd been ill himself and that he'd been working on a book but wouldn't be drawn on the subject. He was thin, and the good side of his face appeared haggard. He smoked constantly, roll-ups which he made with the economy of a prisoner. He didn't eat much of her celebration supper of loin of pork roasted with truffles and he drank heavily but with no change in his mood. He asked if he could stay – he needed a safe place to work. She felt ashamed at having to think about it for a fraction of a second. She showed him up to the attic room. That night she lay in her bed listening to him moving around, pacing, while she thought that he should have been with her, but she didn't want him in her bed. The stranger.

He'd arrived with very little clothing but two large suitcases filled with documents and files. A week later a trunk arrived with more paper. She felt invaded but still bought him a computer. He worked all the time. She heard him clacking on the keyboard at four in the morning. At meals he was distracted and withdrawn. In the afternoons she sat in her own study, looking up in his vague direction and feeling the terrible pressure coming down from the

451

top of the house. The unbearable weight of silent hate. It was overrunning her house, moving between the floors and walls like vermin, infecting the stairs and landings with its sharp stench.

She had to get out. She spent time at Kathleen's shop, confided in her, told her about Voss and how he'd seen off Gary Brock but now she couldn't bear to have him in the house. Kathleen told her to put him out, like a dog at night but never to return.

After a few weeks Voss started to take his meals at different times. He thought that by being absent it would relieve her of his oppressive presence, but it was equally intolerable because then he was *being* absent. He was still there even when he wasn't. This was not how it was meant to be.

She took refuge in the past, leafing through old papers, photographs, trying to recapture a sense of how she used to feel about him because, of course, there was no record, he was anonymous in her life. There were no old letters, no photographs, no mementoes even. Then she came across the letter from João Ribeiro's lawyer informing her of his death, which had happened two years after the revolution, in 1976. She had missed the funeral because, by law, burials have to take place within twenty-four hours in Portugal. João Ribeiro, who'd never taken up the offer of reinstatement to the central committee, had been carried out of the Bairro Alto in his coffin followed by hundreds of people. The lawyer's letter also said that he was holding something for her which had been left in João Ribeiro's possession.

She called the lawyer and booked two flights to Lisbon for 26th June. Voss had become so expert at avoiding her that she had to lie in wait like a hunter in a hide.

'I've bought you a present,' she said.

'What for?'

'Your birthday.'

'My birthday's not for three more days.'

'I know,' she said. 'The present is in Lisbon. We're flying tomorrow.'

'*Unmöglich*,' he said. Impossible. 'My work. I have to do my work.'

'Not *unmöglich*,' she said. 'We're going somewhere very important.'

'Nothing is more important that my work. Once that is finished

452

'. . . only then am I free,' he said, and his voice faltered over that last word as if he didn't believe it himself.

'Are you refusing to accept my gift?'

He looked tortured.

They flew into Lisbon on the afternoon of 26th June. The flight was pure torment for Voss, who had to endure two and a half hours without tobacco. He passed his time rolling cigarettes so that he had a hundred ready-made. They took a cab into the city through Saldanha, the Praça Marquês de Pombal, Largo do Rato and down Avenida Álvares Cabral to the Jardim da Estrela.

She was sitting on the ruined side of his face but she could see his eye, staring out from its gnarled and webbed nest, taking it all in, remembering. His head ducked down as they passed the Basílica da Estrela to catch sight of the façade of his old apartment building on Rua de João de Deus still intact – in fact, untouched, just a little more cracked and crumbled. Only then did she realize the brilliance of her gift. These parts of Lisbon hadn't changed at all in fifty years and some not since the 1755 earthquake.

They turned off into Avenida Infante Santo and into Lapa. The cab threaded through the streets to Rua das Janelas Verdes and the York House. They walked up the same stone steps as the monks had done in the seventeenth century, when it had been the Convento dos Marianos. Voss stood in the old courtyard, beneath the huge spread of the palm tree and remembered all those characters in all those other *pensões* in Lisbon reading their newspapers, waiting for the day's real information which was never in print in front of them.

They rested and in the evening walked back up to the Jardim da Estrela. They touched the tiles of the old apartment building's façade. Voss ran his hands up the iron swans' necks supporting the roof of the now disused kiosk, where he used to buy his cigarettes and newspapers. They sat and had a beer in the café in the gardens. They stood on the spot where he'd given himself up and he raised his eyes to the window of the old apartment, now open to the cool of the evening.

They walked the walk that they believed had been their undoing – down the Calçada da Estrela to São Bento and the National Assembly, into the edge of the Bairro Alto, around the church,

453

along Rua Academia Ciências, up the Rua do Seculo and right into the grid of the Bairro Alto. Andrea ate a meal of *rojões*, cubed pork with cumin, in a Minhote restaurant. Voss watched and drank the best part of a bottle of *Vinho Verde* red from Ponte da Lima. In the lamp-lit darkness they strolled past bars, restaurants and dodgy-looking characters offering a night of *fado*, as if it was a porno movie. They reached the Rua de São Pedro de Alcântara and walked up between the silver rails of the tramlines as they crossed the street to the *miradouro*. They stood at the railings, looking out across the city to the Castelo São Jorge, just as they had stood forty-seven years before, but not touching.

Voss still hadn't spoken much since they'd arrived, but it wasn't the hard, grim, obsessive silence of the month in Langfield. He seemed to be filling up, like a dry clay jug, darkening with moisture as it takes in water from a spring. She leaned with her back to the railings and pulled him to her by his lapels, looked into the good half of his face.

'Is this completely normal?' she asked.

He struggled. His eyes shifted over her face.

'I don't . . . I don't remember the words,' he said.

'You remember them,' she said. 'You told me them.'

'They've slipped my mind.'

'Is this completely normal?' she repeated, shaking him by the lapels.

'I don't . . . I don't know,' he said. 'I've only been in love once.'

'Who with?'

'You . . . crazy.'

He'd said it but it didn't carry the same conviction as forty-seven years ago.

'In that case,' she said, relenting, 'you're allowed into my hotel room.'

He joined her in bed that night and she slept with her back to him, their heads on the same pillow, hands joined over her stomach.

In the morning she went off on her own and found the lawyer's office in the Chiado. He gave her the wooden box, which she signed for. She bought some paper and wrapped it and went on to the bus station and booked two tickets to Estremoz for the next day.

They took the train from Lisbon out to Estoril along the glinting, panel-beaten Tagus, the silver carriages of the train visible ahead as they turned on the bright and shining rails. The surf broke against the Búgio lighthouse in the middle of the estuary and the hump of the sandbank lurked behind like a surfacing whale.

They were horrified by how tacky the casino had become – all naked girls and ostrich feathers. The passage up to the garden of the Quinta da Águia no longer existed. Houses had been built across it and up the hill behind. They had lunch on the promenade. He poked at his sardines. She showed him where she'd lived when she'd been married to Luís and they took the train back into the city in the late afternoon.

When they arrived in Estremoz the next day it was already brutally hot. They took a cab up to the *pousada* within the castle walls and flaked out for an hour. They went back down into the town for lunch and found a dark, cool *tasca* whose walls were lined with terracotta wine jars, each tall as a man. The place was packed with Portuguese, workers and tourists, all sitting on wooden benches and eating vast portions of food.

'Do you see these people?' asked Andrea.

'Yes, I see them,' said Voss, wary.

'What do you think about them?'

'That they might become very fat,' he said, the thin smug man.

'I think they don't give a damn about anything, except the food on their plates, the good wine in their glasses and the people around them. It's not such a bad way to be.'

He nodded and ate a quarter of his grilled fish and a leaf of lettuce.

They took a cab out to the small chapel and graveyard amongst the marble quarries on the outskirts of town. They walked the lanes of the graves and tombs until they reached the Almeida family mausoleum. Voss lagged behind, looking at the photographs of the dead, which were very formal, no better than mug shots, some of them. He fingered the flowers, some of which were plastic and others made out of material. He came alongside her, not knowing what they were doing in this place. She tapped Julião's photograph, faded in the years of draining sunshine. Voss took a closer look, peering at the outline of the face.

'You haven't asked me anything about him,' she said. 'So I

thought I'd start at the end. In his end is your beginning . . . something like that.'

Voss clung on to the wrought-iron bars of the gate to the mausoleum and took in the coffins, more coffins now, and the two urns of Julião and Luís on the same shelf. Andrea took out the old photograph and put in a new one. She handed the old one to Voss. They left the graveyard, Voss's head bowed over the bleached picture, and found a cab to take them back up to the *pousada*.

Outside the hotel she took his arm and walked him past the church and the statue of Rainha Santa Isabel and sat on the ramparts. She gave him the present, which he opened. He admired the African box and thanked her with an awkward kiss.

'Look inside,' she said. 'The present's inside.'

On top was the Voss family photograph. His hand shook as he took it out. His emaciated body shuddered as he looked from face to face, each one with its own sense of triumph at being someone in the family group, in front of a photographer. He took out his father's letters, leafed through them to the one asking him to get Julius out of Stalingrad. He read it, and then his own to Julius and finally the letter from one of Julius's men. He wiped his eyes with the back of his wrist.

'I took them from your room before I escaped on to the roof back in '44. I thought it might be the only thing I'd ever have of you so I kept them. They're yours,' she said. 'You probably don't have anything left yourself.'

He shook his head, chin resting on his chest.

'I lost you, Karl,' she said, standing up, looking down on his bowed head. 'This last time, you've turned up in my life but you're not here. You've been consumed by something else and I want you back. I hope this reminds you of the man you were, because you're still the only one who has meant anything and everything to me.'

They went up to the hotel room. Karl, exhausted, slept on his back with the box on his chest, its contents seeping into him like a new drug. In the evening they returned to the same *tasca* where they'd had lunch. This time he ordered beer and wine. He ate the cheese and olives. He ordered roasted pig's cheeks and ate it all, right down to the crackling skin. He had a pudding – cake with sugar plums – and coffee and he drank a *bagaço*, because he wanted to remember that harsh liquor, his demand for it when he'd been in Lisbon during the war. He still didn't say very much but he looked at her throughout, taking her in as if he'd noticed her for the first time. His eyes were still sunk in his head but they'd lost the haunted look, the tortured, pleading look.

Slightly drunk, they held on to each other and found a small café near some gardens by the barracks and ordered *aguardente velho*, less harsh, more refined, more suitable for pensioners. He toasted her:

'For what you've returned to me,' he said. 'And for reminding me what's important.'

'And?' she asked, severe, but eyes smiling with the booze.

He paused, smacked his lips.

'For being the most beautiful creature on earth that I've never stopped loving.'

'More,' she said, 'I think I deserve more of that stuff. Tell me how much you love me. Go on, Karl Voss, physicist from Heidelberg University. How much? Quantify it. I need measures.'

'I love you . . .' he said, and thought about it for thirty seconds.

'I'm glad this is taking so long to compute.'

'I love you more than there are water molecules in the oceans of the world.'

'Not bad,' she said. 'That *is* quite a lot. You may kiss me now.'

'This work,' he said, as they recklessly asked the waiter to leave the bottle of *aguardente velho* on the table, 'this book I've been working on, that I thought, until this afternoon, was so important, is called . . . I've named it *The Gospel of Lies*. It was to be a personal account of what it has been like to spend my whole life as a spy, always working against the states which have employed me. I thought that this would be the way to make sense of it all. But it wasn't just going to be that. I was also going to make an astounding revelation . . . that for the entire post-war period, until it became unimportant, the Russians had somebody installed at the very highest level of British Intelligence.

'In 1977 I was retired, but I asked to continue working in the Stasi archives. I had already stolen lots of documents, which I kept buried in the garden of a villa Elena and I had the use of on the outskirts of Berlin. From 1977 to 1982 I worked exclusively on stealing documents which would give me irrefutable proof that there was a traitor permanently in the top five executives of the British SIS. In 1986, when Elena fell ill, I took her back to Moscow and there I managed to fit in the last piece of the puzzle. The final and verbal confirmation of all my documentary proof. I spoke to Kim Philby on three occasions before he died in 1988.

'It was difficult to work on the book in Moscow and later, as Elena got sicker, I became ill myself. I have cancer, which at my age is a slow-moving affair, but I've been told that it can suddenly get worse. So I've believed myself to be on this important mission, to tell the world everything I know, but without knowing how long I had to do it.

'I felt compelled to do this work because the man, this traitor, has been honoured by his country for his services and I didn't think it right that such a person should be so highly regarded for sending his own countrymen to their deaths.'

'And now?'

'And now, in the last forty-eight hours I've come to realize something. That what I thought was the most important thing, the work that would have left my stamp on this world, is as valuable as all the intelligence ever gathered and presented to those leaders who demanded it in order to make their brilliant decisions. It is worthless. It is dust. And now that I know that, or rather had you to help me remember it, and with all that you've shown me, with all that you've given me . . . I am, at last, happy.'

Andrea sipped her *aguardente*, kissed him on the mouth so that he felt the sting of the alcohol on his lips.

'But who is it?' she asked. 'You've still got to tell who he is.'

They laughed.

'It is so worthless, such dust,' he said, 'that I don't think there's any point in telling.'

'You'll be sleeping on your own if you don't.'

'I wanted to tell you when we were on that walk yesterday. Our walk through the Bairro Alto. The one where we were seen by the *bufo* who reported it to General Wolters. That, for me, was the most amazing thing that Philby revealed. It was during my last meeting with him. I hadn't told him I'd been in Lisbon during the war. To begin with I thought that would be too risky, but Philby was completely finished by then. A very sad case. I think even the Russians were wary of him by the end. So I told him who I was. I even remembered my codename, because it was such an odd one. I told him I was "Childe Harold". He started laughing, laughing so hard I was worried about him. He grabbed my hand and breathed into my face, "And now we're on the same side." So I started laughing with him, willing him to tell me but not wanting to ask, because asking someone like that is different to them telling. He told me he had given the order that my name should be handed over to Wolters as a double agent and traitor . . . but that it must be done with subtlety. Nothing traceable.'

'Why did Philby want to get rid of you?'

'Because I was stuffing his British agents full of information which could possibly have given us, the Germans, a chance at a separate peace with the Americans and the British. He didn't want there to be any possibility that the Russians would be excluded. So, he ordered one of *his* men to give me up. It was this man who told the *bufo* to report it to Wolters and led to my arrest.'

'I knew it,' said Andrea. 'I knew it would be him.'

'Who?'

'Richard Rose.'

'This is very sad, Andrea, because I know how much this man means to you but . . .'

'Richard Rose means nothing to me . . . even less than nothing now. I invited him to my dinners because he's one of the gang. He's entertaining. But I've spent most of my life not liking him at all.'

'It wasn't Richard Rose. I always thought it would be, because he was so hard in the negotiations I had with him and Sutherland in the Monserrate Gardens.'

'No?'

'I couldn't believe it either . . . that he was already in position at such an early stage.'

'Philby was a liar, too.'

'I've got the documentary proof of his later work, Andrea. All those files I dug out of the Stasi archives. They're all at home.'

'If it's him, I want to hear it from his lips.'

'I'm not sure how wise that is, Andrea,' said Voss. 'Philby and Blake were both ruthless men. They sent hundreds of agents to their deaths, but I can assure you that Meredith Cardew was worse than the two of them put together.'

*   *   *

They slept heavily that night because of the drink. They woke late in the morning and made love for the first time, with the maids singing in the corridors outside.

By afternoon Voss was not feeling well and was in pain. They took a cab all the way to the airport and flew back to London. By eleven in the evening he was in the John Radcliffe Hospital in Oxford. By a quarter past he'd been transferred, in agony, to the Pain Relief Unit in the specialist cancer hospital, the Churchill, where they brought his condition under control. By morning he was stable.

The consultant told Andrea that it could be a matter of days, at the most a fortnight. Voss insisted on staying with her at home. Andrea paid for a private nurse who would come in twice a day. Voss was installed in her bed with a morphine drip, whose doses he could control by a hand-held self-administering device that computed the amount taken so that he couldn't overdose himself.

Andrea didn't go up into the attic. She didn't turn on Voss's computer. She never knew that all his data had been corrupted by a virus and that someone had taken a sample of the documents from the trunk. She stayed in the bedroom with Voss and read to him, because it was comforting to both of them.

At night she made a light supper and before she went up to bed at eleven o'clock, she let Ashley out into the garden. She stood at the back door under the light, the dog lost in the darkness. It was a balmy night but she wore a cardigan and held it tight around her chest though she realized the cold was coming from the inside out. She had tried not to think it, but she knew she was going to have to do it again. She was going to have to go through that whole painful process once more – coming to terms with the word 'never'. Not in a million years. From here to eternity. An infinity of absence.

She remembered coming out of the Basílica da Estrela back in 1944 having cried herself empty and the feeling of that breeze blowing straight through her. Had that been bad? Not entirely. There'd been a freeing up, a loosening of the moorings, her ship still linked to the landmass of her grief but the instinct already there to move on. That was her generation. Don't make a fuss. Get on with it. And now? After a life led with love hanging by a thread. And old age, and the only possible end of old age.

In the afternoon she'd walked through the graveyard of the

church looking at the headstones of married couples, wondering if this was a grim thing to be doing. She noticed that if the woman died first, the man always followed within a year. If the man died, the woman did not go gently into her husband's night. The women hung on in their decrepit bodies, hearts thumping through the years.

She was going to finish life how she'd started it. Alone. Except that this time there were connections and an image came to her of roped climbers up a sheer wall and the looks of encouragement between them.

She shouted for Ashley.

No response.

'Bloody dog,' she said, and set off down the path.

She found him by stumbling over his supine body. The dog was warm but completely inert and she could tell by the light coming up the garden from the back door that if there was any life in his visible eye it was the tiniest crack. She picked him up. Quite a weight for a dachshund. She went back to the light, inspected him briefly under it and took him inside and laid him on the refectory table at one end. She looked at him intently for some sign of what it was that had struck him down. The warm night air blew against her back. She prised open his jaws and saw vestiges of red meat in his teeth and, in the instant that it came to her that he'd been poisoned, a white silk scarf floated down in front of her eyes and snapped tight round her neck.

She grabbed at the reins of the scarf behind her neck and found that a pair of strong, male, gossamered hands held the loop of silk. She tried to move but the taut body behind her jammed her against the table. She kicked back at the shins, saw a pair of mahogany Doc Martens. He pushed her forward again with his hips, bending her down over the table so that she felt her last chance was to get her legs up on to the table, try to scrabble across it. The powerful hands reined her back, bore down on her. She rolled back towards him, clawing at his shoulders, trying to weaken him in any way she could but the fight was going out of her. Her face was swelling, her vision darkening at the rims. Blood blackened in her head and through the narrowing tunnel she saw his face. She mouthed his name with her thick, purple lips. Her last word, a soundless question:

461

'Morgan?'

Voss woke up. The only light in the room from the red digits of the clock which read 00.28. The pain had woken him. He clicked on the morphine dispenser but this time he didn't feel the trickle of Lethe, as they'd begun to call it. He looked at the pillow next to him. Empty. He moved his arm, which swung freely, and saw in the weak red light that the morphine-drip tube had been cut. The pain in his side was crushing, as if there was a steel hand in there relentlessly closing on an organ. He threw back the bedcovers, turned on the reading lamp, saw that the overhead drip-feed bag was empty when he knew it should have been at the halfway mark.

He launched himself out of bed, sent the drip clattering to the floor. He called out, 'Andrea!'

It was a weak cry. The steel hand was crushing the breath out of him as well. He reached the door frame, the cut tube, still with the intravenous needle taped to his arm, whipping around his face. He staggered down the stairs and turned into the kitchen and saw the bodies on the table. The dog at her feet.

What is she doing?

A spear of pain shot through his chest, so sharp and fast that neon flashed in his brain. He staggered to the edge of the table, gripped it with his fleshless hands and looked down into the face that was hers but not.

He coughed against a pain that was far greater than anything the steel hand could produce. He coughed against a whole agony in his chest, the departure of possibility, the flight of future. Drops darkened on the wool of her fuchsia cardigan as he put his face down to hers, touched her cheek with his good cheek, felt the residual warmth. He lay next to her on the table, clasped her hand in his and for one bright moment felt happy, saw her falling through the bubbles of water as he rushed down to meet her, to bring her up, to bring her back to the light. And then the pain in his chest tightened but this time didn't let go and, although he didn't want to resist it, his body arched against it, the last pain. And through it he saw her across the river from him, on the opposite bank, waving.

*　　*　　*

462

Morgan Trent, who'd been sitting at the dark edge of the room waiting for his bit of sadistic amusement, came forward. He inspected the bodies, drumming his chin with his fingers. He saw the hands clasped. How sweet, he thought, how very sweet. He looked over the faces, found himself mildly curious at the quizzical smile on the good side of Voss's face. As if he'd seen something. Received a welcome.

He checked for a neck pulse. None. He went up to the attic and brought down the trunk, which he passed over the wall into the garden of his rented cottage. He returned for the two suitcases of documents. He went back a third time, planted his foot firmly in the flower bed outside the dining-room window and broke a pane of glass. He climbed in through the window and walked out of the front door, closing it behind him.

He put the suitcases and the trunk in the back of his car. He removed the Doc Martens and put on a pair of crêpe-soled shoes. He trotted down to the Brocks' house and put the Doc Martens where he'd found them, in the garage. He drove to Swindon and made a call from a public phone box. They exchanged passwords and he said: 'It's done, I'm dumping the paper now.'

The nurse found the bodies in the morning. She had her own key. She called the police and an hour later three officers were standing around the bodies on the refectory table.

'You know what this looks like to me?' said the DC.

'Apart from murder, you mean?' said the DI.

'The way the bodies are positioned, with the dog at their feet, and the fact that he's holding her hand . . .'

'Odd that.'

'. . . it looks like a tomb,' he said. 'One of those old tombs, carved in stone. You know, the knight in armour and his lady wife.'

'You're right,' said the DI, 'and they've always got those little dogs at their feet.'

'There's a poem written about that,' said the third officer, who was young, new in the job.

'A poem,' said the DI. 'I didn't know they read poetry at Police College these days.'

'They don't, sir. I got a BA in General Arts from Keele University. We read a few poems.'

463

'All right,' said the DC, thinking – acceptable.
'I only remember the last line.'
'That's all right, we don't need the whole damn thing.'
'*"What will survive of us is love . . ."*, sir. That was the line.'
'Well, that's a load of crap, isn't it?'

Oxford Times 3rd December 1991
At 11.30 a.m. in the Oxford Crown Court Gary Brock was sentenced to life imprisonment for the murder of Karl Voss and Andrea Aspinall.

Oxford Times 3rd February 1992
Morgan Trent and Kathleen Thomas would like to announce their forthcoming marriage to take place at Langfield Church, Oxfordshire on 28th June 1992.

The Times 30th June 1993
On 28th June 1993 Sir Meredith Cardew died peacefully at home. He was 84 years old. There will be a memorial service at St Mary's in the Strand on 15th September 1993.